PRAISE FOR *Island of Exiles*

"Readers won't be able to put this book down, as the excitement begins from the first page and only grows from there. Cameron expertly blends worldbuilding and intriguing characters with page-turning action scenes and a story that builds in tension and complexity. The novel's commitment to diversity adds new dimensions to the story, as the cast is entirely nonwhite, and the clan recognizes nonbinary gender identities and complex sexual orientations. The lexicon of unique terms and concepts may be intimidating to some readers, but the vocabulary adds fantastic texture to the world without distracting from the plot. This is rare gem of a book that has a lot to offer readers, including magic, action, and intrigue on the edge of a knife.
A fresh, original series starter, bolstered by a dynamic protagonist and a welcome sense of depth."
—Kirkus, Starred Review

"I was consumed by the savage mysteries of Cameron's harsh and haunting fantasy world. A story of love and loss as searing as the desert heat."
—Diana Peterfreund, author of *For Darkness Shows the Stars*

"Harrowing and heartfelt. The intricately realized world of *Island of Exiles* crackles with harsh magic and gripping suspense."
—A.R. Kahler, author of The Immortal Circus series

"*Island of Exiles* is imaginative, bold, and as electrifying as a Shiara storm."
—Lori M. Lee, author of *Gates of Thread and Stone* and *The Infinite*

"A beautifully wrought fantasy filled with magic, rebellion, and romance, plus a strong, butt-kicking heroine to root for!"
—Lea Nolan, *USA Today* bestselling author of *Conjure*, *Allure*, and *Illusion*

"Erica Cameron's *Island of Exiles* is a remarkable achievement: a fantasy world so richly imagined, so finely detailed, and so strikingly original, even the most incredible elements feel totally real. The energy of the desosa will tingle along your skin as you race through this amazing book, and at journey's end, you'll long for the sequel so you can immerse yourself once more in the mysteries of Itagami!"
—Joshua David Bellin, author of the Survival Colony series

"Island of Exiles has everything I've been looking for in a fantasy—powerful characters, magical powers that make me itch with envy, and a spoken language that is as intrinsic to the story as it is beautiful."
—Amber Lough, author of *The Fire Wish* and *The Blind Wish*

Also by Erica Cameron:

Island of Exiles (The Ryogan Chronicles, #1)
Sea of Strangers (The Ryogan Chronicles, #2)

Assassins: Discord (Assassins, #1)
Assassins: Nemesis (Assassins, #2)

Taken by Chance (Laguna Tides, #1)
Loyalty and Lies (Laguna Tides, #2)

Sing Sweet Nightingale (The Dream War Saga, #1)
Deadly Sweet Lies (The Dream War Saga #2)

A glossary and index of key locations, characters, and phrases is included at the end of the book.

THE RYOGAN CHRONICLES
BOOK 3

WAR OF STORMS

ERICA CAMERON

This book is a work of fiction. Names, characters, places, and incidents are the product of the author's imagination or are used fictitiously. Any resemblance to actual events, locales, or persons, living or dead, is coincidental.

Copyright © 2018, 2023 by Erica Cameron. All rights reserved, including the right to reproduce, distribute, or transmit in any form or by any means.

Edited by Kate Brauning
Cover design by Cait Greer
Interior layout & design by Cait Greer

Ebook ISBN: 979-8-9884387-2-4
Print ISBN: 979-8-9884387-5-5

First Edition November 2018
Second Edition June 2023

This book is dedicated to those who followed me on this voyage,
to anyone who risks taking a journey of their own,
and to everyone who's looking for home.

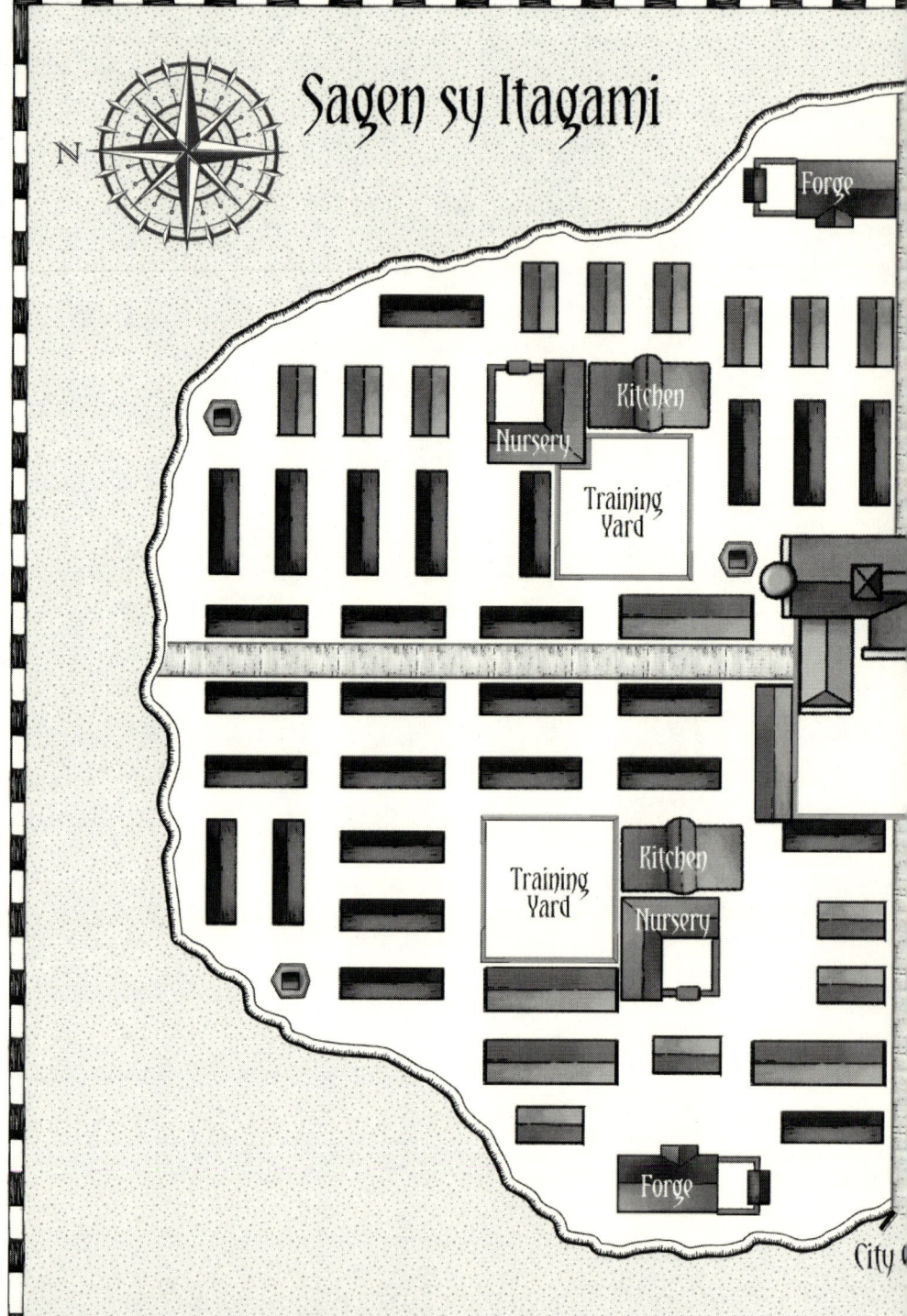

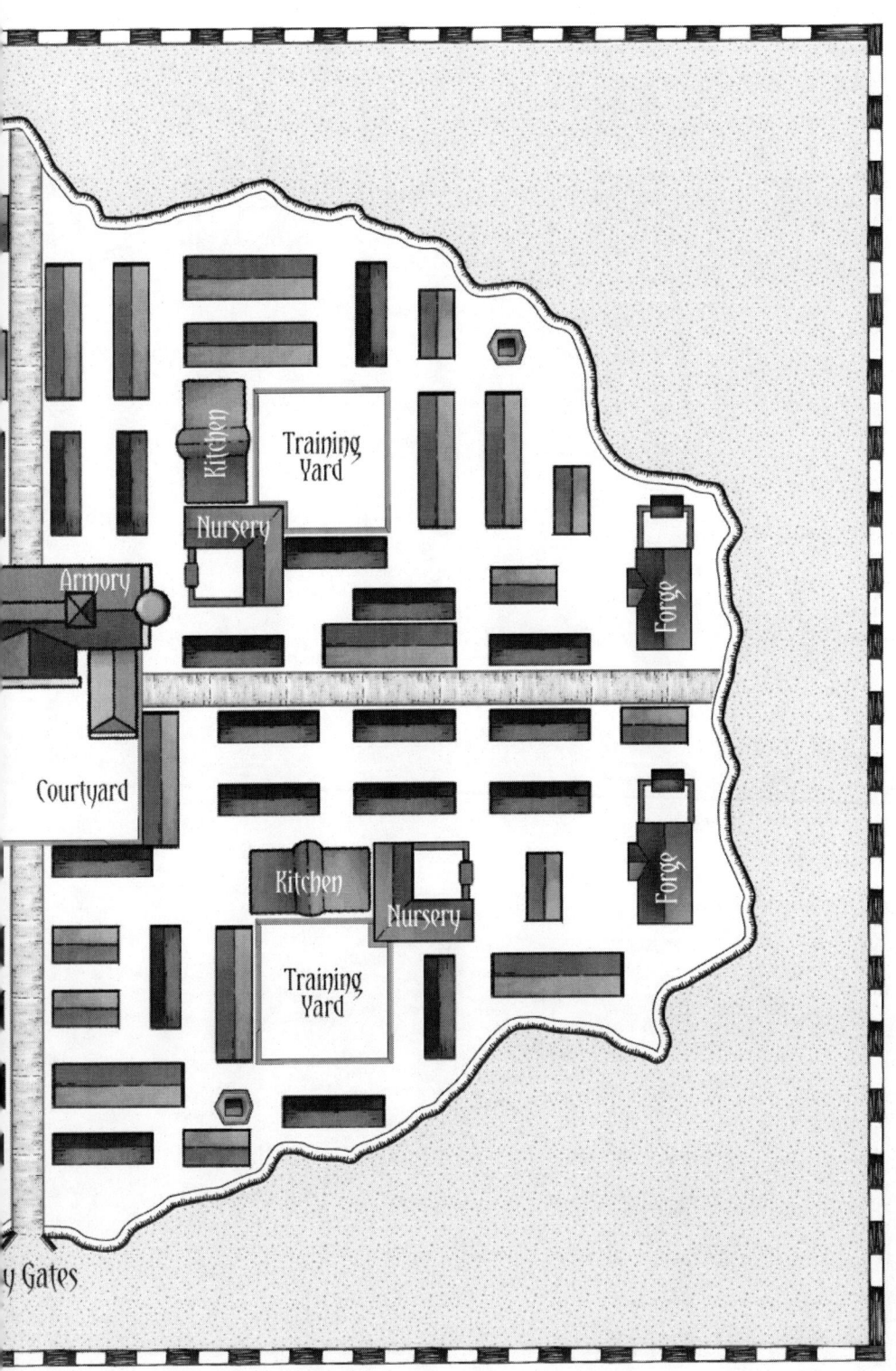

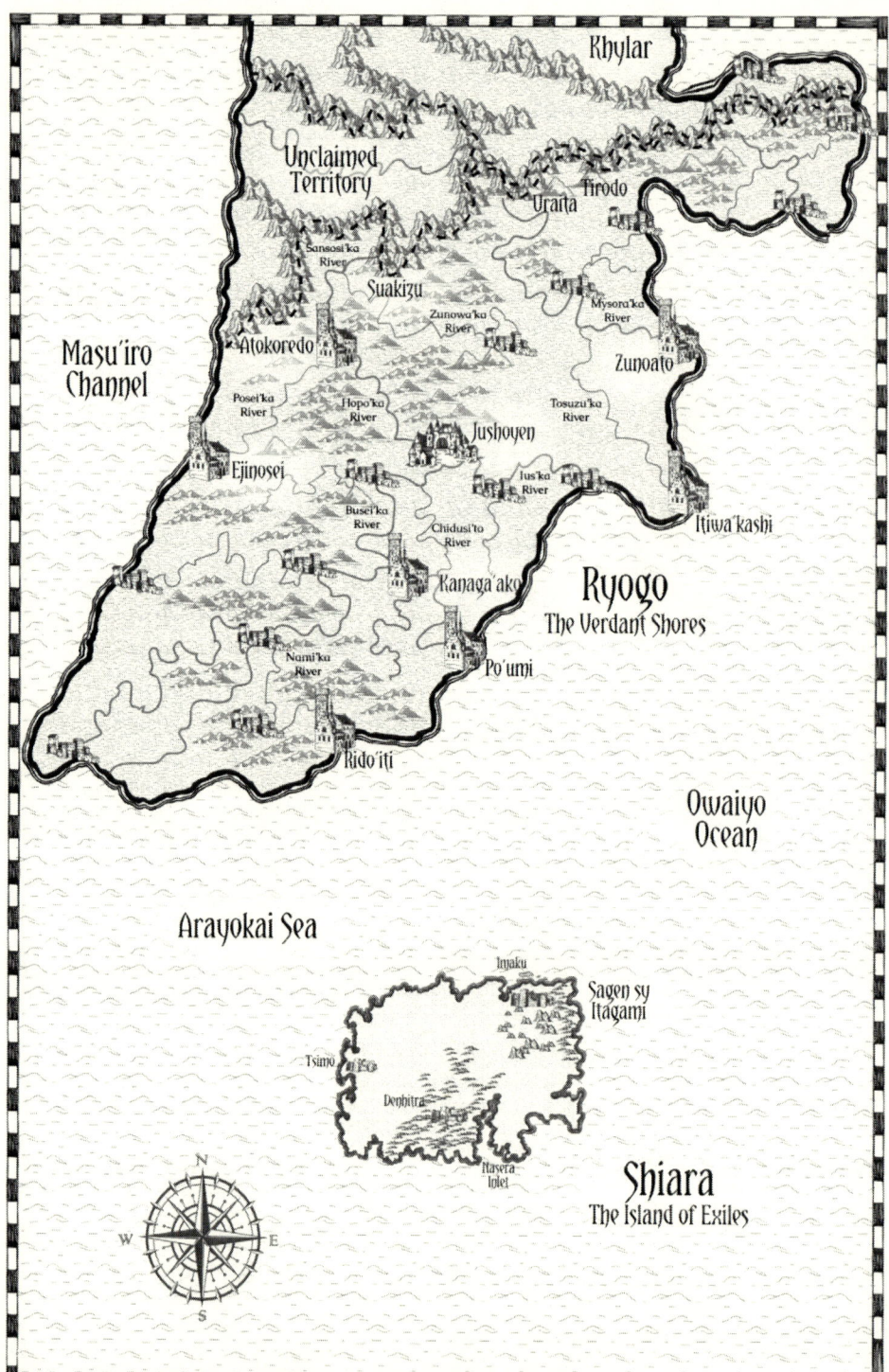

Who are the Kaisubeh to control our lives with such heavy hands while denying us the least proof they exist? Essentially, we're expected to unquestioningly follow beings about whom we know nothing real.

The teachings the kaiboshi claim our gods left behind contradict themselves, which just proves the kaiboshi are as greedy as they are ignorant. The stories I learned as certainties growing up in the north are treated like frivolous folklore in the southern provinces, and that's nothing to the differences between our beliefs and what the nomads or anyone outside Ryogo calls truth.

Maybe the reason we still tell tales about gods no one's heard from in ages is because we don't want to accept the truth—the Kaisubeh are dead. Maybe they've been dead for the last three thousand years, since the schism that broke the world.

If that's true, what I'm attempting is the only way humanity will ever be unified again. If what I created in Kaisuama does what I intend and Chio wakes up from this sickness transformed, then Ryogo will finally get a chance to meet their Kaisubeh. We will lead them, kicking and screaming if we must, and we will make Ryogo more powerful than it has ever been before. After, the world itself will fall at our feet, and the generations that follow will barely remember the names of the so-called Kaisubeh.

They'll tell stories about the Miriseh instead.

— EXCERPT FROM THE JOURNAL OF VARAN HEINANSUTO WRITTEN 3205 A.S., SEVEN YEARS BEFORE THE BEGINNING OF THE GREAT WAR AND TWELVE YEARS BEFORE THE BOBASU'S EXILE

PROLOGUE

Lightning cracks through the sky, fast and close. Thunder is a continuous rumble that shakes the foundations of Shiara. Every rock on the island trembles and vibrates, and Yorri has felt it for so long he can't remember what it's like to be still.

Days. Weeks. A moon cycle or more. Yorri can't be sure how long ago the Miriseh abandoned him and the other prisoners in the mountains, leaving them to the torment of the elements. The storms haven't broken once.

Thunder vibrates through the air and the ground. Heavy raindrops batter him from above. Lightning blazes overhead, leaving glaring streaks even against Yorri's closed eyes. He wishes he was numb to all of it. Shouldn't he be by now? He's not. Whatever power heals the burns from lightning strikes and keeps him alive without food also seems to make him feel each drop of rain as if it's the first to strike. It makes each deafening crash painfully fresh. Lack of sleep should've sent him into delirium and unconsciousness ages ago, but the fresh sparks of pain continuously shock him into alertness, and his mind processes each moment in perfect clarity.

He wants to scream, to struggle against the magic binding him to the black platform he's laid out on. Instead, he presses his lips together to hold back outbursts of agony and anger. He doesn't think anyone is guarding the valley, but he can't be sure, and he refuses to give the Miriseh the satisfaction of screaming for the help no one is going to give him.

Swallowing the pain, he tries to find something else to focus on. The only option, though, is staring at the others trapped on their own platforms. Some are as still as their stone beds, but others thrash and flail, arching up against the cords binding their wrists and ankles to the rock, their mouths open in shouts Yorri can barely hear over the thunder.

If Khya were in my position, she'd find a way to free herself from this, he thinks. *By now, she would've found a way to free us all.* He knows his sister sees him as the problem solver with a mind that can see its way out of any situation, but this... What the bellows is he supposed to do about this? Not even his enhanced strength can break his bindings, and the storm isn't the only anguish he's suffering.

The ache in his chest has been getting worse. Between his lungs is a spot where a pale-yellow warmth bloomed when he bonded with Sanii, but they've been apart for too long. The connection has stretched and strained and soured. The spot has grown cold. It's sent out barbed vines; they wrap around his lungs and heart and slowly constrict. He didn't notice at first—not in the midst of the storm. Now, it's impossible to ignore.

The only way he has to mark the passage of time is the steady increase of that pain and the water slowly filling the small, rocky valley. Now, swells lap at the base of his black stone bed. Wind gusts force waves of water to crest over him. When the water covers him completely, will it bring death or just a new kind of torture?

Lightning strikes the closest peak. Thunder cracks and rumbles. Huge chunks of stone break off the slope, dropping into the valley below. Several land in the water, sending up massive waves. One cracks off a piece of the platform closest to Yorri, missing the prisoner's hand by inches. One falls straight on someone else's leg, crushing it completely.

I can't do all *the work, little brother.* The whisper sounds like Khya, and his sister's voice soothes even though she's not here; all he's hearing is what he guesses Khya might say. *I'm fighting to save you. The least you can do is help.*

We never gave up on you, Sanii, his sukhai, would likely add. *Don't you dare give up on us.*

Tessen's imagined voice throws down a challenge. *Khya always bragged about how smart you are, Yorri. Prove it.*

But he can't. There's no way to win a fight against magic, a mountain, and a storm.

He stares at the bloodied mess of the prisoner's crushed leg, only blinking to clear the rain from his eyes. Over time, the flattened, pulped places round out and the skin smooths. The injury heals completely; only their torn pants and the faint bloodstains not washed away by the rain prove it happened at all.

Yorri huffs, and then he laughs. He laughs despite how the pain between his lungs pierces and pulls. In part, he laughs because of it. His pain will never be enough to kill him. His injuries will always heal. He can't die, and for some Kujuko-cursed reason, he doesn't even have the partial oblivion of false unconsciousness anymore. He's awake, he's aware, and he's watching as the water gets higher with each hour of rainfall.

For how long, he wonders, will he be able to drown?

ONE

Rido'iti is burning. And all I can do is watch.

Our position is a hundred feet up and half a mile away from the city, up on a ridge that overlooks the streets and the ocean beyond. Smoke rises from the city's buildings. It's so thick not even the driving rain can keep it from climbing to join the storm clouds. The darkness continues out to the horizon—the ocean is a seemingly endless stretch of white-capped water so dark it's nearly black.

We've barely moved for the last two hours. Sanii is as mute and still as the nearby Zohogasha, the statues of the Kaisubeh standing sentinel on the coast. Etaro holds Rai tight, face turned against her shoulder. Nearby, Zonna and Natani stare at the city below us, unblinking. Tessen leans against me, his breathing shallow and too quick, his body trembling.

When Varan's army landed, we stayed because I needed to see what he would order his nyshin mages to do. And if they would listen. A small part of me had hoped, despite knowing exactly how well the citizens of Sagen sy Itagami unquestioningly follow orders, that those I once called clan would *look* at where they were. I'd hoped they would see that the city they'd been commanded to decimate was defenseless, its people weak and unprepared. I'm too far away to watch individual reactions, but the army didn't seem to hesitate before the slaughter of Rido'iti began. Now, only ruins, blood, and ash remain.

Despite the water running into my eyes, I barely blink as my gaze traces the narrow, twisting streets dividing the tightly packed, sharp-peaked buildings of stone and wood—or the lines of what's left of them.

We reached this height while the Itagamin army was still marching across the ocean, and the wide thoroughfares were nearly empty then; the raging storm had driven everyone indoors. Even in the darkness of the storm, I could see the bright paint on the structures and count the trees lining most roads. It was easy to imagine what this place might've looked like on a sunny morning with a harbor full of ships and a city full of life.

I'll never see it like that.

Fire has engulfed most of the city, crawling from building to building with the help of brutal gusts of wind and the magic of the kasaijis. The flames are so thick and hot not even the rain can put them out. It'll extinguish itself eventually, but only after everything it can consume is gone. No one is here to douse the flames anymore. The citizens have either fled or died, and the Itagamin army is already leaving the chaos behind to move north, away from the roiling ocean and into Ryogo.

My only memory of Rido'iti will be a city consumed by flames and ruins.

"How many do you think died?" Etaro asks.

"Too many." I close my eyes. Acrid smoke burns my nose, the scent full of burning wood, roasting flesh, and singed hair.

At least the screaming has finally stopped.

"What do you want to do, Khya?" Tessen's voice is so low that I might not have heard the question if he hadn't rested his forehead against my temple. "We need to go, or we'll get caught by their scouts."

I nod to let him know I heard, but I don't move yet. We were so close. After four moon cycles in Ryogo, hunting secrets and building weapons, we had finally been about to get on a ship and sail home. When we reached Rido'iti, we found an army instead. There's no way for us to get back to Shiara—for *me* to get back to Yorri—now. Even if there is a ship in the harbor that hasn't been broken into pieces by weeks of vicious storms, we *can't* leave Ryogo to the revenge of the bobasu. Despite only having the faintest idea of how to stop them.

We never planned for this. And it's ridiculous that we didn't. Or maybe the others *have* been considering this kind of failure. I was too focused on saving Yorri to worry about the rest of the world. Even now, if

I found a ship, I'd be tempted to leave this place behind.

Love is pulling me to cross the tumultuous ocean to save Yorri.

Duty is pushing me to get ahead of this army and destroy Varan.

Choosing one means turning away from the other, and though I'll hate myself for failing Yorri again, I won't be able to live with myself at all if I leave Ryogo to die. I thought Varan wanted to take over and put himself in the Jindaini's place. That's hard to believe after Rido'iti. Looking down at the smoldering city, it doesn't seem like he wants to rule the Ryogans, he wants to rule *Ryogo*. And he doesn't care if there's anybody left alive in it to follow him.

I watch the last squads of nyshin leave Rido'iti as I step backward, deeper into trees. "We'll head north and try to catch up with Wehli, Lo'a, and the others before they get too far inland. Whether we find them or not, though, we have to go to Jushoyen."

Jushoyen, the city at the center of Ryogo, is where their leader lives.

"It won't be an easy trip. We'll have to cross half the country." Rai's round face is pinched and spattered with mud. She between me and Etaro, who's still pressing close for comfort, and then she tilts her head to the north. "It's going to be especially hard if we have to move fast enough to stay ahead of *them*."

"Easy or not, we need to go." I turn north, bringing up my wards for the first time in hours and drawing them in tight to our bodies to make it easier for us to pass through the dense forest. The magical shields will not only keep off the driving rain, they'll keep my friends safe if we run into trouble.

"But, Khya, we can't—" Sanii cuts emself off, but I hear what ey didn't say. Sanii's the only one who is as horrified as I am by the thought of missing our chance to go back to Shiara. I'm making the right decision to head inland and warn the Ryogans, but seeing the lines of strain marring eir long face makes me wince.

My heart cracks, and my resolve weakens. I remember Yorri and the others trapped on those platforms on Imaku, and I've been desperately trying to avoid picturing the awful places Varan could've shoved my brother. All the agony and indecision I've been trying to squash since we first saw the empty harbor and the incoming army rises and chokes me.

Yorri is my brother, but he's Sanii's sukhai, eir soulpartner. To me, missing him is like missing half my heart; for Sanii, being apart must feel as though it's slowly eroding eir soul.

Swallowing hard, I step in front of em, stopping only when we're so close the toes of our boots are nearly touching and I'm looking down into eir big eyes. "I know. I know, and I hate this, but what— When I think about what Yorri would do if he were here, I can't believe…"

Ey flinches, eir hand pressing hard against eir chest as eir small frame seems to collapse in on itself. "You can't believe he'd leave when he might be able to help. Because he wouldn't."

"Especially not when he had a way to know without a doubt we were alive." Which all sumai partners do. As torturous as it must be for them to be apart, Sanii told me moons ago that so long as ey was focused and functional, Varan hadn't found a way to kill the immortal born. I would know Yorri's life had ended the moment ey dropped to eir knees, keening and begging to die. It hurts to even allow for the possibility, but I've already proven immortality has limits.

Sanii looks south, across the towering waves toward Shiara and Yorri, and rubs eir hand in circles against eir chest. Then ey nods. Determination settles over eir face as ey turns north. Rai and Etaro, still holding hands, follow em into the forest.

Natani, who's been nearly silent for hours, gives me a long look, the expression in his dark eyes unreadable. "Do you really think we can make a difference against an army?"

"No, but I don't plan on stopping the *army*. All we need to do is destroy the bobasu." And all I have to do is find a way to make that happen.

I have to find a way to make that happen.

Blood and rot, how am I possibly going to make that happen?

But Natani nods like he expected my response, and then he trudges after the others. Zonna, though, is watching me, his expression carefully blank. The raw pain that's burned in his eyes for the past five days is now banked and hidden behind a wall as impenetrable as my wards.

"I don't know what I'm doing." The words tumble out before I can stop them. Thankfully, only he and Tessen are close enough to hear me; admitting the depths of my uncertainty feels like quitting. It *is*, in a way— it's giving up a lifelong goal—and I hate myself for it despite knowing how poorly the reality of my old dream has settled on my shoulders. "I don't want this. I thought I did—growing up, I always wanted to be a leader one day—but now... Zonna, it should be you. You have the seniority. You have the experience. You know so much more about, about *everything*, and I think..."

Something flickers in his eyes, sadness, but not the deep loss that's been consuming him. This seems more like empathy. "You think what?"

"There's only a few of us against ten bobasu and an army of thousands, and we're relying on a weapon we don't know how to deploy." I grind my teeth, frustration and fear mixing painfully in my stomach. "I think *you* are our best chance at getting to Varan."

"You're fooling yourself if you think anyone, even me, can get to Varan without going through his army," Zonna murmurs. "And in five hundred years, I've never seen anyone rattle Varan's foundation the way *you* have, Khya." He steps closer and reaches out, but he doesn't put his hand on my shoulder until I nod. "I'm not the person who needs to be leading us. You are. Even if it seems impossible right now."

Tessen huffs. "Telling Khya something's impossible is the fastest way to make it happen."

I don't think that's true this time, but his faith is heartening. I reach out and brush my fingers along the back of Tessen's hand. It's a shame I can't absorb the confidence he has in me as easily as I can soak in his body heat. To me, it feels like I've been stumbling along ever since Sanii discovered Yorri had been captured instead of killed. Even though we've made it this far, I feel like I've failed far more than I've succeeded. The costs of those failures outweigh anything we've gained. I don't think there's anything I can do to make it up.

And yet no one who's able is willing to take this responsibility from me. Not Zonna, and definitely not Tessen. I glance at Tessen anyway. His smile is grim and stressed. "I'll follow you anywhere, Khya, but I'm not a leader. I never wanted to be."

Biting back everything I could say to make him change his mind, I follow the others.

The ridge had been rocky and stable underfoot. Between the trees, that solidity vanishes, and the mud gets deeper. It sucks at my boots and makes each step an effort. I shiver and pull my sodden coat tighter around my body.

It's not like my wards help with this; they don't contain warmth unless I make them keep out everything, including air. It seems like the storm is bringing the temperature down. The boots and the layers of thick, padded cloth took some getting used to, but I'm glad Soanashalo'a found them for us. Even with them, the wet and the cold seep through everything and bite at my bones.

I thought immortality would make me nearly invulnerable, but even though I know the cold won't kill me—not much can anymore—it doesn't seem to make a chill any easier to handle.

"You can't get warm, can you?" Zonna climbs over a fallen tree, his gaze flicking back to me. I don't answer as I follow him over the massive trunk. He nods as though I did. "This is something you'll have to get used to."

"What is?"

"Feeling everything fresh." He looks at his hands, flexing and clenching them as he talks. "Pain is usually sharper the first time you experience it, isn't it? Most people I've met can brace themselves for certain kinds of agony, push the feeling aside and ignore it. That's because their body adapts. Their mind adjusts. They learn to handle misery." Then he drops his hands and lifts a shoulder. "Or that's what it seems like they can do. I can only guess."

My stomach drops as another shiver rattles my bones. "It *never* gets better?"

"It won't anytime soon," he admits. "You can train your mind to ignore certain signals, but it's not easy, and it won't happen quickly."

I fold my arms, hiding my clenched fists and trying not to clench my jaw, too, but it doesn't stop my anger from spreading. "So, suffer in silence. Is that what you're saying?"

"No, I'm just trying to explain what's happening and why. If you don't understand, the sensations are going to distract you when we need your attention elsewhere."

Because you aren't willing to take over and give me a minute to breathe. The thought is uselessly spiteful. I bury it and consider what he's saying instead. It makes sense and it doesn't, especially considering I've trained myself to work through pain once already. "It hurt every time an Imaku-stone arrow hits my wards, but I got past it and learned how to block them. Why can't I do the same with cold?"

"Because it's physical, Khya," Zonna says over our squelching steps. "The arrows are different. What you feel when one of those pierce your wards *seems* like pain because your mind can't understand it any other way, but it's not physical because your wards aren't. *Those* will feel the same as before. The only difference there is that the well of energy you have to draw from will be deeper."

"At last. Good news," I mutter. It *is* good, I just wish someone had warned me sooner. Though, to be fair, I'd been dying when they gave me the susuji. There hadn't been time for a breakdown of penalties and benefits.

"There's always more good news eventually." His voice is soft and low, barely carrying over the sound of the rain. "It may not come often, but I promise there will invariably be more."

It sounds like a meaningless but reassuring adage, but the look on his face is too intense. This means something more coming from him, and I slowly realize it means something more to me now, too. The timeline of my life has the potential to stretch for ages, but my mind hasn't adapted yet. I'm still thinking in moons and years instead of decades and lifetimes. Maybe I don't yet fully believe I have that much time.

But that's not what I need to focus on now. "So what else should I watch out for?"

"Hunger will hurt, but you'll never starve," Zonna says after a moment. "You can go about two weeks without sleep before you begin to see things that aren't there, and close to three before your body shuts down and makes you rest. No injury I've seen can kill you, not even losing a limb. Suzu once regrew a finger after it was sliced off in a sparring match. However, every hurt will feel like the first you've ever experienced. It'll take you a long time to get past that because all of it will be more painful than you can understand yet."

He's right—I don't understand yet. I'm also not looking forward to the day that I do.

I don't know what to say, and he doesn't add anything else. Moving faster soon takes all our concentration, fighting through the tightly packed forest and against the thick mud. The wind is at our backs, but instead of urging us onward, it feels like the breath of a bellowing beast chasing us deeper into Ryogo. The thunder's cracks and rumbles seem like its growl as it hunts.

The comparison should be ridiculous—overwrought in ways that only breed fear and end with death—but it's all too apt. We *are* in the forest with a monstrous beast, it's just one with twenty thousand pairs of hands and feet instead of four, and ten thousand bodies instead of one. No matter how much I've learned in Ryogo, I'm not sure my wards are strong enough to protect us. If this beast catches us, we'll be consumed.

I pass Etaro first. Then Rai soon after. It takes me a few minutes to realize I haven't picked up my pace by much; the others are slowing down to let me overtake them. It makes me grind my teeth in frustration when each of them gives way, but there's no point in protesting. *Someone* has to take charge if we plan on surviving the day, and right now that someone is me.

Keeping us traveling the right direction isn't easy, but I head northwest along the coast until I spot a rock formation I remember. It marks a turn. Earlier, it'd taken us maybe half an hour to get from here to the cove west of Rido'iti, but the journey back has been at least twice that. Maybe longer. It's upsetting, because Rai was right—we have to move fast to stay ahead of the army and away from its scouts. My decision to act as witness for Rido'iti instead of running as soon as we spotted the invasion has cost us precious time. Now, downed trees, sagging branches, thick debris, and deep mud keep slowing us down.

My choices have put us in danger yet again.

The forest is so dense even the lightning's flashes of light struggle to reach the ground. As I wave my hand to catch Tessen's attention, I have some hope that he doesn't notice my shivering. I gesture to the path, hand signing a question: *Clear?*

Closing his eyes, Tessen listens to the world ahead. I listen, too, but without the power of his basaku senses, all I hear is wind whipping through the trees, raindrops smacking against leaves, ocean, and rock, and the near-constant thunder rolling overhead. It's so overwhelmingly loud I can't even hear my own heartbeat thudding quick and hard through my body.

"I think we're clear for half a mile, but that's a guess. The storm is—" Tessen flinches at a particularly close peal of thunder and rubs his ears. "I don't know what's coming."

We haven't known what's coming for moons now, I almost say. I bite the tip of my tongue to keep the words back and nod instead, trying to think. Staying here isn't an option.

I order Tessen to lead us on, and I stand back to let the others pass. Etaro comes next, and then Zonna, Rai, Natani, and Sanii. I put myself at the end of the line because if the army is behind us, I need to be the wall between them and my squad.

As we walk, one mile and then two, I glance forward at Tessen as often as I look behind. I know him well now, so by the set of his shoulders, the speed of his steps, and the angle of his head, I'll know he's spotted danger ahead before he can send a message down the line. Even with his senses hindered by the storm, Tessen's our best chance of an early warning.

And we desperately need one.

On the ridge over Rido'iti, the horror of everything we were seeing distracted us; there might've been moments when we weren't as concealed as we should've been. Tessen may have been the only basaku the clan has seen in decades, but he wasn't our only riuku mage. There are at least a hundred unikus with enhanced sight and dozens of orakus with overpowered sight, hearing, and scent. Plus, everything we know about tracking, evasion, and fighting was learned from someone in that army. We're still young. There was a lot we hadn't learned yet. Underestimating our former clan members now would be dangerous.

Still, if I were invading Ryogo, I'd order a quick, straight strike to Jushoyen, so I could cut out the heart of this nation. Deviations would be a waste of time unless I spotted something dangerous enough to be worth eliminating. I assume that's Varan's plan, too, which means we might be safe if we continue moving parallel to the army. *Might* be safe. I'm not risking my friends' lives on an assumption. Despite having learned how to use my wards in ways the mages of Sagen sy Itagami never conceived of, I shouldn't think we can simply—

Tessen's posture stiffens. He hesitates before taking a step. It's all the warning we have.

Someone else's ward flares to life, encircling and trapping my squad. More than a dozen Itagamin nyshin drop from their hiding spots in the trees, safe on the opposite side of the shield.

Heart pounding, I flood my own ward with desosa, reinforcing my protections. More nyshin move in from all sides, weapons drawn and magic ready. The air around us crackles as dozens of mages draw on the desosa. Flames appear in the kasaijis' hands. Lightning gathers around the ratoijis' bodies. Sharp stones and deadly arrows hover in front of the rikinhisus. The ground rumbles as the ishijis shove their power into the stone under us.

My heart stutters. Blood and rot.

Fifty-four nyshin—nearly three full squads—have us surrounded, and two of the squads are led by members of the kaigo council, the yellow stripe running down the center of their tunics' hoods a clear marker. I track them as they move closer, but it isn't until one stops, pushes their hood back, and pulls the atakafu scarf from their face that I recognize her.

"I almost didn't listen when my scout reported seeing a group dressed like the people in the city but carrying Itagamin weapons." Anda steps closer, toes mere inches from the nyshin ward. "But here you are. Somehow not dead yet."

"Do you think you're going to change that now?" This woman gave birth to my brother and me, but she was nothing more than a distant figure in our lives. Anda and Ono were interested in us only when our successes added to theirs, and I cared solely for their respect. When I left Sagen sy Itagami, they weren't on the list of people I knew I'd miss.

Part of me wonders what her orders are, though I guess it doesn't matter. She won't succeed. She's a strong rikinhisu mage and a brilliant fighter, but nearly everything about me has changed since I last saw her.

I smile, and my expression feels closer to a teegra baring its teeth than anything else. "I might be harder to get rid of than you expect."

Sanii and Zonna are as indestructible as I am; I'm not going to tell Anda that, though. I'm also not going to think about who else is standing with Anda or what we might have to do to them simply because they believe what they were taught, trained, and ordered to believe.

"Varan has ordered you to return," Anda says, her voice loud enough to carry to most of the gathered nyshin. "None of you will be hurt until you face the Miriseh yourselves if you surrender to the clan's authority."

"We're not going anywhere with you. And whatever 'authority' Varan once had over us disappeared as soon as we discovered what he's been hiding." Although I feared I'd hesitate the first time I faced one of my old commanding officers or falter the first time I had to put my squad's lives over my clan's, my conscience hardly twinges. Anda isn't fighting for the good of the clan, she's fighting for Varan's petty vendetta and his catastrophic war—it's those who follow her who are oblivious. I raise my voice, projecting over the storm and hoping everyone can hear me. "Do they know? Have you told them what Varan's been hiding on Imaku for centuries? Did you even *look* at the people you slaughtered in Rido'iti?"

"Enough!" Her bellowed command instantly halts the restless shifting that swept through the nyshin. Jaw tense, my blood-mother shakes her head. "Such a disappointment."

She raises her hand. The nyshin attack, launching a barrage of fireballs, lightning bolts, and projectiles against my ward. They must step through their sykina's ward to do it, so for a split second, each one of them is vulnerable.

My wards don't have that restriction.

Rai's flames blast the rikinhisus' projectiles out of the air, and the heat forces the mages back. Etaro uses thick sticks and debris to knock people off their feet. Tessen shouts warnings about the next wave of strikes. I create smaller wards in midair, blocking lightning and creating invisible walls that shock those who slam into the barriers.

Anda's orders get sharper. Angrier. The nyshin's responses get slower. Warier. We're young and, in their eyes, inexperienced. They clearly expected us to fall quickly under their onslaught, but now they're eyeing us like true threats.

Tessen moves closer, murmuring updates in Ryogan and telling me who, exactly, we're up against. I breathe deep, drawing on the sparking desosa surrounding us as an idea forms. Still speaking Ryogan, I relay new orders to Etaro, opening the pouch strapped to my thigh and activating the wardstones inside. Etaro will shoot the stones through the sykina's ward, and the impacts should shatter the shield, landing beyond the nyshin. Then I can use my wards to trap *them*.

Tessen's attention fixes on one nyshin south of us. "Khya, wait, there's—"

A nyshin bellows an order. Anda's regimented ranks shatter as a third of the soldiers turn on the others. Confusion locks me in place, but my eyes dart from one furiously fought battle to the next until the leader of the splinter group shouts again. Ryzo.

A new warmth floods my veins. Ryzo may not have followed Tyrroh out of Itagami, but he's always been my friend. Now he's here, helping us. If I don't help *him*, the other nyshin will tear him apart. I refuse to allow that while I'm here to stop it.

I scream, "Etaro! Go!"

The wardstones rise from my thigh-pouch and shoot away in all directions. Their power is connected to mine, and I sense each impact like sparks of pain inside my chest. Although passing through the nyshin's ward slows the stones down, it doesn't stop them. Some slam into the nyshin's chests. Others embed themselves in tree trunks. Some keep going until they get swallowed by the muddy ground. I use them as anchors, running my magic through them and raising an impenetrable ward around Anda's squads.

The pitch of the battle changes, the frantic energy of a life-or-death fight snapping through the air like deadly magic as my friends join Ryzo's team, and together we fight against the nyshin we once fought with.

From the center of my squad, I deflect and defend, pouring energy into the wards, enough to shock the nyshin unconscious when they crash into the invisible shields. An arrow breaks against my wards, directly over the center of Rai's throat, and I gut the rikinhisu who shot it. Blood spreads across the front of their slashed tunic, darkening the wet fabric. Their hands press against the wound, and their eyes widen in shock as they collapse.

Then I'm left facing Anda. Around us, her nyshin are falling fast.

She's back a dozen feet, sword up and dark eyes flashing with anger. Her hair, the same brown-black as mine, soaking wet and sticking to her dark skin. For a second, the image flashes me back a week. All I can see is Tsua and Chio kneeling on the wet ground with pure anguish on their faces and black veins spreading under their skin as they slowly died. Then Anda shakes the thick strands out of her eyes, and the image shatters.

Tessen screams my name. I catch movement to the left—the second kaigo is coming in fast, their sword aimed straight for my heart. I throw a ward up to block the inbound blow before it can come close. The kaigo slams sword first into the shield. Impact breaks the path of the sword, but training keeps the kaigo's grip tight on the weapon. Which gives it the force it needs to careen sideways and slide deep across Anda's chest.

I blink and step back. Even as I watch Anda stumble, eyes wide and hands dropping her blade, I can't quite make myself believe what I'm seeing. All the uncertainty I hadn't felt before rushes in now. Anda looms giantlike in my memory, as powerful and untouchable as the Miriseh used to seem. When this fight began, I somehow couldn't see this moment. Now, I can't look away. Tessen takes out the kaigo who tried to kill me, and blood spatters against my ward, but I only see it in my periphery. My attention is entirely on Anda.

She touches her chest. Her hands come away dark with blood. Eyes wide and breath coming in fast, pained gasps, she stumbles again, but one bloodstained hand gestures sharply toward her fallen zeeka sword. The short blade rises, the tip pointed at my head.

"You—you can't be allowed to…" She closes her eyes. The sword trembles between us. "You can't— This can't—"

Anda sways. In my periphery, the last of her nyshin fall. Anda tries one more time to aim her sword and thrust the blade toward my head, but it's as though that effort is what finally breaks her. Her knees buckle. The sword drops. Anda collapses so heavily the mud splashes up, dark brown spots smacking against my ward. I look away as the spark in her eyes fades and her life seeps out of the gash in her chest and into the muddy forest floor of Ryogo.

TWO

Fifty-four nyshin surrounded us moments ago. Thirty-five of them are lying on the ground now, unconscious or dead, their beige nyska-cloth, Itagamin tunics stained nearly black with blood and Ryogan mud. My chest aches at the sight, but I can't close my eyes or look away. They aren't supposed to be here. None of us should be here. These lives were only lost because Varan couldn't see the good in what he'd built on Shiara. All he'd seen was his own exile. I grew up believing in something beautiful, but because of his heedless persistence, even the good parts of his lie have been crushed to worthless rubble.

"Khya?"

I tear my eyes away from the lifeless forms, finally looking at the faces of the nineteen nyshin left standing. I recognize all of them, but there are seven who've placed themselves ahead of the rest of the group, and my breath catches at the sight of them. Yarzi, Syoni, Vysian, Remashi, Donya, Amis, and Ryzo. *Ryzo.* I never thought I'd see him, or any of them, again.

"Ryzo." I cross to him, my arms held out, and he meets me halfway, gripping me so tightly he lifts me off the ground. "What are you doing here? How did you find us?"

"Who else but you would be mad enough to stand on a cliff in the middle of a storm watching an invasion?" His cheek presses against mine.

I close my eyes and fight the burn of tears. "As soon as I heard where Anda was going, I made sure we went with her."

I can't believe he's here. I squeeze him tighter before he puts me down so the rest of our former squadmates can engulf me in equally tight hugs. Everyone is pressing in close, his squad and mine, and it's like being surrounded by a physical sense of home.

I end up next to Ryzo again. My heart is skipping, and my skin is tingling, and I watch everyone talking excitedly, but it's so hard to believe this is real. Etaro introduces Zonna and Sanii to the new arrivals. Rai stands at the center of a tight circle, hands waving widely as she talks. Tessen is standing with Amis, whose oraku abilities make his senses second only to Tessen's, and their attention is focused outward, watching our backs in case another wave of trouble is about to crash over us. The sight of that watchfulness frees me to ask the questions I desperately need answers to.

"Ryzo, why— You didn't—" I stop and swallow, trying to organize my thoughts, because I need to know. How is this possible? We were cornered, and we weren't doomed, but the odds were bad. "How are you here? And why did you help us?"

The conversations around us falter. All eyes lock on me, but I don't look away from Ryzo. I used to know his face in minute detail—his strong, square jaw, his sharp nose, and his straight eyebrows—but it's been a year since we were anything beyond squadmates, and it feels like I haven't seen him in a lot longer than that. He almost looks like a stranger now.

"Tyrroh told you the truth, but you didn't leave with him." I try not to say it like an accusation, but it feels like one anyway. "And then you came here with the army?"

"Khya..." He looks down, his face pinched.

"We watched Rido'iti, and— I don't understand. None of it, Ryzo. How could..." I shake my head, trying to think around the chaos of today. "Were you part of that?"

"Khya, *no*. Bellows." He runs his hand over his close-cropped hair, glancing at Yarzi before he meets my eyes. "Do you remember when I ran into you and Tessen in the undercity?"

It takes me a few seconds, but then I do. Tessen and I had been in a rarely used section of the tunnels coming back from meeting with Sanii. "You were following Tyrroh."

"Because a few weeks before, I thought I saw—"

"Him and Daitsa talking to the Denhitrans." We'd been in the mountains chasing a Denhitran squad, and Ryzo had come to me with a gnawing worry—he was sure he'd seen Tyrroh conferring with the enemy. I convinced Ryzo not to report it. Blood and rot, this feels like it happened ages ago, but it's only been moons. Looking back, I can guess what happened next. "You thought he was working to undermine Itagami, so when he came to you with a story about the Miriseh's secret plans and wanted you to run away to meet the supposed enemy, you didn't believe him."

"You'd just *disappeared*, Khya, and nothing had changed in Itagami yet." Ryzo's plush lips thin, the lines around his eyes deepening. "It wasn't until after he'd left that we couldn't…"

"We couldn't deny it anymore." Yarzi steps forward, strands of eir long hair sticking to eir oval face. I shiver at the sight of those dark lines on eir sandstone skin, but push the memory of black veins and brutal death away again. That's not what's happening here.

I grind my teeth and wish I could wipe those memories from my mind. I refuse to look at Zonna, because no matter how badly the deaths of Tsua and Chio are plaguing me, it must be so much worse for him. I don't want to see that pain in his face. Or the blankness he uses to mask it.

Yarzi keeps talking. "The storms have been relentless since you left, and the city was going to die if it didn't change. Everyone was thrilled to have a way across the water and somewhere to escape to, but the first trial failed less than a mile out to sea."

"How many died?" Etaro quietly asks. I barely keep myself from wincing at how closely the question mimics what ey asked barely an hour ago as we watched Rido'iti burn.

Ryzo closes his eyes. "Over a hundred. Only the quick thinking of a few dozen rikinhisus managed to get the rest of us back to the shore before we drowned."

"That's why it took so long." Tessen eases closer, so close I can feel the heat of his body against my chilled skin through my layers of cloth. "We'd wondered, but if the first trial failed, it makes sense. Varan would've been more cautious. He would've tested his plan better."

"Exactly. And he was furious between those tests." Ryzo exhales heavily, his eyes opening but his posture drooping. "I regretted not following Tyrroh out of Itagami—and I hated myself for ever doubting him—but the Miriseh and the kaigo watched every way out of the city after he disappeared. Very few squads were allowed out. So I tried to take over where Tyrroh left off."

"Leading a squad?" Rai asks, confused.

"No—well, yes." He glances at the nyshin behind him. "I was placed in command of what was left of our squad after I proved my loyalty."

"Proved it how?" Whatever the task, it can't have been easy.

"I…" Ryzo trails off.

When it doesn't seem like he's going to start again, Yarzi explains for him. "He told them Tyrroh had been trying to convince us Denhitrans weren't the enemy, and he told them where Tyrroh was planning to take everyone."

"Is that *all* you told them?" I narrow my eyes, watching Ryzo shift uncomfortably.

"Nearly." He looks away before seeming to force himself to meet my eyes. "The only other details I knew were where I'd seen Tyrroh in the undercity and that he planned to head to Denhitra from Itagami. It seemed to be enough for Varan."

"It was," Yarzi agrees. And then ey adds, "After Ryzo took a public beating, a punishment for 'inaction' according to the kaigo."

"Ryzo." My own back aches thinking about the pain of that. Public punishment was never excessive, but they made sure the memory of it lasted, both in the minds of the clan and on the skin of the convicted.

He shrugs as though it was nothing, and his lips part to speak. Then, one of the nyshin nearby begins to stir, struggling to push themselves off the ground. Yarzi's bare, muddy foot snaps out, catching their chin and knocking them unconscious. Ryzo winces at the *crack*, his mouth snapping shut again.

Rai sighs. "I guess it's a good thing Tyrroh didn't tell us about Yorri or Imaku until we were away from Itagami."

My chest aches, and the grief at Tyrroh's loss rises up anew. Tyrroh didn't tell anyone about Yorri until they'd committed to following through because he was trying to protect him. And me. He always tried to protect me, and I wasn't strong enough to save him.

My heart cracks when Ryzo looks around and asks, "Where *is* Tyrroh? I owe him more than one apology."

"I..." My hands clench. My breath rattles in my chest. "Ryzo, I tried, but he..."

"He died weeks ago," Sanii finishes solemnly. "The Ryogans have arrows even Khya's wards couldn't stop, and one of them struck his chest. We couldn't save him."

Grief etches itself deep in Ryzo's face, and the flicker of his eyes gets faster, jumping from face to face. "What about Wehli? Miari? Daitsa?"

"Wehli, Miari, and Nairo are with friends, and hopefully safe." I look north, wishing I could see for myself now. We've lost too many people already. I need to make sure they're okay. But Daitsa... "Daitsa, Keili, and Thelin died before we ever left Shiara."

"Bellows, Khya." Ryzo's shoulders sag, and he covers his eyes with his hand. "I'm so sorry. I wish I had left with Tyrroh when— I should've been there to—"

"Hey, no. Stop." I stuff my own guilt down and step closer, not touching him but making sure he feels me in his space. "Varan controlled *everything*. He only told us what he wanted us to know. You did the best you could."

"No, I didn't." Ryzo's hand drops. He straightens, meeting my eyes. "But I can now. I can come with you. We all will. The army is heading for a city called Jushoyen, and we can help with whatever impractical plan you've got."

Yarzi and the others are nodding, and I exhale.

"Yes. Yes, of course. It'll be a relief to have so many people I trust at my back. Blood and rot, Ryzo. There's so much I need to tell you." Plus, Ryzo was Tyrroh's second-in-command, his nyshin-pa. He's a leader. Maybe *he'll* be willing to take some of this weight off my shoulders.

"No," Sanii suddenly cuts in. "They should go back to the army."

"What? Why?" I turn to face em, my heart rate jumping. Sanii wouldn't suggest this without a reason, but I want Ryzo and the others with us.

"Taking down an army is impossible. So is getting *through* one. However, if Tessen still has Osshi's garakyu...?" Sanii glances at Tessen, who nods. He retrieves the small, clear sphere from his pack and tosses it to Sanii. Ey holds it up, balancing it on the tips of eir fingers and holding the sphere out to me, eir eyebrows raised. "If we had someone inside the army who we could communicate with at a distance, then maybe the impossible becomes a little easier."

A smile spreads across my face as I take it. "You are just as brilliant as my brother."

Sanii's expression softens into a pleased smile. Then Ryzo asks, "What is that?"

I extend my arm, the sphere cupped in my palm. "It's called a garakyu, and it's a desosa-powered way to communicate across miles, even for someone with no magic."

"How is that possible?" Ryzo reaches out to brush his fingers over the cool surface.

"Explaining it would take more time than we have," Sanii says before I can answer. "Trust us—it *does* work, and it'll be far better for us in the long run if you stay with Varan."

Ryzo meets my eyes, two deep furrows appearing between his brows.

All I can do is nod. "I hate for you to leave, but I think Sanii's right."

"Okay, but look around us. What exactly am I supposed to tell Varan about them?" He gestures to the bodies strewn between the trees, and I grimace.

I don't know what to think or how to feel about the death surrounding us. I was taught to obey my superior officers, and that the clan comes before our lives. The beliefs were engraved in me, but I also know getting rid of Varan's most ardent supporters is the only way to purge the clan of his influence. Still, I just can't stop thinking about how much blood is now mixed with the mud under my boots.

Sanii bites eir bottom lip as ey thinks. "Tell him Anda ordered your retreat when it looked like she was going to lose."

"Yes. Give him a version of the truth," I agree as a story blooms in my mind. "Tell him there *was* a group with Itagamin weapons near Rido'iti, but it was Ryogans who'd either found or stolen our weapons. If you claim Anda ran into an ambush, you can tell him that even though the regular citizens are defenseless, he should be wary of the soldiers. They have weapons capable of breaking through wards—arrows with black stone heads."

"You can even prove it to them." Etaro steps forward, an Imaku-stone tipped arrow with a black-painted shaft in eir hand. "Tell them you pulled this from one of the dead."

Yarzi takes the arrow, narrowing eir eyes and peering at the tip. Then, without warning, ey spins and slams the stone head into Anda's unmoving chest. My stomach turns; I want to rip the weapon away from em, but I don't dare touch that stone. When Yarzi rips it free, drops of dark blood fall, splattering on Anda's brown skin until the rain washes it away.

"What are you *doing*?" Not even after the most brutal of battles has anyone from Itagami ever defiled one of the dead.

"Ono was her sukhai, right? So he knows she's dead." Yarzi slides the arrow into the quiver at eir back. "He's also an oraku, and he'll recognize her scent on this now."

Oh. I hadn't thought about that—not the idea of scent, but the fact that my blood-parents are sumai bonded. Their souls are bound together, just like my brother and Sanii, and one sukhai always feels the loss of the other. Ono knows Anda is dead, and I'm sure he's already on his way to find out what happened. So long as the shock of her death didn't kill him, too.

"If Ono's coming here, we need to leave. Now." Because he won't be coming alone. To avenge his sukhai, he'll drag half the Itagamin army with him if he can.

"At least this time the rain will help us," Tessen mutters. When I look at him, wondering why, he shrugs. "*I'm* having trouble picking up scents and following trails in this, and not only are my senses better than anyone else's, I've spent the past few moons learning this place. They haven't. We can use the rain to help us evade them."

"And we'll delay them more." Determination hardens Ryzo's expression. "Show me how to use your little Ryogan message ball and then go. Now that I know you're alive, I want to keep you all that way."

Relieved he's not fighting our plan, I help Sanii explain the garakyus. It takes longer than I like, because we also have to teach them how the Ryogans use words to shape and control the desosa—the energy created and used by the natural world, and the source of all magic. Itagamins are taught to mold desosa like it's clay. Ryogans try to siphon and contain it like it's water. It takes several minutes for Ryzo to understand the theory behind the magic and memorize the garakyu's call and answer phrases.

Then, I give him one more task. "Slowing the army down is a good start, but the only way we'll be able to save Ryogo or any part of our clan is if we erode the nyshin's trust in their leaders. Don't put yourself at risk, but try to make them see the people here aren't enemies, and almost nothing Varan told them about Ryogo is real. I think making them understand that what they expect from this place isn't possible is the only way we'll be able to convince them to follow us home."

"If they can't see that on their own after Rido'iti," Ryzo mutters, "I doubt anything I can tell them will make a difference."

"You have to." Because if we can't convince them, we won't be able to save any of them, and no matter what happens to Ryogo, my entire clan really will die.

There's one truth we could share that would all but guarantee that the clan would begin to splinter, but our immortality isn't a secret I want to reveal yet. If the clan knows, Varan might find out, and this is one of the few surprises we have in the fight against him, so when Sanii catches my eye and makes a slicing motion across eir forearm, thin eyebrow raised in question, I shake my head. Thankfully, no one notices the exchange.

Ryzo finishes fitting the garakyu into his belt pouch and steps closer, lifting his hand. He doesn't touch my cheek until I nod permission. Smiling sadly, he brushes his calloused fingertips along the sharp line of my jaw. "Take care of one another, yeah? It's going to get dangerous."

"We've been dealing with Ryogo's version of dangerous for moons." I place my hand over his, pressing his palm against my cheek. "I'm more worried about you. You're the ones going back to the people who ordered a massacre."

Ryzo closes his eyes, and the others shift, many of them looking east-southeast, toward Varan's army, or where they might be now. No one tries to tell me I'm wrong.

We say goodbye—though I don't want to let them leave—and then they're off, Ryzo leading them away.

"Why didn't we tell them we found out how Varan created immortality?" Sanii asks quietly. "Ryzo wanted a way to convince the clan to abandon Varan, and the quickest way would be to prove the myth of the Miriseh is a lie."

"Exactly. Ryzo would have to *prove* it." I glance at Sanii, crossing my arms. "How can he prove anything without one of us as evidence? If he tries to claim we've become immortal without proof, it'll probably only convince people he's lying."

Sanii looks conflicted, but nods. It's okay. I'm not entirely sure I'm right, either.

But there is one thing I do know. "We also don't want to warn Varan we're fighting on a level field now."

At that, Sanii's expression calms, and both of us turn to watch the last of Ryzo's squad disappear between the trees.

"I think seeing them was as close to home as we're ever going to get," Rai murmurs.

"No." My stomach constricts at the very thought. "We'll get back to Shiara. We have to."

I have to, and I will as soon as I've done everything I can here. I have a promise to keep.

But no matter how determined I am to follow through on my vow, I can't erase the fear that I'm not right this time.

I can't help fearing none of us will ever see home again.

THREE

Tessen is leaning against a nearby tree, his head tipped back and his chest rising and falling fast with each harsh breath. "The forest smells like rot."

We've been pushing ourselves all day, and he and the rest of the squad are on the edge of collapsing from exhaustion. The only thing threatening Zonna, Sanii, and me, though, is the constant cold. It sinks into every muscle and deep into my bones. The chill is so painfully pervasive that it's hard to think, but I can pull my thoughts together when I try. Tessen's words make it worth the effort now.

"Rot," I say, just to be sure I heard him right. "The whole forest?"

He tilts his head toward me. "It doesn't smell the same as on Itagami, but I'm almost sure there's rot in every area we've passed through. It'll be worse on the farms if the forest is already beginning to decay."

I wince. The same thing happened in Itagami, and Varan used it to kindle fear in the clan. Starvation is a dangerously potent motivator. It was strong enough to goad the nyshin across an ocean.

"Well, when we find someone in charge, we'll try to remember to mention that." If they'll listen to a single word we say.

He nods, pulling his chapped lip between his teeth and glancing off to the side as new lines appear on his forehead. It's an expression of suspicious concern I've seen directed at me too often. This time, he's looking at Sanii.

"What is it?" I ask.

"I don't know. We should keep an eye on em, though. It's almost like ey's hiding an injury, but that's impossible." His expression makes sense now; he's not suspicious, he's confused. The only weapon that can harm Sanii is safely locked away. Then, Tessen says, "If ey's in pain, it has to be because of the sumai. Ey's been away from eir sukhai for more than six moons."

I feel the corners of my mouth pulling down despite trying to keep my face neutral. "I don't understand why they did it."

For a heartbeat, Tessen goes still. He doesn't even breathe. "You don't?"

"They knew they'd have to spend nearly every day apart." Sanii had been placed yonin, the lowest of the three classes in Itagami, and my brother had been nyshin. If anyone had discovered their relationship, it would've gotten both of them in serious trouble. "It'd get harder, not easier for them to be together as Yorri rose through the ranks."

"Maybe that's exactly why they did it." His tone is unexpectedly subdued, and he still hasn't looked at me. "*Because* they knew there might not be any other way for them to be together. And they loved each other enough to risk anything to change that, even if only in the afterlife."

"Maybe." I don't know what else to say. An ache is settling in the center of my chest. The afterlife. When Yorri and Sanii bonded, they did it believing they'd spend eternity together in Ryogo. Sanii knows the lie of that now. How will ey explain it to Yorri?

Even if they made the decision in pursuit of forever, it doesn't seem like they thought about the consequences at all. They risked their lives and their souls without considering the years of pain they'd be putting each other through *before* eternity. It doesn't make sense. The very last thing I want is to be a source of hurt in someone I love, and that's what a sumai bond does, eventually and inevitably. It caused pain almost immediately in their case.

But my understanding or lack of it doesn't alter what's happening now.

"Let me know if anything with Sanii changes." When I step away from the tree, Tessen gives me a long look. I feel the weight of his gaze even as I walk away.

It's been about a day and a half since we left the southern shore, so we *must* be close to catching up with Wehli, Miari, Nairo, and

Soanashalo'a. As soon as the others finish eating some of the strips of dried meat we have left in our bags, we keep moving.

Finally, several hours later and miles farther north, Tessen spots the hanaeuu we'la maninaio wagons in the distance. Excitement flares through me though they're still too far for me to see. We won't be any safer in those wooden boxes on wheels than we are on foot, but we'll be a lot warmer in those small spaces. And we're mere moments from seeing Wehli, Miari, Nairo, and Soanashalo'a again.

The trees thin another hundred feet on, and I can make out flashes of color ahead. There are three brightly painted, intricately designed wagons in a clearing, and Wehli, Miari, and Nairo are standing guard. Several hanaeuu we'la maninaio are spread out behind them. Relief almost buckles my knees. They're okay. They look dirty and exhausted, but they're here.

Weapons come up when they hear our approach, but as soon as we're close enough for them to see our faces, they sheathe their swords and rush forward to meet us. I extend my overhead wards as far as I can, shielding them from the hard rain. Miari, Wehli, and Nairo reach us first, but Soanashalo'a is only a few steps behind.

"We have a lot to tell you, but we need to leave as soon as possible, Lo'a." I talk before anyone else has a chance to.

My words stop them abruptly. Soanashalo'a recovers first, signaling to a man named Shiu to prepare for our departure. Another gesture sends two others running back to the yellow wagon my squad has been calling home since the day we met the hanaeuu we'la maninaio. Then she looks at me, her golden-brown eyes worried. "What happened, Khya?"

"Rido'iti is gone." I hate dropping the news so bluntly, but there's no way to soften it. "Varan ordered it destroyed, and the clan obeyed."

"Blood and rot." Nairo rubs his hand over his mouth. Miari and Wehli press closer to his sides, eyes wide and bodies tense.

"Worse, we were seen. Two kaigo squads nearly caught and executed us." Rai smiles grimly. Miari sucks in a sharp breath, stepping forward with hands outstretched, like she wants to check us for injuries. Rai waves her off. "We're fine."

I nod. "Because we had help. Which is our good news."

"Good news?" Wehli straightens, his square chin lifting.

"Ryzo showed up with the rest of our old squad," I say, managing a smile. "They turned on the kaigo's nyshin to help us escape."

WAR OF STORMS

"What? Where are they? Are they following?" The questions come fast from all three. Soanashalo'a stays silent, but I can see the same questions in her eyes.

"No, they're not." I hold my hands up to keep them quiet. "I'll tell you everything, but *after* we get moving."

They snap their mouths shut and jog toward the wagons. Soanashalo'a issues a series of orders in her flowing, lyrical language, sending the rest of the hanaeuu we'la maninaio hurrying off. The two she'd sent to our yellow wagon are just finishing their work when I step up to the door. One is carrying a large, steaming bowl to the narrow table usually kept folded up and stowed, and the other is laying out thick, colorful blankets and various changes of clothes on the two platform beds.

The temperature inside the wagon is a shock after the cold air outside. A wash of heat hits, stinging like I'm standing naked too close to a fire. I flinch but force myself to keep moving. Feeling everything fresh, Zonna had said. Bellows, he was right, and not just about this. So long as I'm in command, I can't afford to allow myself to be distracted by this. Learning to cope with this must be a priority.

I step past Soanashalo'a's people, shedding my damp outer layers and grabbing a blanket to wrap around my shoulders. Then, I take a slice of spiced meat from the bowl and gratefully chew the first cooked food I've had in days.

The interior of the wagon is comfortingly unchanged and familiar. The deep beds extend from the narrow end of the wagon, directly opposite the door. The padded bench attached to the left wall looks invitingly soft, and the black stove just to the right of the door is already crackling with fire to warm the small space. Everyone follows me inside, and the interior becomes uncomfortably packed in seconds, but my body has begun to adapt to the temperature. The body heat added to the fire's warmth is beginning to feel nearly blissful. Even the knowledge that I must go outside again isn't unbearable when I get to come back to this.

"I need to check the trunk." Inside the thick wooden box strapped to the rear of Soanashaloa's wagon is our collection of Imaku stones.

"No, *I'll* check it," Tessen insists as he pulls on a dry shirt. "You can follow me if you have to, but for both of our sakes, please don't go anywhere near that box."

Considering I don't want to go near those stones in the first place, it's an easy concession to make. The buzzing power scrapes against my skin when I'm close to them until it feels like I'm slowly being broken down layer by layer. It's like the stone is sentient and waiting for its chance to attack. Tessen has said he feels it, too, and it makes him uncomfortable, but we both know it can't hurt him. I go with him when he leaves the wagon, a blanket wrapped around my shoulders and a ward enveloping us both. I'm glad, however, to stay a few feet behind him.

When we laid the pieces of Imaku's black rock over the katsujo and drew the vein of power's impossibly potent desosa into them, the stones transformed into weapons capable of destroying an immortal. *I* am an immortal. Despite the wardstones I laid in the box to serve as both a lock and a shield, the stones' energy leaks through like it's reaching for me. It bites with teeth sharper than any animal, but no wounds appear on my skin. It burns hotter than a towering bonfire, but the heat does nothing to warm me.

I thought the stones' power felt like vengeance made tangible when we first succeeded in creating these weapons. Vengeance is enraged and uncontrolled, though. This power feels much more like a predator waiting in the shadows for the right time to strike. Strike it will, but not yet, not here, and not against us. We hope.

I shiver in the aching cold and pull the blanket tighter around me as Tessen runs his hands over the wood.

"It's as secure as we can make it." Tessen touches the center of the trunk one more time before he steps back. I nod and glance around the temporary camp. The ukaiahana'lona—massive horned beasts used to pull the wagons—are hitched in place and the three-wagon caravan is ready to move, so we hurry back to our wagon and climb in. This time, the transition to the heat of the wagon isn't as painful. I wasn't out there for long, though.

The ukaiahana'lona bray, and then the wagon creaks and groans around us, jolting forward before I have a chance to brace myself. Tessen catches my arm and helps balance me until we reach a seat. Natani, Rai, and Etaro are perched on the upper bed, Wehli, Nairo, and Miari sit on the lower, and Sanii is sitting next to Zonna and Soanashalo'a on the bench. Tessen and I take the two foldable chairs that had been hanging on the wall. Sanii is already explaining what's happened since we split up, so I let em continue.

After a few minutes, Soanashalo'a gets up and moves carefully toward the stove to finish preparing the rest of the meal. I doubt I could cook while the wagon shifts and jolts like this, but despite her constant glances at Sanii, she moves with the ease of long practice and continues tossing items into the large clay pot on the stove. Soon, the enticing scent of spiced meat, vegetables, and rich grains fills the wagon.

Wehli, Miari, and Nairo interrupt Sanii to ask questions. Soanashalo'a stays quiet, but the worry lines on her face get deeper. When Sanii is finished, I finally ask, "What is it, Lo'a?"

"Aside from the world being on the brink of ruin?" She covers the pot before she sits down, strain surrounding her eyes. "Maybe we made a mistake. Was Osshi Shagakusa right about warning Jushoyen?"

"I don't know. We *can't* know." But I've wondered the same thing.

Osshi is Ryogan, and he kept pushing us to go to the Jindaini, the leader of Ryogo, and reveal everything. He was so committed to that goal, he abandoned us and headed for Jushoyen on his own. If he was granted an audience when he got there, I doubt it went well; the Ryogan tyatsu were still wasting their time chasing *us* a week ago. Which isn't surprising. His stories must've seemed impossible, and he barely had any proof. Maybe it would've gone differently if we'd been there, but what might've been doesn't matter, because it never can be again.

"I do think that's where we need to go now, though," I say. No one looks excited about the idea. No one protests the plan, either.

But Soanashalo'a exhales heavily. "Are you sure we should be heading for Jushoyen now?"

"We?" I ask hopefully. She and her family have carried us all over Ryogo, and their help made half of what we've accomplished possible, but I would've understood if Varan's arrival changed things. "It'll be safer for you if you don't come, Lo'a."

She searches my face consideringly. The rest of my squad watches, quietly waiting.

"It is not for us to know what will be remembered by future generations." She looks around, her arched eyebrows raised. "This, though? I believe what you and your friends are doing will become the seeds of legend for the next several centuries, no matter the outcome."

"And you want your name in those stories, too?" It was the kind of dream I might've had once. Now, I'd happily forego all recognition if someone else wanted it instead.

"I want to watch the truth unfold," she says. "Your name will be remembered for ages, but the truth of your story will only happen once. I want to be there for it. Others will get the story in pieces that will be diluted or distorted with each retelling. I want to be the first to tell your story, if I live."

"Oh, really?" The corners of my mouth twitch, but I can't quite smile. "And how are you planning to distort the truth?"

"I think I will make you taller," she says with mock seriousness.

Tessen laughs. I straighten in my chair, pulling my shoulders back and lengthening my neck. "I'm not tall enough already?"

"Definitely not for someone about to become a legend." She winks. "Maybe I will also give you glowing eyes and claws that extend like a cat's and rip your enemies to shreds."

"Ridiculous." I smile and relax again. "No one will believe you."

"I've met you. I believe it," Tessen says. Rai, Etaro, and Nairo immediately agree.

"See, Khya?" Soanashalo'a nods at my supposed friends as she gets up to check on the food. "Besides, I can be very believable."

"*That* I believe." And I do, but the lightness of the moment is already beginning to fade as the problems of tomorrow fill my head. What would Tyrroh or Tsua do if they were here? What questions would Yorri ask? I tap a rhythm on my knee and try to think. We're already on the only path I can see. "When we reach Jushoyen, we'll warn the Jindaini like Osshi wanted us to originally. The Ryogans must have a way to send out alarms in times of emergency."

Soanashalo'a sighs. "We will probably have to convince them to release Osshi, too, or rescue him ourselves if they refuse."

Rai snorts. "Why the bellows would we want to do that?"

"He abandoned us, Lo'a." I shake my head. "Then he helped the tyatsu spy on us. The ambush his choices led us into killed someone in your family."

Tessen nods, expression grim. "He's caused us enough trouble. We don't need to invite him back to cause more."

"My family's debt to him was cleared weeks ago." Soanashalo'a stirs the contents of the large pot. "But you still owe him a favor."

"Why is that?" Sanii's voice is unreadably even.

"For introducing you to me." Her smile makes it hard to tell if she's serious or joking. "His trip to Shiara also made it possible for you to get here, and his research helped guide your journey to find a weapon against immortals. Plus, as many problems as his decision to leave caused, you must admit he was not entirely wrong."

I don't have to admit anything. "I'm more worried about beating Varan to Jushoyen than I am about finding Osshi."

"Speaking of worrying, what about the Ryogans' little spies?" Etaro looks up even though Tessen would've warned us if there was anything hiding in the trees. It had taken us moons to realize the Ryogans had hidden garakyus in the trees at strategic points throughout the land, a way to monitor their people and the strangers who pass through their territory. Those magical spies were how they found us over and over again, but Tessen eventually learned how to spot them before they spotted us. He should still be searching for them…unless he forgot about the danger; I almost had.

The more decisions I make, the deeper the truth settles on my shoulders—I shouldn't be in command. There's so much more I needed to learn before becoming the nyshin-ma of a squad, but one by one, those who had been leading us have died, and Zonna—who by age, experience, and right should be in charge—refused to take over. It's fallen to me, even though I can't even keep something as important as the network of garakyus in mind.

Exhaling heavily, I rub my forehead and try to focus. "I don't want to make it easy for the tyatsu to find us, or warn the Jindaini we're coming, but speed seems more important than secrecy. Ryogo has bigger things to worry about now than us, don't you think?"

They agree. However, if a tyatsu watcher sends a force after us now, that will tell us something, too. If, in the face of Rido'iti's destruction and Varan's push toward the capital, the Jindaini sees us as an equal threat, then meeting with him is going to go even worse than I expect.

And I'm already expecting it to fail. Explosively.

FOUR

A loud gust of wind slams against the wagon. It rattles and begins to tilt. I slam my hand against the wall, barely catching myself before the wheels reconnect with the ground and the whole box jolts. For the last hour, the wind has been blowing crosswise to our path, and sometimes the blasts have been so fierce it felt like we'd be lifted off the ground and slammed into the trees.

Tessen grips a shelf and leans closer to the window. It's open to give him a better chance of spotting incoming trouble, but I warded it against the storm. He asks, "Am I imagining things, or does it look like all those trees are beginning to slant?"

The caravan has been traveling north for about three days, and the landscape has become increasingly hilly. The trees, though, have always jutted straight toward the sky no matter how tall they grew or how steep an incline they were rooted into. Here, the trees are tipping over, some nearly uprooting from the land sustaining them. This whole swath of the hillside looks one strong gust away from tearing loose and tumbling down.

"That can't be good," I murmur.

"If the forests are rotten and tearing out of the ground, the farms have got to look like lakes with bits of green trapped in them." Worry etches itself deep into Tessen's brown skin. I wonder if he's asking himself the same question I am—if a land so green is suffering under this onslaught of rain, how much worse off is Shiara right now? Then he shakes his head. "Even if we figure out how to push Varan back out to sea, I don't know how this land can recover from what he's done to it, Khya."

Surprise quickly congeals into frustrated hurt and spreads through me too fast to quell. My hands clench. "And what, exactly, am I supposed to do about that?"

Tessen's eyes dart to mine and then away. Around us, everyone else has stopped. I haven't been truly angry at Tessen in a long time, since before we left Shiara. I am now.

He knows I've been floundering for days, trying to get *someone* to take some of this responsibility from me, yet he's telling me about another problem, one I doubt the Kaisubeh themselves could solve, as though I'm supposed to slot it into my plans and fix it somehow?

Expression unreadable and eyes fixed on mine, he clears his throat. When he speaks, his tone is awkwardly cautious, like he thinks I'm standing on the edge of a precipice and the wrong word will push me over. "No one expects you to *do* anything about it. But we already decided to tell the Jindaini about the rot in the forests. This is just another sign of the same problem. Knowing about it before you face him can only help."

I close my eyes and force myself to take a long, slow breath. A vicious voice in my mind wants to throw my question about Shiara at him to make sure he's thinking about home with the same worry, but what will that help? We can do even less to help Shiara than Ryogo.

"Feeling everything fresh," Zonna had said, but in this moment, I realize I haven't just been suffering from the cold. Every experience and emotion has been more powerful, the good and the bad, and they've been harder to push aside. Rido'iti didn't just crack my foundations, it left gaping holes I'm only now seeing, only now understanding I don't know how to fill.

And my uncertainty is making me lash out at Tessen. I verbally throttled him, and almost said worse, for no reason. There's no excuse, not even what I saw in Rido'iti; he saw the same thing, and he saw it with more clarity and in sharper focus than anyone else.

"You're right." I say it quietly. The words are intended for him, not the rest of the squad, but the others are too close to avoid overhearing. "I'm sorry."

Tessen nods, but his expression is still blank except where the corners of his mouth are turned down. Is he angry with me? I can't tell, and I hate not being able to read him. What's worse is feeling like he's purposefully hiding his thoughts from me. I could push this and force him to react so I can tell if he forgives me, but I won't when we have an audience. That he really wouldn't forgive. I take another breath and force myself to walk away.

With all ten of us stuffed in the wagon, it's not easy to move without getting in someone's way. Everyone shifts aside for me now, though. Quickly. As I pass, Etaro watches me with a wariness I don't like seeing. I drop my gaze to the floor, avoiding looking at anyone else as I climb up to the higher bed and push myself into the corner.

The domed roof makes it comfortable to sit upright in the center of the bed. In the corner, my head brushes the roof unless I curl into a ball and rest my forehead on my knees. Strangely, I feel a little better once I've wrapped my arms around my knees to block out the light.

Get a grip. They're all counting on you, so you had better not fail again.

All of us have lost too much already.

The bed shifts under someone's weight, and the warmth of another body settles at my side. It can only be Tessen. I don't think anyone else would willingly put themselves this close to me right now. Even Tessen keeps a few inches between us and stays silent for far longer than I expect him to. Minutes pass with only the sound of our breathing, and then he exhales, the breath so long and slow it sounds more like a plea for patience than anything else.

"We're only a day out from Jushoyen, Khya."

"I know." It comes out almost like a whine. I curl myself tighter and bite my tongue.

"Then that's how long you have to find a way to get your head out of Rido'iti."

"You really think that's possible?" I lift my head to glare at him, and I don't even try to keep my tone level. "Have *you* forgotten it?"

"I didn't tell you to forget it. None of us will ever forget, but we're not living on that ledge, either." He runs his hand over my hair and pulls me closer, letting me hide against his broad chest instead of in the circle of my own arms. "You aren't responsible for what happened in Rido'iti. If we could have done something to stop it, we would've. That day is not a failure, and it's not a sign that someone else needs to be in charge. You've been leading us since before we left Shiara, Khya. Tyrroh just never bothered to tell you."

That makes me pull back. "What are you talking about?"

"When did Tyrroh last give you an order? Honestly, he'd been treating you like you were equals for moons." Tessen runs his fingers over my hand, his eyebrows raised. "You looked to him for permission out of habit, but he never told you to do anything you weren't already thinking would be a good idea. He also never disagreed when you came to him with a plan."

Is Tessen right? I never saw it like that, but I can't deny it's objectively true. Tyrroh's motivations, though, can only be guessed at. It's hard to believe he'd leave me in charge of even a single person if he were still here. Forget an entire squad.

"He had faith in you, Khya." He isn't smiling, but the disconcerting blankness is gone from his face, and that eases my mind as much as his words. "He believed in you, and so does everyone else. You've got one day to figure out how to make yourself believe. Or at least hide the fact that you don't."

Tessen is right. Out of every challenge he's ever thrown at me, though, this one is asking so much more, and I don't have the first clue where to begin.

FIVE

Jushoyen has walls. The thick stone barrier rises at least sixty feet and cuts a misshapen circle through the sprawling city.

From a hillside to the south, we can see roads running in concentric circles that ring the wall and continue outward. Inside the wall, the layout is far less organized. Closely packed buildings are shoved between roads that twist with the same unpredictability as plant roots, and the structures are mostly white with sharply sloped black wood roofs. Outside the wall, the buildings go from small, unpainted structures that look unstable even from a distance, to sprawling, carefully maintained compounds surrounded by swaths of land and hidden away behind their own walls.

The wall and the way the city is divided are completely unlike any other Ryogan city we've seen. Because of *course* this place must be made of the unexpected. I spent most of yesterday trying to do what Tessen suggested, centering myself and erasing as many doubts as possible. I couldn't clear away everything, but I managed to quell the worst of my fears. Now, seeing Jushoyen, much of that work is breaking down and washing away.

Most of the cities we've passed since Rido'iti have either been empty or in chaos as people fled. Here, gray-clad tyatsu patrol Jushoyen's streets, directing the stream of citizens into the walled portion of the city.

There are far more people than could possibly live in the surrounding buildings, many of them with massive packs on their backs and more bags gripped in their hands. They're being herded behind Jushoyen's walls as though they'll be safe there.

I grind my teeth, hating the very sight of those towering stone barriers. They're not enough to stop an army like Varan's, but they *are* one more thing slowing us down when we're already running out of time.

"Walls?" I look at Soanashalo'a, eyebrows raised in silent question. I hadn't thought to ask her about defenses before—no other city has had any—but she also hadn't mentioned them. "The other cities barely seem to be guarded by tyatsu, let alone walls."

"Their leaders live here. This is one place they actively protect," Soanashalo'a says as we study the city from a mile away. "The palace where the Jindaini and his councils live is surrounded by another set of walls. Not as high or as thick, but still formidable."

Once she mentions that, I can pick out the wall and the buildings it protects from the chaotic maze of structures.

"What about using one of the rivers to get in?" Tessen points toward the wide strip of water winding up to and straight through the city.

"Usually, that route is better guarded than the main gates." Soanashalo'a narrows her eyes at the watery pathway. "The Ryogans care more about taxes than visitors most days."

I don't know what taxes are, but unless it's a type of protection the Ryogans use on the river gates, they don't matter. What matters are the city's three entrances, the guarded gates, and the dozens—maybe hundreds—of armed tyatsu on the wall. And she's right. It looks like the tyatsu on tha gates and near the water are checking *every* visitor. Swarms of people are being let into the city, yet at the gates themselves, the line slows to a crawl as the guards stop every person to talk to them. No matter what we're wearing or how well we've managed to learn Ryogan, we will never pass as locals.

Digging the heels of my hands into my eyes, I try to see the city like a puzzle. The problem is I was only ever passable at puzzles. I'm not my brother.

What makes the situation complicated isn't just the wall but the city itself. To reach the Jindaini, we don't just need to get into the city unseen, we need to get through it, too. I'm not sure if even Yorri would be able to find a way to walk to the Jindaini's palace without catching any attention. Not on a day when everyone is on high alert and the streets are so packed that I can't use my wards to hide us from sight. After all, invisibility doesn't make us any less solid.

It's too bad we can't fly. Tsua might've been able to get us to the palace by lifting us over their heads, but Etaro isn't as strong as she was. Ey could maybe get us over the outer wall. There's no way, though, that ey could keep us aloft all the way to the palace.

The sounds around me shift, snagging my attention. Underneath the wind is a whispered conversation. Zonna and Soanashalo'a are standing close together, their heads tilted toward each other and their expressions intense. A second later, Tessen's focus snaps in their direction, his eyes narrowed and his head cocked. When he strides toward them, I follow.

"Yes, but how sure are you it's gone?" Zonna is asking as we get closer.

"How can I be sure of anything?" Strain adds lines around Soanashalo'a's eyes and wrinkles to the narrow bridge of her nose. "This all happened before my grandmother's grandmother's grandmother was born, and no one in my family has ever set foot in Jushoyen!"

"What aren't you sure about?" I hold my breath and hope.

Soanashalo'a rubs her temple. "A rumor of an ancient tunnel running for a mile and connecting the Kaisubeh Tower in the center of the city and the palace in the northern quarter."

"And the Kaisubeh Tower," Zonna begins, stressing each word, "sits on the bank of the river, which is the only way we'll get into the city unseen. It's the best plan we have."

It's the only *plan we have*, I almost point out.

"You would need to find the tunnel first. And you still must get through the gates on the river, which is *not* going to be any easier than on land," Soanashalo'a insists, "so unless you can hold your breath long enough to walk more than a mile underwater, you need a better plan."

"Why does anyone need to hold their breath?" Sanii asks, just as the same realization sparks in my mind. "Khya's already figured out how to bring air underwater."

I have, in a way, but I never thought I would use it like this.

Soanashalo'a is waiting for an explanation, so I tell her the story of our escape from Imaku. By the time I'm done, everyone else is leaning in to listen, too.

Moons ago, we tried to get Yorri off Imaku, the barren prison island Varan had trapped him on. The only escape left was over the edge of a cliff and straight into the ocean. We survived because I managed—barely—to shape a shield that would keep water out and a bubble of breathable air in.

Then, the bubbles of air had been at the mercy of the currents. I didn't have the power to direct them, and only had Tessen and Sanii were with me. Now, given Etaro's skill as a rikinhisu, directed control and decent speed might be possible. Even if the gates guarding the river extend below the waterline, which is how I'd build them if this were my city, it won't stop us for long.

"So, we have a way in through the river," Sanii says once I'm done. "What exactly will we be looking for once we reach the tower?"

Zonna and Soanashalo'a share a long look, his eyebrows raised and her head tilting in capitulation. He runs a hand through his black hair, long enough now to brush his shoulders. "Hopefully we'll know it when we see it."

Soanashalo'a laughs disbelievingly. "If this works, it really will be a story for the ages."

I smile despite their uncertainty, hope kindling in my chest.

Sooner than I thought possible, the plan is laid out and everything is ready, but we haven't yet plunged into the frigid river. Which means I have a few minutes to stand in the shadows of the trees and question everything.

It's cold here, and we're damp despite my wards—to truly keep us all perfectly dry, I'd have to somehow keep us in midair as well—but getting soaked is the worst anyone will suffer right now if my wards fail. Once we're in the river, the bubbles of air my wards create will be the only reason anyone can breathe. We'll be traveling under the murky surface of the river. It'll be cold, dark, and utterly uncomfortable.

This is one of those moments Zonna warned me about.

I don't know how to prepare myself for what's coming, and I *have* to be prepared. If I lose focus for even a second, my wards will fail. If my wards fail, the water will engulf us. Someone I care about will drown. None of us know how to swim.

"I don't know if I can do this." Tessen is nearby, his posture as stiff as stone and his gaze locked on the sluggish water, but the words are shaky and so quiet I almost miss them.

Bellows, I am such a fool. If anyone here other than Sanii and Zonna can understand the overload that's been crushing me, it's Tessen. His senses are more powerful than I can imagine, and they've been overwhelming him for years. He's spent almost half his life learning how to cope, how to shift his focus and ignore the incredibly loud signals his mind receives, and even he slips sometimes. An unexpected raucous sound can drop him faster than a knife blow. Too much input can force him to retreat so far into his own mind that he can't feel anything. No matter how bad I think this trip is going to be for me, it'll likely be so much worse for Tessen.

It took him moons to handle everyday life when his senses first overwhelmed him. I want to ask for advice, but not now. I don't even have hours to work with; I have minutes. Besides, even though it might help calm Tessen down to focus on teaching me new tricks, we don't have enough time—we have no idea how close Varan is to catching up with us. I still need to soothe his fears before we embark on this mission, though. Thankfully, he already gave me advice.

Pretend, Tessen told me. He said to pretend if I couldn't make myself believe. At least I don't have to pretend to believe in him.

Forcing my own gnawing anxiety aside, I grip his face between my hands. I need him calm. If he panics, it'll only make mine worse. "You *can* do this. Breathe, keep your eyes closed, and focus on me. If you get through this without panicking, I will make it up to you."

"Yeah?" He laughs shakily. "How exactly?"

"Remember what you asked me at celebration? The last *four* of them?" Celebrations only happened once a moon in Itagami, and they were the only night we performed the tokiansu—the warrior's dance. Tessen asked me to dance four times before we left Shiara. I said no every time.

Confusion creases his face for a second before he begins to smile, the expression weaker than usual. "Will you finally say yes if I ask you to dance, Khya?"

"*If* you don't panic, and if we survive Jushoyen and everything coming for us, then yes."

Still smiling faintly, Tessen stares into my eyes for a long moment. Then he nods. My own disquiet eases as he visibly relaxes.

It's so strange. I distrusted and envied him for years, and even in the beginning of this shift in our relationship, our bond was more about challenging and antagonizing each other than anything else. Now, the world is challenging us, and he's one of the only people I trust to help me rise to meet it. I didn't want him with us when Sanii and I started this a year ago. I don't want to even consider his absence now.

He's one of the few who can comfort me without making me feel weaker. Although he's better at accepting help than I am, the same might be true for him.

Natani is nearby, and I lift one shoulder, trying to ignore the unexpected flush of embarrassment rushing through me when I realize he's likely heard every word of the conversation. He doesn't tease or joke, though. Instead, a slight smile softens his strong face and he says, "You can always draw from me if you need it, Khya. Between the two of us, we should be able to get everyone into the city without getting wet. Or," he looks at our perpetually damp clothes, "at least, not any wetter than we already are."

He's a zoikyo, a mage who specializes in enhancing the power others wield. With his hand on my arm, I'll be able to pull in more desosa than I could on my own. It's how we got through Mushokeiji prison without being spotted, and yet I somehow didn't think about his skills while we were making plans today. In an instant, the embarrassment I'd felt becomes gratitude, and I murmur my thanks before I head deeper into the woods.

It's time to say goodbye. Succeed or fail, Soanashalo'a, Shiu, and the other hanaeuu we'la maninaio won't be waiting around. They're taking the wagons and most—but not all—of our weaponized black rock and moving north to stay ahead of the army. We likely won't catch up to them until we reach their hiding place deep in the Mysora Mountains, but neither will Varan. Hopefully, he won't even know to look for them. Nothing we had with us on the Rido'iti ridge hinted at the ties we've formed with the hanaeuu we'la maninaio.

"I do *not* like sending you in there, Khya." Soanashalo'a wraps a thick coat around my shoulders, holding it for me so I can slip my arms into the sleeves, and then she grips my arms once the garment is in place. "This feels too much like I will never see you again."

"You will. It's not easy to hurt me, Soanashalo'a Shuikanahe'le." I brush her long, dark hair behind her ear. "I'm worried about *you*. Ryogo is panicking. Please, be careful."

She smiles but can't quite hide the fear in her golden-brown eyes. "I will if you will."

Pulling on the front of my coat, she brings my forehead down to touch hers, and I feel the barest brush of a kiss before she pulls away. Without another word or glance, Soanashalo'a walks to her wagon, gets in, and closes the door. Less than a minute later, all three wagons are rolling deeper into the forest and out of sight.

It's time for us to go, too.

We step into the river a mile and a half south of Jushoyen. It's strange to watch the water react to my wards, moving away from and around us as soon as my magic touches it. My shields force the current to change and create space for the air we're taking with us to the river bottom.

Last time I did this, it was on instinct and only for a minute or so. Now, I need to hold a ward around nine people while fighting against the distraction of the aching cold and resisting the crushing weight of the river. And it has to last.

Even with Natani's hand on my elbow and a steady flow of desosa running through that connection and straight into my ward, this isn't an easy trick. All my focus narrows to holding the ward and walking forward, placing one foot in front of the other. I'm barely aware of much beyond Natani's grip on one arm and Rai's hand on my other, both gently guiding me, and of Tessen and Etaro's quiet conversation. Etaro propels us forward and clears our path when necessary, and despite how much Tessen clearly hates being closed in on all sides by cold, crushing water, he's skillfully helping Etaro navigate us around massive rocks, broken boxes, and other wreckage that's settled to the bottom of the murky river.

Twice I catch my thoughts slipping, fixating on the ache in my joints or the bumps rising on my skin instead of the desosa-fueled wall keeping us from drowning. Dragging my mind back to my ward and to my next step gets harder each time. It makes the journey seem endless, especially since the water only gets more clouded as we travel, not less. I can't see a rot-ridden thing. I'm sure Tessen knows how far we've come, but I've got no idea until something solid emerges—stone pillars and thick lines of metal. We've come farther than I thought. A mile and a half. We've reached the border of Jushoyen.

The columns at the river's edge are wider than two people standing abreast, and the metal gate is solid, even though it only extends a few feet below the surface of the water. We could simply walk under it, but the Ryogans have proven dangerous when we least expected them to. Just because we can't see more protection doesn't mean it's not there.

"What are we facing, basaku?" I ask.

"There are guards above and something…" Tessen squints at the water below the grate. "I think it might be a spell to act like a tripwire, something to send up an alarm if it's disturbed."

"Bellows. Of all the times for them to use *magic*," I mutter, pulling away from Rai's hold to rub my eyes. "I'd have to shift the ward to get us past. I don't know if I can without risking water bleeding through."

"Hold on. I think I can do something." Sanii steps up through the group, Zonna only a pace behind em. "Tsua and Chio taught me about different kinds of traps, and they talked about something like this."

Last year, when ey faced the herynshi—a trial every Itagamin citizen faced to decide their rank and fate—ey was deemed powerless and placed yonin, the lowest class. They were wrong. First, Sanii learned how to create light, and since we landed in Ryogo, ey has learned how to sense the desosa and use it to work Ryogan spells. Tsua, Chio, and Zonna taught em well.

After conferring with Zonna, Sanii tries several spells in succession, each one spoken in a quiet murmur. Finally, a web of red-gold light flares and dies. Tessen exhales, a little of the tension leaving his shoulders, and I know Sanii shut down the trap.

We cross into Ryogo's most protected city literally under the tyatsu's noses.

The first change I notice is the debris. There's so much more of it here. Broken boards of wood and pieces of cloth float on the surface, and smaller pieces drift on the currents below. Etaro works twice as hard now to clear the way. Boxes, wagons, and sometimes the remains of whole boats litter the sandy bottom. Small boats and larger ships float above us, and pillars supporting wooden platforms obstruct our path. More than once, Miari must break a block of stone into rubble for us to fit past the clutter.

My body is processing so many sensations at once I don't know how to separate them anymore. Water is pressing against my wards on all sides, trying to crush them and me, but we're walking more on my ward than on the ground, giving me a strange sense of weightlessness, too. The bumps rising on my skin and the tremble in my muscles might be from cold or from the buzz of power flowing through me. I feel the drain of the work

I'm doing as clearly as I sense the steady flow feeding into me from Natani and the desosa soothing and healing my tired body and fading reserves. Until now, I didn't know it was possible to be literally trapped in the center of a cycle of exhaustion and energization, endlessly rolling from one to the other. It makes what I can see of the world seem dreamlike, and the longer we walk, the more heavily I lean into Rai's guiding hand.

Finally, Tessen spots the faded red posts marking the dock at the Kaisubeh Tower, and Etaro, despite how drawn and tired ey looks, lifts us closer to the surface. We break through the water under cover of the red wooden planks. Tessen shifts through our group to get closer to the shore. I turn my ward bubble into a bowl that breaches the surface so he can climb up and get a look at what we're facing. I take a deep breath, flinching when the cold air bites my lungs. It hurts, but I don't care. It's the first fresh air I've breathed in hours, and it helps my sense of the world begin to settle again.

As Tessen pulls himself onto dry land, I wrap a layer of wards around him, pulling desosa in and bending the energy to protect Tessen from harm and sight. Only once he's surrounded by my magic can I keep myself from lunging for him and pulling him back into the river with us. Now, at least I'll feel any attack against him well before he does.

He disappears, and for minutes there's no sign of his return. I can track his movements by my sense of his ward, though, so I know the instant he finally reappears. Once I know he's safely hidden, I lift the invisibility. He immediately signals the all clear.

We climb from the river, and I encase us all in the same protections I gave Tessen. Then, we follow him across the garden surrounding the Kaisubeh Tower.

Safely in the building's shadow, a weight lifts from my shoulders. Even keeping the whole group invisible seems easy now compared to fending off the crushing weight of the river. I slowly ease away from Natani, lessening the amount of power I'm taking from him until I can safely let him go. Sighing with relief, I lean against the building and look up at the blood-red, fourteen-story, many-sided tower rising straight toward the lightning-filled sky. We made it this far. Now we only need to find the hidden, forgotten tunnel to get us across the city and into the palace about a mile and a half away. Should be simple.

Kaisubeh, please, help us. I don't know if the Ryogans' gods actually hear prayers, but trying won't hurt. *Help us save the people Varan is trying to kill.*

"Zonna, follow Tessen in," I whisper. "You need to be ready to tell him where to go."

A flash of uncertainty crosses Zonna's face, but he nods and shifts closer to Tessen, murmuring something I can't hear over the storm. While they confer, I look at the city itself.

In the sun-bright flashes of lightning, the scene feels like a series of nightmarish murals instead of anything real. The rain and the cold should've driven people off the streets, but every thoroughfare is packed. Hundreds of Ryogans fill the city, all of them wrapped in layers of thick, sopping-wet cloth. The massive packs they're bearing bulge at the seams and must be heavy with water. Some make wild gestures seemingly aimed at the faces in the windows overlooking the street, as though they're begging those people for help. Others desperately and futilely try to shove their way into buildings already stuffed so full even one more body might buckle and break the walls. The streets and the buildings are bursting, just like Jushoyen itself. No matter how impenetrable the Jindaini thinks his walls are, herding people into Jushoyen is only making it easier to wipe out the Ryogan population.

We've got to convince them to evacuate.

Tessen gives us the signal to move. I linger a little longer, my attention fixed on one point in particular. Unlike the streets, the garden surrounding the tower is almost empty. People peer out through the tower's windows, watching the chaos in the city, but the only people outside are black-clad soldiers guarding the gates, keeping the masses out despite their shouted pleas for help. It's enraging. How can the kaiboshi claim to serve the gods or the people of Ryogo while refusing to help them now? It's like there's no sense of clan here, no sense that anyone is willing to put themselves at risk to protect the whole of Ryogo.

Shuddering, I pour more energy into my ward. Keeping us safe is the only control I have.

Instead of heading for the ground floor doors, Zonna aims for a smaller building attached to the tower by a covered walkway. The wide doors open to reveal a ramp descending at a gentle, curving slope. Made of smooth gray stone and polished wood, it's an easy path to travel. We move quickly, pausing only at intersections for Zonna and Tessen to read inscriptions on the walls. Wrong guesses force us to backtrack three times, but the halls are mostly empty, so we only have to scramble for cover once, when someone in a white floor-length tunic and a deep green sleeveless overrobe hurries by.

"One of the kaiboshi," Zonna whispers after they're gone. "The green robe marks them as a servant of Seisho-fu, the Kaisubeh who watches over growing things."

I nod. It's good to understand who we'll be facing if we're found, but hopefully we won't be staying long enough for the information to matter.

After one more wrong turn in the labyrinthine halls, Tessen and Zonna lead us into a windowless room lit by glass globes hanging from the ceiling and oil lamps on the walls. Elaborate murals and intricate etchings surround us, most of them faded and worn, and the center of the room is dominated by row upon row of shelves. What I don't see is anywhere else we can go; the archway we entered through is the only one in the room.

"The passage should lead off from this room." When Zonna looks around, though, he's frowning, and lines radiate out from his dark eyes.

"Not what you were expecting?" I ask.

"No, but I'm sure this is the right place. My parents described that mural exactly." He points to the south wall where someone, with arms outspread, seems to be making a whole forest sprout. "We need to go deeper underground, but they must've walled off the entrance."

Tessen and Miari move off to search. Between Tessen's powerful senses and Miari's skill with stone, they'll find it if it's here. Shivering, I pull the coat Soanashalo'a gave me tighter, hoping it doesn't take them long. It seems colder here than it was outside. I don't like the blankness returning to Zonna's face, either. The fathomless darkness in his eyes that appeared after the deaths of his parents had begun to recede the last few days. I don't want him to fall back in and get lost again.

"What was this before?" I ask softly. Zonna blinks, confused, so I clarify. "This room. I'm guessing it wasn't always a storeroom."

"It was a prayer and purification chamber." He casts a slow look over the shelves crowded with boxes, baskets, and jars. "Tsua told me this was a sacred, solemn place where people came to meditate and divine the will of the Kaisubeh. This…this use would horrify her. Imagine how you would feel to find the saishigi chamber turned into this."

My lip curls in disgust. The saishigi chamber is where citizens who died honorably were cleansed and given their final rites. Before my faith in Varan and his followers shattered, the saishigi rites were something I valued deeply, the honorable end to a life of service, and a way to provide for the clan one last time. Even knowing the truth about Varan, it'd be appalling to see someone shove extra iron ore or bags of nyska grain into the chamber as though the purpose and intention of the space didn't matter.

Zonna tilts his head, his expression clearly saying, *Exactly. I thought you'd understand.*

Tessen snaps his fingers, the sharpness of the sound in the otherwise quiet room catching our attention. He's found something.

I move closer, but I won't be needed at first, so I let Etaro pass me to join Tessen and Miari at a wall. Natani steps in behind her, hands lifted as though he's preparing to feed her power if she needs it. Miari settles her palms against the surface and glides her hands along the stone, feeling it in ways I doubt even Tessen can. Then she steps back, arms straight and braced.

Nothing happens for one heartbeat. Two. Four. Then, cracks appear—the straight, even outline of a wide door. As soon as she's finished, Etaro moves in, disconnecting the stone from the wall and, after raising it several inches to keep it from scraping across the floor, shifting the slab into the space beyond.

I step toward the revealed passage and glance at Zonna. He doesn't seem happy exactly, but his eyes gleam as he stares into the coal-black tunnel ahead.

"I can hear water." Tessen is focused on something beyond the darkness ahead. Only when he's sure no danger lurks in those shadows does he lead us in. Zonna and Sanii rush in next, and I'm only a step behind them. Once the others are through, Miari and Etaro linger by the entrance. As soon as we're inside, they replace the heavy stone and seal the passage. No one will know we were here once they're done.

With the passage closed, the darkness is suffocating. It's like the forgotten caves under Itagami, where the darkness was so total it became hard to remember where my own limbs were. Relief only comes when Rai, Nairo, and Sanii provide light, the kasaiji with fire held in their palms and Sanii with eir desosa-fueled glow. Then, we move deeper underground.

The wide passage gently slopes downward, curving until it feels almost circular. It doesn't get any warmer as we descend. Thankfully, the temperature doesn't drop, either. There are carved words and colorful murals on the walls, but it's hard to see details in the shifting light. I get a sense of flowing rivers, lush farms, and beautiful figures who tower over the verdant landscape.

Just as the soft babble of water gets louder, I realize the walls have gotten farther apart and the slope is leveling out. We must be almost there.

"This used to always be open to supplicants," Zonna murmurs. "We should be coming to another chamber, one that draws water from the river. Beyond it will be rooms the kaiboshi used to use, but I don't know for what. Neither of my parents ever saw beyond the river room."

I don't know what to say. Zonna doesn't seem to notice my silence, and yet I can't stop my mind from churning, trying to come up with a response as we reach the end of the descent. Then our mages' lights flare to fill a much wider space. My breath catches, and I stop thinking.

Bellows, this feels so much like home.

The massive chamber is open and undivided with high, domed ceilings. It wouldn't have been out of place under Sagen sy Itagami. At least two hundred people could fit in this room at a time, so it should feel empty with only the nine of us here, but the soft splash of water over rock before it drops into the clear pool somehow makes the room feel welcoming. It's as though the cavern itself is glad to be occupied again.

I shake my head to banish the ridiculous thought and concentrate on real details. Similar to the banks of a river, the stone floor slopes down until it disappears into the pool. The water might be siphoned off from the river above us, but if that's true, something in the ground filters and cleans it before it falls gently down a rock wall and into the wide pool. This water is flawlessly clear and sparkles in our lights. There's an etching behind the waterfall, but whatever was once carved there has been nearly erased by hundreds of years of slow erosion. It's beautiful, though, even in disrepair. What must it have been like when the benches lining three sides of the room were full, and the murals covering the walls and the ceiling were bright with fresh paint?

Zonna stands in the center of the room, turning slowly. I want to ask if he's okay, but before I can speak, he shakes himself and strides toward the dark archway opposite the one we entered. The rest of us follow.

Instead of murals and etchings, doors line both sides of this hallway.

From the paths worn into the stone, it seems like this place was once well used, probably filled with noise and life. Now, even our soft steps seem too loud in the stillness.

Tessen and Miari open every door and touch every wall, searching for anything hidden. According to the stories Zonna and Soanashalo'a remembered, even when the tunnel between the tower and the palace was regularly in use, the entrances were kept well hidden and secret. Or mostly secret; the stories had to have come from some source, after all. The lack of details leaves us searching room by room, eliminating possibilities until only three are left.

Tessen and Miari walk the next chamber slowly, their fingers trailing along the wall as their eyes scan every surface.

After two circuits, Tessen mutters, "Not here," and strides out.

We all scatter to clear a path for him and Miari. They repeat the process in the second-to-last room, searching with senses and with magic, and finding nothing. Then, in the last room, because of course it has to be the *last* room, Tessen stops and presses his ear against the stone.

"The other side is hollow," he says quietly. "I can't tell if it's a room or a passage."

"Let's find out." I look at Etaro and Miari. "Ready?"

Miari moves toward the wall and presses her palms flat against it. When Etaro helps her move the block of stone, they reveal another passage just as heavy with darkness as the first.

Tessen signals for us to wait and then walks in. The black swallows him within fifty feet of the entrance, maybe less. I make myself wait where I am, no matter how much I hate letting him out of my sight while we're stuck in enemy territory. His call of "All clear" comes quickly, and I jog forward with Rai walking beside me to light the way. Once everyone is inside, Etaro and Miari reseal the exit, hopefully leaving everything exactly as we'd found it.

With any luck, it'll be as though we were never here.

With any luck, we won't have to use this as an escape when the Jindaini chases us away.

SIX

Although the passage is far from straight, we walk for more than a mile without seeing any rooms to investigate or branching tunnels. Then the passage slopes up and the smooth floor becomes a flight of steep stairs. At the top is a dead end. Another wall. If the old stories are true, the palace should be on the other side. The tunnel should've taken us safely across a quarter of the city, from below the multi-story Kaisubeh Tower to inside the palace grounds.

A barrier of stone might be the only thing standing between me and the Jindaini.

Tessen runs up the stairs first and then presses his hands and one ear to the stone, eyes closed and breathing slow. The rest of us stay back to give him space.

When he finally pulls back several minutes later, his jaw is clenched. He runs his hand over his black hair—long enough now to cover the tops of his ears—and exhales. "The storm makes it hard to be sure of anything, but I think I heard people nearby. I don't know how many, and I don't know where exactly we'll be when we break through. It's outside, though."

"Is there another way?" I try not to let my tone slip into a plea. Both Tessen and Zonna shake their heads, so I force myself to let it go. "We'll have to take our chances, then."

"If we're spotted, we only have to be quicker than the guard running to report us." Zonna looks at me. "Just be ready to ward against the Imaku-stone arrows."

"I know." But I look at the others anyway. I wish I had more choices. Invisibility isn't a real option this time since we're going to have to create a large and very obvious hole in a wall in order to escape this passage. "I can block the arrows, but it's better if they never connect with my wards. Deflect as many as you can."

The others acknowledge the orders and prepare, drawing weapons and readying magic. Tessen trades places with Miari and Etaro. In a few seconds, Miari's magic sends deep, straight cracks through the stone, then Etaro helps her shift the slab of stone aside.

Blindingly bright lightning flashes across the coal-black sky. A blast of freezing wind blows into the tunnel. Shouts of alarm fill the air.

"Blood and rot," Tessen curses. "*Run!*"

I add another layer of protection to my wards and sprint after Tessen, aiming for the red-roofed building on the other side of a small garden. An arrow strikes the grass inches from the edge of my ward with a solid *thwack*. Etaro sends the next five careening off course. Even more arrows are blasted out of the air by Rai's and Nairo's fireballs. The rest strike my ward, but they do no more harm than sand, scattering around us. These aren't the arrows the Ryogans developed in Mushokeiji, their prison for mages. These don't have the power to slice through magic. They don't stop coming, though. They fall like rain until the ground is riddled with them.

With a sharp gesture, Etaro lifts the arrows up and sends them all shooting back the way they'd come. The guards shout, and this time their voices are filled with terror.

More than a dozen tyatsu pour out of the building ahead, their swords drawn, but they wield the weapons with the skill of Itagamin children. Wehli, moving almost as quickly as he could before he lost his arm and thus his balance, darts through the squad and strips weapons from seven soldiers in a blink. Miari and Nairo easily get the rest before most realize what's happening. All thirteen guards in the garden are defenseless in less than two minutes.

I look at Etaro. "Can you get them out of our way?"

Grinning, Etaro widens eir stance and raises eir hands, palms up. The tyatsu lift off the ground and fly backward, screaming. They smash into the archers still firing at us and land in a heap on top of the wall. We sprint toward the building before they have a chance to recover. We don't drop their weapons until we're inside. Enemy swords or not, training won't allow me to drop a well-made blade into the mud.

Tessen leads us down two hallways and up steep wooden stairs. On the second level, a squad of tyatsu is guarding a door, weapons drawn and fear shimmering in their dark eyes.

"Put down your weapons or we'll take them from you," I warn them.

Their leader gives a shaky order to charge. I step aside and let Wehli pass.

His balance is shakier here where he doesn't have the space to move as freely, yet he's still fast enough to shock the tyatsu. He grabs their weapons out of their hands and jams them blade-first into the floor, creating a perfect row to block their retreat. Wehli didn't leave a scratch on any of them, yet they're so flustered no one struggles when we tie them up nor do they protest when we order them to sit against the wall like misbehaving children.

"Good work, Wehli." He's had a hard time adjusting since the accident in Kaisuama that crushed his arm beyond even Zonna's ability to fix, but he's done it well. I haven't always made a point of telling him so. He grins at me, and the expression gets brighter when he sees the pride in his partners' eyes—then again, Miari and Nairo rarely look at him with anything less.

Tessen gestures to the door the tyatsu had been guarding. "There are at least three people inside."

I take a deep breath and kneel in front of the lock. My cold fingers fumble with the ties on my belt pouch at first, but soon I have my set of lock picks out. The guards probably have a key. It's doubtful any of them would tell us where to find it and searching every pocket on every guard would be too slow. More tyatsu are on their way, I'm sure, but it won't matter. If the Jindaini is here, I'll ward us all inside until he listens.

As soon as the lock unlatches, I push open the heavy door.

And flinch at the blast of orange energy shattering against my wards.

I keep my eyes locked on the Ryogans standing opposite the door as I hold up a hand to stall my squad.

"I don't recommend doing that again." I take a step into the room and feel my friends keeping pace. "And don't call for help. No one will be able to get in here until I let them."

The windowless room is nearly empty, just blank wood walls, a bare wood floor, several brightly patterned cushions, two light globes hanging from the ceiling, and three people pressed against the opposite wall, one standing guard over the other two.

The mage is in front with their hands held out in front of themselves magic building around them. Behind are two others. They're crouched and cowering, their eyes wide. One of them is wearing robes made of silver-gray fabric that shimmers faintly in the light and with patterns done in multicolored threads run down either side. The other is dressed in simpler robes of black and gray—nearly the same shades as their long hair—and I think I see a garakyu clutched in their tightly closed hand; they thankfully don't activate it.

I dismiss the two in the rear for now and focus on the mage. They're wearing the clothes of a kaiboshi, the white tunic brushing the floor and encasing their arms to the wrists and a sleeveless overrobe, this one of black with borders of white. The desosa around them crackles, and their lips move as they ready a spell. No warning is going to stop them; I know how to recognize a person ready to die to protect someone they love.

They fire spell after spell, each splashing harmlessly against my wards. I reach into my pack and pull out four more wardstones, holding them on my open palms. Etaro doesn't even need me to explain. Ey gestures, and the crystals fly across the room, landing on the floor around our opponents. I snap the ward into place, trapping the Ryogans. All three scream when the mage's next spell smashes against an invisible wall three feet in front of their faces.

"We're in and the door's sealed, Khya," Tessen says in Itagamin.

I drop the shields around my squad and unhook the bag of wardstones from my belt. Etaro takes it, flicking eir fingers to distribute the stones along the walls. Using the crystals as anchors, I ward the room to keep everyone else out before I ask, "Is one of you the Jindaini?"

The mage clears their throat, fear and determination warring in their brown eyes. "If you're going to kill us—"

"I would've done it already," I cut in. "I could snap your necks if I wanted you dead. If I didn't feel like killing you myself, I could watch as Varan demolishes this city. It'd be easier." They still seem ready to argue, so I murmur in Itagamin, "Rai, Nairo? Fire."

Warmth flares at my back. The Ryogans cry out and shrink away. I finally stop shivering inside my layers of clothes as their flames burn away the last of the chill we carried in from outside, and the cold-induced ache suffusing my muscles eases.

"Yes, we could hurt you, but I promise no one in this room will." At my signal, our kasaiji douse their flames, and I miss them immediately. "Again, is one of you the Jindaini?"

The round-faced person in the plain, dark robes stands shakily, and I assume this is the Jindaini. I expected someone a bit like Varan, imposing in stature and personality, but this person is shorter than me by several inches, slightly built, and moves cautiously. When they look up, I notice something strange. A metal circle sits in front of each eye. The circular pieces are connected by a bridge over their nose, and slim metal pieces extend to loop over each ear to hold the whole contraption in place.

When they face us, they're tense like they're preparing for a blow. "I am Jindaini Gentoni Gotintenno. This is my wife, Jintisu Gotintenno, and this man here is Kaibo'Ma-po Yonishi Tsukadesu. Who are you and, if you're not here to kill us, what do you want?"

"Where is Osshi Shagakusa?" I ask.

"In a cell three levels down, awaiting a trial." Gentoni blinks, furrows appearing between his thin eyebrows. It's almost like he answered my question before he heard it. "You're looking for Osshi?"

"Yes. You should've listened to him." I step closer, keeping my gaze on Gentoni even when Yonishi tries to shift between us. "He wanted us to warn you about Varan immediately, but we didn't think you'd believe us. I wish we hadn't been right. He risked everything for Ryogo. Why are you repaying him by putting him on trial?"

"He broke the law." Yonishi swallows audibly. "He went searching for the bobasu and now they're here, and you think that's a coincidence?"

"I know it is." I pause, watching their reactions. "I was there."

Yonishi leans back, his arm reaching for the others as though he's trying to protect them. Jintisu hides behind Yonishi, but Gentoni steps closer to us. They're afraid. Even Gentoni. But it at least seems like they're listening now.

I bite the inside of my lip, trying to find the words to make them understand. "The storms over the past several moons? They're because of work Varan started long before Osshi left Ryogo. Varan has been planning his vengeance for centuries."

"And who are you to know any of this?" Gentoni asks.

"I am the son of Chio and Tsua Heinansuto." At Zonna's words they shrink back; his declaration seems to terrify them more than our kasaijis' bursts of flame. "I was born three years after your ancestors' ship crashed on an island called Shiara."

"And I was born in the city Varan built there. The bobasu have controlled our island for centuries, and I served them until Varan faked my brother's death." Inside, I flinch at the memory, but I keep my face as blank as I can. "We're approaching with words instead of weapons, but we were trained by the nightmares of your past to become the plague of your present. We're here with a warning. You cannot win against what's coming. If you try, Ryogo will suffer for your arrogance."

The Ryogans share several complicated glances, their expressions too full of nuance to be deciphered by a stranger. The fear is still there, as is at least a little disbelief.

Zonna takes another step, closing the distance between himself and them. "Heed our warning or don't, but do not dismiss us. And do not think us weak. I've seen what Varan is capable of. My parents and I suffered at his hands for centuries, and we did everything we could to keep him away from your shores. Osshi's arrival had nothing to do with what's happening now. All Osshi did was get us here ahead of the trouble and give you a chance to defeat them."

"Defeat them." Gentoni grimaces. "Our ancestors tried. Their only option was exile."

"Maybe," I agree. "But it's not your only option now."

"What are you talking about?" Yonishi demands.

"You found a way to hurt the bobasu, didn't you?" For the first time, there's more interest than fear on Jintisu's face.

"Better. We can kill them." I take no small amount of pleasure in the shock shining clear in three wide pairs of eyes. "You were on the right path and using the right materials, but you fear power too much to make anything strong enough." I look at Miari and order, "Show them."

She takes the pack off her back and unlatches the flap securing the main pouch. She pulls out a piece of black rock the size of her fist. Zonna looks away, an all-too-familiar bleak pain back in his eyes, and Sanii and I both step backward, keeping several feet between us and the terrifyingly deadly stone.

A torrent of emotions skitters across my skin at the sight of that rock. I didn't know it was possible to respect something I also loathed this deeply.

It's death—the weapon that took Tsua and Chio away. It's liberation—the tool we'll use to free Shiara from Varan's reign.

"It's the same rock," Yonishi insists.

I almost laugh. "Not even close. We poured far more power into this than your mages would ever be willing to touch."

Questions burn in Gentoni's and Yonishi's eyes, but Jintsu speaks before they can ask any. "But how do you know it'll work?"

"Because we tested it." Zonna's tone bleeds bitterness and loss. "My parents have been working to stop Varan since before their exile from Ryogo, and they willingly sacrificed themselves to test this, to make sure it worked so we—we…"

"We have no doubt a weapon made with *this* will work," I say when Zonna's words fail. I want to comfort him, but I can't now. "We might have time to set a trap for the bobasu, but what's more important now is getting everyone in the city somewhere safe."

"Safer than Jushoyen?" Gentoni asks uncertainly. My stomach sinks. If *this* is the safest place in Ryogo, its citizens are in so much trouble.

"Yes." Scenes from Rido'iti rise before my eyes, and as much as I hate them, I wish Gentoni had seen the massacre for himself. "The army crushed Rido'iti in hours. Your wall will barely slow them down. It'll give you another hour. Or two. If you're lucky."

The Ryogans share a glance, seeming to read each other impressively well. They remind me of some trios in Itagami, people who'd been partners for years. Soanashalo'a has implied Ryogans don't accept anything other than two-person partnerships, but maybe it happens even if it isn't allowed. I suppose it doesn't matter what they mean to one another, but I do hope they have enough sense between them to see we're the only way to save even a small piece of the life they know.

Someone pounds on the door, rattling it in its frame.

I slowly push my wards back, imagining the magic sinking into and merging with the walls and the door. I've only done this a few times, joining my protections to something solid, but this feels *easy* compared to the first time I tried—which makes sense; I don't have to hold out the weight of an ocean now, just keep back a handful of determined soldiers.

The magic settles. Someone slams against the door again. This time they scream. Tessen flinches in empathy; he knows from experience how much a shock from my wards hurts.

Gentoni, Yonishi, and Jintisu are wide-eyed, fear once more filling them.

"They won't be able to get in, but they also won't suffer more than minor hurts," I assure them. "I know this is a difficult decision, but time is limited. Do you know how far north the army has come?"

"They'll be here in less than two days." Gentoni's chin drops, and his voice sounds hoarse.

I look back at Wehli, remembering too well all the nyshin and ahdo with the same speed as him. "There's a chance the advance guard will be here tonight."

"There's no way they—"

"Yes, there is, Yonishi. I promise you." Irritation tingles under my skin like sparks. Those sparks flare hotter when a mage joins the soldiers in the hallway and shoots a sharp spell at my ward. Temper shortening, I gesture toward the sky. Just as thunder crashes. The timing would've made Yorri laugh if he were here, even in a moment as tense as this. "Neither storms nor a raging ocean stopped them. If Varan orders it, his fastest soldiers will be here tonight."

But, bellows and blood, I really hope they're not. There must be at least twenty thousand citizens in Jushoyen. Even with my wards on the walls to give them protection, there's little chance we can get thousands of people to safety in a few hours.

They hesitate, and it seems like they're having another silent conversation. I clench my hands and roll my lips between my teeth to keep my frustrated impatience inside my own head. A decision had better be reached soon, though, or I might scream.

"You're wasting time!" Zonna snaps before I do. "These mages can do things you've never seen. They decimated Rido'iti, and nothing you've thrown at them since has slowed them down! If we don't act soon, you'll lose everything."

"What is it you want from us?" Yonishi faces us head-on, shoulders pulled back and long face set, but he seems to be forcing the words past his lips. He gestures to the rock Miari's holding. "You want us to turn the stone into a weapon?"

"No, you've done enough experiments with it already." Zonna's tone is harsh. Unnecessarily so, even with what we'd inferred from everything we saw in Mushokeiji. I glance at him, shaking my head minutely and hoping he shuts his mouth.

"We will help you protect Ryogo as long as we can, hopefully giving you enough time to evacuate Jushoyen." I infuse my words with as much calm as I can, hoping to counteract Zonna's flare of temper. "You need to save as many people as possible, which means spreading warnings however you can. I'm nearly certain the entire army is on its way to Jushoyen, so the coast is the safest place for your people. Tell citizens to stop heading here. Order them to the edges of Ryogo instead, and have ships there to carry them away if possible. They might need to leave Ryogo entirely." I take a breath, watching their faces carefully. "In return for our help against the army, we want you to free Osshi and give us a crewed ship to carry us back to Shiara as soon as possible."

If they don't listen, I'll have to find a way to send out warnings on my own. There are people in Atokoredo I made a promise to. Osota and Shideso, who helped us even after we broke into their home, need time to get out before Varan hits their city, too. I don't want to let down two of the few Ryogans who have actually helped us instead of hunted us.

But I can't do anything to help them now, so I force myself to refocus. "I'm sorry we didn't listen when Osshi wanted to warn you. I'm also sorry we couldn't save Rido'iti. It's too late to change either of those things, but it's not too late to protect the rest of Ryogo."

"The councils are already meeting," Yonishi murmurs after another pause.

Gentoni raises his thin eyebrows. "You think we should talk to the councils? I only see that ending one way."

Jintisu puts her hand on Gentoni's arm, but her eyes are on Yonishi. "You've always trusted his instincts before. Now would be a bad time to stop."

Sighing, Yonishi pinches the bridge of his nose and then spreads his fingers, running them along his thick, black eyebrows. His chin dips, and one of his shoulders lifts. Smiling grimly, Jindaini Gentoni faces me, his dark eyes glinting behind the glass in his circular frames. "What exactly are you planning to do to help us? And why do you need the ship?"

I exhale a long, shaky breath. This is far from the end of our journey, but it's a step toward it.

Carefully, I explain my plans and make my requests. I hope I'll one day be able to meet with Jindaini Gentoni again and point to this moment in which I offered help and worked to save his homeland.

On that day, once his people are safe, I'll be asking him to pardon mine.

SEVEN

Hammering out a tentative agreement between us and the Ryogan leaders takes about an hour, and tyatsu mages spend the first half of it trying to break down the door. Each blast makes me flinch. They never come close to getting through, though. I'm still glad when, after Gentoni and Yonishi have several tense conversations through garakyus, the situation outside the room begins to settle and the attacks stop.

When we've come as close as we can get to agreeing on what to do from here, Gentoni and Yonishi use the garakyus to issue orders for every non-coastal city to begin evacuation. They also ask for food and other items to be brought to the room. Since I can hear both sides of their conversations, and Tessen can hear the murmured ones out in the hall, I only hesitate a moment when they ask me to release the ward on the room.

A few minutes later, two people wearing beige robes with red waistbands bring us both the food and new clothes—tyatsu uniforms. These are slightly different than the ones I've seen before with a series of stripes in red arranged in a way that seems to denote rank. These also have thick gray cloaks with wide hoods and golden pins to hold the fabric shut. These large clasps bear insignia Jintisu explains mark us as high-ranking officers who serve directly under the Jindaini.

"It will be hard for anyone to see your faces with these hoods raised, but your accents mark you as outsiders, so you'll only be able to hide in sight if you don't talk," Gentoni says as he and Yonishi show us how to wear the uniforms. "This is our best option, though. It'll take too long to talk the fools on the council into saving their own heads."

I don't fully understand the impact the clothes will have until Tessen, Miari, Natani, and I are out in Jushoyen proper. Many citizens are too scared to notice us at all as they frantically fill small wagons with boxes and bags, their actions the first visible ripples of Gentoni's evacuation orders. Others stare, though, watching us pass with varying levels of fear, desperation, and anger. Despite their awareness of us, we're able to move quickly through the city. Though citizens stop other tyatsu with questions or pleas for help, no one approaches us. Without any signal from my squad, people in the streets move aside as soon as they see our borrowed clothes.

There's an edge of barely contained panic in the air. What if orders don't disseminate through Ryogo, or even through the city? I'm not sure I want to see how bad this gets if Gentoni's people can't control the evacuation out of the city. Or what might happen to the people who are only now arriving here, exhausted and frightened and just in time to be turned away. Terror makes people react instinctively, and if they flee without any real destination, the casualties will pile up. There will be injuries from running through dark woods, starvation from insufficient planning, or deaths when groups run straight into a slaughter. Despite the hundreds of hazards waiting out there, the city could become even more dangerous if a petrified populace is trapped inside Jushoyen's walls while death tries to break in and devour them.

Which is why my squad split up. While Tessen, Miari, Natani, and I are working on the city's walls, the others will be helping to speed up the evacuation. Gentoni didn't know about the tunnel connecting the Kaisubeh Tower to the palace. However, our story sparked a memory of other rumors about secrets hidden underneath Jushoyen. I'm hoping they'll find another passage, maybe one leading outside the city.

Everyone in the squad is supposed to be scouting for a way to trap or ambush the bobasu, too, but I don't have hope anyone will succeed. There's not enough time. Even if someone devised the perfect trap, we don't yet have an effective way to deploy our stones against the bobasu. As much as it burns to miss a chance to carve Varan's heart out with a black stone blade, I'm probably going to have to let this opportunity go.

We walk through the city, and I try to watch everything. Tessen, though, only seems to be watching me. For a second it feels so familiar, like the times we'd walk through Itagami. Then he sighs. "You keep agreeing to the impossible, Khya, and it's getting hard to keep up."

Miari smiles and ducks her head, slowing her pace to fall back and give us a little space. Natani slows to stay even with her a second later.

"No one said you had to, Tessen." Although maybe it's one reason why I've always felt so bound to him, even when I couldn't stand the sight of him—he was one of the few who kept up with me and who sometimes surpassed me. We've grown past the need for constant challenge, though, or *I* have, and I'd want him close even if he couldn't keep up anymore.

"Seriously, I just…" Pursing his lips, he shakes his head. "This will *not* be easy, Khya."

"Is anything anymore?"

"No." He meets my eyes, resolve clear. "But we're with you, whatever happens."

"I never doubted it." When his hand brushes mine, I hold on. I wish I could stop walking, press him against the wall, and kiss him until he was out of breath and aching with it. I want to quit worrying for a moment about what's coming and what the Ryogans will think once I start working magic on their wall. If I could, I'd narrow my focus for a few hours to Tessen, to his reactions and his skin and those overpowered senses of his. To finding out exactly what he can take, how far I can push him before those senses are on the point of overloading.

Tessen's hold tightens. His eyes are wide, and he swallows convulsively. I smile at him with far more teeth than usual, and he shivers.

"Oh, save it for later, you two." Miari brushes past us, grinning.

I smirk. "You're just jealous your partners aren't here to look at you like that."

"Exactly," she admits. "So the last thing I need is you two rubbing it in."

Natani laughs as we reach the stairs leading up to the wall and begin to climb. The steps are enclosed, and the passage is wide enough for all four of us to walk side by side, but we stay to the right in single file to keep out of the way of the tyatsu sprinting up and down the steps. Thankfully, although many glance our way, it seems like the tyatsu's eyes catch on the Jindaini's golden insignias and ignore everything else. It probably helps that everyone is too busy looking for a threat from the forest to bother searching for strangers inside Jushoyen. They nod to us respectfully and keep moving.

Despite our limited time, when we reach the top of the wall, I find myself watching the tyatsu and trying to imagine being in their position. It's difficult to do. Physically, Itagami always felt impenetrable, safe in ways nothing else on Shiara was. A moon ago, every person on this wall must've thought this city was just as impenetrable. Varan has destroyed their sense of security already even if he hasn't touched a single stone of the city. My chest aches when I think about what I might realize he's destroyed when I see Itagami again.

Out in the open and high above the city, I'm extraordinarily grateful for the thick, oiled cloaks Gentoni and Yonishi gave us. They keep most of the water off us, which is good since I can't use my wards as a rain shield here. The tyatsu might not look too closely at our faces, but they'd definitely pay attention to four inexplicably dry officers in the middle of a raging storm. What's even better than the oil in the cloth are the spells Yonishi laid into the cloak as soon as he noticed how badly I was shivering. The fabric instantly began emanating gentle heat like Sanii sometimes emanates light. It doesn't eliminate my chills, but Kaisubeh bless it, it certainly helps.

"We'll put the first one here. Are you ready?" I ask Miari. She's carrying a large pack that contains most of our wardstones. I started this journey with only a few dozen, but I've made more in Ryogo, not all of them from crystal. Soanashalo'a gave me the idea for using other natural elements—in this case regular stone—and I'm extremely grateful now; I wouldn't have near enough wardstones for this plan otherwise. When we're done here, though, the only wardstones we'll have left are the ones my squad are wearing.

Miari places her foot where I point—directly in the center of the wide wall—and closes her eyes. When she moves her foot, there's a circular hole in the stone, maybe six inches wide and six deep. I use the voluminous folds of my cloak as a shield, gently drop a wardstone in, and move aside so Miari can close the hole. Then, I reach for the familiar energy of the wardstone, grip one slender thread of its power, and draw the energy with me when we leave. A hundred feet or so away, Miari creates another hole. I drop another wardstone and latch the thread of energy I pulled from the first point to this one.

It's the first link in what will be a very long chain.

We slowly walk the five-mile wall, repeating the process. It pains me to essentially discard dozens of wardstones, but the cause is worthwhile. I can make more. The lives here can't be replaced so easily. Neither can the city.

Initially, I assumed he wanted to rule Ryogo, not destroy it. If that's true, there's a chance—a small one—he'll leave Jushoyen standing if no one is here to fight him for it. Then, when all of this is over, the people will at least have a home to return to.

It's unlikely, though, and not only because he's already destroyed one city. The evacuation of Jushoyen will have to move at speeds only mages like Wehli and Yorri are capable of to finish before Varan arrives. We'll probably be here to meet him, which means holding the city against him, which means goading him into a stronger and more violent reaction simply by resisting. Would it be better to leave the walls as they are and concentrate my efforts on the actual exodus? I don't want my decisions to cause any more deaths. I don't want people to die because I didn't act, either. Tessen and Zonna might believe I'm capable of leading and trust the choices I make, but I don't know if I can handle failing here.

And there are so many ways we could fail. So long as most of these people survive, though, I'll call this day a success.

"Will this be enough?" Natani asks as we place the last wardstone.

"I made them from the katsujo, so they'll last for a while, but against the entire Itagamin army?" I shake my head. "We'll have a few extra hours once they get here."

"Good luck to all of us, then," Miari says as she closes the final hole in the wall's stonework and leaves, heading off to join the search for a tunnel out of the city. Natani and Tessen stay with me.

We'll need luck, but the wardstones *are* powerful. Once I connect the last wardstone to the first, completing the circle, the whole wall seems to vibrate with energy. Pulses of desosa travel through the lines of power connecting one link to the other, binding the ring together more tightly with each circuit. If I had enough time and desosa to draw from—like the vast katsujo vein I used to create these wardstones—I might be able to turn every stone in the wall into an anchor for my shield and build Jushoyen a truly impenetrable protection. I don't have either, so I do what I can. Eyes closed, I rely on Natani to keep me balanced and on course and trust

Tessen to watch over us and for the first signs of the incoming army.

The crackling, lightning-streaked air is overfull of desosa, the kind my training masters always warned us not to use. They told us it was dangerously unstable and could burn a mage to ash from the inside out if they weren't careful. Necessity has taught me how to use it, but Natani's skill as a zoikyo makes it seem easy. For a while, anyway. Repeatedly, we walk the wall and strengthen the links between the crystals, sinking power he feeds me into the ring. Before the susuji, I would've collapsed from exhaustion after laying half the wardstones. Now, I have to be careful not to overwork Natani, because I could keep going for hours.

"It's good none of the Ryogans can sense desosa. We'd *never* be able to explain what you're doing if they could feel this. Honestly, I'm surprised they can't." Tessen shudders. "How many more times do you need to circle, Khya?"

"As many as possible." We're halfway through the third circuit. "Once we finish this loop, I need updates from the others, and we have to—"

Tessen stops short, and I barely keep from slamming into his back.

"What?" I scan the land beyond the wall for anything that could cause the distress I feel in Tessen. There's nothing, no hint of danger I can see.

He steps toward the wall's outer ledge, and the tyatsu posted there move out of the way. "I thought I saw movement in the trees."

"*In* the trees?" I keep my voice quiet and stop pouring energy into the wall, gathering it into a ward around the three of us instead. If the first wave of Varan's army is out there, I am not leaving us exposed, no matter how suspicious it might make the tyatsu to see rain curving around our bodies instead of falling on them.

He nods, attention fixed on the forest. "It's just flashes, but the color is close to nyska cloth. It works as camouflage in the desert but doesn't blend with anything here."

"How many?" I ask.

"There's... No. Of all the rot-ridden—" His murmurs sound like he's counting. "There's at least twenty, and that's just what I can spot from here. Not even I can see *through* things."

"Disappointing, Tessen," Natani mutters absently. "I actually believed those rumors."

I can't see what Tessen spotted no matter how hard I try, but I trust his senses. Unfortunately, that means Varan's advance guard is here. The army won't be far behind.

Crossing the width of the wall and leaning over the opposite ledge, I look down into the city. Every building is ablaze with light, creating a bowl filled with a beautiful golden glow between flashes of lightning. It illuminates the movement in the streets. From what I can see, the evacuation is moving smoothly, the flood of people flowing steadily north. But there's still enough people below us to absolutely pack the sreets. My chest clenches. There are so many people still trapped inside Jushoyen. Soon, I'll have to hold the wall against the incoming force. Varan must push through me to get what he wants.

I wish I could see the city drenched in sunlight instead of rain and walk the streets on a day when I don't have to fight through panicked crowds, but Varan will demolish the city exactly like he did to Rido'iti. By tomorrow, all of this will probably be gone.

I take a deep breath and find my garakyu. With just a few words, colors fill the once-clear glass globe. A second passes. Two. Then Yonishi's face fills the sphere.

"You'd better have a way to speed up evacuations," I say. "We've just run out of time."

He flinches. "I'll spread the word. What do you need us to do?"

"Tessen needs a better line of sight. Get him to the top floor of the Kaisubeh Tower. Or the roof, if it's safe." There's a long pause, and then Yonishi's face settles into determined lines. He nods, promises to meet Tessen in the tower's gardens, and ends the connection. The garakyu becomes a clear globe of glass again.

Tessen's eyes narrow at me while I put it away. "And what will you be doing?"

"Making sure the wall stands as long as possible." I've warded someone twenty or fifty feet away from me, and I've pushed a ward until it encompassed an entire ship, but I'm not sure I could reach across the miles between the Kaisubeh Tower and the wall. It isn't a risk worth taking. If I'm directly over one of the crystals, and I have Natani to boost my power, I have a much better chance of holding my shield against the army. For a while.

Tessen's gray eyes are shadowed. "I don't like scattering ourselves so much."

"You think I want to be here with *them*?" I jerk my chin toward the tyatsu who are watching us with growing unease. It's hard to forget the squads of men dressed exactly like this who have chased us across Ryogo for moons. It's harder to forget a tyatsu killed Tyrroh.

Tessen only looks more worried. I sigh and ease closer to him, lowering my voice. "I'll be fine. We just need to be ready to run when time is up."

His expression turns incredulous. "Run *where*?"

"That depends on whether or not Gentoni and Yonishi keep their promise of a ship." I've already been delayed too long. I've got to get to Yorri and free him before Varan finds a way to stop me.

Then Tessen nods and turns to leave. I'm the one who ordered him to go, but seeing him walking away fills me with a shiver of terror. *I'll* be fine, but what if this is it, our last moment together?

I grab his hand. He glances back, frowning. I'm being ridiculous, but I can't make my grip loosen. My mind scrambles for something to say, something other than "don't leave." He has to leave just like I have to stay.

"I just... Once you get there, ask Yonishi for a garakyu and try to reach Ryzo. He might be able to tell us exactly where the main army is and how much time we have left." I grip him tighter and press a kiss to his cheek. "And be careful. Please."

"I'm not the one on the front lines, Khya." He brushes his cheek against mine. "I'll never forgive you if you let yourself get caught, oh deadly one."

"Then I'd better be ready when Varan gets here." Another kiss, this time against his cold lips, then I can finally relax my hold on him. "Go. And tell Ryzo to cause some trouble on my behalf."

"Now *that* is an order he'll like obeying," Tessen says wryly. Then the quirk to his mouth falls flat. He brushes his thumb along the back of my hand. "I'll see you soon."

Not soon enough, I think as I watch him go.

Tessen jogs back to the stairs and descends. Once he's gone, all Natani and I can do is wait. I could walk the wall again, but this is where Tessen spotted the nyshin. I want to stay here until he directs me somewhere else. I don't want to discuss what's coming, and I don't want to stand here in silence until Varan attacks. For a whiule, though, I can't think of anything to say.

"What do you miss most about Shiara?" The question pops out before I know I'm going to ask.

"The sun," Natani says immediately. "Or being dry. Or the food." He stops, considering, his straight brows furrowed. "All those, but I miss the sun the most."

I smile. "I'm starting to think it's something I dreamed up. I used to wish for shade, but now I think I'd give up a lot if I could stand in sunlight for an hour. I mean, do you remember—"

Yonishi appears at the top of the stairs, and my mouth snaps shut. His bright white robes are glaringly out of place here. He walks with calm confidence, and the guards part to let him pass, each murmuring "Kaibo'Ma-po" and bowing their heads respectfully. I'm surprised when he stops to talk to each. Only when he gets closer can I hear what he's warning the tyatsu: "Tusenkei Khya and Tusenkei Natani are going to be working magic, and they are *not* to be disturbed. Protect them by whatever means become necessary."

Pleased at being called a mage and not an *evil* mage by a Ryogan for once, I smile.

He continues his slow progress, leaving a lot of tyatsu behind him who can't seem to keep from staring at Natani and me. Yonishi's posture and pace don't change, but when he's left facing us, his expression turns hesitant. "What else can I do to help?"

Nothing, I almost tell him. But then I remember the spells he blasted at us this morning.

"You can do magic." The words come slowly as ideas form. "Put your skills to use, and pull in any other mages, too. Find a way to speed up the evacuation and protect the evacuees."

"I'm not sure if..." He hesitates, looking toward the Kaisubeh Tower.

"I know most Ryogans fear magic, but you can't hold back today." I step closer, challenging him. "If you don't use every resource you have, you'll have to live the rest of your life thinking about what you could've done here but didn't."

Yonishi stares at me, eyebrows high. "How old *are* you?"

That...is not the response I expected. "Um, it's the fourth moon cycle of the year, right?" When Yonishi nods, so do I. "Then I turned eighteen three moons ago."

"I can't imagine any Ryogan eighteen-year-old being in your position and succeeding," he admits.

"Then you've been meeting the wrong people, Yonishi." I think of Ahta, the ebet child who survived with eir mother in the inhospitable Mysora Mountains for years, and I think of Soanashalo'a, who isn't Ryogan but who grew up here, isn't much older than me, and serves as the voice of her people. "I've only been here for a few moons, and I can name two."

He drops his gaze, a flush of color spreading across his beige cheeks, but the embarrassment is quickly replaced by resolve. "I'm already coordinating with every mage in the city, but I'll reach out through the garakyu network and ask others to protect the refugees once they're away from Jushoyen."

"That will help." Depending on what exactly the mages can do. "Also, if you have any weapons like those stone-tipped arrows, use them. And don't forget the other part of our deal."

He only looks confused for a second. "The ship? Our usual lines of communication are unreliable right now, and we're trying, but—"

"No. Well, yes, we'll need the ship soon, but I meant Osshi." I glance toward the palace. "Everything's happening fast. Don't leave him in whatever hole you threw him in."

Panic flashes in his eyes. I'm pretty sure he *did* forget.

"D-do you want me to have the guards bring him here?" he asks.

"What he does once he's free is his own choice." I may understand why Osshi felt he had to betray us, but I can't forgive his abandonment or forget the ambush he helped lead us into. "He'll probably want to make sure his family is safe. Unless they're under lock and key, too?"

"They are, but not here." Yonishi bites his thin lip and won't meet my eyes. "They're in a city to the south."

"I hope for their sake it wasn't in Varan's path," Natani mutters in Itagamin.

I agree, but there isn't anything we can do about that now, so I keep my thoughts silent. Yonishi leaves soon after, disappearing into the staircase. Then, exhaling slowly and trying to clear my mind, I move to the closest wardstone and stop with Natani by my side. We're blocking the center of the busy pathway, and more than one person shoots us an annoyed look when we refuse to step aside. Thankfully, Yonishi's orders keep the tyatsu from disturbing us.

I need to focus, so I wrap myself in the spell-warmed cloak and sit down where we are despite the obstruction it causes. Sitting makes it easier to block everything around me out and concentrate solely on the power beneath me, the energy Natani channels into me, and the crackling desosa swirling around us. Natani stands guard over me with his arms crossed to discourage anyone from bumping into me at the wrong time.

An hour later, someone wearing kaiboshi robes approaches holding a large box. "Excuse me, Tusenkei Khya, Tusenkei Natani, but Tusenkei Tessen asked me to bring you this."

Curious, I open it and smile. Tessen's taking care of me even from more than two miles away; he sent food for two—grains, fish, greens, and two flasks. I can go without, but Natani can't, and this is more than enough to allow us to save some for later, which is a very good thing.

I don't think we'll be leaving this spot for a long time.

EIGHT

I lose track of time as I pour desosa into Jushoyen's wall faster than Natani can pass it to me, and faster even than the susuji can refill my own well of power. I'm stiff, aching, and tired when something vibrates against my hip. It takes several confused seconds for me to realize it's my garakyu. Someone is trying to reach me. I nearly fumble the sphere when I take it out of my belt pouch, but I manage to keep my grip. When I activate it, the swirl of color inside quickly settles into Tessen's face.

"Incoming. Two and a half miles out. Southeast and..." His head turns, and the lines around his eyes etch deeper. "It's multi-prong. Mostly spread between the south and east. More coming from farther west. Probably others."

"Have you reported it to the tyatsu commander?" Even as I ask, a ripple of tension travels along the wall as new orders are relayed, and I know his answer.

"Yes." He looks at me through the garakyu, fear in his eyes. "Contact in less than a minute, Khya."

I glance at Natani, and when he nods, we go back to work. Energy swirls around us, all of it pouring into the veritable river of desosa now flowing through the wall. The stream of power seems to travel through the ring of wardstones faster with each new drop of desosa we add. At the start, we were building a foundation, letting Jushoyen's wall adapt to power it's never felt before, and then I reinforced the wall itself, pushing my ward as deep as I could make it go, but I haven't activated the wardstones themselves. Until now.

The wardstone underneath me is a bonfire coming to life. It sends a spark through the ward ring that sets the desosa in the wall ablaze. My ward forms in a spiral, spinning higher and lower simultaneously. No one can see it, not even me, but I imagine this is what sitting inside a tornado must be like. Then the shield begins to close. The spiral curves inward until it becomes a dome protecting everything inside Jushoyen's walls. Not even raindrops make it past me.

"Bellows, Khya, what did you *do*?" Tessen laughs, the sound breathless and shocked. "They definitely felt it, too. They stopped."

I don't answer. I can't. Too much of my focus is on my wards. This is more than I've ever tried to do before. I'm protecting tens of thousands in a city spanning miles, and the drain of this task is only getting worse. I doubt I'd be able to keep myself upright without Natani standing behind me as a counterbalance.

Time slides through my fingers. I can't even seem to keep count of my own breaths or heartbeats to mark its passage. There's too much else to distract me. I feel lives inside the ward like moving sparks of energy and see them like bright stars against the black inside of my eyelids, each blazing bright and flashing in and out of existence so fast they're impossible to track. At the edge of the city, they slam against my ward, each one an impact and a burn. I flinch and resist, but it's like hundreds of fists are pounding on the inside of my skull.

"You did too well, fykina." A voice in my ear. Hands on my shoulders. "People need a route out of the city, but you sealed us in. Can you open a path without collapsing this bubble?"

I can't answer.

"Khya!" The world is shaking and screaming. I try to tell it to stop but— "*Khya!*"

My head is still filled with sparks, and I can't remember how to move my tongue.

"No, I can't get her to listen to—" Natani protests. "Well, then *you* try!"

"Khya, *focus*." A new voice, farther away, but deeply familiar. Tessen. He pulls my attention like the first voice couldn't. "People are throwing themselves against the ward trying to get out. Find Miari's wardstones, and create a hole where you find her. There's a tunnel. She's guiding people through. Do you understand, Khya?"

I try to nod. I must succeed, because there's a sigh of relief. Then Tessen clears his throat. "Good. But brace the wall, Khya. They're closing in fast. Keep her safe, Natani."

Natani's laugh is a little frenetic. "I'll try. How is everyone else faring?"

"Sanii just left," Tessen says absently. "Ey's determined to find a way to slash Varan's throat with an Imaku shard, but I don't think there's— Bellows. Is that Ono? He looks—"

"How far, Tessen?" Natani tightens his hold on me.

"Less than two miles," he says. "They're moving slow. Trying to figure out how to get past the ward, I think."

"Can they?" Natani asks.

"Eventually." I can barely form the word, but Tessen hears.

He huffs and says, "Hopefully not soon," so he must've understood.

"Tell them," I murmur, trying to gesture to the tyatsu. "Tell them. Coming soon."

Swallowing, Natani switches to Ryogan and calls out to the tyatsu. They don't even seem to blink at his accent. Instantly, those closest shout the warning down the line.

"Oh, blood and rot." This time, Natani's voice tremors. "Khya, brace!"

Twenty bolts of lightning strike the ward. They're like white-hot daggers driving into my arm. I scream. Shouts rise around me. Orders. Questions. It blurs into a senseless cacophony. The next barrage of strikes hits the same spots, like they're aiming to shatter my wards by weakening one point. I dive deeper into my mind to protect myself from the pain and the pressure. I lose sense of anything beyond the desosa channeling through me into the wall and the bruising grip Natani has on me. Until the impacts change. And spread.

Fire. Rocks. Lightning. Arrows. Swords. Bodies. I feel each one on my ward. I *feel* them. Somehow, more than ever before, I am my ward and my ward has become an extension of me. My muscles tense. My teeth grind. My bones rattle. My mind shakes free of my body and rises above the city. I float, drawn toward the heart of Jushoyen until I'm directly above the Kaisubeh Tower.

I look at my hands, or the approximation of them made of pale white light. How strange. This has happened before, but only when I siphoned power directly from a katsujo vein. I didn't know I could do this without one. Am I pulling in the same amount of desosa I'd draw from a katsujo? Maybe breaking away is the only way my mind can cope with this kind of force, by leaving my body behind until the work is done.

But I wish it hadn't happened now. I don't want to watch this.

Jushoyen is surrounded, and swaths of the outer city have been pulverized into piles of smoking rubble. Nyshin sprint through the few intact sections, hauling themselves onto roofs to take aim at my ward. Hoods dyed indigo or striped with yellow appear randomly, each in constant motion as the Miriseh and the kaigo relay orders.

From where I float, the invaders look small enough to be flicked aside, but the damage they're causing is already immense. My height and distance, though, allows me to see a pattern. The fiercest attacks against my wards all come from the nyshin closest to a yellow or indigo hood. As soon as the leaders move away, the attack slows and weakens. It could be part of Varan's plan, it could be Ryzo and the ripples of dissension I hope he's been spreading…or maybe the nyshin have begun questioning Varan on their own.

Hope swells through me. I can't trick myself into believing we might win—losing today is quickly becoming inevitable—but it does mean I might be able to keep this fight going for longer than I'd thought possible. It also gives me hope that, when this ends, the clan I once loved truly can be saved. Some of them, at least.

Movement draws my attention. It's closer than it should be, as though someone is climbing into the air to reach me. Relief fills me when I look down. Tessen is climbing to the roof of the Kaisubeh Tower. Once he's stable, he reaches into the packs on his belt and removes two garakyus, both filled with color and active, and then he turns in place slowly before he raises both glowing globes closer to his face.

"You're not even going to secure yourself to something, Tessen? And you call me reckless," I whisper, though he can't hear me.

But he looks up, expression uncertain. It seems like he's staring directly at me. Then one of the garakyus flash and his attention refocuses beyond the wall.

I want to stay with him and make sure he's safe, but somewhere else, someone is saying my name. Over and over and *over* and—

I jerk sideways, sliding and slipping and falling. Falling. Farther and faster until I slam into something warm, soft, and solid.

Hands rest on my shoulders, and a chest is pressed against my back, and there's cold stone under my legs, and chilly air expands my lungs, and voices ring in my ears, and I *am* again. It still takes me several seconds to recognize Natani's shouted words. I force my eyes open. Moving is impossible. A warm weight is locked across my chest and—

"—stop this! Khya, we need to run if you can't! *Khya?*"

Natani isn't shaking me. The wall is shaking all of us.

"Ishiji are—" He shudders with the motion of the wall, but his hold on me never falters. "They're trying to rip the stones out of the walls and break it into pieces under us!"

"Can she hold it?" the closest tyatsu asks, stark fear in their voice.

I nod jerkily, trying to sink back into the pure, distant focus I had before. "A while. I can..." I swallow and close my eyes. "A while."

But then the ground shudders. Ripples. Cracks.

My eyes shoot open, my pulse pounding in my ears. "What?"

"Oh, no," Natani breathes.

Tessen curses through the garakyu Natani must've dropped in my lap. "Varan's not aiming for the wall. I think he's trying to crack the ground beneath the city."

If he does that, the tunnel Miari created will collapse and my ward won't matter—all it'll do is give us a bubble of air to breathe while we're buried alive in the ruins of Jushoyen.

Blood and rot, I should've guessed something like this might happen. Varan is ruthless. I should've had a plan in place for this, and now people who could've survived today are going to die. The tears building in my eyes burn. He's had five hundred years to plan this, to learn how to master and expand his powers. I've had five moons. No matter how powerful I've gotten or how much I've learned, Varan is stronger. Why did anyone ever think I should lead us against him?

I have to get everyone out of this city now. This can't become another Rido'iti.

"Evac—evac—e—" I swallow, giving up on the word. Thankfully, Natani understands and passes the order on to Tessen. They relay orders and bellows instructions, warning everyone it's their last chance to get out alive. They'll have it so long as I can make this ward last a few more minutes.

I press both palms against the wall and release *everything* I have into the ring of wardstones. But the effort is too much, even for my newly enhanced endurance. The edges of my vision go black. Then more. More. I think I might be falling.

"Get up! Khya, *up*!" Natani pulls on my arms, yanking so hard my shoulder pops.

"Help them!" someone nearby shouts. "Get them out of the city!"

Yes, I want to say. *Get them out. Get everyone out!*

More voices. Overlapping orders. And then there are more hands on me, several people lifting me off the cold stone. Me, I realize then. They were talking about getting *me* out.

When we move, it feels like flying. My eyes are open, but all I see are flashes of light and glimpses of buildings. Faces with too-wide eyes and mouths open on screams—people I'm supposed to be protecting. I need to get up. I have to—

I pull in air, feeling the desosa I gather pool under my skin and sink into my bones. With each breath I let energy fill the well I drained and feel my body heal from the strain. Never have I come back this quickly, at least not before immortality ran through my veins. Now, the farther I get from the circle of wardstones, the better I feel. By the time my bearers reach the mouth of the tunnel Miari opened in the center of the city, I remember how to talk. Moments later, I can walk with only a hand on Natani's shoulder for balance.

"Where are the others?" I ask, even though I really want to ask, *Where's Tessen?*

"Tessen is behind us. He's coming."

"*What?* He's not here?" I straighten as much as I can and look toward the tower, searching. My heart rate jumps erratically. Panic buzzes through me until it feels like every inch of my skin is vibrating.

In the distance, something explodes.

"Come on! We have to go." He drags me down into a crudely carved tunnel.

I yank my hands away from him and stop. "No. I'm not leaving him here, Natani!"

Another thunderous crash above us. The tunnel trembles, dust and shards of stone shaking loose. It sounds like Jushoyen is collapsing, and he wants me to abandon Tessen?

"Khya, go!"

My heart skips a beat. That was Tessen's voice. But where— The garakyu. I snatch it from Natani's outstretched hand.

Tessen is looking up at me from inside. Deep worry lines I'm becoming uncomfortably familiar with are etched between his straight brows, but his voice is steady. "Go with them, Khya, *please*. I'll be right behind you. I spotted a group trapped by rubble. I couldn't leave them. We have a way out, though. I'll find you. Go, and I'll meet you on the way to the Mysora caves."

Natani pulls again. Although I want to find Tessen, knock him on the back of the head for putting himself at risk, and drag him out of Jushoyen, I go with Natani.

My eyes don't leave Tessen's. "I'll never forgive you if you get yourself killed."

"I love you, too, okhaio." His gray eyes burn into mine. His words knock the breath from my lungs. He's gone before I can respond, the connection severed and the glass sphere empty.

I love you, too, okhaio. Okhaio. Beloved. Dearest one. Treasured love. Tessen has never called me that before. Has never said he loved me, either. Why the bellows would he do it for the first time now?

Because he's afraid he won't ever see you again and won't get another chance to say it.

No. Stop. I push the thought aside and focus on the tunnel, the crowd of Ryogans ahead, the feel of cool glass gripped tight in my palm, or on anything except the pain in my chest.

Except, Tessen's goodbye sounded far too much like a *goodbye*.

"Where's the rest of the squad? Do we know how many Ryogans got out?" It's an easier question to ask than, *Do we know how many we're leaving behind to die?*

"Everyone checked in with Tessen a few minutes ago," Natani says. "They're out of the city or headed that way."

"I heard a report that at least two-thirds of the inner city was emptied," one of the tyatsu adds.

Two-thirds. It's so much less than I'd wanted to see escape, and so many more than I'd dared to hope. I take another breath, feeling a little steadier on my feet.

Everyone is probably fine. Everyone is probably fine. I mentally scream the words to block out the rumbling behind me and the extra dust in the air. We didn't save the city, we didn't save all the citizens, we didn't trap any of the bobasu, and we don't even know if Gentoni, Yonishi, and Jintisu survived let alone if they'll be able to find us a ship, but as of this moment, all my friends are fine. Plus, I remind myself, the Ryogans finally know we're on their side, so for the first time since we landed here, we won't be tracked and hunted like animals.

It's not much, but it'll have to be enough. It's all I have to hold on to as we flee.

NINE

Natani and I emerge from the tunnel on a hillside north of Jushoyen that's protected by thick forest. Miari stands at the entrance, hurrying escapees along. Two large groups of citizens are splitting off, stumbling in their haste as they follow their tyatsu guides. Those guides seem to be the last tyatsu in the area other than the wall guards who helped us escape. I expect our tyatsu to run after one of the departing groups, but they linger.

"Clear?" Miari asks, looking into the tunnel.

"Clear," a tyatsu confirms.

"Don't worry. Tessen has another way out," Miari murmurs to me. Then she steps into the mouth of the tunnel and presses her hands against the stone and dirt walls, her eyes closed. Even with her reassurance, my heart still stutters when I understand what she's about to do.

I feel a pulse roll through the desosa as she shoves power into the ground, shooting threads toward the city like a system of roots. All the warmth of my spelled cloak seems to vanish in an instant as a chill rushes over my skin. The ground rumbles. The tunnel collapses with a blast of air riddled with gravel and dirt.

You'd better know what you're doing, Tessen.

We leave as soon as the rubble settles. It's a surprise when the tyatsu who helped get me out of the city come with us instead of fleeing to the coasts, but maybe it shouldn't be. If I were in their position, I'd stay close to those leading the fight, too. Unfortunately, some were injured today—mostly from accident or panic—and Zonna isn't here to heal them. None are as used to pushing through exhaustion, pain, and hunger as we are, either. We must rest more often than I'd normally allow because they're with us.

At least the rests give me plenty of chances to try reaching Tessen, Sanii, Rai, or anyone I haven't seen since Jushoyen. They were all alive right before the city collapsed. I refuse to believe anything's changed, but when I reach out with the garakyu, my calls go unanswered. Each time, the swirl of colors inside the clear globe turns a dull gray. They're out of range. It doesn't make sense. Wehli, at least, should be gaining on us.

When we stop for dinner, I glare at the gray globe and shake it out of sheer frustration. "I thought these worked over fifty miles."

"Only some, Tusenkei, because it depends on how they're made." The voice nearly makes me jump; I hadn't expected anyone to answer, but Davin does. He and his shift-partner Atsudo had been stationed closest to where Natani and I worked on the wall, and since our escape, they seem to have appointed themselves as the intermediaries between the tyatsu and us. "Simple ones only work over a couple miles. Better ones communicate over five or ten miles. The ones capable of more must be made with the best glass, and it's usually only ships and soldiers who carry those."

I don't understand how glass is made. I didn't even have a word for the stuff until Osshi taught it to us—we don't have anything like it on Shiara. Now, I wish I'd asked for more than the material's name. "How far do you think this one reaches?"

He holds out his hand, but when I pass him the garakyu, he gently tosses it to Atsudo with a shrug and a simple, "She's better at this than I am."

Smiling, Atsudo holds it up to the firelight and studies it for a minute. "It's not one of the best. I'd say it can't have better than a five-mile reach." Her tone is almost apologetic as she tosses the spelled ball back to me.

I grind my teeth and resist the urge to chuck the ball at the nearest tree. Not knowing what's happening to Tessen, who I'm still planning on yelling at for calling me okhaio when he thought there was even a chance he might die, is absolutely hateful. I need to know what's keeping Sanii, who has helped hold me together for the past year. And Rai and Etaro, who gave up everything they knew simply because I needed help, should be here where I can protect them, not off risking their lives by themselves. My fist clenches tighter with each thought, and I eye the closest tree, mentally aiming my throw as soon as the garakyu is back in my hand, but angry outbursts won't benefit anyone. They'll only unnerve the tyatsu more.

I put the garakyu away, making sure it's settled against my hip so I'll feel the energy inside buzz if someone tries to reach me. Closing my eyes, I rub my temples and try to focus on the people with me, who still need my protection, and on what we're going to do once Tessen and the others keep their promises and reunite with us.

And blood and rot, Tessen, you had better *keep your promise.*

The relentless pace I set exhausts everyone else to the point of muteness. In the silence, I'm left with too much space to think. Worry continues to consume me despite how hard I try to beat it back. At each stop, I try to reach out missing friends. They don't answer.

I force myself to focus on Varan instead. He won the day. Jushoyen is his. Ever since the army landed, we've been assuming Jushoyen has been Varan's primary destination. There's a chance he'll linger over what's left of the city if that's true. It's a small chance, though. Ruling Ryogo might still be his ultimate goal, but he seems determined to raze it to the ground first. It makes me wonder what he plans to do with the land after, though.

Varan isn't known for being forgiving, and my squad and I have killed two of his kaigos *and* we dared stand against him at Jushoyen. Even if he stays near the city's ruins, he'll send a good portion of the army to hunt us down.

I keep urging everyone faster.

At the end of the third day, we meet up with another tyatsu squad and halt for just long enough to share news and supplies. I half expect Davin and Atsudo's squad to follow their people when our groups split again, but they don't.

"Are you sure?" I ask Davin as the other squad leaves, heading east.

"Please, Tusenkei Khya." He bows his head. Nearby, Atsudo does as well. "Let us come with you."

I try to look at their faces, but all the tyatsu have followed Davin and Atsudo's lead—they're bowing, heads down and hands stacked in front of their chests, palms up like they're making an offering. Clearing my throat, I search for something to say. There has to be a way to make them see reason. "None of you know magic, and swords won't win this fight. Plus, there's no one in Ryogo Varan wants dead more than us. If you come with us, chances are you'll die."

"Then we'll die fighting to protect our home alongside the tusenkei with the best chance of winning." Atsudo meets my eyes with surprising resolve. "It'd be an honor to give our lives for something so important."

The welfare of all over the survival of one, and sacrifice for the good of the clan despite the desires of a few—they were codes drilled into us in Itagami. Since we left Shiara, I've been questioning the reasoning behind all Varan's lessons, but apparently the tyatsu are trained to believe the same thing. Maybe this wasn't based *solely* on manipulation. Maybe his ideas about protecting the many were born at home.

But as noble as Atsudo's resolve is, I've seen other beliefs the tyatsu hold, and some of them are vicious, ugly, and dangerous. If they come with us to the Mysora Mountains, there are things they need to know, and several realities they need to prepare for.

"Tyatsu have been hunting us since we landed here. Our only allies were people you neither like nor respect, but they're our friends. They've helped us protect your land. *They* have, when you would've killed us without listening to a word we had to say." I pause, letting the words settle. "Anyone who follows us has to accept and *respect* the hanaeuu we'la maninaio and a child your people think is a curse from the Kaisubeh."

"They found a hinoshowa?" someone in the group murmurs.

"Yes, we found a child you call that ugly word. *We* call Ahta an ebet and a blessing. A squad of tyatsu slaughtered eir mother for helping us." I hope my words land like whips, each one sharp, accusing, and painful. "They sliced Dai-Usho nearly in half and left her to die. And then they burned down the house she'd built to protect her child from Ryogo. Ahta barely escaped the same fate, or worse."

I honestly hope I never learn who's responsible for what happened to Dai-Usho. If I do, I will happily show them exactly what that kind of pain is like.

Taking another breath, I remind myself *those* tyatsu aren't the ones standing before me. Just like they've probably been reminding themselves my squad isn't the same as the ones who've invaded their homeland. If they can look me in the eyes and agree to my demands, I won't slip away in the middle of the night and lose them in the forest.

"When the tyatsu pursued us, your outcasts took us in, so if you come with us, those are the people we'll be meeting. I'll break the legs of *anyone* who insults, threatens, or hurts someone I consider a friend." I stare down any tyatsu who meets my eyes. "If you can't forget whatever dreck and lies your minds have been filled with concerning ebets and the hanaeuu we'la maninaio, leave. Go find your families or help the evacuation. You don't have to come."

There's a weighted quiet. Several of them glance around, like they're trying to gauge the others' response before making their own decision. Then Atsudo gracefully drops to her knees, head still bowed though she looks up at me with eyes gleaming with mischief. "I never believed those stories anyway, Tusenkei. I'd be glad to meet your friends."

Her declaration causes a ripple of murmurs. Although a few do leave, most of the tyatsu lower themselves to their knees, sinking into the thick mud.

Bellows. What have I done? I was expecting either agreement or dismissal, not some sort of obeisance. This wasn't what I wanted. Why do people keep thinking it's a good idea to put me in charge of their lives moments before I realize I don't want the responsibility? It was hard enough to make decisions when I was only immediately concerned with the welfare of my squad. Now, for a while at least, I'm in control of more than two dozen people.

Natani catches my eye and raises his eyebrows, gesturing to the supplicants like he's silently asking, "Well, what do we do with them now, Khya?"

I wish I knew. This almost feels like the beginning of an army. How long can this truce last, though?

I have a stone that will kill Varan, but no way to use it.

I'm in the middle of a war, but I have no idea how to win.

And when I'm honest, my goal is the same as it was a year ago: save Yorri.

Jindaini Gentoni promised me a ship, and as soon as he hands it over, I'll sail straight through the storm, back to Shiara. I've left my brother there too long already. Yorri was the one with the ingenious mind for puzzles and invention. Once he's free, he'll help me come up with a plan to turn hunks of rock into the brutal weapon we need them to become, and then we'll sail back to Ryogo and kill Varan.

Maybe then, armed with death and backed by the thirty-nine immortals Varan's kept prisoner, we'll be able to do more than watch and resist and run for our lives.

Maybe then we'll stand a chance of winning.

TEN

The trek north gets harsher with each mile, but for what seems like a day and a half, we don't see another soul. No refugees and no nyshin. We trudge up slick hills and pick our way through dense forests, entirely alone as far as I can tell.

I refuse to let the silence make me overconfident, though. We travel as fast as I can push the large group, barely stopping until we reach a protected clearing on the bank of the Hopo'ka River. I think it'll be safe enough to rest here for a day or so. It'd better be, because we've reached it none too soon; I don't know how much farther the Ryogans will make it at my pace.

Our general lack of preparedness hasn't helped matters. None of us were ready to leave Jushoyen. My pack is in the palace where I left it, and none of the tyatsu had the time to grab anything from their homes before we fled the city.

Even though the clearing is enclosed by a mountain on two sides and a thick line of trees on a third, it hasn't been kept dry. Without bedrolls or a kasaiji to start a fire, we're going to be spending yet another night sleeping on wet ground and shivering. Miari started sniffling yesterday like she was fighting off a sickness, and several Ryogans began doing the same today. If Zonna or Ryzo were here, they'd be able to heal everyone in a few seconds. Without them, all I can do is hope it doesn't get too much worse before we find one of our hishingu again.

Trying to protect the others as best I can, I use my last few wardstones to shield the camp from danger and sight. Tessen, Sanii, and the others know we'll stop here and will probably aim for the same resting place. Anyone else looking for us doesn't wish us well.

Invisibility is draining to maintain. The task makes me regret the loss of my other wardstones even though I don't at all regret what I used them for. It'd be easier to keep the camp hidden if I had more than the handful Miari and Natani had been wearing. Some is better than none, though, I suppose. Natani would let me draw more power through him if I asked, but I don't want to yet. He hasn't had enough time to rest since our work on Jushoyen's wall. Neither have I, but I can push myself harder than I can push him.

I've taken two of three watch shifts each night while the others rested, and I've tried to take only enough food to keep the Ryogans from noticing I'm not eating. Exhaustion has settled into my bones as an unyielding ache, but it's not unbearable. In a way, it's good. I haven't yet had to test most of my new physical limits since the susuji. Only my magical ones. This trek is giving me a better sense of how far some boundaries have extended. Hopefully, I can keep pressing on until my friends return.

When I finish setting the ward, I walk to one of the clearing's stone walls and climb to a ledge. I settle in to wait, absently rolling my garakyu between my palms. The ledge perfectly lines up with a gap in the trees, giving me a view of at least a portion of the forest, and since this is a campsite the hanaeuu we'la maninaio often use, I can't help wondering if they designed it this way or if nature happened to shape itself into something so extraordinarily useful.

Natani joins me after a while, though there's barely enough space for both of us. For a moment he's silent, then he sighs. "I know you're stronger than us mere mortals now, but you should get some real sleep."

Never show weakness to those who follow you, Itagamin wisdom insists. *If you admit to fear or doubt, you won't be the only one questioning your decisions.*

But I can't be the distant, emotionless, confident shell I always thought I could become once I was in command. Those in my squad aren't just subordinates, they're friends, and they're the only support I have. I can't pretend seeing the destruction of Rido'iti and Jushoyen isn't tainting my thoughts. I can't pretend the constant peril my friends are in isn't a strain. If I have to keep leading us all into greater and greater danger, I also can't feel like I'm in this alone.

"Not yet. I need…" I close my eyes and tighten my hold on the glass sphere. "If I sleep before I see them or get word they're okay, I won't actually sleep. Too many nightmares."

"I'm going to have nightmares for years even if they all get back here safe," he says with a harsh laugh. "That doesn't mean I can stop sleeping. You shouldn't, either, even if you *can*."

"I know, just…just a bit longer." I sit up straighter and return my attention to the forest and the path my friends had better appear on soon.

Hours later, I finally spot movement. Someone is out there. They're wearing gray cloaks exactly like the one still keeping me warm in the freezing air. I shift to get a better look and count the moving shadows. I come up several short. Natani and I share a look—and the depth of the exhaustion bruises around his eyes shocks me. I'll order him to rest. But *after* we figure out who's approaching. And who's missing.

We're waiting at the edge of my ward when Zonna leads Nairo, Rai, and Etaro into the camp minutes later. Everyone but Zonna looks ready to collapse where they stand, but they're here and they're whole. Rai and Nairo immediately set the stack of wet wood in the center of the clearing ablaze, which earns a tired cheer from the tyatsu, and Zonna heads for the several tyatsu who are, by now, desperately in need of a healer.

Etaro stops by my side and leans into me so heavily it seems like I'm the only thing keeping em upright. "It's so good to see you, Khya."

"Me? I've been worried sick about *you*." I wrap an arm around eir shoulders to help balance em. "Have you heard from anyone else? Tessen, Wehli, and Sanii haven't caught up to us yet."

Ey shakes eir head. "We took the long way to avoid the nyshin scouts. They're everywhere. We tried to reach you with the garakyus, but we were out of range. Then…"

"It's okay." My gaze keeps straying to the trees. No one is out there. The only movement is the shifting branches. I hold Etaro tighter. "It's been too long. They should be here."

Rai approaches from the crackling campfire, rubbing her hands together. "It'd only be 'too long' if we knew what Tessen planned on doing after he left Jushoyen."

If he got out at all. I can't make myself voice the fear—it might become real if I say it out loud. "And I don't know if Sanii and Wehli are with him or on their own, and—"

"Bellows, Khya." Rai faces me, her forehead creased. "You've never been such a worrier."

"I never had this much to worry about before."

She tilts her head, acknowledging the point, and then she rubs her hands over her round face. "I never wanted a major command, you know. I would've been happy never rising higher than a nyshin-ma. I couldn't understand why you wanted this much weight on your shoulders."

"On Shiara, I wouldn't be in this position for another decade." Maybe longer. My promotions would've come over the course of *years* instead of moons. The weight of the role might not have felt quite so heavy then. If I were more used to bearing it, maybe responsibility wouldn't feel like a boulder tied to my throat dragging me under water.

"Khya, don't. Whatever you're thinking, just..." Etaro sighs and straightens until ey can look at me, eir naturally narrow eyes thinning to slits. "I never wanted your role, but I always knew you'd excel at it. You're doing everything right, okay?"

Rai moves to stand in front of me, leaning in until our foreheads are almost touching. "Even now, looking back and knowing what we do, I can't think of many decisions I would've made differently. Whatever happens, know that."

"Thank you." I shut my eyes and close the distance between us until my forehead rests against hers. I can't help asking, "What *would* you have changed?"

"That whole keeping secrets from friends thing you were doing back in Itagami when this started." She gives me a look that screams *don't even try to deny it.*

Smirking, I shake my head. "I already apologized. I'm not doing it again."

"Who said I was asking you to?" She kisses my forehead and then steps back.

Calmer now, I order them to rest and make sure the others are doing the same. Atsudo helps pass out what food we've gathered, and soon my friends—including Natani—are asleep.

I consider climbing back up to my perch on the mountainside, but

Atsudo and Davin's hesitant approach stops me.

"We were wondering," Davin begins, his deep voice rumbling, "if you would tell us about the place you come from. All we know about the bobasu are the legends, and I never thought— Well, they seemed more exaggeration than truth. Now…"

Atsudo picks up. "If we're going to war, we need to know who we're fighting."

I don't want to relive the past year *again*, but given the choice between agonizing over Tessen, Sanii, and Wehli or letting the tyatsu distract me with questions…

Though I gloss over details and sometimes jump centuries with a single statement, I tell them the whole story from Varan's persistent pursuit of the Kaisubeh to now. I explain how Varan used us to breed stronger mages and warriors, and I talk about the kind of training we underwent. But what I spend the most time discussing is magic.

"We don't fear power on our island, we praise it," I explain. I also try to define the desosa, the elemental energy all magic—and life itself—comes from, but it's like describing air to a fish. The way we teach young mages to think about the desosa and their abilities is utterly foreign to the tyatsu. Ryogan mages think of the desosa like water in a river, and they use words and potions and cords to create borders and banks. Everything is about control to them. To me, desosa is like the air in my lungs, and I'm no more in control of the desosa than I am of the wind.

Ryogans who *can't* work magic don't seem to think about the desosa at all, which I don't understand no matter how hard I try.

Hours into my impromptu lesson, the garakyu in my hand vibrates and swirls with color. I jump up midsentence and run toward the edge of my ward, eyes locked on the globe as I nearly shout the activation spell. My heart pounds as the colors coalesce into Tessen's face. He looks even more exhausted than Rai and Etaro did when they found us, but he's alive. He's *alive*.

"Where are you?" I demand.

His smile turns crooked. "It's good to see you, too, Khya."

"You're okay? Are the others with you?" If he's able to reach me with the garakyu, he's got to be within a few miles. I hear others behind me coming up to listen; I ignore them.

"Yes. Sanii, Wehli, and…" He moves his arm, and a new face comes into view—Ryzo, smiling tiredly. A knot in my chest loosens. He's alive. I didn't send him back to the army to be killed. Seeing his face, shadowed with exhaustion though it is, is a huge relief.

But it makes no sense to see them together. "What happened, Tessen?"

"I was about a mile out of Jushoyen when Ryzo contacted me," he says, bringing the garakyu back toward his own face. "He'd been part of the group ordered to hunt us down."

"Capture or kill," Ryzo says. "You're lucky I like you more than Suzu, Khya."

"Like that's hard to accomplish. Is that why it took you so long to catch up?"

"No. We were spying." And the curve of Tessen's lips tells me exactly how much he enjoyed the work. "After what Ryzo told me, I wanted to hear it for myself."

"What, that they're hunting us? Not exactly a surprise."

"I don't think you understand how badly you've spooked them, Khya." Ryzo leans into view, a vindictively happy grin slashing across his face. "Bellows, you spooked the entire clan. No one knew a ward like that was possible."

"What are you talking about? There's a ward-wall surrounding our entire territory on Shiara." It stretches for dozens of miles—far longer than the one I created in Jushoyen.

"Sure," he says, nodding with mock seriousness. "And it breaks if you throw too many rocks at it, needs constant upkeep, and requires every *single* sykina and fykina in the clan to help maintain it. You, though. Khya, you protected an entire city with just a few wardstones."

"It was the only chance those people had of getting out." I swallow hard, shaking my head. "I couldn't stand by and watch while they— I had to, so I did. But Ryogo won't last much longer. The only way this stops is if we corner the bobasu and crush them."

Though Tessen is in view, Ryzo is the one who says, "Luckily, we have an idea."

"Well, we're waiting for you. Hurry up and get here so you can tell me about it." I look around and remember the shield. "If you can't find us, use this again. I have the hide-in-sight ward up."

Tessen nods. "We're only two or three miles away, so we'll see you soon."

The sphere clears, and my breath whooshes from my lungs. My hands are shaking, relief and adrenaline making my body buzz. He's safe. They're all safe—even Ryzo—they're almost here, and Tessen, a ridiculous overachiever as always, is bringing me a way to crush the bobasu.

Having a plan, even a vague one, will be heartening. We've barely been able to do more than flee since Rido'iti. This is the first moment in a long time I've felt like, when I reach out, my hand might close on something solid. Of course Tessen is the one to throw me that lifeline.

A little more than an hour later, I see them through the thick rain—three gray-cloaked shadows and a lot more in the pale beige clothing of an Itagamin nyshin. That isn't just the six others I expected to follow Ryzo, this is at least three whole squads. I shift the ward, creating a hole in front of me. It had been a feat of will to do inside the Jushoyen ward, but here it feels as simple as opening a door.

The instant Tessen walks through, I yank him into a hug so tight I must be hurting him. I can't make myself loosen my hold. We're vibrating, and my mind flashes back to the Jushoyen wall shuddering under my feet. It takes a moment to realize it's Tessen. He's trembling so hard it's shaking through both of us. My hands move over his back and through his short, black hair, checking for injuries even though Ryzo would've healed anything deadly long before now.

"I don't like worrying about you making it back in one piece." My words are barely more than a breath, but this is Tessen. He heard. I can't help wondering if he hears what I kept back, too, because I'm still furious when his goodbye echoes through my mind—*I love you, too, okhaio.*

His arms tighten around me, and he hides his face against my neck for a long moment. "Definitely one worry I don't miss having."

"If we had any more of the susuji with us now, I'd make you take it." At least then it'd be harder for him to die and leave me. What little of the immortality potion we have left, though, is stowed in Soanashalo'a's wagons, and despite having most of the materials to make more in the packs Tessen rescued from Jushoyen, there's one key ingredient we won't find here. Or anywhere for miles, if my sense of the katsujos is right.

He takes a deep breath and brushes his lips against my throat, just under my ear. "And I'll do it as soon as we're somewhere safe."

Somehow, his words feel like an apology, not for what he said, but for when he said it, and for the fear demanding he say it then. I pull away, touching his cheek to let him know I understand. I don't know if I've forgiven him yet, but now isn't the time for this conversation.

Only after I pull my eyes away from his face do I see what I missed as Tessen approached. There are *far* more people than I spotted at first. In addition to the other Itagamins who followed Ryzo here, there are two full squadrons of tyatsu, all of whom seem to be a bedraggled honor guard of sorts for Gentoni, Jintisu, Yonishi...

...and *Osshi*.

My heart lurches painfully when I meet his eyes. I can't believe Osshi dared to come here. He's soaking wet and shivering, his long, black hair hanging in sopping locks. I'm relieved he's not trapped in the ruins of Jushoyen, but I also can't tell if I'm capable of talking to him without screaming. Or breaking his nose, his arm, and possibly several ribs.

I take a step forward. Tessen holds me back, his lips brushing against my ear as he whispers, "Breathe, oh deadly one. He's already suffered. Nothing we can do is worse, and nothing he can do now will hurt us."

Breathing I can do, but it's probably safer to ignore Osshi for now. I walk to Gentoni instead. "I didn't think we'd see you again. How'd you three end up following Tessen out here?"

"It seems as though the safest place in Ryogo is wherever your people are," Gentoni says, bowing his head with deep respect. "Tusenkei Khya, what resources I have left are at your disposal, and my people will be in your debt for generations if you help us stop Varan."

We've been trying, I almost say. Instead, I force my face to stay blank as I nod. "I appreciate that. I'll let you know what we're going to need."

In addition to the ship he promised.

Once I'm sure everyone is inside the clearing, I seal us inside the ward. This space is wide enough for at least sixty hanaeuu we'la maninaio wagons, all the beasts that pull them, and everyone who lives in those wheeled boxes, but there must be several hundred people here now, and it feels crowded.

Practicalities fill my mind with new worries. We don't have enough food. How are we going to travel in secret with so many? There are only two hishingu in my group, and dozens of sick and injured to care for; how long will Ryzo and Zonna last at this rate? Even Zonna must need rest eventually.

I wonder, too, how many of the newcomers know who we are and what's happening. Am I going to have to retell my life's story again? My last question at least gets answered quickly. Atsudo and Davin approach the leaders of the new squads, and I overhear enough as I pass to know they're filling the tyatsu in on all the necessary details.

My reunited squad also does as much as they can to make things easier. After a brief conversation between Syoni and Miari, the two ishiji head to the stone wall and begin carving more space out for our group. Amis, who's an oraku nearly as powerful as Tyrroh was, talks to Tessen about how best to split the watch shifts. Yarzi, Vysian, and Remashi begin unpacking the food they brought or caught while Donya—Ryzo's kasaiji— is setting up additional campfires. Those who've just arrived eagerly crowd around each new blaze.

As soon as Miari's sure Syoni has the stonework under control, she whistles a sharp, three-note tune, catching Nairo's and Wehli's attention. They quickly follow her into the quasi-privacy of the trees at the opposite end of camp. The unexpected separation has been a strain for them, one I understand too well. Tessen and I haven't been together as long as those three have, and I hated being apart from him after Jushoyen. The uncertainty has left me continuously in need of reassurance. Every few minutes, I'm fighting the urge to touch him to remind myself he's here, safe and whole. Rai and Etaro at least had the good fortune of risking their lives together the past few days.

I busy myself helping prepare food instead of giving in to the urge to follow our trio's example by dragging Tessen into the woods. When it's ready, the first plates go to Gentoni, Jintisu, and Yonishi—the habit of respecting elders and commanding officers is ingrained. The first few moments are silent as everyone begins to eat. I hate it. I have to bite my tongue between my teeth to keep from demanding details of what happened while they were gone.

Tessen must sense my impatience, because he begins to talk between bites. "Ryzo managed to get close to Suzu and leave an active garakyu hidden in her pack just before the assault began. Jushoyen isn't their final goal. They're heading north. Ryzo didn't hear where, but I have a guess."

"Kaisuama," I murmur, rubbing my forehead. Literally every single thing happening now is because of what Varan did in Kaisuama over five hundred years ago. I don't want to be dealing with the results of his second visit five hundred years from now. "He really will be unstoppable if he gets back there. Look what he did the last time!"

"Well, not everyone is heading to wherever that is." Ryzo's face is lined with worry. "They're furious, Khya. Tracking you has become the priority for almost every oraku."

"The rest of them appear to be after me," Gentoni says with a grimace. "I didn't even know what an oraku was until today, and now I'm being pursued by a horde of them."

And they're the worst to be hunted by. An oraku's enhanced senses may not be strong enough to challenge Tessen's, but their powerful sight, hearing, and smell can track a single enemy target across miles of rocky desert. "We'll have to hope the rain and the strangeness of Ryogo throws them off our track."

Tessen is in the middle of swallowing another bite of food, so it's Sanii who says, "Or we use them to lead the bobasu exactly where we want them to go."

"You make it sound so easy. But getting the bobasu somewhere is only half the problem." Sighing, I turn to Tessen. "Tell me your plan, basaku."

"It'll be a waste if the bobasu don't join the hunt themselves," Tessen warns, "but if we can get everything set up in time, it should work."

I listen closely as he, Sanii, Ryzo, and the others lay out their idea. Though some details are vague, I can see the shape they're describing. It's a beautiful combination of simple and complex, and it seems like it really does have a shot at working.

"When this is over, will you keep your promise of a ship?" I ask Gentoni once I understand what needs to be done. And how little time we have to make it work.

"Khya." Gentoni leans in, his small eyes focused intensely on my face. "If you end this invasion, I will give you a *fleet* of ships to carry you around the world if you want. I can't promise them tomorrow, but you'll have them."

I only need a ship strong enough to survive the storms between here and Shiara, but I won't turn down a fleet if he puts it under my command. With a fleet, I can take the entire army home. If they're willing to follow me when this is done.

And if there's anything left to go home to.

ELEVEN

For the rest of the night, I don't let Tessen leave my line of sight for more than a few minutes. I try to hide my watchfulness at first, but the third time I create an excuse to stay by his side, he gives me an affectionate smile and sighs my name with a hint of exasperation. I don't know why I bothered trying to fool him. Tessen has always been able to see through my masks.

"You enjoyed it, didn't you?" I ask when we're finally alone, mostly to keep him from asking me anything—he'll either want to know why I'm suddenly stuck to him, or why I haven't repeated the endearment he'd used before Jushoyen fell.

Tessen blinks. "Enjoyed what?"

"Eavesdropping again." It used to be a habit of his. He brought me key details more than once because of his oversensitive hearing and his tendency to snoop. In Ryogo, we haven't had to put that talent of his to use as often. "You missed it."

"I like being useful," he admits. "Almost as much as I like knowing things."

"You brought Gentoni and the tyatsu commander back with you. That was absolutely useful." Tyatsu-ge Chirida is a force—a tough, practical, and highly intelligent woman. When we started discussing the specifics of our new plan, she was the one who knew where we could collect the garakyus we needed. She also, on Gentoni's orders, taught us tricks most Ryogans don't know about the spheres, and demonstrated how to use them as watchers and spies.

"Well, we'll be in Atokoredo soon. Then we'll see exactly how useful I've been." Tessen glances out over our large camp. He's worrying about the plan, about how many of the people with us will die because of the plan, about what might happen to anyone who hasn't evacuated Atokoredo before we arrive. I know that's what he's thinking, because I am, too.

We approach the outskirts of Atokoredo after a long day of hard travel, and what we see eases one of the concerns from my mind. The city has been utterly abandoned.

This is my second visit to this city, and both times have been under the cover of darkness and shrouded in rain. The storms had been following us north the first time we came here, and they struck Atokoredo the same night we did. We barely saw anyone on the streets. It's why I didn't notice the echoing emptiness of the city at first—I've never seen its streets full of life. There's definitely a difference, though. It hadn't felt this hollow when we came moons ago to collect—to steal—the last ingredients we needed to re-create Varan's susuji.

This abandonment means people are listening to Gentoni's warning, though. And the desertion is good for us—we won't be risking any Ryogan lives in the crossfire.

The silent city is unnerving. Most of the doors are either unlatched and swinging in the wind or lying on the ground, broken off their hinges. Debris litters the streets. The Hopo'ka River has flooded its banks and engulfed low-lying sections. We're heading to the center of Atokoredo—one of the city's highest points—but dead ends, water, and rubble continuously reroute us. Not all this damage could've been caused by the storm. A lot seems to be the result of sheer panic. Thankfully, the one thing I don't see is bodies. I breathe a sigh of relief and pray Osota and Shideso have made it to safety.

Sanii stumbles. Instead of recovering and pushing on like ey always does, ey stops, hands pressed to eir chest, face pinched with pain, breath coming in sharp pants, and body curled in as though someone just jammed a knife into eir stomach. Seeing eir agony sends a spike of pain through my own chest.

The day I drop to the ground and start begging you to let me die is the day you'll know we've lost. That's what ey told me moons ago.

I call for Zonna as Tessen and I close in, bracing Sanii. "What—"

"Stop, don't, I'm—I'm fine." The words come out between breaths as Sanii forces emself upright again, but ey can't seem to keep the wince of pain off eir long face. "And get that look off your face, Khya, Yorri's fine too. I think."

"You're not fine." Tessen beckons Zonna closer. "Your heart is racing, and you're sweating. No one should be sweating in these temperatures."

Ey huffs a laugh, the sound breathless and strained. "It won't kill me, and it's nothing anyone here can fix."

"It's Yorri. Something happened to Yorri. Tell me what happened!"

Tessen grabs my arm, hauling me back. The uncertainty in Sanii's large eyes is startling. Only then do I realize how close I'd gotten to Sanii. Or that I'd been yelling at em.

"All I know for sure is he's still alive. Everything else is..." Ey presses eir hand flat against the center of eir chest. "The longer we're away, the worse it gets. It's like there's a hole in my lungs. I can't breathe right anymore. If it wasn't for the effects of the susuji keeping me going, I doubt I'd still be standing."

"Are you..." I close my mouth, swallow, and try again. "Is it just because of the separation, or is something wrong?"

I shouldn't ask. Even if something has happened, what can I do? Our plans in Atokoredo won't work nearly as well without my wards, and even if we had a ship, leaving now wouldn't mean getting to Shiara in time to stop anything happening to my brother now. It took almost two weeks to get from Shiara to Ryogo's southern coast, and Atokoredo is about as far north as we can be while staying within the boundaries of Ryogo.

"I think—I *hope*—it's just distance and time, but I can't be sure." Sanii rubs eir chest. "I knew you'd worry too much if I told you, but it's getting harder to pretend I'm okay."

Blood and rot, I am *never* doing this to someone. I don't want to be the cause of anyone's pain, but especially not someone I love. There are so many ways a sumai bond can cause pain, and from what I've seen, the bonuses don't come anywhere close to outweighing those. The one advantage was the promise of forever and the afterlife in Ryogo, but what does that mean now? None of us has a clue what might come next anymore.

"Let's go," Sanii says before we can respond. Ey starts walking, but before we follow, Tessen gives me an unreadable look. I raise an eyebrow at him, not sure what he's trying to say. He shakes his head and moves after Sanii.

I push my thoughts aside; there's no time for anything but the present now.

We find shelter in a building near the center of town, and despite my own impatience to see tangible progress in setting our trap, I don't even let myself make a face when everyone settles down to rest for a few hours. The Itagamin army will have to stop for rest, too.

Once she's had a chance to sleep and eat, Chirida leads us to a tyatsu armory. The building is as squat and unadorned as she is, and also like her, it turns out to be far more interesting on the inside than I expect. In Chirida's case, this is because of her tactical insights and her unflinching honesty. In the building, there are weapons. Lots of them. Swords hang along one wall above shelves of daggers. Opposite, bows of different styles hang above two massive buckets of gray-fletched arrows. The rear wall is stacks of boxes and barrels, while the shelves filling the center hold uniforms, armor, and—set in specially carved divots—garakyus.

We claim the garakyus first, but then Tessen veers toward the rear wall. He crouches to peer at one of several large, sealed barrels, his finger pressed against the tip of his nose like he's trying not to sneeze. "What's in these?"

Chirida purses her lips, but her hesitation is short-lived. Gentoni ordered her to help us, after all. "It's a special powder. When packed into a tight space"—she points to a narrow tube and a small ball, both seemingly made of metal—"and given a spark, it explodes."

"You explode things. On purpose?" Explosions on Shiara are devastating accidents. The buildup of gases or sulphur plus too much summer heat once collapsed a network of tunnels and killed several dozen people.

"Sometimes," Chirida says. "If necessary."

At first, it's hard for me to see how it would ever be necessary, but then it begins to make some sense. In Itagami, kasaijis are responsible for everything from lighting lamps to creating columns of molten flame capable of wiping out enemy squads. Ryogans seem to only use magic if there's no other way to accomplish a task. Without kasaiji and ishiji to reshape their land, it makes sense that they'd find some other way to bend the world to their will.

"This might be perfect." Tessen runs his hand over the side of the jar, but his gaze is distant. "When did your people start using this, Chirida?"

She shrugs. "Somewhere between three and four hundred years ago."

Tessen smiles. "After the bobasu were exiled, then. It's likely they don't know it exists. They won't be looking for it, and they won't know how to react to it."

"What are you thinking, basaku?" I ask.

"That I've found a new way for Rai and Nairo to amuse themselves."

"Have you heard from Wehli's team yet?" I ask Tessen. We sent him and a few others out hours ago to serve as scouts and to do what they could to give away our location. A trap isn't much of a trap if no one ever walks into it.

"They're on their way back. Whoever's following them is less than an hour behind."

A distant *woomph*. A flash of light.

Oh, no. Pulse picking up, I run toward the source. Only when I'm close enough to hear Rai's cackling laughter do I slow my pace. Rai, Etaro, Natani, Nairo, Donya, and Miari are sitting in a large circle in an otherwise-empty room, and between them is charred stone and a small jar of black powder.

I sigh. "I didn't think we had enough for you to be playing with it."

Rai doesn't even try to suppress her grin. "We won't be able to use it if we don't understand it."

"And we're trying to make sure these do real damage." Miari holds up a handful of what looks like thick black needles. "With*out* destroying half the city."

She's been working with the small supply of black stones from Imaku we have with us. The hand of the Kaisubeh may be on these stones, but she's right—that'll only matter if they strike their targets. But she had another project, too. "Is everything else in place, Miari?"

"Your wardstones?" She rolls her eyes and flaps her hand as though waving me off. "I finished a while ago. I thought you knew."

Miari took the last of my wardstones—the ones my squad used to carry with them—and embedded them in a circle through Atokoredo. They cover a much smaller area than in Jushoyen. This time, I simply need to keep the incoming force in place long enough to aim Miari's shards of stone at the heart of every bobasu in Atokoredo.

"And we only have an hour left?" I ask Tessen, grimacing when he nods.

Any trace of a smile fades from Rai's face. "An hour is cutting it close. We're about to put everything together, but the powder is sensitive. We can't move too quickly, or all this might go up too soon."

"You'll have to risk it." I grind my teeth, regretting the sharpness in my tone. Taking a breath, I try again. "We must be ready. This might be the only chance we have."

Wehli skids to a stop in the doorway, almost falling before he catches himself with his right arm. His wet, empty left sleeve flies up, sticking to his chest, and I can see a rip where it must've gotten caught and come untied while he was running; he's taken to keeping it pinned down since he lost his left arm in Kaisuama. He flicks the cloth away with an annoyed grimace.

"We got lucky." He takes several deep gulps of air, still slightly out of breath. "They're wary of us now. The scouts have been ordered to stay back until the main force arrives, so we have a little more time than I thought."

"Do you know who's coming?" I send a prayer to the Kaisubeh for luck. I'll be thrilled if all ten bobasu are here. I'll be satisfied if we only get Varan and Suzu. All the bobasu need to die, but although the others are dangerous, everyone else simply follows where those who lead.

"My line of sight wasn't clear enough. Between the trees and the mountain's incline, I—" He shakes his head, a flash of frustration flashing across his strong-featured face. "I'm not as fast as I used to be, and I'm not Tessen. At least one of the bobasu is leading them, but—"

"But they didn't send the entire army, so there's no way all ten will be here." Eyes closed tight, I pinch the bridge of my nose. "We'll do what we can with what we have. It's all anyone can do," I mutter to myself.

Then, I signal Natani to follow me and leave them to their work.

The building we head toward used to be where the city's governing council worked. It's not quite large enough to comfortably hold our whole group, but it offers protection from the storm and access to a storeroom of food the locals didn't have time to completely empty.

I pass warnings to the nearby tyatsu as Natani and I walk through the building to where the Jindaini trio has been resting, making sure they understand their roles in what's coming. I also remind them this is their last chance to leave. "Staying is risking your life. You may be soldiers, but every Itagamin picks up our first blade when we're five. We train every day until we turn sixteen, and then we join squads where our work becomes a matter of life and death. Nothing I've seen in your training can match up."

They all acknowledge the warning and go back to work, scrambling to finish their tasks. None of them leave, not even Gentoni, Yonishi, and Jintisu. Chirida wanted them far away from Atokoredo, but we couldn't spare an escort, and the hanaeuu we'la maninaio's cavern in the Mysora Mountains is a well-kept secret. I don't want to send them there without me or send someone from my squad away with them. As a compromise, they agreed to hide in a windowless, underground storeroom below the Kaisubeh Tower as soon as danger was imminent, so that's where they head as soon as I give them the latest update.

As soon as their honor guard has escorted them away, I leave Natani to rest while I go back into the city to prepare. I double-check the wardstones. I direct placement of the powder-and-stone-filled weapons Rai has made. I let myself be seen and desperately try to keep the anxiety gnawing at my mind from showing on my face. More than once, I've caught people watching me as though they're gauging how scared they should be by how close I seem to losing control, and not just Itagamins. The tyatsu, too, seem to have decided to take their confidence as well as their orders from me. Thankfully, I have practice appearing far more fearless than I feel.

Two hours later, Amis and Tessen signal the approach of the army. Our time is up.

At my signal, everyone scatters. Earlier in the day, the tyatsu scrounged clothes from the houses in the city to conceal their uniforms. Now, they spread throughout Atokoredo, hiding in sight. They'll light lamps and make just enough noise to create the illusion of life in the empty city. We're hoping it'll keep the nyshin from guessing what's waiting for them here.

Once everything is in motion, I head up to the third floor of the building we've been using as our central quarters. Tessen and Natani are there, collecting the last of what they need.

"How much time left now?" I ask Tessen as they work.

"Twenty minutes? Fifteen, maybe." He bites his full bottom lip, peering south through the window. "Safer to assume less."

Nodding, I look at Natani. We served together under Tyrroh for nearly a year, and he was always the squad's sturdy, silent support. His terra-cotta skin is chapped from cold and wind, and the beard on his jaw has grown in dark and full in the last few moons. Despite the exhaustion, the stress, and the losses of the past year, he meets my eyes with the same quiet patience he had at home when the worst we had to face was a Denhitran raiding party or an angry teegra cat.

"Are you sure you want to stay with me for this?" I ask him. "You know I tend to attract trouble." That'll be especially true today. Varan must've ordered them to take me out—specifically *me*. Every nyshin heading here will be looking for me.

"We'd willingly follow you into Kujuko at this point, Khya." A wry smile twists Natani's lips. "If I can help, there's no way I'm leaving you."

"Fair enough." I force myself to smile even as my heart sinks at his choice of words. I don't want my choices leading my friends anywhere near the nightmare of Kujuko—whether it exists or not. "I had to ask."

We've all made our choices, and the only way left to us now is forward.

I pull out the garakyu Chirida gave to me, one designed for tyatsu commanders. While most of these spheres can connect to just one other at a time, this is slightly larger than any other I've seen and allows me to link to five other garakyus. I won't be able to see anything happening elsewhere like I can when talking one-on-one, but this will keep us in contact constantly.

"I'm setting the last garakyu and the black-powder ball," Etaro reports as soon as everyone has sounded off. "All forty are set where you wanted around the city center."

"Just in time," Yarzi says. "I have movement on the southwestern road."

"And more to the southeast," someone else murmurs.

I glance at Tessen, and he nods, leaving with a garakyu of his own gripped in his hand. The Kaisubeh Tower has the best view here, too. He'll help me direct everything from there.

While he heads to his perch, Natani and I climb out the window and up to the roof. Only because my ward protects us from the blustering wind can we make the jump to the next roof. Our boots slip on the slick slope, and we immediately slide down. I throw my weight forward and reach out. My fingers latch on to the rounded peak of the roof, and my body thuds against the side hard enough to expel the air from my lungs. Breathing deep, I haul myself up and manage to get both feet on the narrow peak. Natani is already up, balanced and watching me closely. Once I've stabilized, I rise to walk south, moving slowly until Natani and I get our balance.

I nod to Rai, Nairo, and Donya as we pass above them. All three kasaiji and the few Ryogans capable of working a simple asairu spell—a weak imitation of a kasaiji's power—are each positioned near a cluster of black-powder balls. I try to spot the weapons, but Etaro fixed them under the eaves of buildings and behind piles of debris. They're well hidden, even when I know what to look for.

"I see Ono." Yarzi's report is so quiet I have to hold the globe to my ear to hear over the storm. "I recognize at least two other orakus. Watch what you say from here out."

"Mytua and Wyrin," Ryzo murmurs when he spots two of the bobasu.

"Suzu," Syoni adds.

"I see two indigo hoods," Amis, one of our own orakus, whispers. "Can't see their faces."

"Five bobasu including Suzu?" Rai laughs softly. "You must've scared Varan even more than we thought, Khya."

Maybe. If he were truly worried, wouldn't he have come for me himself? I don't know what will draw him into a trap if my show of defiance at Jushoyen wasn't enough.

I can't think about that now. Dealing with what's in front of us will be hard enough.

Natani and I move toward the southern edge of my wardstones enclosure. Updates keep coming in, and my mind struggles to make sense of it all. A group of nyshin to the west. The directed lightning strikes of a ratoiji to the south. I place each report on my mental map of the city and issue new orders in a rapid stream.

Yarzi screams and then curses. "Rot-ridden oraku!"

"What happened?" I slam to a stop and peer south. I see nothing but roofs and rain.

"Spotted," ey huffs. "Then a kasaiji almost got me. They're inside the city. Be ready."

"Khya! Empty the southwestern buildings!" Syoni warns. I pass the order on, and the tyatsu barely get out before the ground trembles and cracks under that section of the city.

Tessen takes a shaky breath. "Bellows, there's a lot of them. I haven't seen an end to the nyshin's line yet."

"Tell me when that changes," I order before shifting my attention to the next problem.

Nyshin swarm the city. There are hundreds, maybe a full third of the army, and they're intent on destroying us. Varan may not have come himself, but to split his focus like this and send *this much* of his force after me, he's got to be scared. Which means I really am doing something right.

This fight still needs to end fast. The longer it lasts, the greater the losses will be.

My heart pounds harder in my chest with each streak of lightning, each column of fire, and each distant scream. Some of the people fighting on my side today are going to die. Some of my *friends* might die—none of them have wardstones anymore. They gave them up for the sake of the plan, and if they duck right instead of left or fight when they should flee, they could die. Zonna is the only one I don't have to worry about. Even Sanii is vulnerable if ey gets caught in a blast meant for the bobasu. I try not to think of the possibilities, but every face—even Chirida's, Atsudo's, and Davin's—rises before my eyes. I force myself to push them aside.

"Where are the bobasu?" I ask Tessen as I jump to the next roof, wincing as several arrows ricochet off my ward. I run across the roof crouched to make myself a slightly smaller target. There's a clatter nearby, metal on stone, but the street below is empty. I signal for Natani to keep an eye on the rear. "Are there still only five?"

"So far," Tessen reports. "I think we—"

His words are lost in a thundering bellow, a rage-filled battle cry.

"Khya! Right!" Natani screams.

I spin, breath catching in my throat as I reinforce my wards and draw one of the two short zeeka swords attached to my belt, the garakyu still clutched in my other hand. Ono leaps from the roof on the opposite side of the street, blowing past Natani and lunging at me. I deflect the blow, and the edge of his long tudo blade misses my throat by inches, skittering off my ward.

My blood-father howls in wordless fury, his eyes wide and red rimmed. He looks nothing like the man I once admired. Frustration buzzes through me. I can't be distracted now. Everyone is waiting on my order. Ono surges forward, wildly swinging his long tudo and the shorter zeeka. Natani parries one blade, and I try to duck away from the other.

My foot slips on the wet roof tiles.

Arms thrown out, I slam my foot down, praying for traction, and thrust away from the building, leaping across the narrow street. I don't make it far enough to land on the next roof. Desperately, I drop my sword and grab for the gutter of the eave. My grip slips. The jarring halt wrenches my shoulder, the pain a sharp burst of heat washing my vision white and making me scream, but the moment slows my descent. I drop to the street without breaking my ankle.

Ono isn't so careful. He launches himself from the roof, landing in a crouch less than a foot from where I dropped, and the angle of his fall looks painful. My vision is still speckled with dots of white as my shoulder sends sharp throbs down into my hand and up my neck, but Zonna's warning rings in my mind, too: don't get distracted.

I force myself to move. Grabbing my zeeka, I bolt up the empty street. Ono isn't far behind. My vision clears as desosa pools in the joint, soothing and healing the torn muscles. The farther I run, the louder Ono's furious screams get. It's almost entirely wordless agony, but sometimes I catch words—curses, bloody promises, and his sukhai's name.

If I had the chance, I'd kill only the bobasu and let every other Itagamin live. They only knew what Varan told them, and they're only partially responsible for the destruction of Ryogo. But Ono is a kaigo, one of the elder council who knew more of the truth than anyone else. He let one of his children be imprisoned on a desolate rock in the middle of the ocean, and now, consumed by the loss of his soulpartner and half of his own soul, he's trying to murder his eldest. Even though *I* didn't end

Anda's life, I was there. I hadn't saved her, and I dared stand against Varan and the elders in the first place. Since Ono can't find the "Ryogans" we blamed, he's determined to destroy me. In this state, he won't stop until either I'm dead or he is.

Gritting my teeth, I let instinct and training take over. Turning sharply, I jump and twist sideways to plant my foot on a wall. I push off, spin, and slam my booted foot into Ono's head. He stumbles. I pursue.

My zeeka swings down, the tip aimed for his throat. Gracelessly, he parries, his expression warped by fury. My blade moves in fast, practiced sweeps and thrusts he's too slow to counter. I draw blood from his arm, his throat, his chest, and his thigh before I finally slash through cloth and skin and muscle and vein, leaving a deep line of solid red across his chest and a stunned look in his eyes.

Ono stumbles, his back thumping into the building behind him. His tudo clatters to the cobbled street. Slowly, he lifts his hands to the wound. Both palms come away covered in so much blood even the rain can't immediately wash them clean. His knees buckle, and he slides down to the street. His eyes never leave mine, not even after the life has gone out of them.

As soon as I break away from his unseeing stare, panic constricts my chest. Where's Natani? He should've been behind me.

No. There's a body in the middle of the last street, unmoving. Their clothes are dark with water, but an even deeper stain is spreading over the cobbled stones.

I *run*, calling Natani's name and praying he'll respond. Sliding the last few feet, I fall to my knees by his side. As soon as I see him, I stop breathing. There's no use calling Zonna or Ryzo. Not even magic can save someone when a blade opens a throat wound deep enough to show bone. I place my palm on his chest, nearly crying when the power I'm so used to feeling under his skin isn't there. What's under my hand now is just a shell.

I don't have the first clue anymore what happens when we die or where we might go.

"Khya? Khya!"

I look down, jolting when I see the garakyu still clutched tight in one hand. Tessen is screaming at me when I finally lift it to my ear. "Khya, *wards*! Now!"

Whatever our fate, I hope it's a good one. Natani deserves peace.

I suck in a sharp breath and close my eyes. The wardstones shine in my mind like stable sparks. It only takes a touch to turn the sparks into a conflagration. The ward rises and spreads into an impassable, invisible wall encircling half a mile of Atokoredo.

"Ready?" Confirmations come in quickly. "Tessen, on your mark."

"You have to get out first!" Tessen shouts. And he's right; I need to get out of here before our kasaiji light this whole block on fire.

Forcing myself to stand, I sheathe my zeeka and tuck the garakyu into my shirt. I'll come back for Natani when this is over. For now, I leave him where he fell and run.

I turn into a narrow alley, launching myself at one wall. Pushing off hard, I leap and grab hold of the eave of the opposite roof. I nearly lose my grip on the wet surface, but I scramble up, hauling myself onto the steep slope. I crawl to the peak, jump to stand on the narrow, flat surface, and run toward the Kaisubeh Tower, retrieving the garakyu from my clothes.

Just in time to hear Tessen bellow, "South quarter, *now*!"

Fire flashes behind me. I skid to a stop, crouching and putting my hand down for balance. Ten explosions boom in quick succession, each one sending reverberations through the city and my bones. There are screams, but I can't tell if they're from pain, fear, or surprise.

"North and east, go!" Tessen shouts.

More fire. More explosions. More screams.

Bodies, weapons, and magic strike my containment ward from both sides, those trapped desperate to escape, those outside the wall frantic to free them.

"Rai, west quarter!"

Another round of bright lights and booming blasts rolls through Atokoredo.

Screams of anguished torment draw me around the next corner. I move cautiously, careful to stay low and avoid being seen. Then I see the source of those sounds.

The bobasu. Three of them. At least some of Miari's stone shards must've struck skin, because Mytua clutches her throat, collapsing to her knees and bellowing her pain to the stone street. Nearby, Wyrin is pressing one hand to his cheek and the other to his stomach. Lines of black show between his thick fingers. The third is lying on their stomach, desperately trying to reach the wounds across their back.

They're barely bleeding—no one who was hit is—but these three who proclaimed themselves Miriseh centuries ago and believed themselves as invulnerable as gods, *these* three are suffering something I wish I didn't have to witness again. No matter how much I hate the bobasu for everything they've done, each tortured scream makes me flinch.

I jump to another rooftop to search the rest of the city. With each street I pass, I search for another indigo hood and a face I haven't seen in moons. But I don't see her.

"Who has eyes on Suzu?" I shout into the garakyu. Negatives come in from everyone. I climb to a higher perch. "Keep looking! She can't've gotten out, can she?"

"Maybe," Wehli says. "If she caught a ride with a kynacho."

And there were more than a few of them in the Miriseh's and kaigo's squads. Kynacho have the strength of ten or twenty people and blink-and-you-miss-it speed. They're invaluable. Yorri is one, and for the brief, shining moment he served as a nyshin in Sagen sy Itagami, he answered directly to Kaigo Neeva. Tessen's blood-mother.

My free hand clenches into a fist. Was it my fault they escaped? I knew Natani was beyond saving, and I still spent too long at his side. I didn't hear Tessen's call for the wards right away. If I'd reacted instantly, like I should've, would Suzu have been caught?

"Now, Khya," Tessen says.

Swallowing my questions, I reach into my belt pouch for another garakyu, a smaller-than-usual one with a special purpose. When I activate this glass globe and begin to speak, my voice comes through every garakyu in the city.

"The Miriseh always told us they were immortal—all-powerful and as timeless as the plateau from which they carved Itagami." My words echo through the empty city, and the barrage of blows against my wards slows. I hope that means they're listening. "They lied to us about that just like they've lied to us about everything."

I pause. No sound rises from the city except the storm. Atokoredo is as silent as it was when we arrived. But they *need* to know this. They need to know everything. It won't convince most of them today—not even after witnessing our so-called immortal leaders die. There's a chance they'll carry my words back to the army and unheedingly carry on the work Ryzo's squad has already done.

"Do you even know where you are? You're standing in Ryogo, and it's not what Varan promised it would be. The Miriseh aren't the gatekeepers of paradise, and this isn't the afterlife. Ryogo is simply the place where they were born. They committed treason against their people, killed and stole and destroyed, and they were exiled for it. Centuries ago. Now they're using you to take over a land that doesn't belong to us, and you're letting them."

I walk along the roofs, looking down at every person I pass. Some of the Ryogans watch me pass with wide eyes I don't know how to meet. I ignore them for now—their reactions don't matter; they can't even understand what I'm saying. I'm speaking Itagamin, not Ryogan. Some of the Itagamins I don't recognize, their skin, their clothes, and their shivering marking them as clan, but their faces unfamiliar. I pass dozens of nyshin, and one of the kaigo, and none of them so much as lift their sword to threaten me.

"The Ryogans are running from us. We've walked out of their legends as murderers and monsters, and they're more defenseless than children. We don't belong here. None of this is ours to take. Home is hundreds of miles south of here, but we can't go there while the Miriseh live. They won't allow it. Even if they do retreat to Shiara, they'll only wait for us to die and try this again with a new generation."

I reach the building closest to the Kaisubeh Tower and quickly climb down from the roof. It only takes a moment to run across the street and through the courtyard, aiming for the staircase winding up the side of the multi-faceted red tower. Charred spots and broken beams are the only signs of the explosions that rocked the center of Atokoredo. I glance at those spots, but mostly keep my eyes on the nyshin as I climb. The Itagamins trapped inside my ward have to hear what I'm saying, look at what's happening, and ask themselves what the real truth is.

"If you're questioning them the same way I have been since the first out-of-season storm struck Shiara, surrender. Stay. Help me end a war that never should've started. If you think I'm lying, leave. Run back to Varan now and tell him what happened here. Warn him what will happen to *him* if he doesn't leave Ryogo. Watch and listen to what happens next. Ask questions. Remember what I told you. You'll see I'm right."

I reach the fifth story of the tower and stop, standing at the railing and looking down into the streets. They're far more crowded than they were when I reached the Tower, and more nyshin are coming. Hundreds of eyes are now locked on me.

"I'm going to destroy Varan for what he's done to Ryogo, but also for what he's been doing to the citizens of Itagami for five centuries." I take a breath, remembering the brush I had with the power Ryogans call gods. Varan is nothing compared to *that*. "Tell him the Kaisubeh are real, and they've given me exactly what I need to destroy him."

Then I hold my breath, drop the ward, and pray.

TWELVE

Most of the nyshin flee, chasing after Suzu as soon as my ward is gone. It's exactly what I expected. They've served the Miriseh and the kaigo their whole lives. For most, breaking that loyalty won't be a choice they make in a moment. Even having a few dozen ask to join us surprises me; I'd only expected half as many. Although I don't turn them away, I do make sure Tessen and Amis—Ryzo's oraku—know to watch them for a while. I don't want spies in my army.

Only after they're dealt with do I finally get to check on my own squad. My friends. Everyone who fought in the streets was injured. Some, like Yarzi and Syoni, merely have scratches on their faces and arms from the explosions, but when I see Rai, she's walking with a limp and her clothes are so covered in blood I stop breathing for a moment.

I rush to her side. She bats my hands away with a grimace. "Stop, I'm fine."

"Ryzo healed the worst of it, Khya," Etaro adds. "We just don't have anything else for her to wear yet. She really is okay. Or she will be once she gets food, sleep, and a deeper healing."

"Not necessarily in that order," Rai grumbles as she hobbles away.

After a quick glance at me and a tight attempt at a smile, Etaro hurries after her and loops eir arm around her waist to hold some of her weight.

"Your face was just starting to lose that look. Don't wallow in guilt again." Sanii stops in front of me, and I blink; I hadn't even realized ey was nearby. "Nothing about today is your fault." Then ey seems to reconsider. "Except for the fates of the bobasu. *That* you can partially take the blame for. Or the credit."

"I…" I close my eyes and rub my hands over my face. "Natani was with me. I should've been able to protect him, and I didn't. How is that not my fault?"

Sanii exhales, and ey's standing so close I feel em droop. "Everyone knew the risks. We all chose to fight today just like we chose to follow you across this cold land. There's one thing I don't think you fully understand yet. However you feel about it, you've ended up in command of this mission." Ey pauses, and the silence stretches so long I finally make myself meet eir eyes. Only then does ey say, "What must we do for our leaders besides follow their orders?"

"Die to protect them." But I don't want anyone dying for me. What makes my life so much more important than theirs? I don't know what to say to em about it, though, because I know I won't be able to convince my friends to stop throwing themselves in front of blades meant for me. I'd do it for any of them, after all.

Someone calls my name before Sanii can speak again. Eir full lips quirk with a smile that looks almost smug as ey reaches out to me. I accept, gripping eir small hand tight before I move toward the tyatsu.

More dead have been found, and there's little chance these are the last of them.

I order a thorough search of the city through every street still accessible and every building still standing. Into alleys. Up on rooftops. The search becomes more complicated when I see our explosions have collapsed more buildings than I'd thought at first; some of the dead might be lost under rubble.

"Do the best you can," I tell those still searching. "Whoever you find, bring them to the courtyard near the Kaisubeh Tower."

Two hours later, I'm standing in front of a row of bodies. Natani and the other Itagamins are separate from the rest. He isn't our side's only loss—there are forty-three, twelve Itagamin and thirty-one Ryogan—but he's the only one of *my* squad, the ten who've so willingly followed me up and down this foreign land for moons. In Itagami there'd be a ceremony and a blessing before the bodies were laid in the saishigi core and allowed to serve the clan one last time by feeding the soil of the farms that kept us all alive. Here, there's only one way we can offer them the same final gift.

Ignoring the curious and doubtful looks we're getting from the tyatsu, my squad surrounds Natani and the rest of our dead, creating a wide circle around which I build a ward to keep the rain and wind at bay. Rai, Donya, and Nairo use their fire to evaporate the water clinging to everything, but they don't light the pyre yet. They're waiting for me to say goodbye.

Except, I don't know what to say. All the prayers we'd once speak and blessings we'd once have laid on our lost friends are worthless, nothing but lies constructed by Varan and the bobasu to reinforce the stories they told us. Now, I just need to find a way to say goodbye in some way that feels right.

I kneel at the feet of the fallen and close my eyes.

"May what the Kaisubeh give you be every bit the paradise Varan once promised Ryogo would be," I pray in Itagamin. "May whatever comes next be full of peace, bounty, and truth in all the ways this life lacked them."

I stand to rejoin the circle, inserting myself into the space between Tessen and Chirida. Tessen presses close on one side, not holding on to me, just silently offering warmth and support.

"I am so sorry for your losses, Khya," Chirida murmurs in Ryogan.

"As am I for yours." She lost so many more than I did. Even if she may not have called any of the tyatsu lying in the courtyard friends, they were still her people. Her soldiers.

"Their deaths will be mourned, but you did something incredible here." For the first time since we were introduced, she smiles at me. "You gave my people hope today."

"I..." My gaze flicks back to the line of dead, confusion locking my tongue in place.

"In centuries, the best weapon we ever came up with was the arrows the tyatsu tell me you swat out of the air like insects." Gentoni steps around Chirida to look at me, his expression almost proud. "In a few moons, you created something that actually *kills* the bobasu."

"We're already in your debt for so much. By the time this is over, I don't know how we will ever be able to thank you." Chirida bows her head, a new respect in her posture. Then she, Gentoni, Jintisu, and Yonishi shift back to stand with the tyatsu.

"They're right, but I know it's not that simple." Tessen rests his head against mine. "I'm sorry I wasn't there to help save Natani."

"I don't know if anything would've saved him. You didn't see Ono, Tessen. He was—" I shudder, wishing I could forget the frantic, mindless agony my blood-father had been suffering. "I doubt he'd slept since Anda died, yet he was unstoppable. I've never seen that kind of rage. That's why I've never understood how anyone could risk a sumai bond."

Tessen stills, tension creeping into his muscles. I look at him sharply, afraid he's been hiding an injury, but he clears his throat and says, "Your brother thought it was worth the risk."

"And now Sanii is spending half eir energy every day hiding how much it hurts to *breathe* without him." I shake my head, looking toward the line of dead. Yorri was—*is*, I sharply correct. *He is*—braver than me in a lot of ways. He's also more naive. He never seemed to truly understand the dangers of Shiara and seemed to take it on faith that everything would be fine simply because it always had been. Until Sanii was placed yonin, his unfounded optimism never seemed to waver. Maybe that's why he thought bonding with em would work out even if they had to spend the rest of their lives sneaking around to be together. "I could never bring myself to cause that kind of pain to someone I love. I don't understand how anyone can."

"You—" He's cut off when Rai, Nairo, and Donya pour fire into the center of the circle.

Flames devour the dead, quickly burning them to ash which Etaro, Vysian, and Remashi collect. The three rikinhisus use their power to pull the fine gray dust off the ground and pour it into several empty packs. Like we did for Tyrroh, Chio, and Tsua, we'll spread these ashes as we walk, allowing their bodies to serve the world one more time by feeding the forest.

The tyatsu look disturbed—though I'm not sure if it's because of the pyre or the ash collection—and it makes me wonder how different their rituals for the dead are. Thankfully, no matter what they're thinking, they hold their silence until we're done. This is how we mourn. It gives death meaning, and it's what Natani expected. It's the last gift I can give him.

Once the packs of ash are secure, I head for Chirida. She's separated from Gentoni's group and is speaking to several of the tyatsu commanders, but she steps away from her conversation as soon as she notices my approach. I stop by her side and ask, "Is there anything you need from us in order to give your tyatsu final rites?"

"Thank you, but no. I've had groups working on that already, and they should be done soon. It won't be the full ritual the fallen deserve. Under the circumstances, though…"

"There isn't anything else we can do," I finish for her.

"Exactly."

"We'll need to leave soon after you're done, but I hoped you would know where we could find more of the black powder nearby. We used nearly all of it today."

"I'll have to ask around to see if there's another stockpile nearby." She studies my face for a moment. "Is that all you need?"

"No," I admit after a moment. "I need to talk to Gentoni and the others, too."

Chirida nods, beckoning Gentoni, Jintisu, and Yonishi closer. I'm unexpectedly nervous, and they seem to sense it. They straighten, their focus narrowing in on me. Being tense won't make the conversation any easier, but I can't help it. I have no idea how they'll react, and I can't bring them to the Mysora cavern unless they agree—it'd be a flagrant betrayal of the hanaeuu we'la maninaio's trust if I did.

Gentoni reaches us first. "Is there a problem?"

"Not yet." My answer only confuses them, so I press on before my uneasiness transforms into anything more. "I'm headed to a place the hanaeuu we'la maninaio have used for centuries, usually to hide from you. You have to understand what Lo'a and her family are risking if they let a Ryogan—but especially someone in your position—see their safe haven. Protecting you and your soldiers now *cannot* cost them later."

There's a pause, and another silent conversation between Gentoni, Jintisu, and Yonishi like the ones I saw when we spoke at the palace. It ends faster than I expect.

Gentoni straightens his shoulders and looks at me with somber eyes. "Not only will I promise there won't be any trouble or retaliation, but I swear to you on the lives of my children that, if I survive this, I'll see to it all the trade agreements with the hanaeuu we'la maninaio are rewritten more equitably, I'll lift the remaining travel restrictions, and I'll grant a number of licenses to ensure the families traveling continuously within our borders have the protections and rights of Ryogan citizens." He purses his thin lips, glancing again at Jintisu and Yonishi. "I've never approved of the history Ryogo has with their people, but before now there was no real way for me to effect changes like this."

"And now, legends have forced everyone's hands." Jintisu nods solemnly. "I know our history with the hanaeuu we'la maninaio has taught them to be wary of Ryogan promises, but we swear no harm will come to them because they've shared this secret."

"You'd better keep that promise," I warn even though I'm relieved beyond words at their easy capitulation. "And you'd better be ready to travel hard, too. It wasn't an easy journey last time, and we were inside wagons. On foot, it'll be dangerous even with my wards."

Gentoni nods, setting his shoulders and immediately beginning a discussion with Chirida about provisions to keep our ever-growing group fed and warm. Orders soon snap out like the cracks of a whip from the commander, and her tyatsu jump to obey, organizing parties to raid the city for what we need. As they work, I walk Atokoredo with Zonna, Sanii, and Tessen, looking at the damage. Though most of the blood spatter has been washed away by the rain, the black-powder explosions left a mark on the city that will be harder to wipe clean. Even in areas where none of the buildings collapsed, there are gouges in the stone walls and char marks that spread along the surfaces like growths of mold.

"Suzu's going to warn Varan about everything." I clench my fists but try to keep my expression calm. "Once Varan knows we can kill him, he'll be even warier and harder to trap."

"Yes, but that means he'll be thinking about the possibility of his own death when the returning nyshin tell him what you said." A fire burns in Sanii's eyes, and eir breath comes faster. "When they start asking questions for the first time in their rot-ridden lives, or when they look at Ryogo with confused, uncertain gazes, he'll know they're seeing all the ways he's lied. You planted doubts that will spread and grow. I'm guessing more of the clan will hesitate next time he orders them to crush a city, and some will walk away from him completely. Soon, he'll be alone in a land he doesn't know anymore, and all he'll have are his Miriseh and the knowledge that we're hunting each and every one of them down."

Zonna murmurs, "From eir lips to the Kaisubeh's ears."

I just hope they really are listening.

THIRTEEN

I was right to warn the Ryogan leaders before we left Atokoredo. Two and a half days we've been traveling and still we trudge on, climbing higher and higher into the Mysora Mountains.

Miari recovered our last wardstones before we left Atokoredo, and now they're being carried by my squad, who are purposefully spread throughout the line to give me a sense of where our cavalcade begins and ends. Trees around us bend and sway in the storm's gale. My shields are the only way to protect us from getting picked up by the gusts and blown off the mountain or blasted by the lightning. Strikes against the mountainside send chunks of rock tumbling down. Twice, those boulders would've crushed several people. Once lightning missed the mountainside and struck the road. My wards keep us from losing lives, but we'd better get to the cavern soon. I can't save anyone from sheer exhaustion.

"I don't know how anyone is still going," Sanii murmurs late in the afternoon of the third day. "I doubt I'd be able to keep my feet if not for…"

For the immortality healing strained muscles and keeping our hollow stomachs from eating themselves. Ey doesn't say that aloud, though; no one outside our original squad knows the bobasu and Zonna aren't the only immortals in the world, and we'd like to keep it that way for now. Still, for a trek as hard as this one, I'm incredibly glad for the strength the susuji gave us. If I collapsed, so would my wards. Then, everyone else truly would be in trouble.

Tessen's raised hand closer to the front of the line catches my eye. When he sees me looking his way, he points to a bend in the rising path. We're almost there.

I smile for the first time since Atokoredo. Pushing forward through the crowd, I signal for the Ryogan leaders to follow me forward as I pass them.

The entrance to the cavern is a narrow crevice, barely wide enough for a hanaeuu we'la maninaio wagon to fit through, and the relief of being between folds of solid stone is staggering. Or it would be if I wasn't suddenly facing two dozen tense, angry, frightened hanaeuu we'la maninaio, all of them with weapons drawn and magic ready.

I pull the necklace Soanashalo'a gave me out from under my clothes, letting the pendant rest against my cloak like a silver star on a black sky. Then I raise my hands, both empty of weapons, and reinforce the ward between us and them as I cautiously shout one of the few phrases I know in their language. "*Mouka'a ka lea'i malohakama. Soanashalo'a ai sha Shuikanahe'le opili napuna ki'i ame'eola ona mouka'a.*"

Two people at the back of the group begin shouting her name. Thankfully, Soanashalo'a must have been nearby, because she's there an instant later, raising her own hands and clearly urging the others to stand down. "*Ou'a ka lea'i shohikino. Alakosha naho olea'o ano'a ke mouka'a shahi'i alasha'ino.*"

As soon as they ease back several steps, she rushes forward, her arms outstretched. I open my arms and let her shorter, rounder frame collide with mine.

"*Alua'sa liona'ano shilua'a shomaihopa'a mouka'a.*" She whispers the words like a prayer as she squeezes me. "You should have been back days ago, Khya." Then she pulls back, her worried expression getting tenser when she takes in the mixed group behind me. "You should have been back with fewer people, too."

Fewer Ryogans, she means.

I speak quietly, the words meant solely for her, and hope she hears my sincerity. "I wouldn't have brought them here if they hadn't made very serious promises first, Soanashalo'a Shuikanahe'le."

She considers my words and the strangers for several seconds before she finally nods and takes my hand, guiding me deeper into the cavern.

The hanaeuu we'la maninaio guards don't stop us from entering, but their weapons don't lower, either, as they move aside to let us pass. Gentoni, Jintisu, and Yonishi walk through the gauntlet with their eyes lowered respectfully, and Chirida seems to be trying to follow their lead, but she can't quite hide the tense readiness filling her muscled frame.

"Where have you *been*?" A small blur races past, arms outstretched for Etaro. Ahta, the young ebet we met on the edge of the Nentoado region of the Mysora Mountains, crashes into one of eir favorites. It's hard not to smile at the scene and the joyous relief on eir face to see us, but the tension surrounding our group can't be allieviated by something so ephemeral.

"You had better come this way," Soanashalo'a says uncertainly, drawing my attention away from Ahta and leading us toward a growing group of tense, wide-eyed elders. Hoku and Akia, whom we've been traveling with for moons, are among the last to arrive, and both look shocked. Their words sound like admonishments even if I can't translate them. The rest of the elders are silent, but the anger flashes in their eyes like black-powder sparks.

I stop a few feet away and greet them in their own tongue before formally introducing Gentoni, Jintisu, and Yonishi and quickly explaining the promises they'd made. Quiet had fallen over the cavern at our entrance, and my voice carries across the massive stone room. Surprised whispers ripple outward immediately. Once I'm done, I hold my breath and hope the hanaeuu we'la maninaio will accept the deal I'd dared to make on their behalf.

At first, neither Soanashalo'a nor the elders seem to know what to make of the story. The distrust I expected is there, but the longer I talk, the more it seems mixed with hesitant hope. The elders ask for a moment and turn away from us, conferring quietly with one another.

Soanashalo'a, though, looks at me with a gleam of hope in her eyes. "*Alua'sa liona'ano shilua'a shomaihopa'a*, Khya. I knew you would be responsible for great things, but this?" She laughs breathlessly. "If these promises hold, you may have changed the fate of my people."

"The promises will hold," Gentoni quietly insists. "It's far past time for this pact."

Even if the hanaeuu we'la maninaio elders don't agree, they seem to be willing to listen, because they ask for the Ryogans to follow them deeper into the caves.

"Get everyone settled if you can, Khya." Soanashalo'a squeezes my hand once before she, a little reluctantly, begins to leave. "It is probably best to keep groups separated until we can figure this out. Food, especially, is going to be a problem. We were not ready for so many."

"We brought some rations with us, but I think everyone's so tired they'll sleep first and worry about food later."

She nods and points to where I should set up the Ryogan camp, then she follows the other elders and Gentoni's group toward the privacy of the smaller caverns that branch off from the larger space. I can guess it will be hours before we see any of them again. It'll take more than a short chat to undo generations of distrust.

I have plenty of my own work to do once they're gone—the confused and anxious hanaeuu we'la maninaio keep coming to me for assurances their refuge hasn't just been invaded.

"No one is in danger here," I promise repeatedly. "You're helping them now, and when we all come out the other side of this war, there will be a debt to be repaid. This is a good thing."

While I talk and calm and soothe, my troop of Itagamins and Ryogans somehow, despite their exhaustion, keep their feet long enough to lay down bedrolls, set clothes out to dry, and unpack the food we have left. Rai, Donya, and Nairo also arrange and light several fires while Miari and Syoni create a long line of hooks in the cavern's wall to hang bags and cloaks. By the time the last group of hanaeuu we'la maninaio return to their own camps, mine has been completely set up without a single bit of effort from me.

I survey the rows of bedrolls bearing exhausted soldiers, and my stomach clenches. I've spent almost an hour promising dozens of people everything will be fine, but it's an impossible vow to have made. How can I possibly defend this many people? On top of the more than three dozen Itagamins now under my command, there are over a hundred Ryogans in the cavern and nearly twice that many hanaeuu we'la maninaio. They're as safe as they can be here, but if Varan discovers this place, not even my wards will save them. And he *will* find this place if we give him enough time. After Atokoredo, it's not like he doesn't have several new reasons to hunt me down.

Sitting next to Tessen, our backs against the wall and our weight leaning into each other, I let plans form slowly in my mind only to be torn apart in seconds as soon as logic is applied. There must be a way to move forward from here while protecting those under my command. It takes an hour for me to see what needs to be done, and I should've admitted it to myself sooner.

My friends need to become immortal before we go any further in this war.

The problem is that even though we have the instructions and the ingredients to make a susuji, the potion to create immortality, drinking it is an immense risk. Immortality isn't guaranteed. In order for the human body to sustain near-eternal life, the susuji must make all-encompassing changes. Yes, my squad will be protected from so much danger if the susuji makes them invulnerable, but first, they'll have to suffer through a days-long evolution. Some people don't survive the process.

Is it worth the risk? There's no way to know for sure, and there won't be until I can look back on the whole year and weigh out losses and gains. Which is why I won't—and would never—make this an order. They'll each make their own choices, same as they have every step of this journey. I will ask, and they will answer, and I have no idea how the conversation will go.

"You've been thinking loudly." Tessen's eyes are closed, and his head is tipped back against the wall, but his attention is still on me. "What has you tied up in knots now?"

"Something I need to talk to everyone about." I touch his wrist, and he turns his head, opening one eye to look at me. "Help me gather our squad? Just the original nine—" My stomach flips, and I correct myself. "The eight of us. We'll meet in one of the alcoves."

Although he sags against the stone for a beat, exhaustion in the line of his shoulders as much as it is in the lines around his eyes, he pulls a reserve of energy from somewhere, straightening and running his gaze over the crowded cavern. "What about Ryzo? Cutting people out of the loop didn't help us before. I don't think it'll do us any good now."

I hesitate. Doubts rise in my mind like a plague of insects, burrowing into my thoughts and showing me every way this choice could go wrong, but all I say is, "It's about Kaisuama. Do you think we should bring anyone else in?"

"Yes," he says after a moment. "Ryzo first, and then we'll see. More is probably better if we're going to survive this."

Although I nod, I must not do a good job of keeping my uncertainty off my face.

Tessen frowns. "There's more. What are you so worried about?"

"*Immortality*, Tessen." I don't understand how the idea doesn't worry him. "We're asking our friends to risk their lives, to possibly die. As if that isn't bad enough, we'll have to live with the consequences if this works. Yes, we need to better our chances against Varan, but what happens when this is over? If even one of us decides to play gods the way the bobasu have—"

His eyes widen the longer I talk, the words pouring out in a rush I can't seem to stop.

"We can kill most immortals, sure, but we already know it doesn't work on everyone. If we're right about why Zonna survived, it won't work on any other hishingu, either. And people change, Tessen. Not always for the better. If we give someone the potential for centuries, they might not willingly give up that chance. I know we have to fight now, but we can't ignore how what we do today could impact the next hundred or *thousand* years."

Sighing, he squeezes his eyes shut and rubs his temples. "I remember when the biggest problem in my life was convincing you not to hate me. Never thought I'd miss that."

"I never hated you." I ease closer to him, resting my hand on his hip. He startles, but relaxes as I brush my other hand over his shaggy curls, and his gray eyes soften when they meet mine. "I envied you, Tessen, and I wanted to be better than you, but I never *hated* you."

There's very little he could ever do to make me hate him.

He smiles gently, catching my hand and bringing it to his lips to press a kiss to my palm. Still holding my hand between his, he casts another glance at the people around us. "I still think Ryzo. He's cautious, and I doubt he'll unthinkingly jump into a life as long as Zonna's."

"And he'll be a better gauge of the others." I squeeze his fingers. "You're not wrong."

"Neither are you. I know it's a lot to ask of everyone, and I know we need to be careful, Khya. We will be. I promise." He brushes his lips against mine, the barest of kisses, and then he heaves himself to his feet and heads toward the wagons where Sanii and Etaro are sitting with Ahta, both smiling tiredly at the little ebet as ey tells them a story, eir hands gesticulating wildly.

I collect Miari, Wehli, and Nairo, and together we trudge deeper into the mountain. Many of the chambers closest to the main cavern have been claimed by couples or families, but it isn't long until the rooms are as empty as they were the night I dragged Tessen down this hall for a chance to be alone. Soanashalo'a and the elders are still down here somewhere, but they're probably a lot deeper into the mountain than this. I only walk until the sounds of conversation in the main cavern fade and then pick the first cave I see. Soon, everyone is gathered, and I find myself looking for the missing faces—Natani, Chio, Tsua, Tyrroh. My heart aches as I wrench my mind back to the present.

Ryzo doesn't know the truth about what Zonna, Sanii, and I are, and I know he won't believe this without proof, so I pull out my anto, running my fingers along the dagger's cold, curved blade, and try to brace myself for the pain.

"Ryzo, watch." I push my sleeve up and drag the sharp edge of the anto along my arm.

Simultaneously, Ryzo and I curse. Pain I haven't yet relearned how to ignore sparks through my entire arm. I hiss and clench both fists to keep from pressing my hand against the wound. Ryzo rises to his knees as blood wells from the deep cut, spills over, and runs in warm rivulets over my brown skin. Before he can dive in and heal me, Etaro grabs the back of his tunic. "You're supposed to be watching."

He settles, but his eyes jump between my face and my arm. The pain shifts from sharp lines of fire to a throbbing ache which then mercifully fades to nothing once the desosa pooling under the wound seals it. When I wipe the blood away, I leave clean, unscarred skin behind.

"Khya, what— How can— But you're not..." Ryzo's eyes bulge. "What did you do?"

"We found the secret of Varan's immortality, and Tessen used it to save my life."

Ryzo blinks, shaking his head like he's trying to get water out of his ears, and I go back to the beginning—meeting Soanashalo'a and traveling to the mountains beyond Uraita, the village where Chio, Tsua, Varan, and Suzu were born. I tell him about Varan's notes and of our initial failures— how the potion healed Sanii, even of old, lingering injuries, but didn't make em immortal. After, I explain how stories about the ancient Kaisubeh legends led us into Nentoado, a supposedly impassable section of mountains hiding a vast vein of desosa.

Ryzo already looks awed and baffled, and he's barely heard a portion yet.

Sanii's transformation comes next, and with it our realization that our plans to counteract the susuji with another potion wouldn't work.

"We went hunting for the Ryogans' ancient hoard of Imaku stone and stole as much as we could carry. The Ryogans had been experimenting with it, and they created stone weapons to use against mages. It could shatter my wards before I learned how to block it. I got shot here." I place my hand over my chest, just above my heart. "Another arrow hit Tyrroh. Tessen got to me in time to save my life, but Tyrroh…"

Nothing would've been fast enough to save him.

"Blood and rot, Khya." Ryzo rubs a trembling hand over his mouth. It's several moments before he speaks again. "What's changed? Why tell me this now?"

Everyone else had been slumped or resting against the walls, but they sit up now, the same question in their eyes. So I answer it. "All of you who are willing to take the risk need to take the susuji as soon as we can get to Kaisuama and make more."

Zonna closes his eyes and sighs. Miari sits straighter, her eyes wide. Nairo and Wehli curse and look at each other over Miari's head, but Miari turns to Tessen and Sanii like she's expecting them to talk me out of it.

"And if it kills us?" Rai asks. Neither she nor Etaro look shocked. "It could—you're right about that. Not even you're stubborn enough to will us into being immune to death."

Wehli and Miari laugh, but the sound is buried when Nairo demands, "Tell me *why*."

"Because I don't know what we might have to face between now and whenever this ends, but I do know that Tyrroh and Natani would still be here if they'd done this." I look down instead of allowing myself to search for those missing faces again. "Becoming one of the bobasu is the only way to make sure Zonna, Sanii, and I aren't the only ones in this room there to see Varan finally fall."

"Not bobasu," Zonna corrects softly. "When you transform, you'll all be andofume."

I smile, but I don't know how to say thank you when he looks more resigned than anything else, like we're making a hopelessly foolish choice he knows he can't talk us out of. He's looking back at us from a distance of centuries, though, and he was never given the choice I'm offering my friends now. He was born to it. He was never given a choice at all.

"Well, fine, Khya," Rai says with an exaggeratedly aggravated sigh as she leans back against the cave's wall again. "If you're risking your scrawny neck to see this to the end, I'd better do what I can to ensure you make it."

"Me too," Etaro says with quiet determination.

"It could kill us," Miari reminds them. "And even if it works, we might still die trying to get to Varan. I won't be able to work with the Imaku stone anymore, so setting up traps or weapons to use against them will be nearly impossible. Are you sure about this?"

"At least she's offering us a choice this time instead of running off trying to do something impossible by herself," Rai says.

Tessen snorts tiredly. "Don't give her ideas. She hasn't pulled one of those tricks on me in moons, and I'd like to keep it that way."

"I— Are you both serious? You're going to take it?" Nairo asks Rai and Etaro.

"Either it kills me now, it heals me, or it makes it possible to outlive Varan. If I don't take it, I probably die anyway when we corner the bobasu." Rai raises her eyebrows. "I don't see how this is a choice. At least taking the susuji gives us a chance."

"Well, when you put it like that, but..." Miari glances at Zonna apologetically before she finishes the question. "If we live through this war, the Imaku stone will make sure we're not trapped in eternity? It should work for us, right?"

"Only Ryzo is a hishingu. He's probably the only one who has to worry about facing forever," Zonna says, tension straining his voice. "If we're right about why I'm alive, the rest of you will have the option one day of choosing to be done."

Unlike me. Those are the words hanging heavy in the silence.

"I don't..." Ryzo rolls his lips between his teeth, his focus on Zonna before he shivers and looks down. "If I knew there was an end to it, I'd jump in, but I don't want to live forever. Yarzi and the rest of the squad will help, though. I'm sure they'll volunteer for this."

"How soon do you want to leave, Khya?" Sanii asks.

The others look at me, seeming to brace themselves for me to say,

"Now." Even if we could leave tonight, though, I wouldn't do that to them. "As soon as you're all rested."

I order the others back to the main cavern to rest—even Tessen, though he resists at first. Only Zonna and Sanii stay with me. For an hour, we plan routes and review our stores, especially the ingredients we need for the susuji. Then, we've suddenly finished everything we can do while working only with words. I stand, wrapping my spelled cloak tighter around myself and still shivering. The warmth is fading from the fabric, as is the faint tingle of desosa Yonishi wove into the cloth. I need Yonishi to refresh the spell before I head into Nentoado or pushing through that icy wild will become an unendurable torment. Unfortunately, none of the Ryogan and hanaeuu we'la maninaio elders seem to have returned to the main cavern yet.

I'm sitting near my squad's temporary camp, watching the passage for Yonishi's return and trying not to fall asleep, when Ryzo approaches and sits by my side. "You should be resting."

"I will." Once I'm sure I'll stay warm enough to actually get to sleep in the first place.

"When you leave, you're taking everyone who served under Tyrroh, right?" Ryzo asks.

"Yes." I frown. "I thought that was what you suggested?"

Ryzo's gaze lingers on a hanaeuu we'la maninaio child bringing a steaming bowl to a huddled, miserable-looking tyatsu. "Once you leave, how will we communicate with them?"

"You—oh." Bellows, how did I not think of that? The only Itagamins who speak Ryogan are those who escaped Shiara with me moons ago, which means our departure will leave many behind without a translator. Soanashalo'a understands just a few words of Itagamin. There's only one person who knows all three languages. I never wanted to speak to him again, but there is literally no one else. Not in all of Ryogo.

"Blood and rot," I mutter, rubbing my hand over my face. I'm going to have to swallow a lot of anger. "Give me a moment. I'll be back."

Finding Osshi is harder than I expect. Few people in the cavern know him—only my squad, a few high-ranking Ryogans, and Soanashalo'a's family—and it appears he's avoiding all of us. Finally, I reluctantly wake Tessen up and ask for help.

His expression pinches at Osshi's name, but he does as I ask, carefully scanning faces, sniffing the air, and sifting through the overheard conversations. After several minutes, he leads me to the south wall, lifting his chin toward a corner of the craggy stone wall. He doesn't say anything when I touch his arm and head that direction. I don't see Osshi at first, but then what I'd thought was a pile of wet clothes moves.

His face is drawn, and his cheeks are sunken. His usually beige skin is far too pale, almost gray. Dark hair hangs in wet, stringy clumps around his face, and bruise-like circles make his eyes look like fathomless holes. He blinks several times before he focuses on my face.

"Osshi?" Maybe Tessen was wrong. This doesn't look like him at all.

"Khya." He breathes my name, too many emotions layered in the sound. Planting one hand on his knee and the other on the wall, he struggles to his feet. It looks like it takes far more effort than it should. "What do— I mean, is everything okay? Do you need— Well, no. Of course you don't need my help." His laugh sounds breathless and pained.

"Actually, I do." I clear my throat, a good portion of the anger churning in my stomach draining away. He already looks wretched. "I'm leaving in the morning, and I'm taking everyone who came with us here on Kazu's ship."

He nods slowly, confusion creasing his face. "And you want me to come with you?"

"No. I need you to stay and act as translator. Once we leave, the Itagamins here won't be able to communicate with anyone else."

"Why..." He swallows hard, pulling at his hair. "Why aren't they going with you?"

I get the feeling that isn't the question he truly wants to ask, but it's the one I answer. "They can help protect this place if they stay. And because we're headed into Nentoado."

Since he was with us the last time, I'm sure he can guess our real destination and why we're making the journey. He swallows hard and closes his eyes. "Khya...Khya, I'm *sorry*. I thought— We'd been here so long, and the storms were getting worse, and I thought I was protecting my family, and I—"

"*That* I could've forgiven." My hands close into fists. My jaw clenches. "I understood why you thought you had to leave. What makes me want to drop you in the ocean to drown is what you left behind."

His cheeks flush and then pale in seconds. "I—I didn't—"

"But you did. You chose to leave an active garakyu and gave the tyatsu a way to spy on us. One of Lo'a's family died, and Nairo nearly did, too." I hurl the words at him like daggers. "You backed us into a corner and there was only one way out—straight through *your* people."

His expression crumples. Tears streak down his face in thick streams. "I only wanted Ryogo to know when Varan arrived. I didn't want—" He's pleading, his voice low and desperate. "I told them about it when I confessed everything else, but I never intended it to be used like that, Khya. I swear."

I count the cycles of my breaths, forcing myself to think before I speak. Or scream. Nothing I can say will change what's happened. Plus, his guilt is obvious in every line of his body, and I need him now. Breaking him down further won't help either of us.

Breathing deep, I exhale slowly and try to find a way to make peace. Or create a semblance of it at least. "If you're sorry, help me. Make sure everyone here can communicate. Don't let a senseless fear of magic get in the way of the protection my people can offer. It's the only way any of you will survive until I can finish what we started in Atokoredo."

He nods frantically. "Yes. Of course. I'll do whatever I can."

"Find the garakyu with the longest range and keep a careful eye on it." Ryzo calls my name, beckoning when I look over. I hold up a finger to tell him to wait before I turn back to Osshi. "When we're on our way back, we'll warn you as soon as we can."

He agrees, and already some of the man I remember is reappearing. He's gaunt and tormented, but his posture is stronger and his gaze steadier. Just giving him a purpose seems to have been enough to reignite life in his eyes. I don't think I'll ever forgive him, but the rage I'd felt earlier has tangled itself into a complicated knot with pity, regret, and the thread of gratitude leftover from before Osshi abandoned us.

Remembering everything he suffered alongside us before then, though, I need to say one more thing before I leave. "Osshi, I…I really do hope your family is okay."

"Thank you. I do, too." He closes his eyes, his shoulders sagging as tears flow down his cheeks. "Stay safe, Khya. I hope this brings you closer to finding your brother."

Me, too.

As I walk away, his parting words linger, and I find pity overtaking the confused mess of emotions in my chest. Osshi doesn't have any physical connection to those he loves; he only has hope to hold on to. At least I can be nearly certain Yorri is alive. Despite the moments when the pain of a stretched-thin sumai bond glints like a knife in Sanii's eyes, ey isn't suffering the same agony I saw in Ono when I faced him.

Still, alive doesn't mean well. There's no telling what Varan did to his prisoners after he moved them off Imaku, and no telling how he might've punished Yorri for my supposed betrayal of the clan. I just hope that when—*when*—we find my brother, he can forgive me for failing him the first time, and for leaving him alone since then.

I suppose it's a point in my favor that Yorri, thank the Kaisubeh, has always been far more merciful than I have ever been.

FOURTEEN

The first peak of Nentoado rises into the sky like a blade, a pale gray shadow in a white sky, and its lower slopes are thickly coated in snow. Even though I've made this trip before, it looks impassable, a deadly barrier between us and where we need to be. I shiver and burrow deeper into the cloak Yonishi re-spelled for me. It's a good thing he taught Sanii how to renew the spell when it began to fade or this trip into the mountains would be even harder.

"Khya, look." Rai lifts her chin toward the rest of our group. Yarzi, Donya, Amis, Vysian, Syoni, and Remashi—everyone from our squad on Shiara who wasn't with us the first trip into Nentoado—is staring at the mountain with slack jaws. It's partially the size enrapturing them, since the tallest mountain I've seen on Shiara would look like a tiny dune compared to these peaks, but this shock goes deeper than that. None of them have ever seen snow before.

I smile, glancing at Tessen. He's also watching our friends, his lips curling up at the corners. Sanii's watching too, but eir smile looks more like a grimace and ey's pressing the heel of eir hand into the center of eir chest. As though ey's trying to make it easier to breathe.

It's getting worse.

My smile falters. Sanii hasn't mentioned the pain or done anything much to confirm it, but my surety is bone deep. Pain blooms in my own chest, a hollow echo of what Sanii and Yorri must be feeling. I look back toward our path with a fresh layer of worry on my chest like newly fallen snow.

Trekking through Nentoado is never easy—there are many reasons everyone in Ryogo avoids these passes—but it seems darker and more dangerous than ever today. I don't know if the spelled warmth of the cloak is going to be enough on this trip. The storm blows straight into the side of the mountain, each gust stirring up more and more snow until the air is white with the stuff. I think more is falling from the sky—rain too cold to fall as water—but with the wind this strong, it's impossible to be sure what's coming from above and what from below.

"You're telling me that water can actually get *so cold* it turns into this?" Donya asks.

"All year long," Ahta says. "There's a lot of it now, but it's not so bad. This is soft fluff. Trying to climb up ice is lots worse."

We had tried to leave the child behind—I even threatened to tie em to Soanashalo'a's wagon—but ey planted eir hands on eir hips and reminded us no one knows the mountains bordering Nentoado better than ey does. "And you don't have time to waste gettin' lost."

And ey was right. The symbol Soanashalo'a inked into my skin, directly over my heart, is a hanaeuu we'la maninaio magic Rai and Etaro named boruikku. It's meant to help me find anything or anyone by using a thread of desosa to connect me to the object of my search, and I've used it to track katsujos before. I can use the desosa's pull to direct me toward Kaisuama, but it's a guide, not a map. It won't warn us of dead ends or trenches too wide to jump. Ahta can. Ey's been incredibly helpful getting us to this point. The child is full of surprises, too, like the fact that ey now speaks Itagamin as well as I speak Ryogan, a good thing since the six reinitiated members of our squad don't speak a word of eir native tongue.

"It won't be too bad," Sanii insists, forcing emself to stand straight as ey beckons Donya closer. "I can do more to help this time."

One by one, Sanii refreshes and reinforces the magic in our clothes to keep the worst of Nentoado's icy wilds from gnawing at our bones. I move closer to Tessen once ey finishes with us. He's so shrouded in cloaks and furs and loaded down with packs it's hard to recognize him. Only a small part of his face is visible—his intense gray eyes analyzing everything around us.

As everyone else steps away from Sanii, there's nothing but relief on their faces. It's a stark contrast to the pain, exhaustion, and fear of last time, and it's not just because of the warming spell—now, we know where we're going and can the worst dangers along the way.

Today, my biggest worry is Varan. I'm nearly certain he's heading toward the same place we are—what Tessen and Ryzo overheard certainly hinted at it—but we have no way to know for sure. And no way to know if we're chasing Varan or if he's chasing us.

"Do you think Varan will leave Jushoyen before Suzu gets back from Atokoredo?" Before he knows the extent of his losses.

"No, but do you think Suzu will hold back the kynacho who helped her escape?" he counters.

"No." The word burns, but it's true. She'll push those nyshin for every burst of speed they're capable of, even if the journey drives them straight to the brink of death.

Which means Varan may reach Kaisuama ahead of us—he wouldn't have waited to mourn the dead or protect those he was leaving behind. What might work in our favor is our more current knowledge of Nentoado. His memories are outdated by centuries. It's still a dangerous thought, though. Last time Varan visited Kaisuama, he created immortality and unintentionally killed a whole region of Ryogo. I don't want to see what he might do with the power there after centuries hyper-focused on revenge and destruction.

Rai pulls her thick, warmth-spelled furs tighter. "I can't believe we're doing this again."

"I'm not looking forward to it." Etaro shivers, eir narrow eyes becoming slits as ey peers into the snow-thick air ahead.

"This is the only way we know of to get there," I remind them. Ahta was essential to getting us here so quickly, but ey never ventured past this height. Ey can't offer shortcuts here.

Syoni laughs, sounding unnerved. "Only Khya would promise immortality and put us through a trial worse than the herynshi to get it."

"But only because I can protect you through it." I signal, and the squad moves forward. My wards keep us from being toppled by the brutal wind, but even though the blasts of wind don't hit my body, it still feels like I have to push against it to take each step. The snow shifting and crunching beneath my boots doesn't help; it makes balance a constant battle.

Although Syoni, Donya, Amis, and the others grumble, it doesn't last long. Our years spent running, training, hiking, and climbing don't matter here. This range is so harsh it doesn't leave enough breath for complaints. There's an unexpected benefit to the monstrous height of these mountains, though; they soar so high they hold back the low-hanging stormfront—it crashes against the slopes like a black wave against a rocky shore and then rolls back down into Ryogo like water returning to the ocean.

Either Tessen or Amis is always on watch despite how the winds churn up a wall of white around us. Amis is an oraku, and although his three enhanced senses aren't as powerful as Tessen's, my basaku can't be the only one on guard. And we can't be caught unawares. The bobasu might be coming up behind us, or they could be ahead. When a full day passes without a single sign or sighting, I let myself hope we'll make it to Kaisuama first.

Late on day two, we reach the cliff. *The* cliff. Last time we climbed this, we disturbed a nest of birds whose venomed talons left Chio violently ill. No mortal would've recovered.

"You can ward us this time, right?" Tessen asks.

I nod, eyeing the wall of gray rock like an enemy. "They shouldn't be a problem."

Before, I'd been hungry, exhausted, and nearly frozen. Even holding up a basic ward had been too much for my tired mind to maintain. Today, surrounded by spell-created warmth and constantly healed and refueled by the new ways my body can draw in and use the desosa, no bird is going to break through my shields.

Since drinking the susuji, each time I think I understand my new limits, my body finds a way to adapt. It's as though I've become a magnet for desosa. I pull power in from the world with barely a thought, and it flows through my body like blood. My body has practically learned to consume desosa as it used to need food. I'm beginning to truly believe what Zonna said about immortality and sustenance, too. I think, if I had to, I could be fine for weeks, moons, or maybe years without food or water. Hopefully, I'll never have to test the theory.

Miari and Syoni climb first, each shaping handholds in the cliff that leave me free to sink all my focus into my ward. I'm braced for the birds the whole time. My jaw clenches tighter as I rise, waiting.

The attack never comes. I reach the top of the mountain without seeing a single feather.

It feels like missing a step. Should I be preparing for a sneak attack instead? But these are birds, not enemies. They can't possibly be planning an ambush...can they?

On the wide, flat ledge, Miari is bent over, her hands braced on her knees, laughing. When I hesitantly ask if she's okay, Miari looks up and grins with vindictive pride. "I sealed the rot-ridden things in their little stone nests."

Nairo snorts. "Too bad we can't get rid of Varan that easily."

Although she's nodding in agreement, Miari's distracted, her attention suddenly fixed on the ledge we're standing on. "Khya, does it feel warmer here than it was before?"

I'd thought it was my cloak, but no. The air is gentle and balmy, and the stone is definitely warm to the touch. Although we couldn't figure out a cause last time, we also didn't know about the katsujos. I place my hand over my boruikku and focus.

There. At the heart of this massive mountain is a vast katsujo, probably a segment of the vein that surfaces in Kaisuama. It's buried too deep in the mountain for me to draw from, but I feel it. I smile.

"Is it the katsujo you were talking about?" Syoni presses her palm against the stone.

When I nod, Miari asks, "Do you think it's stronger now because you fixed it?"

"Good a guess as any." The region the Ryogans built Mushokeiji in—their mage prison—began to decay in the decades after Varan's exile, after he broke something vital within the Kaisuama katsujo. If breaching the vein of power could slowly destroy an entire region, it stands to reason fixing it could slowly bring warmth and life to another.

Tessen leads us east along the path that is often no more than a blade-thin ridge of stone. On our last trip, I was beyond exhausted by this point. My hands were cut to pieces by the rock and numb from the cold. My mind was slow to process anything, and the others had to make sure I didn't slip off the side of the peak. Today, I'm the one offering a hand to haul the others up.

Despite their exhaustion, everyone keeps a careful eye on Ahta, though the little ebet rarely needs our help. Ey's spent years living in the mountains and is used to the physicality, used to the cold, and used to the way a single breath doesn't do nearly enough to fill eir lungs. The child keeps up impressively well.

Then, when Kaisuama is finally on the horizon, Zonna matches pace with me to ask, "How much attention have you been paying to Ahta?"

I immediately turn, expecting ey's been injured or worse, but ey's trudging along next to Sanii without complaint. "Is something wrong?"

"No, but I think I know how Dai-Usho survived a wound that should've killed her."

I stop walking. All of us had asked that question when we saw the thick, vicious scar across Dai-Usho's throat. Even with a hishingu's power, Ahta's mother shouldn't have been able to survive a throat wound that deep.

"I haven't had to heal Ahta once, even when everyone else has been covered in cuts and scrapes." Zonna puts his fingers on my elbow and urges me onward. "I think ey's healing emself almost involuntarily. And if it's already this advance, ey probably has the capacity to be a powerful healer. It's possible Dai-Usho's desperate need might've pulled the power out of Ahta—I've seen it happen before. It might've even sparked eir magic to life in the first place."

"It would've been enough for me." The first time I used my wards was to keep a blade away from Yorri's throat. "Can you teach em? We'll always need more hishingus."

"I'll try, but that's not my concern." Zonna glances at Ahta again. "In Kaisuama, someone will suggest letting em drink the susuji—ey's been adopted by the squad already, and they'll want to protect em however they can."

I see his point now. If ey's hishingu, it could mean dooming em to live forever.

Our trip to Kaisuama already has the potential to ripple across centuries, and so much—good and bad—can happen in that span. Time is like the desert wind, it bellows and blows and eventually wears people down until only the core of who, of *what* they are is left. I believe none of my friends could ever become as dangerous as Varan, not even after centuries, but I don't know Ahta the same way as them.

Zonna shrugs. "It's going to come up, Khya. You need to have an answer ready."

Maybe, but unlike all the other moments when I wished someone else would take command, this truly doesn't seem like a choice I can make. Ahta is the one who'll have to live with the consequences.

The look Tessen gives me when I catch up is sympathetic, and I know before he brushes his fingers against mine that he's been listening to the conversation. He leans closer, keeping his voice to a quiet murmur. "You already know what you're going to do, don't you?"

He's right, but I shrug for now.

The closer we get to Kaisuama, the stronger the desosa's vibrations are under my feet. Warmth surrounds me, coming not only from my spelled cloak, but also from the peak of the mountain itself. It permeates my boots and pulses against the soles of my feet like a caress. It makes me shiver. Something about the feeling reminds me of the katsujo far to the south. There, I truly felt a thinking, active presence inside the katsujo. I feel it again now, fainter than when I sank into the katsujo, but real. And watching me.

Is this the Kaisubeh, or is my imagination giving energy a life it doesn't have? More importantly, if the Kaisubeh are watching, are they going to offer help or work against us?

Tessen and I approach the border of Kaisuama Valley with apprehension, leaving the others behind for now. Descending cautiously, we try to avoid the leaves and twigs littering the path in case the valley is already occupied. On either side of the path enormous trees gently sway. Their existence should be impossible at this altitude, but they fill the bowl of the valley.

"It smells different." Tessen stops and breathes deeply, his fingers moving slightly as though he's physically sifting through scents. "Something's changed."

I glance at him. "Should we leave?"

He lifts one shoulder, his expression wary but not afraid, and I swallow the urge to demand more—if he knew, he'd tell me. Halfway down, Tessen stops, expression pinched. "I think it's clear, but I can't be sure from here."

That'll have to be good enough. We signal the others, and they join us quickly. Just as quickly, I layer and reinforce my ward. It's easy here, the air is so thick with desosa my shield is soon stronger than the one I constructed around Jushoyen.

The route is even and the angle smooth, and the air around us is warm and far more breathable than the painfully thin air of Nentoado's outer limits. If I didn't know how high we are, I'd believe this place was at the same level as the sea.

As we carefully continue down the path, I start to notice changes. The trunks of the trees seem thicker. The leaves and the low brush seem denser and more vibrant, too. Stranger, not one leaf, branch, or tree is rotten when, previously, we walked through swaths of death and decay. Unsettled by the sweeping, inexplicable changes, I add *another* layer to my wards, trying to re-create the cocooned safety I once felt inside Itagami solid protections.

"What is—" Tessen stops, his head turning so fast I automatically follow his gaze, expecting to see a venomous bird or some sign of Varan. There's nothing. "You didn't see that?"

"I didn't see anything," Amis interjects even as he turns and scans the area for danger.

"What did *you* see?" I ask.

"Nothing. It—" He cuts himself off with a sigh when I glare at him. "For a second, it looked like the road dead-ended in a wall."

"How tired are you?" Rai asks, laughter in her voice.

Rubbing his eyes, Tessen shrugs. "More than I thought, apparently."

After another hour of careful progress, we finally break free of the trees—and stop.

The clearing at the center of Kaisuama was once a wide oval of broken stone with waves of undulating light pouring through the cracks. Now, those cracks have closed almost entirely, and what light does seep through is steady. I'm only sure it's the same place because sitting in the center of the clearing is the rock I bound here with the niadagu cord.

My stomach clenches at the harsh reminder, and I close my eyes. Memories of Yorri laid out on that black stone platform, wrists and ankles bound with the same red cord, rise in my mind. Binding that stone had left me confident I was mere weeks away from getting back to Shiara, slitting Varan's throat, and rescuing my brother, yet here I am again. I don't feel so sure anymore. About anything.

The touch I felt on the mountain ledge returns, firmer and more purposeful, and my eyes pop open even though there's nothing to see. Energy swirls around me like an embrace, and it almost feels…happy? It's like our return has been long awaited. Bellows, is it possible for a place to change this much in only a few moons? The pain that had rooted deep into this place isn't just patched, it's healed, and I have a hard time believing I had a hand in making it happen.

I want to ask Tessen what he feels, but he's already kneeling on the ground, his hands hovering over the welcoming glow seeping through the stone. There's wonder in his eyes when he breathes, "Khya, this is incredible. I can feel the *light*."

Moving to his side, I crouch and stretch my hand through the glow, trying to feel what he's feeling. All I sense is the desosa. It's stronger than ever before, but maybe that's what Tessen's describing. After all, if light could feel like anything, why wouldn't it feel like magic?

The others are just as awed, but it's different. Most of them can't feel the desosa with the same depth Tessen and I can. Even the ones who were here before didn't feel the thrashing energy reverberating through their bones. They don't know how beautiful this change really is, and I don't know how to begin explaining it to them.

Pulling myself back on track, I order some to stand watch while the rest either gather wood and small stones to create a large firepit in the center of the clearing or set up our camp under the protection of the trees. Then I pull the susuji's ingredients from our packs so Sanii, Zonna, and I can prepare it all. The sooner this potion begins brewing, the better.

By the time we've finished grinding the dried plants into dust and have laid out all the other pieces of the potion, everyone is back. All of them—even Sanii and Zonna—look to me to begin, but I shake my head. "I'm not the one who studied susujis with Tsua and Chio. I'll help however I can, but Sanii and Zonna are in charge of this."

"Oh, I..." Sanii swallows, and eir gaze darts between my face and the brightly burning fire. When ey speaks, it's a series of requests, all of which are swiftly obeyed. Soon, ey gains confidence and requests become orders.

Within minutes, everything is set up and Sanii and Zonna are facing each other across the fire, the rest of the squad creating a wide circle around them. The moment feels solemn despite the heady tingle of the energy still swirling in lazy currents around us, and when I begin to speak, the resonance of my own voice surprises me. "While Sanii and Zonna are working, I'll be warding them. I need you all to be on watch, not only for Varan but for a safe place to hide once the susuji is done. And if any of you think of a way to make this the last place Varan ever sees, then..."

I don't have to say anything else. Everyone understands.

Rai looks around the valley and huffs. "I wish we'd been able to get more of the black powder before we came here. I'd rig every tree in this clearing with one of those explosions."

"That'd only work if we had a kasaiji to light them," I remind her. "And both of ours will be unconscious for days." It'll take at least four days for the susuji to do its work, and maybe longer. It took six days for me to open my eyes again, but I was close to death when I took it.

"Now I wish I'd spent more time practicing Ryogan fire spells." Sanii sighs.

"You can do that later. For now, you have enough to focus on." I look over the group, trying not to let my rising anxiety show. Tyrroh once said leadership is hardest when you're standing on the precipice of a decision and looking down on all the ways it could go wrong while pretending exactly the opposite. I understand now. From where I'm standing, there are so many ways everything could go wrong that it's hard to see the ways this could go right. I need them working on a solution, though, not fixating on fear, so I ignore my own the best I can. "Until it's time for you all to take the susuji, you have your orders—you're on watch, working on a trap, or fortifying a shelter. Let's get to work."

I meet Zonna's eyes, then flick my gaze toward Ahta. Zonna is the one who can best explain to Ahta what a lifespan that stretches into forever will be like. He nods, moving to draw the child away from Rai and Etaro, and I head over to help Sanii set up the rocks and wood that Etaro, Vysian, and Remashi float in from the forest.

"Are we sure about this?" Sanii asks as we work. "About giving everyone the susuji, I mean. I took this risk for Yorri. They're doing it for...what? Revenge?"

I look down at the growing pile of wood. "There's some of that, I'm sure, but more of it has to do with what we learned before we ever thought of revenge. The safety of the clan comes before our lives, remember? Protecting the greater good is all any of us have ever known, it's just that this time, we're protecting ourselves from ourselves."

"Whatever you two think of our choices, Ahta has opted to join us." Tessen steps closer and nods to where Zonna and Ahta are sitting, serious expressions on both their faces. Uncertainty flickers in Tessen's eyes. "Even immortal, I'll worry about em if ey follows us."

"I always worry about all of you." My dread of this moment in particular has been building for a while. Varan gave the susuji to nearly twenty people. Of those, only twelve became immortal. Several were barely impacted. The rest died. Screaming.

So many ways this could go wrong. Such a small chance of this going right.

Donya comes over with Syoni close behind just as Sanii and I finish arranging the metal tripod over the constructed firepit. With a shower of well-aimed sparks, Donya lights the blaze. For a moment, she and Syoni watch the flames grow and consume the thick pieces of wood.

Syoni exhales and looks away from the flames, her gaze moving between Sanii and me. "Whatever happens, thank you for everything you've done. Both of you. I know it's probably been even harder than you've told us, and I know how much you've both lost because you asked questions when no one else did. Just in case something does go wrong with this potion of yours, I wanted to make sure someone had told you thank you at least once."

My mind is still grasping for a response when Etaro approaches with our largest pot floating in front of em, and it's already filled with water.

"Tessen found a stream." Ey gestures, and the pot slowly rises until the handle is sitting inside the tripod's metal hook. "Apparently, this valley has a stream now."

"How can a valley this high suddenly grow a stream?" Donya asks.

"I wouldn't put it past this place to grow wings if it wanted to," I admit, somehow managing the joke around the lump of emotion still lodged in my throat.

Etaro and Syoni leave to help with other tasks, but Donya stays, stoking the fire to make it burn hotter. None of us speak, even when Zonna joins. They simply begin to work, adding the first ingredients as soon as the water begins to simmer. Soon, they're also tossing in flower petals, thin slices of root, and a bowl of crushed leaves.

Four ingredients are the key to transforming the susuji into magic instead of an unappetizing stew—mura'ina oil, rianjuko plants, ojoken root, and majiasu ash. The susuji changes the instant Sanii adds them. A ripple runs through the clearing. I slam my hands down on the stone, convinced for a fraction of a second that the mountain itself moved, but it was the desosa, not the stone. Purple light flares from the pot, and the glow through the cracks left in the stone beneath us blazes brighter.

"Remember, this took my parents two days last time, and once it starts, we can't stop. Not even for a second." Zonna stares at Sanii across the fire. "With Khya on the ward, there's no one to replace you. So, are you ready?"

"As I'll ever be." Sanii rolls eir shoulders, settles into a wider stance, and raises eir hands until ey's holding on to either side of the pot. They tap into the katsujo, and another ripple runs through me, but the power I'm drawing from doesn't drop or fluctuate at all. The amount of power we're using feels vast to me, but to the katsujo, what we're drawing seems to make the same impact as stealing a pot of water from the ocean.

It's breathtakingly different from my first brush with this vein of power. There's barely an eddy or knot to hint at the damage Varan caused centuries ago. Even what I did to fix this place has been absorbed into the katsujo and all but erased.

Kaisuama isn't simply healed, it's perfect.

My katsujo-fueled ward circles the clearing, its border pushed out nearly to the edge of the valley itself. I feel each pulse and shift of desosa here as though it's part of me—more than I even sense my own heartbeat. The major shifts of Sanii and Zonna's work are just as clear as the tiny ripples the rest of my squad's work cause. It's a pleasant surprise, and one that limits the anxiety I might've felt otherwise. The creation of the susuji can't be interrupted, which means no one can enter this valley until it's finished. Splitting my concentration for more than the moments it takes to swallow food and water is too dangerous. If Varan gets here before we have a chance to retreat somewhere safer, my shield will be the only thing keeping him away.

Although funneling power doesn't drain me like it used to, maintaining my ward soon becomes an endurance trial. For two days, I barely move. The others shift around me, and I follow their movements more by the patterns they create in the desosa than by anything I see or hear. The hard stone strains my body, but those aches are minor, momentary annoyances, healed by my desosa-fueled immortality as quickly as the pain registers in my mind.

For days, I use nearly as much power as Sanii and Zonna are diverting into the susuji. The instant that's no longer true jolts through me like an unexpected touch. Power still pours into the susuji, but the flow is slowing bit by bit until it eases down to a trickle and into nothing. I don't do the same, no matter how much I want to drop my ward, slump to the stone, and sleep.

My muscles twitch and vibrate with bursts of power, leaving me both restless and exhausted. I can't let the katsujo go yet. I need to check in with the others, though. Pulling in breaths so deep they make my ribs ache, I watch the glow from the susuji—silver-white now with only a hint of purple—pulse and shift. Relief rises through me, as warm and light as steam. It looks exactly like it did the last time Tsua and Chio made it.

"It worked," I murmur. "This will work."

Maybe if I say it enough times, I'll believe it.

Tessen settles beside me, smiling a little ruefully, and sets a steadying hand on my arm. "Yeah, it did. You found a way to pull off the impossible again, oh deadly one."

"It's not impossible. Varan proved that long before I did." I lean into his solid weight and wonder when my body will remember how to move. "And I didn't do it this time. They did."

"C'mon, Khya." He pulls me so close his lips brush my forehead with each word. "The susuji needs to settle. Make this stone hold your ward on its own for a while so I can show you what we've been doing."

I gather my desosa, imagining it as iron wire. I dig it into the stone and wind it around the valley as far as I can reach. Only when I'm sure it'll hold for a while do I fully shift my attention to Tessen.

"I think you'll be impressed," he says as we near the northern edge of the valley. "Miari and Syoni certainly went beyond what I thought would be possible."

My interest is piqued, but pride overtakes everything else when I see the ingeniously hidden burrow my ishiji built into the mountain. From the outside, it looks like a natural part of the slope. Inside, the stone has been lined with moss and leaves to soften the floor.

The only flaw is the position. "It's so far away from the clearing that we'll never know what's happening there."

Syoni smiles and nudges me closer to a small hole. "Stay here and listen."

She runs back into the forest, leaving a smirking Miari behind. Tessen is watching me with his own amused, pride-filled smile, and I'm glad I don't roll my eyes at him. We should all be proud of our ishiji for this, because it's brilliant. The hollows and holes in the cave's roof are vents that have somehow been connected to various sections of the valley. Sound echoes through them, letting me listen in on conversations happening in three different places. I can't hear every word—the distortion is too heavy—but I can pick out pieces. More importantly, I know there are people out there even though I can't see any.

When she returns, Syoni's grin is wider than ever, and she runs past me toward the rear of the cave and points at the wall. There's a larger shaft here, and this one has hand and footholds dug into one wall. Immediately, she starts climbing.

"Up here's a ledge overlooking the center of the valley," Miari explains from below me. "It's not a perfect view, but it's as close as we could get you without the risk of being seen."

I understand when I see the spot. The trees that block some of the view also provide a little bit of cover for whoever watches from here.

"What about your wards? Will the bobasu be able to feel them?" Sanii and several of the others followed us, and now ey looks at the valley, eir long face pinched. "It's hard for me to feel anything here except the katsujo, but I'm still learning."

"I can feel everything when I'm sunk deep into the desosa," I admit, "but my relationship with this place is…unique."

Zonna nearly laughs. "It's definitely that. I couldn't feel anything but the katsujo when I was using it."

All of us look to Amis and Tessen for confirmation. Tessen doesn't answer; he closes his eyes, his fingers twitching. Amis, though, nods. "I'm the same. Feeling energy over the katsujo is like listening for a whisper over the crash of the ocean."

"If I concentrate, I can feel shifts when people draw on the katsujo, but I have to focus exclusively on that and it's weak." Tessen exhales and opens his eyes. "I don't think anyone who isn't a basaku or Khya will be able to sense anything under the katsujo's hum."

"Maybe it doesn't matter," Sanii says. "With what Khya knows, we could sit with them at their campfire and they'd never know we were there."

My breath catches. I almost laugh at myself for not thinking of this sooner. "You are every bit as brilliant as my brother. Possibly more so—though I'll deny it if you ever tell him I said that!"

"Are you kidding?" Sanii laughs. "I plan on making you tell him yourself."

Ey and Tessen are both amused, but everyone else—even little

Ahta—is watching with varying levels of confusion. Ahta huffs. "Are you gonna tell us or do we have to guess?"

I shoot Rai a glare. "Ey has been spending way too much time with you."

"I think it's fantastic," she says with an utterly unrepentant grin.

Beside her, Etaro rolls eir eyes, fond amusement on eir face as ey explains. "Khya and Lo'a knew each other for less than a day when they managed to combine their magic to protect the wagons. By making us invisible."

"That's…" Amis swallows and shakes his head. "I'll have to see it to believe it. Or *not* see it, I guess."

"Something like that," I agree. "From the inside it doesn't look any different from my usual wards, so you'll have to trust it's working and stay calm if and when we see the bobasu."

"That's important," Tessen agrees. "She can hide us from sight, and noise will be muffled, but if you knock into something, or something knocks into you, they'll know we're there. It's protection, not an excuse to forget everything you know about stealth."

"Yes, Nyshin-pa." Miari smirks as she bestows the rank of second-in-command on him, and chuckles when he blinks in surprise. Even if it was meant as a tease, she's right. If I'm stuck in command, Tessen and Sanii are my seconds. I just don't plan on telling Rai that until I'm out of arm's reach; she might decide to remind me—vehemently—she was in line for the position first.

"So, we have a safe place to wait. What about a trap?" I ask.

My squad's pleased confidence falters. More than one person shifts their weight. Tessen is the only one to speak. "Our plan depends on the kind of risk you're willing to take."

We move back to the cave, and Sanii, Zonna, and I eat our first full meal in days while they tell us every one of the plans they've come up with over the past two days.

There were stone-laced rope webs, shards and stone-tipped arrows rigged on trip wires, and more, but each of them presented problems. For some, a mage with a specific skill had to be there to trigger the trap, but that'll only be possible if we dispense the susuji in groups, which would mean another eight or twelve days spent here instead of only four. Other traps were limited by our supplies. The rest might work, but there's no way to ensure they'll catch a bobasu instead of a mortal, and expending a limited resource on slim chances of victory is foolish.

The urge to cover my face is strong, but I fight against it, mostly because I'm not sure if I'd dissolve into laughter, tears, or incoherent screams once I do. I want to believe in the presence I felt in the katsujo—the one I've been addressing as Kaisubeh even though it doesn't seem like the Ryogans understand their own gods at all—because the Kaisubeh helped us once by transforming the Imaku stone into a deadly weapon.

So help us now, I silently beg. *If you want the bobasu gone, help us again.*

If anyone or anything is listening, they don't answer. We can't come up with a plan that might work. Every idea is torn to pieces. After more than three hours, I can tell more than one of the squad is on the verge of wringing my neck.

"Khya, everything will be fine. The sole thing you're responsible for is warding the cave. Everything else, no matter how it unfolds, is out of your control. We know the stakes and the risks. All of us are volunteering." Tessen's words are calming, and something in his tone makes me think he's also trying to say, "*Breathe, Khya.*"

The knot in my gut hurts to breathe around, though, and each expansion of my lungs aches, but I've made my choice—we all have—and I have to accept that. Focusing isn't easy. Thankfully, Kaisuama is steeped in magic, so contracting my ward to solely cover the cave and adding the layer to shield us from sight is practically effortless. Every stone in the valley seems to be made more of magic than matter.

Which gives me an idea. When I asked about the materials used to create hanaeuu we'la maninaio symbols, Soanashalo'a said, "Anything natural can work, but the materials must fit with the magic you are working." Little is better suited to a ward than stone, so instead of building a shield *around* the cave and the ledge, I sink my power *into* it. There's no resistance, and soon, not even Tessen can see the entrance to the cave when he's outside my protections.

While I was working, Tessen and Amis walked through the valley to erase every sign of our presence, even our lingering scents. It's not easy, but the time is worth taking if it keeps Varan from tearing this valley apart looking for us.

By the time Tessen and Amis return to the cave, sleep mats are arrayed on the moss-covered floor, food and water are ready, and the susuji has been poured into fifteen stone cups Miari and Syoni made for this moment.

Everyone taking the susuji sits in the center of a sleep mat while Zonna, Sanii, and I fill the cups and pass them out. The susuji's light casts strange shadows on my friends' faces, and in an enclosed space, the susuji makes the air smell like growing things, like Shiara once did after the rains passed and the sun called up the life hidden in the island's stone. Almost simultaneously, most of the squad brings the cups to their lips and downs the contents.

It may smell like flowers and magic—a crisp, clean scent that reminds me of mountain air—but it tastes of putrefied meat. Everyone gags when it hits their tongues. Ahta had hesitated, and now ey watches the others with apprehension, biting eir thin bottom lip between eir teeth. Zonna crouches in front of the little ebet, whispering, and although the child's hands shake as ey raises the cup, ey swallows it with a grimace and a hard shudder.

Then only Tessen, Etaro, and Rai are left. The others are already curled on their sleep mats as beads of sweat gather on their brown skin and tremors run through their bodies.

"Ready?" I ask Tessen.

"I don't know, actually." He looks down at the susuji, and the muscles in his throat contract. "Khya, if this doesn't work, I just—"

"No. Don't even say that." I hold his face between my hands, hating how deep the lines of worry around his eyes are. I don't like seeing them there. I don't like thinking about a world without him in it, either. I'd rather take a sword through my stomach than admit it's possible that, in a few days, Tessen won't be here. It's too dark a future. Thinking about it threatens to open the bottomless hole Yorri's loss threw me into, so for once, I force myself to focus on the positive. "So far, every attempt has succeeded. What if just once, we beat the odds?"

He closes his eyes, some of his tension easing. "If there was ever a time for us to get lucky, it'd be now."

"Hey, Khya has the Kaisubeh on her side, right?" Etaro interjects. "And we've been luckier in this valley than anywhere else in Ryogo."

"All true, but Khya being optimistic is weird." Rai shakes her head, careful to keep her hand steady to avoid spilling the susuji. "I still hope she's right, though."

Tessen opens his eyes slowly, his gaze meeting mine and his muscles tensing under my hands. Then he purses his lips as something like regret sweeps across his face.

"What is it?" I move one hand to his shoulder, the other over his chest, and I wish for even a moment of privacy.

"Later. When we're done here, maybe." There's a rueful sigh in the words. Then his head snaps toward the valley. "Blood and rot, they're here."

"They— *Bellows*. Where are they approaching from?"

"The east." Confusion flashes across his face. "I think they came by way of Uraita."

"Why? It'd be such a waste of time." Etaro looks like ey's trying to mentally map their route. I'm doing it too, because Uraita is over a hundred miles east of here.

"It's probably the only way Varan knew how to get here. Chio thought he came in from their village the first time, remember?" Sanii crouches near one of Miari's vents, listening.

Etaro and Rai look at me, and I know they're about to suggest waiting until we know if Varan's presence is going to be a problem.

Shaking my head, I order them to drink. "I promise I won't do anything foolish while you're out. I'll keep you safe until you wake up."

I say it as though it's a certainty, but although I hope that's true, I don't know for sure. The susuji seems to have to break a body down before it can rebuild it, and not everyone survives the process. Sanii and I came through it immortal, and I pray to the Kaisubeh everyone taking it today will, too. If we have to lose someone, if that loss has to be borne…

I hate myself a little for hoping it isn't Tessen, for being willing to trade someone else's life for his. Training on Shiara taught me to value the group over the individual. I can't seem to do that with him, not after the past year. I doubt I could handle losing Rai or Etaro, either. Yes, I would willingly die, if I could, to protect anyone on my squad, but I rely on Tessen, Rai, Etaro, Sanii, and Yorri more than anyone else. Losing one of them would be losing a piece of myself. Even if I didn't die, I'm not sure how well I'd survive it.

They drink, and they quickly fall. Etaro flinches and cries. Rai grinds her teeth so hard I hear it, and spots of blood appear on her lips. Tessen curls into a tight ball and wraps his arms around his head like that can keep the pain at bay. I make myself walk away, joining Zonna and Sanii to see what I can learn from Varan instead.

It takes a few minutes before the indistinguishable murmurs and meaningless noise coming through the vents settle into something recognizable. They must be setting up camp.

Then words echo up the shaft. "Varan, look. Is that…?" Suzu's voice. My hands clench.

"Kujuko take them all. This is one of the cords from Imaku." Varan growls. "How'd he find this place? Chio never paid attention to the old legends."

"Maybe he was more motivated than before." Suzu says something else, the words garbled by echoes and overlapping sounds. "Time changes us all."

"I'm going up," I whisper to Sanii. "Come get me if anything changes with our friends."

After Sanii nods, I climb up the ladder shaft and onto the ledge. My breath catches when I see the valley. There are well over a hundred people down there. Maybe as many as two hundred, because I count at least eight yellow-striped kaigo hoods. I don't see any indigo.

My pulse skips a beat. There doesn't seem to be a single Miriseh in the valley. Impossible. I step closer to the edge, squinting and wishing for Tessen's eyesight. I heard their voices. They *have* to be here.

It's the nyshin who give them away. The respect Varan and Suzu are treated with is obvious, even though they're wearing the same undyed hoods as the nyshin.

I smile. Ryzo was right. This is what fear looks like on Varan, pale and prideless.

The easiest way of identifying the bobasu from a distance is gone, but I know several of them are here, hiding in plain sight and protected by their most loyal followers. I'm glad we didn't waste the time and stone on traps. This isn't the same as the narrow streets of Atokoredo. Here, we'd probably take out more of the nyshin than anyone else, and then the survivors would've hunted us even more relentlessly than ever.

A small group breaks off from the main camp and heads into the trees. Toward us. I check my ward, just in case, before movement in the center of the clearing pulls my attention away from the scouts.

Someone is walking toward the bound rock I left there like a claim, as though that small rock can somehow make this place mine. Even before he pushes his hood back from his head, I know it's Varan. His black hair is longer, hanging past his shoulders now, and he seems smaller than I remember, or maybe thinner. I didn't think stress or starvation could make an immortal wither away. Maybe it's an illusion of distance. Or wishful thinking.

He kneels next to the cord-bound stone and touches it, testing the hold maybe. Anger knots my stomach when he unties the cord and crushes rock into dust. It took me *moons* to master that spell, and binding the rock to Kaisuama was my first success and the first time I let myself hope I might be able to free Yorri when the time came. Varan obliterated it in seconds.

Stiff-backed, Varan stares at the cord in his hand before stuffing it into a pouch on his belt. Then, still kneeling, he moves one hand along the path of a glowing crack. Does he know the angry agony he left behind him here? I can't tell. Strangely, I wish I could ask.

Although Kaisuama itself has been healed, it'll likely take centuries for the more far-flung damage Varan did to reverse itself—if it even can. If he breaks this place again, I might not be able to fix it a second time.

Do something, I beg the Kaisubeh. I don't know what the Kaisubeh are truly capable of, but this can't be too much to ask, not while we're at a true source of their power. *If you don't want him to uncover another secret or create a new weapon, don't let it happen. I'm trying to fight, but I need time. Please.*

Varan must've given orders, because the others are backing away, leaving at least twenty feet between him and them. Barely a second after they're clear, he presses his palms against the stone.

It's like the ledge drops out from under me. Like the air's been sucked out of the sky. I tilt, hand pressed against my chest, and try to stop the spinning in my head. My wards flicker and fade. The light once gleaming through the cracks in the clearing dies.

Oh, no. No. What is he doing? What has he done?

Varan slams his hands down, shouting. The fractures I expect don't form in the stone. It doesn't even dent under his fists.

And then the energy rushes back in like a wave returning to shore. I can breathe, my wards return to full strength, and the ground feels solid again. But Varan is furious. His bellows are wordless at this distance, but he rails against the stone clearing. He got angry the moment the desosa blinked out of existence. It's thick in the air now, though, and he's becoming enraged. Why is— *Oh.*

I don't understand it, but somehow the desosa I feel isn't in the valley. The light in the clearing is still out. It looks like Varan's trying to chase the disappearing desosa by literally digging into the mountain, yet nothing more than fragments break off in his hands. Which only infuriates him more. In Itagami, he could make a mountainside collapse with the press of his hand; here he's struggling to create enough pebbles to fill a single bag.

I laugh. Is this the Kaisubeh answering my prayers? Even if it isn't, this is exactly what I wanted. Better than I knew how to ask for, actually.

It's hard to look away from Varan's spectacle, but I do. Everyone has fled to the forest, even those who could do no more than stagger there and collapse when the desosa vanished. Suzu doesn't brave the clearing for several minutes. She only approaches once Varan's gone still, fists clenched at his sides as he glares at the lightless clearing. None of them so much as glance my way.

Without the distraction of the katsujo's thrum, the Itagamins are too close not to feel the power I'm using, yet they don't. They also don't give up on the katsujo. Each nyshin tests their magic and, I assume, their ability to draw on the desosa. Everyone with a tool gouges holes into the stone. It lasts for two days. In all that time, no one catches even a hint of my power.

Magic. *This* is true magic.

It's almost as though the Kaisubeh have sucked most of the ambient energy out of the air until Kaisuama is as empty and dead as the area surrounding Mushokeiji. There, it's extremely difficult to work even basic magic. It's suddenly the same in Kaisuama.

Nyshin I know are powerful kasaiji light fires with sparks instead of flares of flame. Hishingu resort to bandages when treating injuries. Over and over, the nyshin stumble through tasks they should be masters of, too used to doing everything with magic. They've never encountered a place where desosa isn't simply there for the taking. Until my squad infiltrated Mushokeiji, I never knew such a thing was possible. Maybe that's the point. Varan's actions killed that region, and the Kaisubeh are showing him what he's done.

Finally, on the third day, Varan abandons Kaisuama. I don't move even after they leave. Instead, I stare at the clearing and watch the glow slowly return as I try to think of a plan.

I need a direction to head in. There has to be a way to end this war and give both sides—Shiaran and Ryogan—a chance to see what, if anything, we can salvage of home.

FIFTEEN

Hours after Varan leaves, metal scraping against rock draws my attention to the ladder shaft. Sanii's head appears, and my stomach drops at eir pained expression.

"Who is it?" I demand before ey can speak.

"Just come down."

I don't want to, I don't want another disaster to befall the people I love, but no matter how hard it is, I follow Sanii down. Neither of us speak as we descend. When my feet hit the cave floor, I tighten my grip on the stone ladder, hesitating. What's waiting for me? Who will I lose this time? An image of Tessen, still and silent, his gray eyes dull, is too easy to imagine.

Please not him. It's unconscionable to think, unforgivable, but I can't stop the prayer from cycling and repeating. I can't stop meaning it.

I shove away from the wall and turn, my gaze immediately finding Tessen's trembling, tense form. Alive. He's clearly in pain, but he's alive. Zonna is kneeling beside Amis's limp, lifeless form. For a fraction of a second, I think maybe Amis's eyes will open and we'll realize Zonna was wrong.

"I tried to save him. I couldn't." Zonna sounds far more tired than sad. He's watched people die before. It's an inevitability in one lifetime, and it must become all but commonplace over centuries. "I'd hoped this wouldn't happen."

I'd done more than hope. After the Kaisubeh sucked the katsujo out of Varan's reach, I'd let myself *believe* this wouldn't happen. Throat tight, I kneel by Amis's side and run my hand over his shorn hair. The tight, tiny curls are rough under my palm, and his skin is still warm, but the spark that once animated him is gone. Now, this is just the shell he left behind.

"How are the others?" I ask after a long, heavy silence.

"The same as before." Sanii is sitting with eir back to us, wringing drops of water from a cloth onto Rai's dry lips. Rai smacks her lips and licks them automatically, and Sanii repeats the process. "Most are a little calmer now, though. I think that's good."

Maybe, but I can't make myself leave the cave after that. I sit between Tessen and Etaro for hours, watching both but not touching either. I offer water when their breathing begins to rasp, and bites of food when their stomachs grumble, but mostly, I wait. Wait.

Zonna's head snaps up. In a flash, he's scrambling across the cave so quickly he almost trips over Yarzi's legs. He drops near Miari. I hold my breath.

Syoni wheezes, her breath as strangled as if someone had their hands around her throat. Zonna yanks power from the katsujo so fast I feel it ripple past me like a gust of wind. It doesn't help. The power sinks *through* Syoni without fixing what's killing her. Zonna keeps trying, but Syoni's chest is beginning to rattle with each gasped half breath. Her muscles are curling in, contorting her lithe body into a painfully twisted position. My own body tenses in sympathy. I don't let myself look away until she draws one last insufficient breath and goes still.

It takes several seconds for Zonna to sit back on his heels, another few to move his hands from her empty frame, and several more to finally let go of his grip on the katsujo. If not even that immense well of power was enough to save her…

"Is this going to keep happening? Are we—are we going to have to watch them all die?" I can't keep myself from looking back at Tessen, Rai, and Etaro.

Zonna doesn't answer, and I don't press. I'm not sure I want to know.

We move Amis and Syoni to the cave's entrance, but that's as far as any of us are willing to go from the others. I need to be there the moment one of them—all of them—open their eyes, so I sit next to Tessen with my hand pressed flat against his chest. His breathing is even now, more like he's sleeping, so I count the cycles and wait for anything to change.

Another day, maybe longer, passes between the moment we lose Syoni and the instant Etaro lurches up with a sharp gasp. Eir hands fly out, like ey's warding off an attack. Ey nearly smacks Sanii across the face before there's another sharp gasp and Etaro shudders, pulling in on emself. "Sorry, sorry, sorry," ey repeats quietly.

I shift my weight to get up. Then Miari sighs and turns on her side. I look toward Etaro, but Sanii is there, a comforting hand on eir shoulder, so I stay with Miari. She sits up slowly, blinking, frowning, and looking around the cave like she isn't sure where she is.

"How do you feel?" I lean in, making sure I'm in her line of sight.

She's nodding even as she's still frowning. "It's *cold*."

"Just wait." I try to smile. "If the susuji worked, the cold will get worse."

"Wonderful. Something to look forward to." She shivers again and glances at Wehli and Nairo. "I think I want to wait to find out for sure, though."

Until they can all find out together. I understand that. "All of us will wait."

Etaro and Miari woke up one after the other, and it's enough for me to hope it'll continue like that, but an hour passes before Vysian opens his eyes. Several more go by before Rai gives a squeak, the sound higher than I've ever heard from her before.

As though he's *trying* to be contrary, Tessen is the last to come back to the world.

He exhales hard when his gaze meets mine. "Oh good. You're still here."

"Did you think I wouldn't be?" I slide my hand under his shoulder and help him sit up. He's moving cautiously, like he's injured, and my heart speeds up. He's not dead, so even if he isn't immortal, he should be fine. More than; he should be perfectly healed, all old wounds gone.

"If Varan showed up, and you thought you could get him in a position to kill him…" He trails off, smiling as though he's teasing. The words settle heavily on my shoulders, though I'm not sure why.

"Are you okay?" I ask instead of poking at the bruise his words left.

"Nothing hurts, it's just..." He raises his arms and stares at his own hands, moving his fingers as though he's either testing the air or his appendages. "It's like when I was a kid and the world was suddenly too much to bear. This isn't as painful, but it feels like I have to get used to my own skin again."

"That's good." It must be good. A healing, even one as intense as this susuji, shouldn't change the way he fits into his body. That must mean it worked.

"Since he's finally decided to join us," Sanii begins. Ey lifts a dagger instead of finishing.

Although no one looks happy about the prospect, they gather and unsheathe their daggers. As they do, more than one scans the faces surrounding us, looking for the missing.

Wehli asks first. "Do I need to ask where Syoni and Amis are?"

The glance I cast at the cave's entrance is involuntary, but it's all the answer they seem to need. I clear my throat. "We'll give them their rites later, and spread their ashes around Kaisuama, but first, we need to know where the rest of you stand."

I need to know how many of my friends have become immortal.

Heart racing, I hold my breath and stand behind Tessen. Everyone raises their daggers and slices a shallow line across their forearms. Most of them gasp or cry out, shocked by the pain of the wound the same way I was the first time I got hurt after the susuji. Tessen sways like his legs are about to give out. I don't like seeing them in pain, and yet the sound is so promising. If they're feeling a small cut like this so deeply they *must* have transformed.

Blood pools in the wounds, cutting dark lines across their brown skin, and Sanii hands them each a strip of clean cloth. I put my hand on the back of Tessen's neck and watch over his shoulder as he wipes his arm clean.

No trace of his wound is left.

My breath rushes out in a gust. I slump, dropping my forehead to rest on his shoulder and wrapping my arms around him, one hand resting over his heart. He places his hand over mine and leans back against me. I don't have to tell him how relieved I am he's okay or how devastated I would've been if he'd died or how tired I am after four days of waiting for this moment. I don't have to tell him because he can feel it all, feel the effect my emotions have on the desosa surrounding me and read it like a map. Which is good, because I don't know how to say any of that aloud.

"If I didn't know better, I'd think she was only happy to see him," Rai drawls. "The rest of us might as well be talking strips of teegra meat."

I squeeze Tessen tighter before I let him go—though his words from earlier still circle in my head like mykyn birds on the hunt.

Straightening, the first thing I notice is Rai's expression. It doesn't match her tone. Too serious. Almost scared. I look down. She's pressing the cloth against her bleeding arm.

My gaze jumps wildly from arm to arm. The only other person with an unhealed wound is Remashi. Zonna is somber as he places his hand on each of their arms and forces the skin to close and the cut to heal. *Forces*, because their bodies aren't capable of healing themselves.

It failed. I knew it might, that was always a possibility, but it failed.

I stare at the freshly healed skin on Rai's arm and swallow my rising bile. This was supposed to make her safe. She's as vulnerable as ever, and our mission isn't going to get any less dangerous from here until wherever this ends.

Rai takes a long breath. I only hear it tremble because I've learned how to listen to her.

"So," she says after several seconds of quiet. "What now, Nyshin-ma?"

"Now..." I pause, unsure. "We'll head back to Lo'a and see if Gentoni has found us a ship. Despite this, I want both of you to come with us when we leave." I look between Rai and Remashi. "I won't make it an order."

Rai snorts, a tense smile on her lips. "I've followed you this far. I'm not stopping now."

On the other side of the circle, Remashi nods, but she doesn't speak. She doesn't need to. It's as heartening as it is stressful to know they'll stay by my side until this is truly finished.

SIXTEEN

We've said goodbye to too many friends since we arrived in Ryogo, but in the process, we created a new tradition, one that's all our own. By now, it not only feels right, everyone knows their role in the proceedings. It doesn't take us long to arrange Amis and Syoni in the clearing, say our final goodbyes, and consign their shells to the flames.

I feel so little as the fire consumes two friends, and this is only the start. If numbness can settle over me in a few moons, how must it be for Zonna, who's watched countless people die over the past five centuries?

Everyone is subdued as we gather food and refresh the fire. Only after everyone is settled and fed do I tell them what happened after Varan arrived, but we linger on his failure and the katsujo's reaction. The katsujo *reacted*.

"If I didn't believe in the Kaisubeh before, I certainly do now," Tessen says. "And I'm extraordinarily grateful we don't have to see what Varan would've done here."

"But we do have to worry about what he's doing now, and where we should go." I had been called down to the cave before I came up with anything even resembling a plan. Now, I unroll a map showing Ryogo and the lands surrounding it. "I don't think we'll ever be able to outmatch him in Ryogo. He has too much space to hide in. A lure might work, but he's not a fool. He'll expect a trap. Especially after Atokoredo."

"He's already hiding, trying to keep us from easily identifying the bobasu at a distance. If we give him more time, we'll never be able to find him, so we must force him into the open." Sanii's eyes gleam as ey talks. "His control of the nyshin hinges on his lies about the Miriseh's immortality and the belief that only the Miriseh are granted that gift. If he knew we were heading for Shiara to bring Yorri and the other 'dead' back to life, there's a chance he'd follow us home. And leave the army behind. It's the one secret he'd risk everything to protect."

My heart leaps, and I latch on to the idea. "Plus, once we free Yorri and the others, a fight against the bobasu would be weighted on our side."

"We do know Shiara far better than Ryogo. There's a chance we know it better than the bobasu, actually; they rarely left the city." Tessen speaks slowly, like he's working plans through in his head as he talks. "But do you think *all* of the bobasu would follow us?"

"Who else could Varan bring?" Excitement bubbles in my chest. "The kaigo know the truth, but few of the nyshin do. And only the bobasu are strong enough to take on other immortals. If we're careful, and feed him the right information, the bobasu will come after us with everything they have. We could end this and spare Ryogo the rest of this war."

So many—too many—have died already, and the final battle will be brutal, bloody, and terrible. Moving it off Ryogan shores is best, even if I fear what the nyshin will be ordered to do in the bobasu's absence.

"But even if Gentoni can find us a ship, I don't know how we'll get there." Etaro shakes eir head. "You saw the storms! Immortal or not, can anyone cross an ocean like that?"

"I'll protect the ship," I promise. "But it'll still be dangerous, and I won't order any of you into this. Will you come?"

Lasting silence follows, only broken by Ahta's restless shifting. Finally, Wehli says, "We're always with you, Khya. If you think this is our best chance to end this without thousands dying, then we're in. Just tell us what you need."

Most of the others nod, but Donya bites eir lip. "I'll follow, but none of you were there when we crossed. It was— " Ey shudders. "It was terrifying. I didn't know waves could reach so high. Can even you keep us safe in that, Khya?"

"Yes, she can," Sanii, Tessen, and Rai say at the same time. The three share a glance, amusement glimmering in their eyes.

"I can," I agree. "We have to go back sooner or later, and I'm voting for sooner. Shiara is home, the only place we can go when this is over. Besides, I want to give Yorri and everyone with him a chance to fight the people who punished them simply for existing."

Thankfully, there are no more questions after that. Everyone finishes their food and prepares to leave. While they do, I gather our garakyus and use the katsujo to enhance their range. I also refresh our remaining wardstones and, with Miari's help, create new ones from the clearing's stone. As many as we can carry.

Although I want to leave Kaisuama immediately, I order a night of rest first. Rai and Remashi need it, and so do the rest of us. Of course, no matter how hard I try to sleep, I can't manage more than a short nap. I find myself watching the play of firelight against the cave wall rather than trying to fall back to sleep. Sighing, I give up and quietly make my way outside.

Zonna is on watch at the cave's entrance, and he nods as I pass. He's been nearly silent since yesterday. I'm beginning to worry. His expression isn't nearly as empty and hopeless as it was after he lost his parents, but I don't know how to comfort him. My own mind is too mired in anxiety and strain to come up with anything to say.

I know Tessen is in the forest somewhere, scouting the perimeter in case Varan comes back. Instead of looking for him, I head for the clearing and lie down in the center, folding my hands behind my head and staring up at the blessedly dry, cloud-covered sky.

A scuff of boots against stone warns me someone is nearby a few seconds before Tessen speaks. "Don't tell me you're already becoming a leader who doesn't follow her own orders. You're supposed to be resting, aren't you?"

"Would that I could."

Tessen sits beside me, leaning over me. The light from the closest crack in the clearing is behind him. All I see is a shadow against a dark sky. "What's keeping you up?"

"I don't know." I look away from him, back to the sky. We're so far from home. Would the stars be different here? I know how to navigate by them on my island. Would the same rules apply so far north? It's the kind of question Yorri would ask if he were here.

Thinking about Yorri makes me think about Sanii.

"Sanii's getting worse." The words pop out of my mouth and keep coming, all my worry bubbling up. "I didn't notice until Kaisuama, but ey breathes like eir ribs are broken most of the time. None of the bobasu have sukhai, have you realized that? Maybe there's a reason. Maybe stones aren't the only thing that can kill an immortal. It's never been tested before, but separation is clearly affecting Sanii, so it's probably affecting Yorri, too. It's constant, no matter how ey tries to hide it. What if it gets worse? What if straining the sumai bond too far can kill them?"

"It won't. That much I believe. Up to then, we'll help Sanii however we can until ey reunites with Yorri." His voice is so impossibly calm it almost makes my teeth clench. This is Tessen, so of course he notices instantly and sighs. "It's all we can do, Khya."

"I know." I look at the trees or the shadow of the mountains against the charcoal-dark sky—anywhere but Tessen.

"It's not even about Sanii, is it? Or even Yorri." He scoots closer when I don't respond. "Why do you hate the sumai so much?"

I startle, my gaze snapping back to him. "I don't hate it."

"At first, I thought you were mad because Yorri had been keeping secrets from you," he says. "But it's deeper than that. If it's not hatred, it's something like it."

"You can't just read me and figure it out?" The question comes out sharper and far more mockingly than I'd intended.

"Usually I can with you, but not always. You're complicated. Sometimes what seems like one thing turns out to be something else entirely." His tone is strange, and without getting a better look at his face, I don't know how to interpret his words. I don't know how to respond, either. The urge to apologize is strong, but we've known each other our whole lives, and I won't apologize for being who I am.

Wrapping my dark cloak tighter around myself, I try to figure out how to explain something that has only ever been a feeling in the pit of my gut and a shadow at the back of my mind. "When we were seven, a rockslide took out Suesutu Pass. I'm sure you remember. We lost half a squad of nyshin that day."

"I think I remember that. It was an awful accident." He speaks slowly, obviously confused. "But what does that have to do with—"

"One of the dead had a sukhai, and I was there when she carried him into the city. Her screams were…" I shudder, and this time it has nothing to do with the cold. "It was the day I learned what a sumai was, and no matter what I learned after that day, I couldn't get the sound of her pain out of my head. Nothing about the sumai made sense anyway. Ryogo was an eternal haven for the whole clan, so why would anyone need to bind themselves to someone else so deeply and risk that kind of pain? Now, it makes even less sense. We don't know if there's any kind of afterlife or what happens when you get there. It just..." I shake my head, words failing me for a moment. "I've seen the damage a sumai can do, Tessen. More than once. The thought of causing that agony in someone else is awful."

Tessen is still and silent for several moments, then he takes a sharp breath and asks, "Do you remember how Neeva used to take me into the city?"

"Yes?" It comes out like a question, but I do remember. Tessen's blood-mother hadn't been a kaigo yet, only a high-ranking nyshin, and she'd been more involved in her son's life than most blood-parents. It was noticeable, especially when I'd longed for the same kind of attention.

"When I was twelve, she took me to the bikyo-ko. Do you remember how I was then?"

"It's hard to forget." He'd been insatiably curious and determined to show off his newly acquired basaku abilities—how far he could hear and see, how strong his sense of smell was, and how much better he was than us. Or, at least, that's how he'd seemed to me when *I* was twelve.

"That day, I was there when a newly bonded sumai pair came out of Varan's chambers. They were..." He trails off, and I wish I could see his face. The softness of his voice must be reflected there. "I'd never seen anyone look so peacefully happy. They moved differently, too. I'd seen them before, and they always orbited each other. But after the sumai it seemed like they barely needed to talk. They shifted around each other like they were connected. It was beautiful."

I picture Tessen at twelve, gangly from a growth spurt and overly inquisitive, sneaking into a restricted section of the bikyo-ko and watching this scene with wide, wonder-filled eyes.

"I also saw Sanii and Yorri moments after their bond." His quiet words take a few seconds to land. When they do, they hit like a boulder.

I'd forgotten that. How had I forgotten? Tessen was the one who told me about the bond, and when he did, he admitted that he'd known since the day it happened.

"Your brother always felt like he had to chase everyone else's progress, and it made him wary. He was on guard with everyone but you." He shifts closer. "That day though, he looked... I don't even know how to describe it. It isn't an expression I've seen in any other moment."

Closing my eyes, I turn away, not because I don't want to see him, but because I don't want him to see me. Everything he's saying is true, and yet it doesn't ease the fear knotting my stomach when I think about bonding myself.

I've talked about it before, but only in offhand comments as nebulous as heat waves. I've thought about it, but only the good parts—being able to hold on to someone I loved even beyond death. In a daydream, the pain that death brought never came and I'd never have to face the reality of how easily a sumai bond could tear a soul apart.

"Nothing is certain, Khya, but when has that stopped us?" Tessen shifts, something he's wearing scraping against the rock. "Why are you letting it stop you now?"

"This is different! I'm not afraid of suffering. I'll gladly throw myself into a maelstrom if I need to." My hands are tight fists against my thighs, but my words flow like a waterfall once I start. "How can whatever joy someone finds in a sumai be worth the inevitable agony? And it is inevitable. Even immortality isn't forever. We've proven that. A sumai means one day tearing someone I love in half and leaving them bleeding from the inside out. Because of *me*."

Silence. My own breathing is shockingly harsh in the stillness. When did I start sucking in air like I was sprinting? Why isn't Tessen saying anything?

"What if I told you I was willing?" he asks after so many breaths I'd stopped counting. "What if, for me, suffering that kind of agony is worth it for everything that came before?"

I look at him, cursing the darkness. If I ran the tips of my fingers along every line and curve of his face, would it be enough to read his expression? I'm not usually envious of his power. Now, envy doesn't feel like a strong enough word to explain the yearning I have to see. Maybe then I'd know how to answer his questions.

"Hardship is a constant, but there are circumstances no one should be asked to endure," he says. "When a citizen volunteers, though, honor that sacrifice and their choice."

I sigh. "Quoting Varan? He wasn't even talking about this, he was—"

"Making a point about why we should die to save the clan, I know, but it applies, Khya." He exhales in a sharp, frustrated gust, which quickly turns into a harsh laugh. "This is what you'd do to Yorri, you know—try to protect him from *life*, as if that was possible. I don't know how he endured it for so long without shouting you down in front of everyone."

Me neither. Before we left Shiara, I realized I'd spent most of our lives trying to make sure Yorri became the person *I* wanted him to be, and that epiphany still taints everything he's suffered with the stench of *this is your fault. You did this to him.*

It's part of why I've been fighting the command circumstance has shoved me into and why so many of the big decisions have been requests instead of orders. Guilt over what happened—is still happening—to my brother weighs heavily on my chest.

"I know you're scared, but our lives might last as long as Itagami, so I thought I should tell you I..." He sighs softly. "The sumai pair I saw when I was twelve? You were the first person I thought about. I stood there imagining I was walking out of that room with you."

Shock wipes my mind clean and hollows me out until I am nothing but a cavern his words are echoing through. When he was *twelve*? How could he have been so sure about anything for so long? He can't possibly have been so sure about me.

"You didn't hate me as much back then as you eventually did," he says, his tone wry. "Even last year, though… It's always been you, Khya, and I'm here whether you want forever or not. I love you, okhaio, and there isn't any fate I've seen or heard of that's enough to keep me from wanting you as my sukhai. From wishing you loved me the same way."

As he gets up and walks away, his silhouette catching the light from the clearing in flashes before he disappears into the forest, I realize he left because he knows I won't be able to speak anytime soon. What terrifies me, though, is that his senses might've picked up on something I'm only now beginning to understand myself: I might never be able to give him what he wants.

Maybe, if we'd never discovered the truth about Imaku and the bobasu, this would feel different. It'd be alarming, yes, because the prospect always has been, but not insurmountably so. Before losing Yorri, I believed deeply in Ryogo and the paradise of the afterlife, so I might've been able to convince myself that even the soul-wrenching agony of a sukhai's death would be bearable in exchange for the eternal life we'd have in Ryogo. That kind of faith is hard to find now. There's little I believe in besides my friends. And the existence of the Kaisubeh. To put Tessen at risk of losing half his soul without any clue of what—if anything—might come after it is unthinkable.

But when the impending destruction of the world isn't binding us anymore, how long will he stay if I keep saying no? Worse, if he does stay, how long will I *want* to keep saying no?

It may not be storming in Kaisuama, but the cloud cover is still so thick we can barely tell the difference between sunrise and high noon. In what our bodies decide is morning, we depart the valley for what I hope is the last time. We have a long way to go, a lot left to plan, and not enough time to accomplish any of it.

After the way our midnight conversation ended, I keep expecting tension or even just to find Tessen watching me more often than usual. Nothing changes. It makes me hope no one else notices my tension, how I'm watching *him* more often than usual, or that I don't stand quite as close to him as usual for the first day out. Thankfully, he doesn't let that imposed distance last too long. The tension, however, lingers.

On the third morning, Tessen is still quieter than normal, but I don't let myself watch him. Instead, I stare at the horizon as it slowly shifts from deep black to the dark gray that passes for daytime now. Gray and black and black and gray when all I want to see is an endless expanse of blue.

I sigh. "I think I've started to believe I'll never see the sun again. I'm not sure it even still exists behind all that."

"What?" Sanii blinks, eyeing me uncertainly. I hadn't been talking *to* anyone, but ey must've been close enough to hear. "Of course it does. Just because you haven't seen something in a while doesn't mean it's blinked out of existence."

Pursing my lips, I shrug and keep the rest of my thoughts to myself. We haven't seen Itagami in a long time, either, but that might be gone, or at least so unrecognizable it might as well be gone. We haven't seen Yorri, either, so what does that mean for him?

A few hours later, we walk into the welcoming warmth of the

cavern. In our absence, it's turned into a small city with the wagons serving as physical divisions of the spaces each group has claimed as their own. But that doesn't mean anyone keeps solely to their side, so finding anyone in the ordered chaos takes time. As soon as we locate Soanashalo'a and the Ryogan leaders, I head for the hall of smaller rooms deeper in the mountain. Osshi follows, too, and I don't stop him. Most of these small caves are in use now, but farther in there are still places we can talk privately. And I have a lot to fill them in on.

They knew we wanted a ship, and they assumed we would be sailing back to Shiara, but this is the first time I can explain that we're planning to use our escape to lure Varan away.

Gentoni stares, his small eyes wide behind the glass circles. "Using yourselves as bait is asking too much of someone so young. Are you sure this is the only way?"

"If this doesn't draw him away from Ryogo, nothing will," Tessen answers before I can. I try to hide my wince. That's the one thing we haven't explained yet.

"There's no doubt you're all powerful, but why would you *leaving* Ryogo draw him away?" Jintisu's forehead creases. "It seems like it would be safer for him to stay here."

"I know a secret he'd risk death to protect." But I don't want to tell them what it is. I seriously doubt that the existence of more immortals will sit well. Especially not while the seven remaining bobasu are sowing destruction across Ryogo.

Gentoni looks ready to argue, probably to demand an explanation, but I shake my head. "I can't tell you more, but I promise it isn't anything that'll harm your people."

If I survive, I'll make sure of that myself.

"I can't say I enjoy not knowing," Gentoni says after a moment, "but you've earned our trust. I should try to talk you out of this for your own sakes, but I can't think of any other plan, so I'll do whatever I can to help."

"Thank you, Jindaini." It takes more effort than I like to keep from slumping in relief. "Can we leave in the morning?"

"Will a night be enough rest? The journey won't be easy." The concern on Gentoni's face seems sincere.

"We'll be ready," I promise. We could leave tonight and most of the squad would be fine.

He looks relieved. "Then tonight you should pack the supplies you'll need for ten days."

"We're heading west, correct?" I pause until Gentoni confirms my guess. "Then we probably won't cross paths with the bobasu. Varan was heading east when we saw him. If my guess is right, he's busy setting up a defense right now."

"A defense. Against you?" Yonishi's question carries an insulting amount of surprise.

"Yes. Against me. Against *us*." I gesture to the rest of my squad. "After Jushoyen, he knows he's underestimated me, and he's not a fool. He takes threats seriously."

"My army will likely see you as a threat, too, even if you're traveling with me," Gentoni admits. "They're scattered and scared, and they'll be on high alert."

"Strike first, ask questions later, and hope it's enough," Yonishi says seriously. "We told the Mushokeiji squads to arm as many tyatsu as possible with the Kaijuko-stone arrows."

I shudder, remembering too well the pain of those weapons. They won't kill the bobasu, even if they strike deep into their hearts, but they might knock the bobasu unconscious long enough to give any Ryogans nearby the chance to flee.

The next morning, we leave. All the Itagamins come with us, of course, but so do Ahta, Gentoni, Yonishi, and Jintisu. Of course, the presence of the three leaders mean traveling with a hoarde of tyatsu, too.

Surprisingly, some of the Ryogans are staying behind. When I ask why, Gentoni reminds me he has a promise to keep. The tyatsu still in the cavern will act as mediators if another squad discovers the place. Soanashalo'a appears in the line, bags packed and ready for hard travel. Shiu and several of the others we've been traveling with are standing alongside her as well. It's an odd group, and communication is a confusion of languages and hand signals, but once the journey begins, it's clear every person in our cavalcade is determined to see this through to the end.

Three days in, Tessen signals a halt. I creep up from the center of the group, shivering despite my layers. I kneel next to Tessen and remind myself to have Sanii renew the warming spell in my clothes. To Tessen, I murmur, "Friend or enemy?"

"They're speaking Itagamin, so enemy. But I don't think they're tracking us." He tilts his head to listen, and I signal for silence. Tessen closes his eyes. I grind my teeth, force my hands to flatten against my thighs instead of clenching, and fight the urge to ignore the danger and run. Stopping, even to keep everyone safe, scrapes against my skin like sandstone.

"Several squads are camped ahead, but there's good news—some of them are questioning Varan." He exhales and smiles. "Rumors have been spreading since three bobasu went missing. They're saying, 'It's as if they vanished.'"

"Vanished?" I frown. "I can't believe the bobasu managed to hide their deaths from the rest of the nyshin."

"Clearly they didn't hide everything. There are rumors." Tessen smirks, his gray eyes glimmering with delight. "This is a good sign. They're finding holes in Varan's stories. If they keep digging—"

"Everything Varan has ever told them will fall apart." I speak in Itagamin, conscious of our Ryogan listeners and how they might interpret what I say. "If there isn't someone waiting with the truth when that happens, something provably true, I don't know how they'll react. It could make things worse."

I hope the bond of clan will be enough when they're otherwise surrounded by enemies in a strange land. I was in that moment once, and it felt like a fathomless hole opened in my chest. Only Sanii, Tessen, and my mission to save Yorri kept the betrayal's weight from crushing me.

"We'll find a way to help them," Tessen promises, his own smile fading. But I don't know if that'll be possible. We're leaving. Even if we weren't, most of the clan sees us as the enemy now, and I don't know if I can change their minds fast enough to make a difference.

We go out of our way to avoid the nyshin and continue on, walking along narrow trails and climbing higher into the western Mysora Mountains. Cold, high, dangerous, stormy—they were right to warn us that the trip wouldn't be easy. The afternoon of the tenth day, however, we stand on a ledge overlooking the coast.

Gentoni points to a sliver of water in the distance. "That's the bay. The ship will arrive tomorrow, loaded with enough food and water to carry you home."

"Tsst." Tessen waves for quiet, his attention to the south. "There are people coming closer. I can't quite hear them, but I think they're speaking Itagamin."

"Looking for us?" My heart pounds hard enough to rattle my breaths. If Varan tries to take our ship, I'll rain black rock on his head until it buries him at the bottom of the bay.

"Who *isn't* looking for us?" Then Tessen glances at me. "We can use this. If they 'overhear' something interesting, they'll carry it back to Varan."

I close my eyes, trying to see all the possible outcomes. Varan must follow us to Shiara, but not immediately or we won't have time to free Yorri or devise a trap. He also can't be too far behind us, or we'll be leaving the Ryogans under his thumb too long. The problem is, I don't know what too soon or too long is. I need more details. "Can you tell if they're using garakyus?"

"Not from this distance," Tessen says.

"I'd never seen anything like those globes until I joined you," Ryzo adds. "Doesn't mean the kaigo and the bobasu haven't started using them since I left, though."

"The range will be fifty miles at most, so I'm not sure it matters," Tessen reminds me. "This squad will probably have to travel a quarter of Ryogo to get within range of Varan."

"And it'll take even longer if they don't know where he is." Ryzo gestures vaguely toward Gentoni and the others. "If they get lost, run into dead ends left by the storm, or if the tyatsu purposefully delay them, it could be more than a moon."

"Which might be exactly how long we need." Or not nearly enough time. I grind my teeth, hating the uncertainty. "It's what we have. We'll make it work."

We send the Ryogans and hanaeuu we'la maninaio down to the bay, but Tessen and I keep Ryzo, Yarzi, Donya, Remashi, and all the nyshin who deserted to our side back. My friends glare when I tell them to stay with Gentoni. They don't disobey, but they do order me to be careful—or, in Rai's words, "Try not to be as big a self-sacrificing fool as you're capable of being, Khya."

I roll my eyes and almost turn away, but a thought stops me. "Are you carrying any Imaku rock?"

Rai raises an eyebrow. "Depends on what you want it for."

Calling Ryzo over, I order Rai to give what she has to him and then I warn, "Be extremely careful with this. Keep it well away from Yarzi and

Donya, but you can use it against the bobasu if you have the chance."

"Nothing would convince the clan faster than watching Varan die." Ryzo's expression is serious as he takes the pouch and packs it in the center of his largest bag. "I'll use it if I can."

"I know," I say.

"Good luck," Rai adds before she turns and walks toward the shore.

"So what, exactly, are we responsible for this time?" Yarzi asks.

"Bait laying and dissension." Saying it like that sounds so simple, yet I know what I'm asking them to do is anything but. "Follow these nyshin, and in two days, begin telling the story of our escape. Tell the truth about what happened to those who died in Atokoredo and what I said after the fighting was done. If you act as though you were there with Suzu instead of me, and that you barely escaped with your lives and have been running ever since, they'll believe you."

"And when we keep running instead of staying with them, they'll tell the story to every squad they meet." Ryzo nods. "It'll work, but how will you know when Varan's on his way to you? I don't want you caught unawares, Khya."

"We'll hope Suzu still has that garakyu you left with her; then we'll get some warning when she's in range. If she doesn't, we'll find another way." I reach out, and Ryzo quickly winds his fingers through mine. "You have plenty to worry about keeping yourself alive until we can come back for you. Don't add us to your list."

"The best I can do is try." Ryzo squeezes my hand before letting go.

Yarzi, though, smiles. "You know the only person better than me at spreading gossip and chaos is Rai, so everything will be fine. And once we finish your mission, Khya, I'm sure we can find something else to keep us busy."

"I don't doubt it for a second," I say, smiling back. "Let's move out."

We travel slowly and stay as silent as possible, but soon we're on a ridge overlooking the nyshin camp. I shiver to see them wearing just the simple pants and hooded, long-sleeve tunics we wore on Shiara. I doubt I'd be able to function in only that. I hope they're at least wearing the nyska cloth in layers, because it was made for a desert summer, not this chill. The entire Itagamin army must be freezing, which might help us. A miserable, mistreated subordinate is more likely to turn on their commanding officers. That was one of Varan's lessons. I doubt he thought it'd be used against him.

I point it out to Ryzo and offer one more warning. "Everything about Varan's plan goes against what he taught us about clan. Use it, no matter how much it hurts to watch those cracks spread through the ranks. Bear up or we'll lose any chance of this working."

"Already let you down once." His full lips twist into a sad smile. "I won't do it again."

"If he looks like he's wavering, we'll poke him back into line." Yarzi's smile is forced, but eir determination is genuine. "End this, Nyshin-ma. If anyone can, it's you."

Donya and Remashi smile, too, and it's just as strained. They're faking confidence to ensure I won't worry about them, but despite my own words to Ryzo earlier, that's impossible. I'd be worried even if they were staying with us.

Tessen advises them on the best path to take to intercept the nyshin as though traveling from Atokoredo, and when he's done, all we have left is goodbye.

"You'd all better be here waiting for me when I come back to get you," I order.

"Absolutely, Nyshin-ma," Ryzo says with a wry smirk. Then he leads his small squad down the northern slope. Too soon, even Tessen can't hear them anymore.

"We could wait," he murmurs when I don't move. "I could track them. Then, we could bring them with us after they start the rumors. They don't *have* to stay."

"No, but it's better if they do." Leaving them hurts, but it has to be this way. They can turn ripples of dissent into waves within the Itagamin army. They can protect Ryogan refugees. I can't affect the Itagamin army from Shiara. Ryzo can. The army will be vulnerable once the bobasu leave, not to attack but to information. To gossip. To the revelation of secrets. While Varan and his attendants are chasing me, my friends will be here, undermining his control.

And I have several promises to keep, too—once I rescue Yorri and end the bobasu, I've got to find a way to get the nyshin back to Shiara. At least, with Ryzo's team here, someone might be around to make that happen if I'm not alive to do it myself.

SEVENTEEN

A massive ship appears out of the fog-covered bay, the hull as red as fresh blood. Black stripes run along the side, their passage broken only by windows and other openings on each level—at least three below the main. There's a word written in white near the rear, but the letters aren't anything like Ryogan. Its color, though, is echoed in the white sails that rise above the deck, each rectangular cloth attached to one of the three masts and guided by ropes stretching in every direction.

The Khylarin vessel must be nearly twice the size of the ship that carried us to Ryogo. There's nothing about being on a storm-tossed ship I want to relive, but surely it'll be harder for the storm to wreck something this big, especially with my reinforcements.

The first Khylarin to step on shore is as impressive as the vessel. Though they're stocky, several inches shorter than me, and much paler, the Khylarin moves with confidence and power. Their hair is braided and reaches their hip, and the color is striking. It's mostly soft brown, but there are streaks of pale gold. They stop several feet away, one hand resting on the hilt of a short sword as they scan our group, and their gaze lingers longest on me. I'm not sure why. I'm dressed as a tyatsu, and my hood is up, so what marks me out?

Then the Khylarin shakes their head. "Anyone the Ryogans' strict customs allow to stand equal with the Jindaini and his family must be important."

"She is, Shytari Leowesa," Soanashalo'a calls, moving forward through the group. "She reminds me of you—a woman with power. And right now, she needs your help. We all do."

Shytari tilts her head, and light from our torches catches her eyes. I stare. Her eyes are blue like the deepest parts of the ocean on a bright day. I didn't know eyes could be that color. Then she sighs. "I'm going to regret promising to let all of you on my ship, aren't I?"

"I'll do everything in my power to make sure you don't," I promise. "But if we're leaving, it needs to happen now."

Shytari shakes her head. "We have a problem to deal with first—I wasn't expecting so many of you."

The next few hours are a lesson in a side of leadership I've barely considered before: logistics. Before now, we have simply been scrimping and rationing and hunting as the need arose. That clearly won't work for this many people within the confines of a ship.

Calculations for food and water and sleeping space for Shytari's crew, my squad, Ahta, Soanashalo'a and a handful of hanaeuu we'la maninaio, and the tyatsu Chirida and Gentoni handpicked to come with us take a while to figure out. Then, we do it again, this time factoring in potential loss if the storm cracks a barrel of water, potential delays if the storm blows the ship off course, and all other potential disasters that *might* befall us. I never realized before how much can go wrong if the person in command messes up a simple calculation.

But I don't think about failures now. With resupply plans in place and provision needs set, we're soon as prepared as we can be. I think about where the trip will end instead. Finally, I'm on the edge of having everything I need to finish this.

I shift my gaze toward Sanii, biting the inside of my cheek when ey winces minutely and closes eir eyes. It's too easy to imagine my brother suffering the same pain.

Please, I beg the Kaisubeh, *don't let me be too late.*

Once we're underway, Shytari keeps the ship miles away from Ryogan shores, even in the channel of water separating Ryogo from its neighbor to the west. She keeps the small islands breaking up the waterway between us and them. I almost ask her to sail closer so we can see what's happening, but if we can see land, those on land can see us. The risk isn't worth it.

The farther south we sail, the worse the storm gets, descending on us until it feels like we're sailing into a wall made of lightning. Clouds, rain, and the constant flashes reduce everything to shifting shadows. Checking the ward every few minutes becomes habit quickly, especially after I notice how many other ships we pass.

"What if a ship tries to take ours?" I ask Shytari. What if Varan is chasing us already?

"Even without you, we're not defenseless," Shytari says with a smirk.

And then she shows me the cannons. Cannons are *fascinating*.

I spend several days on the lower deck with Shytari's weapons master and Chirida so they can teach me everything they know about these massive weapons. Tessen, Rai, Etaro, Sanii, and some of the others come, too, listening and asking their own questions. There's nothing close to them on Shiara. Like the black powder, cannons have potential. Cannons could direct the balls of black powder and stone we used in Atokoredo and take out the remaining bobasu all at once. If we can lure the bobasu to the right spot. And if we can get the cannons in place in time. And if the storms haven't sunk Shiara into the ocean.

Eventually, though my interest hasn't ebbed at all, Chirida smiles ruefully and shakes her head. "There's nothing else I can tell you. I've never seen these beasts being built, so I don't know anything about the process." She braces herself on the wide black tube when the ship lurches. "But I do know these won't be easy to move. They're meant to stay once installed. Talking Shytari into giving some up will be harder."

Which I understand. In her place, I wouldn't want to give up my best protection, either.

Then the woman herself walks in. "We're about to leave Masu'iro Channel, and the Arayokai Sea will toss us like a leaf. All of you get somewhere where fewer heavy things can crush you to death. Except you." Her blue eyes lock on me. "*You* be ready to keep the promise you made. If any of my people die, I'll throw you overboard."

It's a threat she can't realistically follow through on and a promise I can't realistically keep, but I still nod. Shytari raises one thick eyebrow, and then she leaves us.

I look down at Tessen, who's sitting on the floor. "How's your stomach?"

"Immeasurably better than last time. An unexpected bonus of immortality, I guess," he says in Itagamin. I'd been bracing for his seasickness to be worse—like our awareness of the cold is—but the susuji must've healed it instead, leaving Tessen no more unsettled than the rest of us. He grips the chain locking a cannon to the deck and hauls himself to his feet. "I'd still hate being on the water in a storm, and food sounds only slightly more appealing than standing naked in a sandstorm, but I'm okay. What do you need?"

"An early warning." We say goodbye to Chirida and head to the main deck.

On the first day, I placed wardstones around the ship, but only the mildest of shields surrounds the ship. It slows the wind gusting across the ship, stops the waves crashing over the deck, and keeps the rain out of everyone's eyes. It does nothing to hold the ship in one piece.

"You'll hear damage to the ship before I can. If I need to shove more power into the layers of wards, let me know."

"No, I'd much rather keep quiet and drown," Tessen drawls.

I roll my eyes and drag him along to check the wardstones I'd secured, and then I lead him to the smaller, raised deck at the front of the ship where Tessen will have a better view and we'll both be out of the crew's way.

"Are you ready for this?" Tessen asks.

I nod, because no other answer is acceptable.

To the east is the gentle slope of Ryogo's southern shore, and it's the last land we'll see until Shiara. Ready for it or not, we're heading home.

The ship tilts as the wave rises, and I tighten my grip on the rope lashed to the mast. My feet slide on the angled deck. Kaisubeh save us; I really do think we're going to tip over this time.

I pour power into the ship's ward, holding my breath because I can't close my eyes. I need to see what it's going to throw at us next or this ship won't make it to Shiara.

Heart pounding, I exhale in a gust as the ship rights itself and immediately begins to slant another direction, tilting me back as it climbs another wave. I desperately miss stone beneath my feet. Even Ryogo's muddy landscape would be welcome, but I long for stone. I wish I could promise myself I'll never step foot on another ship once we reach Shiara. If the past year has proven anything, however, it's that I can't predict what life will demand of me.

But I can't help praying for solidity. *Stone, rock, land. Get me home.*

Memories of Itagami rise in my mind like the waves surrounding us. Sneaking away with Yorri to explore the undercity when we were children. Sinking into the warm waters of the bathing pool after a long day training in the brutal sun. Running through the streets dodging citizens and ore carts. Laughing and drinking too much ahuri wine as I watched my friends challenge each other with ridiculous feats. Even in the open air, on Shiara, I was always surrounded by stone. Solidity. *Safety.*

"Khya!" The panic in Tessen's voice snaps my attention toward him, and wordless shouts rise all around us. Because the ship is inside a bubble of deeply red sandstone.

I gasp, my mind going blank. The stone ripples. Dims. Dissolves. Within seconds, it's gone.

Neeva, is my first thought. Tessen's blood-mother is a rusosa. She created the illusions we faced during the herynshi and— No. That doesn't make sense. She's powerful, but her power worked inside the mind, and never on more than a handful of people at a time. There're more than a dozen people on the deck. All of them are staring up. Besides that, she'd have to be close, and there's nothing but water surrounding us. And of all the illusions she could use against us, why would she bother to pick a bubble of stone?

"What was that, Khya? How did you do that?" He has to scream to be heard.

All I can do is gape at him and stammer. "I—I have no idea."

"Again," he shouts. There's more, but the rest gets eaten by the storm.

Again. But how? I wasn't doing anything except dumping desosa into ward. And thinking about home. About...stone.

Oh! It's just like when we were descending into Kaisuama Valley. Tessen had stopped because it'd looked for a second like the path dead-ended at a wall. I'd brushed it off and forgotten about it, but now...

I grab the loose end of a rope and tie myself to the ship so that a moment of surprise won't get me swept off the ship and tumbled by wave after relentless wave. As soon as I'm secured, I try it again. *Stone*, I think. In my mind, I'm walking through the undercity and remembering the solidity and smoothness of rock under my palms. *Stone and home and stone.*

For an hour or more, it doesn't work. My ward is stronger because of all the power pouring into it, but nothing appears in the sky, not even a flicker and not even for a second.

You failed when you first tried to block the stone arrows, too, I remind myself. *Try. Keep trying. You did it once, so figure out how to do it again.*

This time, I focus on what it felt like when it worked. There was something familiar about it, almost like... *Oh.* Though I hadn't created it the same way, holding the illusion felt like creating invisibility. Because it's all about light.

Understanding rushes through me with a sharp tingle of excitement. My wards are essentially bending energy. What Soanashalo'a taught me, I finally realize, is how to bend light and selectively send things into shadow. If I'm right, creating an illusion will be the opposite, twisting the energy of my wards until it *becomes* light. Neeva's illusions trick minds, and she can only focus on a few at a time. I'm tricking eyes and letting minds come to their own conclusions.

Determined, I take several long breaths and try again.

Color flickers above us. I grin and focus on one, beautiful image. The colors coalesce into a large, bright sun hanging directly over the ship. It's clearly not real—the deck of the ship is no brighter or warmer—but the sun exactly as I remember it at midday in the middle of summer is suddenly and inexplicably *there*. For a minute, maybe longer, it shines like a beacon above us.

And then the ship dips abruptly. The illusion vanishes. I stumble and slide until Tessen's grip steadies me.

"Okhaio, I have never been more in love with you or more afraid of you than I am right now." His words send a delicious shiver down my spine. Then he kisses the corner of my jaw, right under my ear, nipping my skin with the barest edge of teeth, and my body sings. "If Varan doesn't already regret betraying you, he will soon."

No, I silently disagree as I lean back against his chest to brace against the next tilt of the ship. *Varan won't live long enough to regret anything.*

EIGHTEEN

Imaku rises out of the water like a solid shadow, a hidden trap waiting to smash the ship into kindling. Only what Tessen sees during the frequent flashes of lightning keep us from sailing straight into the island that was once Yorri's prison and is now our best source of weapons and the fastest way back into Itagami.

On a clear day I'd be worried the ship might be spotted from the north wall of Itagami, but the storm's chaos is a shield as good as my wards. The waves are taller than the ship. The rain is so thick it seems solid. I can't see Shiara from here. No one on Shiara can see us.

Sanii, though, is leaning over the railing and staring toward Shiara like Yorri might appear out of the darkness. Ey still breathes too carefully and winces with pain ey can't quite hide, but there's ardent hope on eir face for the first time in moons.

"Is it getting any better now that we're close?" I pray for the answer to be yes, for eir sake as much as my brother's. But eir answer is immediate.

"No." Sanii doesn't look away from Shiara. "It's been too long. At this point, I don't think it'll get any better until I can actually reach out and…" Eir lips roll between eir teeth, as though even saying the word "touch" is too painful for em to bear.

"Soon." It's a promise this time. We're almost there.

Shytari guides the ship as close as she can without risking it against the rocks pervading these waters. From here, rowed boats or magic are the only ways we're getting to Imaku.

"I've said this already, but seriously, Khya. It seems like a really bad idea for us to step foot on that island." Worry lines spread out from around Etaro's narrow eyes. "We can't save anyone if we're unconscious."

"That's why I need you and Vysian to make sure we *don't* step foot on that island." I point to a stack of the wood kept onboard for emergency repairs. "We'll use those."

Eir eyes gleam when ey sees where I'm going. "Like Tsua's bridge across the ravine?"

"Exactly." It was the memory of Tsua holding a row of flat stones in midair, creating a bridge between one mountain and the next, that sparked this idea. "Can you do it?"

Ey looks at Vysian, and they consider the problem for a moment before Etaro nods. "If one of us is at the front of the line and one at the end, it shouldn't be a problem."

"Honestly, I'm more worried about how we're going to secure the boats to Imaku without them smashing against the rocks." Sanii peers out at the angry, roiling ocean.

Miari looks toward Imaku, frowning. And she begins to smile. Soon, we have a plan.

Soanashalo'a and several Ryogans offer to come, but I refuse. No one who isn't Itagamin will visit Shiara until I know what's waiting there. It's too dangerous. We know the landscape and will be able to spot trouble well before they could, but there's another reason, too—nothing on this island can kill most of my squad. We're safer there than on the ship with the trunk of desosa-enhanced stones. Only three fist-sized stones are coming with us in case Varan left a bobasu in control of Itagami. They're tucked away in Rai's pack because she's the only one they can't hurt, and everyone knows to keep their distance.

An hour later, my squad is packed into the four boats that sway and nearly topple us as we head toward Imaku. It feels like sailing over mountains. Waves crash into my wards and over them, engulfing us over and over, but our rikinhisus pull us toward Imaku faster than we could ever row. Ten feet from the island, Etaro and Vysian lift the boats into the air.

We jerk when the rikinhisus move us forward. My balance falters. I nearly fall, but Tessen grabs my cloak and holds me up. Up and up we climb, and still the ocean slams into us until Etaro and Vysian drop us onto Imaku. We land on a wide ledge with a shuddering jolt that rattles my bones. The boats immediately begin to slip back toward the water. Miari nearly dives over the edge, hands outstretched. Her palms stop an inch away from the black stone.

Seconds pass. We slip farther. And then I feel it—we're sinking. She's softening the stone just enough to trap the boats and keep the waves from knocking them back into the ocean. Hopefully it'll be enough; we need the boats to help carry everyone and everything I plan on taking back to the ship with me.

Etaro and Vysian focus on the wood next, lifting the stacks out of the boats and shifting them until they're laid end to end. My gaze follows the pale line—the color stark against the black rocks—and stare when I see where it leads.

Blood and rot, we're really here, aren't we? I made it.

Elation bubbles in my chest, but it's tempered by the guilt being here drops on me. This is the ledge we leapt from on our first, ill-fated rescue attempt, and it's the last place I ever saw Yorri. He's not on Imaku anymore. Here, though, I'm closer to him than I've been since that day.

Yorri, I'm coming, and I won't fail you this time.

Walking along the narrow boards of wood is frustratingly slow. We have to wait for Etaro and Vysian to place and secure the boards, and they struggle to keep the slats steady under our shifting weight. I wish we'd left our boots on the boat—I might be able to get a better grip with my toes—but wearing them has become habit and immortality healed the protective calluses on our feet. I can't risk losing focus because I stepped on a sharp rock at exactly the wrong time. And I definitely need my focus.

My wards may protect us from the battering wind, but they can't seem to lessen the waves of hostile desosa emanating from Imaku. It's not the same active rage as the weaponized black rock. The longer I'm surrounded by this energy, though, the tighter the knots in my neck get. My hands begin to shake. My thoughts fixate on the hundred ways today could end in disaster.

Falling off won't kill us, I remind myself. The last time I was on this barren island, I was mortal, and the rock wasn't any kind of threat to me. To most, the black stone of Imaku is just rock that's black. Any immortal who touches Imaku even for a second is forced into unconsciousness. Yorri once compared a single touch to descriptions of Kujuko's eternal nothingness—the place of punishment Varan claimed was waiting for the unworthy and disloyal after death. That power is why Ryogo exiled the bobasu here, and it's why Varan has used Imaku as a prison since then.

No matter how badly I want to rush onward, I take measured breaths and keep to the steady pace Etaro sets, giving em time to settle each new piece of the walkway in front of us and allowing Tessen time to check for traps waiting ahead. It's unlikely Varan would've bothered with a trap or a guard here, but the lack of either as we cross the empty central chamber of the island is a relief.

Then Zonna cocks his head and stops walking. "Khya, will you drop the ward?"

"What? No." The panicked negative is instinctive. It takes me a second to ask, "Why?"

"Because something is different, and—" He shakes his head. "I want to try something I can't do with the wards up."

With a quiet curse, I reluctantly give in. Until he begins to tilt dangerously close to the chamber's wall. I suck in a sharp breath and pour power into my wards, but I'm a second too late. Zonna's hand is already touching the wall.

Nothing happens. He frowns and places both hands on the rough stone. Still nothing.

Tessen makes a strangled noise. "What? That doesn't make sense. The power I feel off this place is even worse than it was the first time and— No! Don't—"

It's too late. No one is fast enough to stop Etaro from touching the stone. And no one is quick enough to catch em when ey crumples to the artificially smooth floor. Our walkway drops several inches. Vysian shouts and tries to regain control. The rest of us drop into crouches and grip the narrow boards, trying not to join Etaro. Rai, though, leaps off our path. Zonna is only a heartbeat behind her.

My heart lurches, but she's not immortal. I choke on a laugh and rub my face against my knee. I never thought I would find a reason to be grateful for that, but here it is. The susuji didn't work on her, so neither does this stone. And, apparently, the same is true for our hishingu.

She carefully picks Etaro up and lays em out on the boards. Vysian's hold on the path is a little shaky. Rai keeps her hands on Etaro to steady em until ey finally begins to stir. It happens slowly, like ey's coming back from a deep sleep, but it *is* happening.

I look to Zonna and try to make sense of everything that's happened in the last… Bellows. It can't have been more than a minute or two. "I don't understand. The bobasu wouldn't come near this island. Even Tsua and Chio talked about Imaku like it was Kujuko itself, Zonna, but you—"

"Used to react to it the same way they did," he interrupts, looking down at the black stone. After a long breath, kneeling to run his hands along the smooth floor. "Varan brought me here after they realized I was immortal. I was maybe twenty-three. He told me to walk onto the stone without warning me what would happen."

"And Tsua *let him*?" I ask.

"She wasn't there. She didn't find out until later. My parents were exactly as mad as you'd think." His smile carries a hundred lifetimes of sadness. Then he frowns at the stone like he thinks it might be tricking him somehow. "This is bizarre. I don't understand."

Neither do I, and I hate having one more puzzle we don't know how to solve.

"We should keep moving." Sanii is near the front of the line, and although ey's crouched low for balance, eir small body is practically vibrating with the need to *go*.

Since Etaro is on eir feet again, looking chastened as Rai yells at em in harsh whispers but otherwise fine, I give the order for em and Tessen to lead us on.

Slowly, we approach the entrance to the tunnel connecting Imaku to Itagami. Tessen stops there and breathes deep. His eyes close, and his head tilts, and his attention focuses on what's ahead of us. My attention, though, strays.

Shards of crystal are scattered across the floor. Holes have been blown out of the wall. Small streaks of gray ash mar the rock, and where once there were shelves is now empty space above piles of pebbles and dust. There are also cuts, the sharp, too-straight lines marking the stone where a tudo or a zeeka sword sliced into the wall.

Those marks are signs of the fight we barely escaped alive the second time I tried to rescue Yorri. Those marks are the only proof I was ever here.

Tessen makes a noise, and my focus snaps to him. Tension radiates from him. Something is wrong up ahead. It's not danger or he'd be warning us to run. Something else is waiting for us.

He looks at me with an apology in his eyes. "Khya, I—"

"No! Etaro, get us down there." My orders lash out.

Ey jumps and rushes to comply, laying the boards out as fast as ey can. As soon as we turn the corner, rage rushes through my body like the heat of a fever. We're staring at a wall of crumbled rock and dirt and an ankle-high pool of water. I want to slam my clenched fists against the stone until it disappears and lets us through.

"Clear it!" I roar at Miari.

Miari jumps and presses her hands to the stone. Too soon, she shakes her head. "Varan did this, Nyshin-ma. If I don't shift it in exactly the right way, the tunnel will collapse. And you know what's above us."

The ocean. Its weight would crush us, and even if most of us didn't die, Rai would. I force myself to relax, but it still takes several slow breaths before the order to push through eases back from the tip of my tongue.

"Sanii, do you remember how to find the entrance to the tunnel Tyrroh showed you?" It was how he got in and out of Itagami to pass information to Tsua and Chio in secret. It was also how he was able to steal food for the voyage to Ryogo. Today, we headed for Imaku first because we needed more of the stone and because that tunnel leads straight into the heart of Itagami. Now, I pray Varan missed the other tunnel.

"We might have to sail down the eastern coast to find a cove Shytari can anchor in, but then…" Ey huffs and runs eir hand over eir short hair. "I've only used the tunnel once, I didn't get there from the east before."

"Tessen will help." It's not that simple, though, not when unheard-of amounts of rain have fallen and washed away any old trails. Hopefully my squad's knowledge of Shiara's landmarks and Sanii's familiarity with Itagami's undercity will be enough. At least, even if we can't get to Shiara from here, we won't be leaving Imaku with nothing.

Miari listens warily as I tell her to break off sections of stone. Etaro trembles when I ask em to help move those chunks into the boats, but despite the fear in eir eyes, ey nods.

I tamp down my frustration and try to reassure them. "We already know it can't hurt us through our magic. Miari wouldn't have been able to anchor the boats if it could, right?"

The reminder soothes their nerves and speeds up their work. Soon, one boat is being loaded with every slab of black stone Miari frees. Rai and Zonna climb into that craft when it's full, and the rest of us haul ourselves into the others.

When we reach the ship, Shytari's crew helps load the stone, and the captain herself is waiting with arms crossed and eyebrows raised. "If you're back already, I can't imagine it went well. Are we running away now?"

"Leaving, yes. Not running." But I automatically look back at Imaku and shudder. A part of me hopes I can run from that island now and never have to set foot on it again.

NINETEEN

Tessen stays by Shytari's side to guide us around the rocks scattered miles out from Shiara's shore. The tide is high, and the waves are rough, so most of the masses are hidden by the dark, white-capped waves. Tessen's the only one who can detect them. He steers us safely around the northeastern tip of Shiara and down the coast until we're sheltered in a harbor.

When I really look at the landscape for the first time, my breath catches. I know where we are. If we walk four miles southwest, we'll be in Suesutu Pass, where I met Tsua for the first time. Three miles straight west will bring us to the plain where Yorri finally manifested as a kynacho and saved my life. Five miles west-northwest is the city I once hoped to help lead.

I *know* where we are. It's dizzying, and I don't know why. Have I gotten so used to being lost I don't know how to handle certainty anymore? Maybe. The longer I stare at the coastline, the red sandstone made dark by rain and storm clouds yet still achingly familiar, the more my eyes burn. The more my chest aches. The more my hands close around the ship's rail, tighter and tighter until my knuckles crack.

Home. I'm almost *home*. My feet will be on Shiaran soil again, and I'll walk through the streets of Sagen sy Itagami one more time. Maybe for the last time if my plans fail. At least I'll die on familiar ground.

Someone joins me at the rail. I don't look until they start to speak. "There's nothing higher than the honor of Itagami, nothing greater than serving the needs of the clan, and nothing more beautiful than the deserts of Shiara."

"Well…" I breathe deep, glancing at Rai before I exhale and turn back to the island. "At least one of those three is still true. It's still beautiful."

"It is, but I miss the sunlight," she admits. "When I picture the Kyiwa Mountains, it's always at dawn with the sun turning them fire red. The lightning doesn't paint it the same way. It makes me wonder…"

"What else the lightning changed?" I finish when she doesn't. "We'll see, I suppose."

"Will you?" Shytari stops next to us, Tessen right behind her. "Who says this route will be better than the last?"

"Fewer people knew about it," I say. "It isn't a guarantee, but the chances are better."

"Hope you're right, 'cause I can't wait forever."

Tessen makes a noise I know is a repressed laugh, but I don't know why. I don't blame her for putting her crew and their ship first.

"How long can you give us?" I ask.

"Hard to say without seeing the sun or the stars to tell the difference between night and day," she admits. "After two weeks, though, I'll be on the verge of running out of food for the return trip. If you're not here before that, I'm leaving you behind."

I nod. "You have the garakyu I enhanced. We'll give you updates when we have them, and if anything changes here, let me know as soon as possible."

"Fair." She pats the belt pouch with the glass globe in it. "Now, get going. You're wasting time talking to me."

Shytari returns to her crew, and Rai moves away to help launch the boats. As soon as they're gone, I look at Tessen. "What was so funny?"

For a heartbeat, it seems like he won't answer. Then he sighs and rubs the back of his neck as though he's embarrassed. "Nothing was funny, exactly. It's just obvious she doesn't know you at all."

I raise my eyebrows. "How is that obvious?"

"You're always worth waiting for." He says it without humor. He says it as though he's positive this belief is a truth everyone should be aware of.

Maybe that's why it hits me so hard, why his words feel like I'm watching the sunrise for the first time in moons.

Bellows. He really does love me. That fact makes me extraordinarily lucky in ways I'm barely beginning to understand. Maybe we'll have time when our mission is finished for me to learn what it means when Tessen adores someone. And maybe I'll have the time to learn how to love him back in a way he deserves.

Some of what I'm feeling must ripple outward, because Tessen blinks, pleased surprise widening his eyes and curving his lips.

"Always the worst timing, Tessen. The *worst*." I lean in to rest my forehead against his temple. He truly is awful about this. Why does he always have to say something that makes me want to devour him when we're surrounded by people and desperately pressed for time?

His hand comes to rest on the small of my back as he laughs softly. "Trust me, I know."

"Maybe one day, timing won't matter so much."

"I hope so." He brushes a soft kiss against my cheek. "You still have a promise to keep."

There are a lot of promises left to keep, so it takes a moment to figure out what he's talking about. I smile.

The tokiansu—the warrior's dance—used to feel like a test or a challenge to me. Watching it was glorious, but I'd only perform it with people who I felt were, on some level, worthy opponents. Tessen asked several times. I never said yes. In Ryogo, when we both needed something to look forward to, I promised I'd dance with him as soon as we had the chance.

My smile falls when I think about what the next few days and weeks might bring. "Do you think we'll ever have another celebration?"

Tessen's gaze shifts to the rocky, water-drenched landscape ahead of us, the storm around us, and the churning ocean behind us. Sighing, he shrugs. "Maybe not a celebration in the way any of us remember, but we will have something worth celebrating eventually. Despite Varan, there's no reason to throw away everything we are. Especially not the pieces we like."

My lips quirk. "Like the tokiansu?"

"Exactly." His eyes gleam. "There's no way I'll let that tradition disappear before I get to see exactly how good you are with a suraki."

I give in and smile. "You might regret that choice when I'm done with you."

It might never happen. Tessen still grins. "C'mon then, oh deadly one. Let's head home and see if the Kaisubeh still like us."

My laughter bursts out so fast I snort. His smile gets wider as we walk toward the others. It's amazing that, despite everything we're facing, Tessen can still make me laugh.

Within ten minutes, we're in the boats and racing toward Shiara once more while Ahta and Soanashalo'a watch from the deck of the ship. This time, at least, none of us have to fear the ground. I leave my boots on the ship and hope to feel solid stone under my bare feet soon.

After Etaro and Vysian lift the boats past the high-tide line, I leap over the side. My bare feet immediately sink into the sand, and I close my eyes. Somehow, even though the sun hasn't hit these shores in moons, it's still warm here. Even the sand was cold in Ryogo. It was softer and finer there, too. Almost insubstantial. I wiggle my toes, spreading them wide and relishing the scratch of the rough grains. The storms have changed the scent of the island, and the landscape seems strange lit by lightning, but the beach beneath my feet is heartbreakingly familiar.

Something inside me settles. I often doubted I'd make it back here—there was too much between me and these shores—but I'm here. I'm home.

I shift my damp cloak aside and press my hand to my boruikku on my chest. Until now, I've used the spell Soanashalo'a inked into my skin to find katsujos. Today, I focus on Yorri.

"He's close." Sanii's whisper catches my attention. I glance down at em. Eir hand is pressed over eir heart, and eir gaze is pointed south. There's no boruikku under eir palm, but maybe ey doesn't need one. Ey's standing on the same land as eir sukhai for the first time in moons. It might be enough for em to know how close ey is to eir partner.

Because ey's right. Yorri can't be more than twenty miles away.

There's one good thing about the Imaku tunnel's collapse—I already have the stone I need, so there's little reason to risk sneaking into Itagami now. All I have to do is turn south and run. Sanii and Tessen are perfectly in step with me, and if the others aren't already right behind me, they will be soon.

The plains surrounding Itagami should've made it easy to move fast, but that was when Shiara was barren and dry. There are deep, swift rivers now that Etaro and Vysian must launch us over. Miari has to harden sinkhole-riddled ground. My ward takes a beating from wind, lightning, and once, the ear-splitting roar of a tornado in the distance. Even Tessen has a hard time avoiding the worst pitfalls. And all of us jolt with the unexpectedly sharp pain of our uncalloused bare feet landing on the rocks in the landscape.

I'm more grateful than ever to Soanashalo'a for the boruikku—if I didn't have a thread of power guiding me to Yorri, we'd never find the way. Desosa pulses along the line between us, thudding in time with my heart. Each time, it seems to ring with Yorri's name.

A mile. Two. Three. There's an off-tone buzz in the air that gets stronger the farther south we travel. It's familiar, and it definitely isn't coming from the storm. We're approaching what's left of the border ward.

Varan's great wall is in pieces.

I shiver and quickly repress the ingrained urge to fix whatever broke here. I was in training for that job once, and I know what a broken wardstone feels like. Three of the eight closest to us have shattered. They were probably overloaded by lightning strikes or cracked by impacts with debris.

Varan used this wall to keep us in as much as he used it to keep his enemies out. A vindictive part of my soul pleased to see it fall.

I keep moving, pushing my friends harder than Tyrroh or our training masters ever did. We leave the plain, and the ground slopes more steeply as we reach the foothills of the Kyiwa Mountains. Up and up we climb, Shiara's familiar red sandstone passing quickly under us.

The higher we get, though, the worse the storm becomes. The gusts are strong enough to pound my wards like a battering ram against a city gate, and I have to anchor my magic into the mountain itself to keep us from flying. Lightning strikes the rocks constantly, breaking off chunks of stone larger than a person and sending the charred boulders into the air. Ryogo's trees protected us from the winds just as much as my wards did, something I realize only now that I'm missing them. Without the trees, I feel exposed.

The journey is a struggle, especially for Rai. She doesn't feel the desosa pulsing under her skin like I do, and it's not rebuilding and repairing what effort and strain bruises or breaks. Etaro and Zonna stay by her side the whole time—ey to help haul her up the mountain when the effort gets to be too much and he to heal what her own body can't. It lets us move without stopping for far longer than I thought we'd be able to.

I pay less and less attention to the landscape as we get closer to the end of the path, watching only for obstructions and danger. Nothing matters except getting to Yorri. I keep a solid grip on my sense of my brother, hating every moment that doesn't take us in the straightest, most direct path to wherever the bobasu left him.

Sanii's breathing is still strained, but eir grin is glowingly happy when I catch eir eye. "We're getting close. Khya, he's *so close* now."

Then Tessen puts his hand out to call a halt. I immediately look up to scan for danger. We're in a narrow pass with high walls to either side of us, and if I were protecting a location nearby, this would be the perfect place for an ambush. But Tessen isn't looking up when he asks, "Khya, do you feel that?"

"No." I reach for the desosa, testing it and the boruikku. Nothing seems to have changed in either. "What is it?"

"It's like…" His eyes are getting wider. "It feels like panic. Pain. A lot of it."

Sanii makes a sound like ey's been stabbed. I swallow every curse and scream that fights to free itself from my lips. That won't help Yorri, and helping Yorri is all that matters. My brother is in pain. For the first time in far too long, I'm close enough to do something about it. I'd fight the Kaisubeh themselves to get to Yorri.

"Where are we?" I ask the group, but I look at Zonna. "What's ahead?"

Zonna looks confused. "There's nothing out here. Never has been."

"Which is probably why he picked this place," Donya says. "No one comes here."

"Why doesn't matter." I look to Tessen. "What can you sense?"

"From here? In this?" He looks around, frowning. "I think there might be a valley there, but there's something else. It almost feels like there's a ward up."

It's hard to pick out of the chaotic desosa and the electricity of the storm, but eventually I feel it, too—the buzz of wards that aren't mine. Varan must have left something behind to keep anyone from discovering this secret. Knowing him, if there's one level of protection, there's probably also something far more dangerous than a ward to get through, too.

Despite how badly my body is vibrating with the need to move—Yorri is so close now, so close, so close—I shut my eyes and think. The ward isn't a problem. I figured out how to pass through Suzu's strongest protections before we even left Shiara. But Varan knows that. I proved to him wards aren't enough protection, and I doubt he's forgotten the lesson.

"Tessen, Wehli? Scout ahead as best you can, but don't touch the ward."

Nodding, they move off, Wehli in a blur of speed and Tessen at a much easier-to-follow pace. Tessen returns first, and the frustration on his face hints that I won't like what he's going to say. "I know there are people nearby, but I can't tell who or how many."

"Are there traps?"

"Definitely. Layered like tripwires, but—" He flinches when a crack of lightning strikes the next peak and then gestures widely to the storm. "Trying to feel something that subtle under all this is as hard as doing it in Kaisuama. And at least that power is stable."

Wehli skids to a stop nearby, and I bite back my response. He's breathing hard as he says, "There's a rise that might be outside the ward. It should give us a better view."

"Show us," I order.

Wehli leads the way, moving so fast I struggle to keep up. Finally, when it seems like we've got to be at least halfway around the valley, he stops and points. Wehli was right—this overlook is outside the ward. I leap for the first handhold I spot and haul myself up the nearly vertical face. Sanii is beside me the whole way, pure resolution sharpening eir long face.

I jam my hand into a crack in the stone so hard it rips my fingernail in half. The shock of pain sparks through my fingers and up my arm. My hand spasms. My grip loosens. I barely swallow my scream, scrambling to grab at the rock and slamming my feet into the stone. *Wards*, I realize. I extend my shield, jamming it into the stone and stopping my fall. Gritting my teeth, I yank my broken nail from its bed, cringing at the fresh wave of pain, and keep climbing.

Zonna had insisted weeks ago that even though most people learn to push their hurts aside, immortals can't, but I don't think that's right. I'm doing it now, ignoring the lingering pain and the aggravating feeling of the nail re-growing as I push myself forward. There were moments before I had a cloak spelled for warmth when I all but forgot how Ryogo's cold bit at my bones. It's a matter of priorities. What does pain matter when I'm so close to seeing my brother again?

Nothing is going to stop me now, not Varan, not danger, and not even my own body. But I must balance speed with caution. I extend my ward farther ahead of us, feeling the buzz of Suzu's barrier ahead. It's meant to keep everyone but the bobasu out. The ward's energy is like dull needles against my skin when my own power touches it. Moons ago, passing through Suzu's ward drained me to the point of exhaustion in seconds. Now, when I guide my whole squad through, it won't take much more effort than holding open a curtain.

Careful to stay outside Suzu's barrier, I lean in to see what's below us. My chest clenches. My hands shake. My throat closes around a sob.

Yorri. He's trapped on a slab of black stone that's sitting at an angle, and he's thrashing against the red cords binding him, his head tipped back in a futile attempt to keep his nose above the water. Rain has filled the valley, and every gust of wind pushes another wave over his face. He sputters and chokes, his body straining for air so hard the muscles in his neck bulge.

My brother is about to drown.

Chest tight and hands shaking, I shove my power forward like a boulder, shattering Suzu's shield seconds before I leap over the ridge. The other side is steep. I practically fall down the slope. Grabbing the rocks would only break my fingers, so I dig my wards into the mountain.

I don't see the traps, but I feel each one as I set it off. They reverberate through the air like the thud of a drum well before I see anything. I throw my shield forward, encasing every person in the valley a heartbeat before smoke pours from three points in the mountains and an arc of lightning shifts, jerking toward the valley like it was yanked from the sky.

Rage and fear boost my power nearly as much as the storm-charged desosa I draw on. The lightning strikes skitter off my ward. The smoke rolls along my invisible barrier and pools where magic meets mountain. I refuse to let anything else harm my brother. None of the dangers will touch any of us.

I push my ward higher and drop the one that had been encircling my squad—everything we need protection from is above us now. Dropping into the flooded valley sends a wave outward. More water crests across the surface as the others splash down behind me. The wave their landing creates washes right over my brother's face.

Panic tightens my chest. I pull power in and reach for him, creating a bubble of breathable air around his head, expanding it to keep the water away.

"Your brother isn't the only one here, Khya!" Rai shouts. "Do something for the others!"

I stumble to a stop and look down. Someone stares back at me from beneath the water.

My stomach drops. Even as I begin to make new plans in the back of my mind and gather energy to create new wards, my eyes find Yorri. I should've known it would have to be this way.

"Sanii, go to Yorri! Miari, drain this!" I bellow, hoping I keep what I'm thinking off my face as I create a ward around the poor soul drowning at my knees. "Break the mountain if you have to, just get rid of this Kujuko-cursed water!"

Sanii sloshes through the water as fast as ey can move. Miari is gone in a flash, disappearing under the water as I create more wards, one around every person I find. Then, the valley trembles. Strong currents form in the water, nearly ripping my feet out from under me. I see Sanii stumble a few feet away. Tessen catches me, and we brace each other in the water rushing to escape through the holes Miari is making. Sanii struggles against the flood, each step taking em one foot closer to Yorri.

While I stay behind, watching, planning, and trying not to feel like I've lost something.

Miari's work already seems to have dropped the water level several inches, so I focus on warding those still trapped. Even some who are under more than a foot of water are fighting, thrashing and trying to escape the stone that's kept them unconscious for…

Wait. What?

I blink, but nothing changes. Although not everyone is fighting, most are, despite being bound to slabs of Imaku stone. How are they awake? The stone worked on them before—I saw proof of that myself—so something has changed, and whatever it is doesn't solely affect Zonna like we thought it did. I raise my hand, reaching toward the closest chunk of black rock.

No. I pull my hand back even before Tessen says my name in a warning tone. There's no doubt this is the same stone, and there's no doubt it'll work against me—this valley is so full of it I can feel its subtly uncomfortable buzz even through the storm's electricity.

I don't know how, but the Kaisubeh have done something to the stone, even though they had to reach across an ocean to do it. I thought I had a sense of the Kaisubeh's capabilities. This, though, is astounding. Is it possible to be in awe of something you're also afraid of? Even at his strongest, Varan never came close to the power of the true gods.

Across the small valley, Sanii reaches my brother and places a hand on his ankle. Yorri goes still the second eir fingers touch his skin. Two heartbeats later, ey's ripping the first niadagu cord off Yorri before ey moves to his other foot.

Tears gather in my eyes. My stomach feels like it's full of rocks. I imagined this moment so many times. Not once did I picture myself passively watching as someone else unbound Yorri. I spent moons mastering the niadagu spell, sometimes ignoring everything else so I could reread the book Osshi found for me about binding, and yet Sanii is the one ripping the second cord off him and letting the torn red fiber drop to the slowly falling water.

Above, the smoke of Varan's trap has grown so thick over the dome of my ward not even the flashes from the lightning break through. The impacts of those strikes reverberate across my ward and straight into my bones, but the hits barely register anymore.

The last of Yorri's bonds is gone. My somewhat selfish disappointment aside, satisfaction bursts to life in my chest, as bright and hot as the summer sun. We did it. I might not have been the one to tear the cords off, but I kept my promise and found a way to free him.

Yorri surges off the stone table so fast he seems to vanish and reappear on his feet. The speed of the move sends Sanii stumbling back, and my stomach drops. He looks terrified, even of em. What's happened to him? I can't believe any pain or trauma could be powerful enough to make Yorri or anyone else forget their sukhai. Bile rises in my throat at the thought of the pain being forgotten would bring.

I take a step forward, not sure if I should head for Yorri or Sanii first, but I stop when my brother blinks. His mouth moves. I'm too far away to hear the word, but it looks like Sanii's name. Nodding slowly, Sanii reaches for him with unexpected hesitance. All eir doubt vanishes the instant Yorri's hand closes around eirs. In a blink, Yorri picks Sanii up, and ey wraps eir arms and legs tight around his body.

There is one thing I never let myself wonder because I hate myself for being so scared of it. I should be nothing but happy to see Yorri and Sanii reunited, but a fear lingers at the edges of my thoughts. Sanii freed my brother, pulled him off that platform, and Sanii is the one he's clinging to as though no one else matters.

Now that they have each other, will my brother still need me at all?

TWENTY

I keep working, reinforcing the ward against the acrid black smoke and removing the wards around the prisoners as their heads fully clear the disappearing water. No matter how hard I try to focus on my tasks and give Sanii and Yorri space, I can't keep myself from looking their way every few seconds. I find myself watching them like they're strangers.

Sanii's personality is so big I forget how small ey is. It's obvious now, Sanii looks as small as Ahta in comparison to Yorri. I never realized the disparity; then again, I've never seen them together before now, either. I'd better get used to the sight soon. It'll likely be years or decades before they can bring themselves to spend more than a few minutes apart, and I don't blame them for it at all.

Just before I head for the first prisoner, preparing to unbind them, I glance at Yorri one more time. I freeze. This time, Yorri's watching me, too. There's so much in his expression, but it's the hurt I think I see there that sends me rushing across the valley.

I run through the knee-high water, my throat closing around everything I don't know how to say. By the time I near him, he's extended one arm, and I stop trying to think of words, accepting the silent invitation instead. Sanii is still clinging to him, and ey barely twitches when I crash into them. Eir breathing hitches arrhythmically; I think ey's sobbing, hiding it against my brother's neck. Yorri isn't crying, but he's so tense his muscles feel like bone under my hands. It makes me pull back to look at him. He barely seems to be blinking. His eyes dart from point to point alarmingly fast. One of his hands is on the back of Sanii's head, and the other is pressed to the middle of my back. I'd forgotten exactly how strong my brother is until now; I can lean back enough to see his face, but no farther.

"Yorri?" I put my hand on his shoulder and squeeze.

He blinks, a tremor running through him, and then his eyes lock on mine. I stop breathing. For one heartbeat—two, three—he stares at me as though he has no idea who I am. My breath catches, but I've already seen him do this, and seen the others do this, too. He'll come back, I tell myself. He'll come back from whatever mental hole he fell into. Another blink, and I exhale in shaky relief as focus and recognition come back to his gaze. A breath. "Khya."

I want to ask if he's okay, but how can he be? What I say instead is, "Sorry I'm late."

"You came." Yorri doesn't smile, but the stress around his eyes doesn't seem as deep. "It would've been so easy for you to leave us here, but you didn't."

"What can I do? What do you need?" The questions burn my tongue the same way the tears I'm trying to hold back burn my eyes.

"You're here, and I'm standing. Other than that, I—" Yorri shudders, and his grip on me tightens. From the pained gasp Sanii releases, his hold on em does, too. "I don't know, Khya. I don't know. I just— It's hard to believe you're real. I've had so many dreams that ended."

I expect more—that ended too soon; that ended in pain—but his mouth clamps shut, and I realize there isn't more. The fact of a dream's end is bad enough when either Imaku or this valley is the reality to wake up to.

Someone approaches, their footsteps sloshing through the water. I don't turn until Tessen softly calls my name. Even then, I can't make myself move away from Yorri yet.

"The others need you, Khya." He seems oddly hesitant to speak. What worries me more, though, is the blankness on his face. "Only you and Sanii can undo the niadagu cords."

I glance at Sanii. Eir face is still hidden against the curve of Yorri's neck, and eir body still locked around him. When I shift away, Yorri turns his face toward Sanii, hiding against em as much as ey's hiding against him. Nothing short of a threat will get them to move. I don't want to leave either, but there's so much work left, and I can't bring myself to ask Sanii to do it.

Nodding, I step toward the closest stone platform, careful to avoid the scattered pieces of black stone. I focus on the person trapped there instead of the distance in Tessen's eyes. I'm not ready to face that yet. "It's always been you, Khya," he'd said, "and I'm here whether you want forever or not." Was he remembering those words as he watched Sanii and Yorri's reunion? I think that's the only thing capable of putting such blankness in his eyes now, but I don't want to know if I'm right. Not yet.

Only Zonna and Rai can touch the platforms, but everyone is working to calm the panicked prisoners. I move toward the closest, murmuring calming assurances to settle their wild-eyed alarm. Then, I touch their wrist and whisper, "Ureeku-sy rii'ifu."

I jerk back, but I'm almost too slow to avoid the arm that flies up. They run their hand over their face, saying something too garbled to make sense of. It's all right. The words likely aren't meant for me.

As quickly as I can, I move from one platform to the next, repeating the spell for every cord on every prisoner. There are thirty-eight in addition to Yorri, and I free them all from the spell Varan used to confine them for so long.

"We need to get them to the ship somehow," Tessen says once everyone is free.

"Somehow?" No one is injured, so it's not like we'll have to carry them. But I was so focused on my work I haven't been paying attention to what is happening behind me.

Some of the prisoners are fighting. Others are curled into balls and screaming. The rest are climbing the mountains, throwing themselves against my ward, demanding we let them go. How had I missed the impacts on my ward? They're weak compared to the lightning still crashing down, but I should've felt them. I should've heard the cries for help. I should've noticed that some of those I released never moved from their platforms. They're alive—their chests rise and fall, and their limbs twitch—but despite my friends' pleas, they stayed exactly where I left them. How the bellows are these people going to follow me anywhere when most won't listen and the rest won't move?

Only a few seem somewhat okay. Like Yorri. They seem tense and vaguely detached, but they're standing, they're calm, and they're watching us with wary hopefulness.

I ease closer to my brother, who's still wrapped around Sanii, though now they seem to be talking instead of simply clinging. Despite the itch to touch his shoulder or grab his hand, anything to assure myself he really is here, I hold back. Sanii needs this more. We were born of the same parents, but they chose each other. Choice can forge a much stronger bond than blood.

So I stay back a few steps when I say, "Yorri, I need your help."

He looks at me, but then I don't know what to say next. He's the only one who can help me understand what these people have been through, but *Help me figure out how to force the people you've been trapped with for moons to move* doesn't seem like a good way to phrase the request. Thankfully, he seems to catch on after I glance at the immortals still using their bodies as battering rams against my wards. I wince in sympathetic pain when someone bashes into the ward and slips, tumbling down the sharp, steep slope. "We need to leave, Yorri, and all of you need to come with us."

Taking a deep breath, he turns his attention to Sanii. Cupping the back of eir head, he murmurs something in eir ear. Several long seconds later, ey slowly—and reluctantly—loosens eir hold. Ey doesn't let go completely, though—their hands lock together so tightly their knuckles go pale, as though they expect someone to try to tear them apart again. No one ever will if I can do something to prevent it.

Yorri climbs up to the point where ward meets mountain first, Sanii's hand still clutched in his, and begins calming those trying to flee. While he's working with them, I stop at the side of a platform and gently try to rouse some reaction from the eerily still immortals. I watch my brother out of the corner of my eye. It takes time, but eventually the impacts against my ward stop, and he eases all six of them down to the valley, repeatedly promising to keep the Miriseh away.

The whole time, Sanii is never out of his reach. If Yorri needs both hands, Sanii shifts eir grip to his elbow, his shoulder, or the small of his back. They lose contact once—Sanii's hand slips off his shoulder when he moves too fast—and their reaction is immediate. Sanii flinches like ey's been struck. Yorri spins in seeming panic. The way he sags when he sees em is heartbreaking. It's as if, for a split second, he believed his sukhai's reappearance was a dream.

None of the other Imaku survivors are faring better. I barely get a reaction out of the ones still lying on the slabs of stone. The screamers have quieted, but many are rocking quickly, their arms wrapped around themselves. Even those who, like Yorri, seem fine don't respond right away when we speak to them. Sometimes they go still, staring at nothing. It's as though they keep forgetting their bodies are under their control now. They don't seem to fully believe that, if they speak, someone will be there to listen.

Even if Varan never touched these people—and how could he have when Varan couldn't set foot on Imaku?—he's destroyed them. Even the most alert are wary to the point of paranoia, watching us like they're waiting for an attack. Or waiting to find out this has all been a hallucination and they're still on their black stone beds. Even with his refusal to stop touching Sanii and his constant need for reassurance that I haven't vanished, Yorri is easily the least paranoid and most functional to walk out of the valley. He's the only one who seems to be improving the longer he's out of the niadagu cords. He's also the one who spent the shortest amount of time trapped by the bobasu's magic.

I nearly laugh. I'd been so naive to think we'd have an army of immortals after this rescue, that they'd rise whole, hale, and ready to destroy Varan. Ridiculous. Even when I worried about what Yorri was suffering, I hadn't truly considered the reality or what it would mean for him, for us, or for people who've been suffering for centuries, people who felt *everything* fresh and didn't have anyone to explain why.

"Warn Shytari," I tell Tessen as we walk, trying to imagine her reaction when these jumpy, bedraggled strangers climb onboard. He nods and does as I ask. Some of the distance is gone from his eyes now, but his expression is still guarded. I'm not used to seeing this from Tessen anymore. It makes my chest tighten, especially because I can't do anything about it now. Instead, I say, "Ask her to empty a room if she can. It might be easier for them to be somewhere quiet."

If we can convince them to get on the ship at all. None of them have ever seen such a thing, and most Itagamins avoid the ocean as a matter of course—it's dangerous, and few of us swim well enough to handle its currents. Asking the freed prisoners to trust me and climb into what will look like a strange building floating on the water is asking for more trust than I've had the time to earn. I can only hope Yorri can help convince them to listen again.

My hope dwindles in the hours it takes to reach the cove. Five of the immortals try to escape. One sprints toward a cliff and might've thrown themselves over the edge if Wehli hadn't been fast enough to stop them. By the time we see Shytari's ship ahead, I fear the moment to come. We might have to force the prisoners onto the ship. Shytari might refuse to let them on board if they keep trying to throw themselves into the ocean. Yet, despite my growing concern, it's still a relief to see a group waiting on the narrow beach, their drenched, dark clothes sagging on their frames.

Soanashalo'a and Ahta are easy to pick out. They tear away from the group, running up the beach toward us. I watched Soanashalo'a's frantic approach, and I'm somehow not prepared for her to barrel into me, wrap her arms around me, and squeeze until it's hard to breathe. Only Tessen's hands bracing my shoulders keeps me from falling flat on my back. To my left, Sanii barely manages to catch Ahta when ey leaps into Sanii's arms.

"Sorry, sorry, sorry," Soanashalo'a mumbles against my throat. "I know you like being asked about touch first, but *alua'sa liona'ano shilua'a shomaihopa'a*, Khya! I was worried!"

I sink into her embrace before she's gotten through more than the first litany of sorries. Smiling, I remind her softly, "Not much can hurt me now, Soanashalo'a Shuikanahe'le."

"I kept telling myself that." She pulls back, her round face pinched. "It got harder to believe after the first few hours."

"It's not over yet." I squeeze her arm one more time, and then head for my brother. It'll take more than one trip to load us all, so I'll stay on the beach until everyone else is on board. I'm hoping Yorri and Sanii will go first, though.

Yorri's listening to Ahta, nodding as the young ebet talks, but his gaze keeps straying toward Shytari's ship. As I approach, I hear Sanii and Ahta identifying different pieces and insisting it's capable of carrying us across the ocean. Yorri looks at me with awe in his eyes when I stop next to him, and there's a smile finally beginning to appear on his lips. "See, Khya? I told you there was something beyond Shiara."

"You were right about more than that." There isn't time to go into it all now, though. "I need to stay here, but I want you and Sanii on the first boats out. Ahta, too. You can be there to help the others get settled. I don't want anyone getting hurt because of an instant of panic."

For a long moment, he searches my face, but then he nods. "Don't linger, Khya."

"I'll see you soon, little brother." I smile and squeeze his shoulder, not letting my expression fade until his boat has pushed off the beach. Tessen and Soanashalo'a move to flank me, silent bolsters until the boats—all but empty once again—have turned around to head back.

"It is not what you expected, is it?" Soanashalo'a asks.

"Things rarely are." I try to sound unconcerned, but Soanashalo'a cuts me a knowing glance and Tessen's mask cracks a bit, understanding shining through his expression. Closing my eyes, I let my own posture droop and admit some of the truth. "I never considered those powerful enough to scare Varan would need our protection even after we freed them. I should've. Now I might've just given us one more front we have to fight on."

"They could surprise you," Tessen says. "We have to wait and see."

As though we have the time to wait for anything. I open my eyes and scan the beach. My heart picks up when I don't see Yorri anywhere. My lips part, and I'm about to call his name when I remember. He's ahead, safe on the ship already. Exhaling, I ask Etaro to speed up the progress of the boats if ey can. Yorri's only out of sight, not gone. He's really here, alive and as well as I could've hoped. I succeeded, even if success doesn't feel like I expected.

I'm the last to step back onto the ship, and I find Shytari and Chirida waiting.

"Is this the secret?" Chirida watches the last Imaku prisoner disappear through the door to the lower decks before she turns back to me. "When you told Gentoni you knew Varan's secret, I expected something more than this."

Gritting my teeth against the curses building on my tongue, I urge both women to follow me to the rooms Yorri and the other immortals have been given instead of interrogating me on the deck. One of the knots of tension in my chest loosens when I see Sanii, Ahta, and my brother passing food out. I see the same relief I feel reflected in Yorri's eyes.

"What did you find, Khya?" Chirida watches the newcomers, gaze jumping from the two in the corner with untouched food in their hands to the ones along the far wall watching her with the same suspicion she's showing them.

My explanation is halting, but eventually I find the words to reveal, for the first time, the secret I've kept out of every recitation before now—immortals can be born, and my brother is one of them. Varan's secret to immortality is no longer a secret, and my squad has used it. Chirida's eyes narrow when she hears. Shytari seems dubious until I slice a thin line across my forearm and heal before her eyes.

"You just keep getting more interesting," Shytari says after a full minute of silence.

Chirida's expression still hasn't relaxed. "Should we start calling you bobasu now, too?"

"No." I spit the word, disgusted by the idea.

"My parents called themselves andofume because they wanted to separate themselves from Varan, but changing the word couldn't alter the fact that their lifespan came from the same source as Varan's." Zonna's quiet words land like a stone in water, but they send out stillness instead of ripples. "Their immortality wasn't in their blood the same way it's in mine."

Or like it's in Yorri's. And like it isn't in mine. I lower my eyes, frowning. Chio and Tsua told me to call myself andofume, but it isn't true. There's a distinction between immortals, and I don't fall on the same side of the line as Zonna and my brother.

"Maybe that's what kept you alive." Tessen's words pull me out of my thoughts, but it takes several seconds for the meaning to sink in.

"Kaisubeh bless it." I rub my hand over my mouth. "That makes sense."

"Imaku wasn't a danger to Zonna, but Etaro dropped as soon as ey touched the stone." Sanii looks between Yorri and Zonna. "It'd explain why they were awake in the valley."

But when did that change? Swallowing, I ask Yorri, "Can you guess how long it's been since you woke up?"

"I don't know." Yorri breathes slowly and grips Sanii's hand. "It has to be three moons."

"When we found the southern katsujo," Sanii sighs.

"And made the first batch of stones." It's where I thought I felt the Kaisubeh—or some other presence or being or god—reach out and touch us. "What if the Kaisubeh did more than we realized that day? If the old legends about the creation of Imaku are true, why wouldn't the Kaisubeh be able to change it?"

Shytari and Chirida follow the conversation with their eyes, but neither speaks.

The silence that settles leaves me room to think, and there's plenty to consider. If the Kaisubeh did alter the stone, it impacts *everything*. It means we have andofume on our side who are truly more powerful and invulnerable than Varan. They'll be able to wield stone shards like daggers if they need to. On the other hand, nothing can kill them, so if my plan fails, I'll have led the andofume back into Varan's reach, and he'll make sure they spend the next several hundred years *wishing* they could die.

"We need to warn Ahta," I murmur to myself. Next to me, Tessen nods. "And we need to adjust the plan. There were yonin who helped us before. If we can sneak into Itagami and find them, they might help us again."

"No. Not there. None in Itagami." Heads turn, including mine. One of the andofume sits in the corner, their head resting against the wall. It doesn't seem like they've moved since we entered the room let alone spoken, but no one else could've spoken.

"What's your name?" I ask gently.

"Been there too long lying on the rocks." The bedraggled survivor shudders and turns their face toward the wall. "'Arinri knows too much,' they said. 'She'll tell too much.' They were right. I told. I told and screamed but no one hears no one hears nothing."

Talking to her feels as dangerous as waking someone who's sleepwalking, as though any sudden noises could startle her into hurting herself, but I need more than what she's giving me. "Arinri, you said no one was in Itagami. What did you mean?"

"Yonin. Looking for yonin, but no one there. Flee, fly fled. Denhitra," Arinri mutters to the wall. "Not all. Many. Many in Denhitra. Too many people now. Can't last. But there."

I want to demand an explanation, but I keep my voice soft and gentle as I ask, "How do you know that?"

"See it. Always see answers when people ask questions." Arinri pulls at her long, matted hair and shakes her head. I don't think she's talking *to* me. It's more like she's talking to herself and just happens to be doing it out loud. "Akuringu know. We know. I can't say what I know, just dream answers and keep quiet, but I know. It kept me sane, the seeing. I could see the world even after they took it away."

My heart leaps. Akuringu is a rare mage designation for those who can use the desosa to see dozens of miles away. More, if they're exceptionally powerful. If Arinri can see all the way to Denhitra, then she's *very* exceptional. And this gives us a direction. Denhitra could give me the fighting force I thought I'd find when we rescued Yorri.

"It's been decades since an akuringu of any real power was born in the clan." Etaro looks awed, eir narrow eyes almost round. "How long were you on Imaku?"

"Long. Too long. Nicer there, though. Like it better than the storm place." She shudders.

Looking at Zonna, I ask, "Will the Denhitrans help?"

"To get rid of Varan?" Zonna nods. "Absolutely."

"Good." I nod, trying to think. "If the yonin are there, they can tell us what happened in Itagami after we left, too. And I'm sure they'll help even if the Denhitrans won't."

"Tell me where to go." Shytari stands and looks at Tessen. "I'll need you above. My lookouts can barely see through this blasted rain."

He rises, and many of the others do, too. I catch his hand to hold him back. He tenses, looking at me with surprise. "What's wrong?"

"Nothing, I just…" I squeeze his fingers. "Be careful, Tessen."

The detachment that's been in his eyes most of the day cracks and crumbles away, something painfully like relief replacing it. He brushes my cheek with the back of his fingers, smiling. "I'm not the one known for taking unnecessary risks, oh deadly one. I'll be back. You're not getting rid of me that easily."

I catch his wrist and pull him down, pressing a quick, bruising kiss to his lips before I rest my cheek against his. "I don't want to be rid of you at all, okhaio. Never believe otherwise."

His breath catches. For a moment, he isn't breathing at all. Then he relaxes. He slumps against me, his face tucked against my throat. He brushes a kiss there, so light and quick I barely feel it, and a tremor runs through him. When he straightens, his smile is almost peaceful.

"Keep your wards up," he says, still smiling. "I don't want to learn how to swim today."

"As if I'd let you try," I mutter, nudging him away. He winks and strides away, his certainty suddenly returned. Zonna is the last one out, and he gives me a small, complicated smile as he closes the door.

Yorri huffs something almost like a laugh. "I guess you finally gave in to Tessen, huh? Took you long enough. He's been sighing after you since we were kids."

"Yes, well…" I shrug, trying to ignore the warmth in my cheeks and hoping my embarrassment stays off my face. "It's been a long year."

All my brother's good humor vanishes. "Only a year? It feels…" He closes his eyes, seeming to sink into himself for a moment. "It seemed like longer."

"Are you okay?" It's a ridiculous question.

"As okay as I can be after moons of starvation and dehydration while people either jammed weapons into my chest to—I don't even know why. Make sure I was still alive, maybe." His tone is even. His eyes have gone distant again. My own chest twinges, remembering pain from a wound that didn't even leave a scar behind. I rub at the spot as he continues. "In a way, leaving us to the storm was better. At least I had water. And the lightning rarely hit us."

My wards come up around him before I even realize I've begun. For all the good they'll do. His injuries are well past gone, and even the moment they happened, he wouldn't have needed my protection. But I can't help it. Except for starvation, I know all those pains too well. I clench my fists in my lap and imagine a slow, agonizingly painful death for every person who dared lay a hand on my brother. I will deliver those deaths, but I can't do it now.

"I wish that hadn't happened," I manage to say. "That pain is awful."

His eyebrows rise. "You sound like you know."

My hand rises to my chest before I can stop the motion. "Unfortunately, I do."

"It's why she's immortal," Sanii says, shifting closer. "It was the only way to save her."

"Bellows, Khya." Emotions play across Yorri's face so fast I can't follow them. And then he smiles, reaching out to place his hand over mine. "I can't leave you alone for even a minute before you're getting yourself into trouble, can I?"

"That's absolutely the other way around." I force myself to tease him despite the guilt I haven't entirely let go. "I let you go on *one* mission without me, and look where we are."

His smile stays, but his eyes are conflicted. "It's not like there was anything I could do."

It's not a statement, I realize after a second. He's asking me to honestly answer a question—is this his fault?

"There wasn't anything you could've done. None of us would've been ready for danger to come from the kaigo. That kind of betrayal was unthinkable. And there's so much we haven't told you yet. " I turn my hand under his to grip his fingers. "Varan used the clan as an experiment and as weapons in his war. Without everything that's happened to you, there might not be anyone to stand against him. The end is worth our pain. If we win, Shiara might finally get a chance to grow without Varan's control."

"And if we lose, everything we know and everyone we love will be gone," he murmurs, the worry he's kept hidden until now bleeding into his tone and appearing around his eyes.

"Doing nothing guarantees failure," I remind him. "And the greater the possible gain, the more devastating the potential loss."

Yorri relaxes again. "Since when do you quote our old training masters?"

"It's practically become habit for her." Sanii's smiling when ey says it.

"You hush." I wave em off, but I can't protest something I know is true. "It's not my fault they were right more often than not."

"You've grown up." Yorri grins, truly looking like my brother for the first time since we found the valley, and tears swiftly gather in my eyes at the sight. "I'm sure they've always been right. You never admitted it before, though."

"Probably not." But mistakes weren't something I allowed myself before, and I didn't understand the consequences of failure, either. Now I know both, and worse. But I don't want to think about war or loss or failure or mistakes now. My brother is finally here. I have both a ship and a destination. For this one moment, I want to revel in feeling like I did something right.

"It's so good to see you, Yorri." I swallow, tightening my hold on his hand and trying not to feel relieved when he grips me in return. "I missed you."

"I missed you, too, and it seems like I missed a lot more than that." He squeezes my hand and manages a smile. "Tell me more about these tricks Sanii said you've learned, instead. Something about making people invisible?"

I laugh and spend the next hour doing something I never thought I'd get the chance to do again—showing off to impress my little brother.

TWENTY-ONE

The next morning—or maybe later; it's hard to tell when lightning is the only illumination from the sky—our ship pulls into a harbor Zonna believes is as close to Denhitra as we can get. Soanashalo'a and Ahta want to come with us, but I talk them out of it. The andofume aren't as easy to convince. All of them follow us off the ship.

Once we're on land, Zonna and Tessen take the lead. Zonna knows this region best, and he guides us to a path through the mountains that often doesn't look like a path at all. It's narrow—sometimes narrower than the width of one foot—and it makes travel slow. What surprises me most are the andofume. They don't just keep up; some seem to be getting stronger.

The immortals didn't like the ship. Only a few complained in words, but it was clear in all of them. They hated being trapped in a small room that moved with the waves and was surrounded by water, and I can't blame them—it must've seemed like I took the worst parts of both of their prisons and combined them. Having time to get warm, eat something, and sit in relative quiet, however, does seem to have done wonders. They're so much better on solid ground than they were before. Not once do Wehli or Yorri have to stop them from running away.

"Almost home," Zonna says as we round a corner and finally see a sign of life.

There's a bridge ahead. It's intricately designed, with lengths of chain and rope stretching in multiple directions to anchor it to the mountain, but it's so narrow only one person can pass at a time. Handholds at different heights offer people stability as they walk across the floor of rope, chain, and iron plates. There are gaps because the plates seem to be set to match the stride of someone slightly shorter than me. I have to watch every step—which means staring at a drop of several hundred feet—to make sure my feet land on the plates instead of between them. Tessen is somehow as surefooted as someone who's crossed this treacherous bridge many times before.

Until I extend my wards across the entire gorge, gusts of wind shift and rattle the walkway like a boat in a stormy ocean. How do the Denhitrans deal with this every day? Thankfully, we close the distance between us and something solid faster than I expect. Armed Denhitran guards are waiting for us. They're eyeing us with the same suspicion we would've shown them moons ago if they'd marched straight up to the gates of Itagami.

"Dria'ampha, mafanatra," Zonna shouts when we're twenty feet away, calling for peace and naming them friends. "We're all here to help."

Their stances relax instantly. Despite his greeting, I almost think Zonna's going to walk right past the guards, but he pauses between them and says something too low and quick for me to catch before he walks through the gated arch and into the tunnel beyond. Sconces line the striated stone walls, only ten feet apart or so, lighting the way. The passage is wide enough for three to walk abreast. The roof, though, can't be higher than six and a half feet; I don't have to straighten my arm to touch the stone.

Near a bend in the tunnel, the light changes. The flickering glow of fire is replaced by a steadier, paler illumination. It reminds me of the light globes I saw in Ryogo, which doesn't make sense. Tessen seems just as confused. Zonna, though, is smiling.

"It is like Ryogo," I breathe as the source comes into view. A glowing crystal like the ones I used for my first wardstones is embedded in the ceiling. The light is as steady as the Ryogan lamps. The color, though, is closer to sunlight. "I didn't know this was possible."

Zonna smiles. "I guess the world hasn't shown you all her surprises yet."

I raise my eyebrows. "Don't even try to claim you've seen all of them."

"I wouldn't dare," he says, laughing, "but I have seen this place, and although Itagami is impressive, there's something special here." He sweeps his arm wide. "Welcome to Denhitra."

My gaze follows his gesture, and then I can't look away.

Tsua, Chio, and Zonna told us stories about their life here, but they didn't tell us what the place looked like, so I pictured the city in a hidden valley or spread along the southern coast. I was wrong.

The citizens of Denhitra have claimed the center of a mountain.

I can't tell if it was hollowed by nature or magic, but the mountain is a massive, imperfect ring of stone that's open to the sky. Rain pours through the hole in a column as thick as a waterfall. Wide ledges line the sloped mountainsides, and dozens of bridges like the one we used to get here stretch across the central gap, disappearing into the falling water.

We came in on the top level of the city, and when I step to the edge and look down, I see a massive lake. It's incredible. I'd build here for that water source alone. This is a stronghold to rival Itagami, and a city capable of withstanding all but the longest and most brutal sieges.

Zonna frowns when he sees the lake, though. "There should be farms down there. We've always had a lake, but drains kept it from drowning the farms in the rainy season." He closes his eyes and curses. "I'd hoped those would hold."

Bellows, how have they kept the city fed? There are dozens of people nearby—all too thin and all watching us with suspicion—and hundreds or thousands more on the other levels. Without farms, there's too many people. Not enough food.

A wall near the tunnel has a dozen circular pieces of metal embedded with faintly glowing crystals. The guard stationed there shifts a cover aside and speaks into the opening beneath it, and I realize they're sound shafts like the ones Miari and Syoni built in Kaisuama. They must be used to send messages within the city.

"Have you come to collect the refugees?" another guard asks Zonna.

"What refugees?" he asks.

My heart pounds, and I look again at the people surrounding us, searching for faces I might recognize. People from Tsimo would rather die than abandon the peninsula they've claimed to the west, so there's only one place on the island refugees could've come from.

"Itagamins." The guard looks from Zonna to us, confused. "You didn't know?"

"Do you know how…" Sanii glances northeast, toward Itagami. "How many fled here?"

"More than six hundred fifty," the other guard says, apparently finished with their report. "Reeka led them out. It hasn't been easy with them here, but we couldn't send them back."

Reeka. I know the name. She helped Sanii and me during our first search for Yorri, and it doesn't surprise me to hear she took charge of an escape. But what prompted them to leave? And six hundred fifty people is barely a portion of the yonin who would've been left behind when Varan left. Where's everyone else? And what were they running from?

The guards' focus shifts, and I follow their gaze. Three Denhitrans are striding toward us, parting the gathered crowd. They're scowling until Zonna jogs closer, his arms open wide. One Denhitran exclaims with joy, running to give Zonna a tight hug. They cup Zonna's face, and it almost looks like they're checking him for injuries—which is ridiculous for so many reasons—as they speak in a flurry of Denhitran.

It's been a long time since I've heard so much of this language, and their conversation is fast—my ears stumble over the words. I catch Tsua's and Chio's names, though, and I see the distress on their expressions when Zonna murmurs a response. Whatever he says next shifts the group's attention to us, and the one who seems the oldest of the three steps forward.

"I am Ralavanona. This is my husband Ahnatiolio, and Zonna is speaking with Soaholia. She wasn't sure we'd see our andofume again." Ralavanona frowns. "And it looks like she was partially right."

"I'm sorry." I clear my throat, not allowing myself to look away from their eyes. "We're still mourning their loss, but it— Is there somewhere else we can go? There's a lot to explain."

"Yes, of course." Ahnatiolio puts a hand on Ralavanona's arm. "Follow em up to the council room, and we'll meet you there in a moment."

Although Ralavanona casts a glance at eir husband, ey nods.

"Before we go, I wonder if I can ask a favor." I glance at the andofume, but I don't explain who they are yet. "Do you have a room away from the storm some of us can rest in?"

After conferring with Zonna, the elders seem to decide on a place. They offer to guide us there, but Zonna declines. He knows this city better than anyone else alive. Although most of the squad will follow the elders to their council room, I go with Zonna and the andofume.

Maybe I should ward the barrier between them and the rest of the city. My wards won't just keep everyone else out, after all, they can also keep the andofume in. Given their current state, there's too big a risk they'll violently defend themselves if someone spooks them.

In many ways, the layout of Denhitra is similar to Itagami with part of the city open to the air and part enclosed in stone. It seems like most of the population lives and works in the spaces overlooking the interior of the mountain, tunnels deep within the peak. The passages are wide, labyrinthine, and lit by a combination of torchlight and crystal lamps. I was hoping the familiarity of a place like this would appeal to the andofume, and I was right. They seem calmer, maybe because of the quiet. It's peaceful here apart from the murmur of distant conversation and the sounds of our own footsteps.

Our journey ends at a large room that once might've been used for storage. Sanii uses a Ryogan spell to light the torches, and we settle the andofume inside. Yorri stops to speak to several who—like him—have come out of their ordeal scarred and scared but far from broken. When we leave, they shut the door behind us, and lock it. I wish I could ward the room for them, but despite practicing, my wards still don't last long once I leave. Maybe it wouldn't be a good idea anyway. With a ward up, there'd be no way for them to get out without shattering the shield. I don't want this temporary safe haven to turn into yet another prison for them. Zonna leads us back the way we came, but Sanii is the one directing Yorri. He's holding eir hand and walking sideways, his gaze on the andofume's room long after the tunnel's curves hide it from sight.

This time, I pay more attention to our surroundings and the people we pass. Everyone is gaunt and subdued, their embellished tunics, wraps, and skirts too big for most of their frames. They all recognize Zonna, and they step aside to let us pass, their heads lowered. Zonna nods to most, greets others by name, and looks stiffer and more conflicted with each step.

While Varan was building Itagami in his image, Zonna and his parents were here, helping Denhitra protect itself from the bobasu. I knew that, but watching him see how the city and its people have changed for the first time since he lost his parents drives the point home like a tent spike into stone.

I catch up with him and wait for a break in the crowd before I say, "Before we reached the bridge, you called this home."

"It is. I was only forty-three when we came here, so I may have spent my childhood watching Varan carve Itagami from the mesa, but Denhitra…" He runs his fingers along the wall, a gentle smile on his lips. "I love this city."

"You seem close to Soaholia." We enter a curving stairwell and begin to descend. "Have you and she been friends for a long time?"

"Friends." Zonna huffs a laugh. "We're that at the very least. I was present at her birth and helped raise her and her sisters. She's one of the oldest citizens, though, and most of her generation has already been returned to the land. I wasn't sure she'd still be alive."

"How did she take the news about your parents?"

He smiles sadly. "She isn't sure she wants the honor of outliving Tsua and Chio. I told her I hadn't wanted it either."

"It'll be worth bearing if you can outlive the bobasu, too. Right?" My skin buzzes with nervous energy. I *need* to hear his answer. For a while, he'd been so depressed and detached I worried he'd become nothing but a walking shell. I need to know he has a reason to live.

Fervor kindles in his eyes, and I breathe a little easier. Until he says, "Don't worry. If it's the last thing I do, I'll make sure every bobasu dies before me."

Rage and revenge won't carry him beyond this last battle, but I swallow my protests as we leave the staircase and walk the curve of the lower—and more crowded—level. We'll simply have to help him find a new mission when this is finished, something filled with hope. But that's for later. Now, we have more stories we need to tell.

The room we enter is a large square with a fireplace in the center of one wall, rows of shelves along another, and a low table surrounded by cushions filling the space between. All three of the elders are already waiting for us. When Ralavanona gestures there, I nod and sit in one of the few open spaces.

"We've heard a lot about you, Khya," Ahnatiolio says as he sits beside Ralavanona. "Tyrroh talked about you, the strongest fykina the clan had seen in ages. We weren't surprised when Tsua brought back stories about you, too. Still, I don't think anyone expected you to be the one to set all this in motion."

My lips part, but I don't know what to say. It's bizarre to think stories of me traveled across Shiara. It's painful to think the people who told them are gone.

The same realization seems to hit Ahnatiolio, because he frowns. "Are you sure Tsua and Chio... I mean, I hadn't thought it was *possible*. They've been here since before my grandmother's grandmother's grandmother was born."

I glance at Zonna, my chest tightening as I watch the increasingly familiar blankness descend over him. Clearing my throat, I nod. "We're sure."

The elders lower their heads, lips moving in what might be a prayer. There's real pain in their expressions, and their postures sag, so I keep my silence, giving them the time to grieve old deaths that are brand new to them.

When they look up again, Ralavanona and Ahnatiolio focus on Zonna, their expressions expectant, but he shakes his head and glances my way. It's a simple, silent gesture, but it carries so much weight—the person who by value of age, power, knowledge, and experience should be leading this discussion is deferring to me.

I don't protest, not even in my head. I take a breath and go back to the beginning.

I've told this story so many times it's begun to feel like someone else's history. The Denhitrans ask dozens of questions, making us go back to events I brushed over too quickly. Yorri is watchfully silent, reminding me of how he was during lessons, absorbing all the information before working through the details on his own. It worries me, though, when I catch up to the present and he still hasn't said a word. Especially since I can't read his face.

The Denhitran elders aren't any easier to interpret even as Ralavanona places eir linked hands in eir lap and asks, "What do you propose we do next? I need to know your plan has a chance of success before I ask my people to risk their lives for it. Convince me, young one."

I take a moment to order my thoughts, and then I lay out everything that needs to happen before Varan catches up to us. The only thing I don't—can't—say is "The plan will work." That isn't a promise I can make, so that hope, I keep to myself.

TWENTY-TWO

For hours, we go over our situation from every possible angle. We eat while we talk, and although most of us could push on for another day without stopping to sleep, rest is a necessity for the Denhitrans and Rai. We make plans to reconvene in several hours, and then they retreat to their rooms, their shoulders and their eyelids drooping.

As much as I hate the delay—time is slipping away faster than sand in a desert storm—I'm also grateful for the break.

"Do you think they'll help?" Sanii asks as we leave the council room.

"I think we'll have to turn people away." Yorri says it with a certainty I wish I felt.

Zonna is nodding. "It's in the stories they tell, if you listen. They've spent centuries resisting Varan's control of Shiara. He and the bobasu are invaders who tried to take this island from the Denhitrans and Tsimosi."

"I hope they'll let us stay when this is over," Tessen mutters. "We have to get the army out of Ryogo, and they never want us to come back. If we must make the same promise here, I don't know where else we can go."

"No one who's heard what happened in Ryogo is going to welcome Itagamins onto their land." Sanii leans more heavily into Yorri's side.

I snort and shake my head. "That's putting it far too mildly."

Zonna leaves then, heading off to check in on friends, and the four of us continue on to the room we've been assigned to share. As much as I wish I could have a moment alone with my brother, I can't bring myself to even hint Sanii should leave. I also don't protest when Tessen comes with us.

For a while, I let their words wash over me, my mind lost in the past. Only when the muted sound of their conversation disappears do I realize they're looking at me like they're waiting for a response. The worry and guilt that's been building since the night I learned Yorri had died tumbles out; all I can think to say is, "I am so sorry."

Yorri blinks and cocks his head. "For what?"

"For letting them take you." I can't keep the words back anymore. How is it not obvious to him? "And because it took us so long to get back to you."

"Bellows, Khya, stop. Please." My brother exhales and rubs the bridge of his nose. "Don't do this to yourself. It's not like you were spending your days... I don't know. Trying to build yourself a pair of mykyn wings." He drops his hand, and his eyes find mine. "Everything you were doing was important, and every day it took was necessary. You had your own trials."

And then his expression relaxes. An almost playful light glints in his eyes, and his tone becomes annoyingly reasonable. "Besides, crossing an ocean and discovering another land takes time."

"I'm being serious," I snap.

"I know. So am I, mostly." He reaches for me, stopping less than an inch from my arm. The gap closes only when I move into the touch. I want to say something, to explain it's not just how long I took to get back, it's that I let this happen to him at all. I keep my mouth shut because I know the first thing he'll ask is, "Well, how could you have possibly stopped it?" and even looking back with everything I know now, I don't have an answer.

"I'm not going to tell you I wasn't angry, because I was," Yorri says, finding words before I do. "I didn't know what was happening at first, and then, after a few weeks, I couldn't track time well anymore. It got...endless. It was awful, but you spent all your time working out how to get back here." His grip on my arm tightens. "Why should you need to apologize for that?"

"Yorri, I..." I look away, my stomach churning. I don't know how to break apart and name the emotions knotted in my chest. Tessen eases closer, leaning against my side. I'm grateful for the reassurance even as I cringe—it means he sensed the pain I'm in. No matter what's happened in the past year, it's nearly impossible to stop thinking of myself as a nyshin, and nyshin aren't supposed to admit to pain. Pain was weakness, and we were never allowed weakness.

But as I'm turning Yorri's words over in my head, my breath catches. I sit up, staring at him and afraid of the answer even as I ask, "You were aware? I'd thought it was possible—I felt like something yanked my mind out of my body when I tried to cut the niadagu cords on your wrist, and it happened again at the katsujos—but... Were you aware the whole time?"

I want him to say no, but instead his hold on Sanii tightens and he nods.

"It was like being stuck in a dream, except sometimes I *did* dream, and I would wake up exactly where I'd been before. I could hear and see everything—and feel it all, too—but I couldn't *do* anything." Then he looks at me and tosses a small piece of cloth at my chest. "Don't you dare apologize for that. Being aware meant I saw what happened when you came for me the first time. There was nothing you could've done differently, not with what anyone knew at the time."

Looking down is easier than trying to meet his eyes. I've grown almost comfortable in command and used to taking responsibility for the consequences of my decisions, but that hard-won logic doesn't seem to apply when my brother is involved. Forming sentences with actual meaning also seems to be a skill I lose around him now—I can't think of a single thing to say.

"Khya?" He waits until I look at him to speak. "How much more is there? Is it just Ryogo and Khylar or are there other lands, too?"

"Far more than we got to see." My stomach settles enough for me to smile back and mean it. "We'll show you a hanaeuu we'la maninaio map later. The world is bigger than even you can imagine."

His straight eyebrows rise. "Really?"

"You'll love those maps," Sanii assures him, stroking his arm with eir fingers. "As soon as I saw them, your reaction to them was all I could think of."

"Me, too, and with more than just the maps," I admit. "There was always something I wished you could've seen for yourself."

"Maybe one day." His smile softens. I see resignation in his eyes; it's like he no longer finds it so easy to hope escaping Shiara is possible. Maybe part of him is still trapped on Imaku, strapped down and consciously unconscious. I'll find a way to fix that eventually, but it can't happen until this whole crisis is behind us one way or the other.

"Do you think the andofume will answer questions?" I ask. His expression turns hesitant, so I try to explain. "If all of them were aware, they might know something that could help."

"I don't know. I wasn't there long compared to some, but it's…" His lips disappear between his teeth, and his eyes close tight. "It's hard enough reminding my body it can move. For most of the others, anything beyond that is going to be impossible for a while. At least."

Some haven't moved at all yet. It's like they've sunk so deep into their own minds they've forgotten they *have* bodies. I don't think I want the answer, but I make myself ask, "Will you tell us more, then?"

Yorri's eyes open warily. "About what?"

"What happened to you."

The creases around his eyes and mouth vanish, the muscles along his jaw stop moving, and his blinks slow. It's as though he's erasing all sign of emotion from his expression. When did he learn how to do that? He was never good at this before.

Tessen leans into me, and the weight and warmth of his body give me the strength to speak. "The times my mind left my body, it was disconcerting but not horrible. I was aware of physical sensations, but never overwhelmed by them. Was it like that for you?"

"No," my brother huffs.

Then Sanii murmurs something. Yorri blinks, and Tessen brushes his thumb along the back of my hand. The harshness of my brother's expression eases. He takes a slow breath, his shoulders drooping.

"I felt everything as though I was awake. I couldn't not. It was the same for the others, I think." His head falls to rest against Sanii's as though it's too heavy for him to hold up anymore. "Maybe you're different because you're a fykina, or maybe what happened to you didn't last long enough—I don't know. There hasn't exactly been time for us all to compare experiences. Even if there had been…" His eyes close, and he shudders. "I'm not sure I want to know how bad it was for anyone else."

Bellows. My breath stutters, and my heartbeat quickens. Tessen's thumb presses against the pulse point in my wrist, but he doesn't speak. I draw on his strength and continue, keeping my voice as gentle as I can. "You don't have to talk about it anymore if you don't want to, but if you were aware of those around you and could hear what they said, I thought you might know something we could use."

Yorri's lips twist into a wry smile, his face still turned against Sanii's shoulder. "You think too much of me if you honestly think I can untangle the last year. Moments stand out—like when you three were there on Imaku—but most of it is in out-of-order bits and pieces. Everything was overwhelming. All I know for sure is that even though none of the bobasu visited Imaku, but all of them were there when we were carried into the valley."

Sitting up, Yorri shoves his hair back absently. It's long, almost to his shoulders. Some sections are still matted flat from moons trapped against stone, and other sections curl in tight ringlets that fall back into his face as soon as he drops his hand to his lap. "I'll try to remember, but that's all I can promise."

"It's all I can ask."

"I think we're all forgetting something," Tessen says. "The bobasu were captured because of the stone from Imaku, so Varan knows exactly what it does to the mind and how much a person can hear and remember. He's lived through it. I don't believe he'd let anyone hear anything he didn't want them to know."

Blood and rot, he's right. Can even Varan be that constantly wary, though? Time blurs memories, and distraction eliminates caution. "Focus on the trip to the valley, Yorri. If the bobasu let anything slip, it would've been then."

I don't want to press him anymore, so until he remembers, I'll have to get more information from another source. "There are Itagamins in this city, ones who must've had a compelling reason to flee their home," I say as I stand. "It's probably a good idea to ask what drove them out before we head back."

"Sleep would be a good idea, too," Tessen says, even as he stands, too. "Who knows how long we'll have to push ourselves once we leave here? You need rest."

"I need information more. We have to know what we're walking into."

Despite his initial protests, Tessen follows me when I leave. Yorri and Sanii stay behind.

Most of the Itagamin refugees are on the lower levels of Denhitra. Heads turn as we pass. We had been burning up in our Ryogan layers, so the Denhitrans had given us clothes to change into. They didn't have enough full outfits for all of us, though, so we've ended up in a mishmash of pieces from Itagami, Ryogo, and Denhitra. I recognize some of the faces around me, but it takes them a second—and sometimes third—look to recognize us.

Those who do surge closer, their voices overlapping as they try to ask questions and give us information all at once. It takes a few seconds to sort through the sounds and several more to get them to answer the question I have: "Where is Reeka?"

The clamor rises again, all of them anxious to not only tell me where she is but how she saved their lives. Their adoration is obvious. She's spoken about her like an ages-old legend, but she's not even twenty-five yet. It makes me remember Soanashalo'a's words about watching the truth unfold for herself so she'd know later where reality ended and exaggeration began. What I hadn't understood then is what it might be like to be the subject of those stories and myths. It's a lot of pressure to bear and a lot of expectations to meet. In a different way from my own trials, Reeka's been surrounded by it for moons.

Reeka finds us before we can extricate ourselves from the throng. The crowd parts for her, and she nods her thanks even as she keeps her attention on Tessen and me. I'm impressed. Whatever she's lived through the past year, she seems to be bearing up well under the strain. She smiles to see us and leads us to a small room nearby, one she seems to have to herself, an oddity in such a crowded city.

"The others insist," she says when she sees I've noticed. "They call it an honor of rank. But you didn't come looking for me to ask about my sleeping arrangements."

I wish it were so simple. "I need to know what's happened in Itagami since we left."

Reeka nods. Although she seems surprised, she doesn't answer right away, either. She pushes aside whatever is making her hesitate with a few deep breaths and begins to speak.

"After Varan and the nyshin left, things deteriorated fast. The army took most of the food, and the ahdo in charge didn't realize how little was left until the army was already gone. Order held for a while. We survived on what rations were available, and we hunted what we could, but it wasn't enough. The ahdo..." She laughs, the sound harsh and bitter. "Well, they weren't going to starve themselves to save us."

"Eventually, it got so bad I was finally able to convince everyone to sneak out of the city and head here." She looks up, her dark eyes filled with pain. "We should've left sooner."

My heart aches. I recognize the heavy guilt she's carrying around with her. I've borne the same burden most of this year. People died, and she's convinced herself she could've done something to prevent it. "It's amazing you convinced them to leave at all."

"Maybe." Expression closed off in a way that ends this part of the conversation, she shrugs. "You're headed back, aren't you?"

"As soon as we can arrange it, but we learned from an akuringu that some of the clan was here. I wanted to find out why before we tried to get into Itagami," I explain. "One of the advantages we have over Varan is that we have the time to see what's changed since he left. I want to find a way for us to use it against him."

We talk to Reeka for hours, discussing the best approaches and pulling details about the state of the city from her. The longer we talk, the more an unshakable suspicion takes hold of my mind. I don't say anything to Tessen, though, until we leave her to get some sleep.

"I'm afraid of what she wasn't saying," I murmur in Ryogan.

"I don't think it's a dangerous secret. She seemed sad, not guilty." Tessen glances back. "We'll see the truth for ourselves soon enough."

On our way back to our room, I pause at the edge of the level, looking down at the water-filled basin. It's hard to look at that water with anything but dread. Even if we win, will it matter? If the storms have destroyed our chances of growing anything here this season, we'll have to abandon the island. If we don't, we'll perish clinging to these shores.

I rub the back of my neck and exhale slowly. Maybe Soanashalo'a will know a place that might be willing to take us in or some *other* isolated island we can move to. And maybe Varan will surrender as soon as he sees me. At this point, one feels just as likely as the other.

TWENTY-THREE

There are more discussions of plans and possibilities when the elders wake up. In the end, the Denhitrans give us everything we ask for and more. All the Itagamin defectors, half the andofume, and hundreds of Denhitran soldiers will follow us out of Denhitra. Essentially, it's everyone who can be spared and is physically able to manage the trip while carrying enough food for two weeks.

We leave the mountain city and take the first steps of what I hope will be one of the last journeys I have to take for a long, long time. But we're not heading straight for Itagami. I need a katsujo first. None of us were sure one existed on Shiara—wouldn't Varan have found it?—but as soon as I used the boruikku to focus the desosa, I felt a tug in two directions, west and north.

Without knowing exactly where they were, it took Tessen and me a while to decide which way to go. The problem was the possibility of reaching the ocean before the katsujo. If it was under the ocean, that would explain why Varan never used it and why none of us—not even Tessen—ever noticed the tingling vibration of such immense power. But Varan is probably on his way—he could be here tomorrow for all we knew. There's no way to— *Oh.*

The idea is beautiful in its simplicity. It takes my breath away even as it makes me want to pound my own head against a wall for not thinking of this earlier. It only makes me feel a little better to know Tessen hadn't suggested it, either.

Sometimes, to avoid something, you have to find it first. If I use the boruikku to locate Varan, I'll always know where he is in relation to us, and I should be able to at least guess at his distance. Even if all I learn from the hanaeuu we'la maninaio spell is that he's really far, closing in, or around the corner, it'll be more than we have now.

"What is it?" Tessen is watching me closely, the expression on his face shifting between confusion and concern.

I explain as quickly as I can, stumbling a few times because the hows of the idea are only just beginning to take shape in my mind, but Tessen catches on fast. His eyes pop open wide and he grabs my tunic, hauling me in for a kiss.

"Brilliant," he murmurs against my lips before he pulls away. "Bellows, Khya."

I grin, giddy with his fervent praise and the flush of finding a solution. The relief becomes even headier when we test my theory. I was right. It works.

But Varan is far closer than I hoped he'd be.

"He won't be here tomorrow," Tessen says after a moment of heavy silence. "At least we know that for certain now."

Yes, but he might be here in the next few days. It's hard to tell exactly, but the pull of energy through the symbol inked over my heart tells me Varan is far closer to Shiara than he is to Ryogo. He took the bait and is following us into the trap, so we'd better get the trap finished before he gets here.

I take a breath and pick a katsujo. "We're heading north."

Although I want to take the ship, there's no way we could fit several hundred people onboard. Instead, I use the garakyu to fill Shytari in on the details and tell her to head in the direction of Itagami while we leave Denhitra on foot.

We slowly reverse the trip we took a few days ago, only this time, I'm at the head of an army. In narrower mountain passes, the line stretches out so far behind me I can't see its end. A year ago, I never would've believed this moment was possible. I would've laughed if someone had described it to me, thanked them for the inherent compliment, and forgotten about it. Now, tremors of excitement fill my chest—all these people are willing to follow *me*. It's thrilling...and terrifying. I'm not scared the same as I would've been a moon ago, but I can't stop wondering how many won't live to see how Shiara transforms once Varan is gone. If they die, how much responsibility will I bear for their loss?

"What are you getting yourself so upset over?" Yorri's question yanks me from my thoughts, and I blink. I hadn't even realized he'd caught up to me.

"What makes you think I'm upset?" I'd been trying to keep it off my face.

"I may not have seen you in a long time, Khya, but I know how to read you." He gestures to my face. "It shows in your eyes."

"It's my misfortune to be constantly surrounded by overly perceptive people," I mutter, gripping an outcropping of rock and hauling myself up the next rise. "I'm trying not to think about how many of these people won't see next week because of me."

His eyes narrow. "If anyone dies, it'll be because they chose to."

"Better to die for a purpose than live in fear of the end." Another quote from our training masters. Their lessons held many truths. What would they say if they saw how I now interpreted them, though? "You'd tell me if you thought I was making a foolish decision, wouldn't you?"

His eyebrows go up. "When have I ever held my tongue when it mattered?"

"Never." I'm blessed with friends who don't hesitate to tell me the truth, even when I don't want to hear it. Or cursed with them. It depends on the day. Today, I'm grateful.

Once Tessen and I have a better idea where we're going to end up, we give Shytari a more specific destination. Her ship is waiting for us by the time we get close to the strongest point of the katsujo. Etaro and Vysian rush forward to help Shytari's crew haul the heavily laden boats onto the beach. They stop short when they realize what exactly those boats are filled with—piles of Imaku stones. Rai is the one who takes over, ordering people in to drag stones up the beach. Everyone obeys her snapped shouts without question. Most of my squad stays well back as they work. I move closer, taking the long way around to reach the last in the row. Chirida and Shytari's boat isn't filled with rock at all.

"Is that a cannon?" I ask, incredulous. It'd seemed so unmovable before.

"Yes, and just one so far." Shytari runs her hand along the weapon's dark metal. "Getting these off the ship isn't easy. I wasn't about to waste time if you didn't have a way to get these beasts from here to wherever you need them. I certainly can't move them past this point."

I shout for Etaro and Vysian, and when they arrive I explain what I need from them.

Etaro frowns. "Moving one cannon won't be a problem, but several dozen? Fast isn't possible with that much weight, especially not carrying them inland to Itagami from here."

"And definitely not if we're balancing the chunks of Imaku stone, too," Vysian adds. "Moving it all piece by piece is possible. It would eat up far too many hours, though."

Rubbing my forehead, I try to think. This is like one of Yorri's rot-ridden metal puzzles—all the pieces are in front of me, but I can't see any way to untangle them. I wish—*oh*. My hand drops, but my heart rises. I don't have to wish my brother were here. He *is*.

"Yorri!" I beckon to him as soon as he looks over. He jogs closer, Sanii only half a step behind. I blink, surprised to see even that much space between them. I explain what we need as soon as he stops in front of me.

"I can carry one of these, but there has to be a faster way." His words seem like thoughts spoken aloud as he steps forward to run his hand over the cannon. I smile to see his puzzle expression take over his face. Eyes focused, lips pursed, eyebrows pulled together—this is the look he got as he taught himself how to pick a lock when we were kids. This time, the consequences of the solution he finds will be a lot bigger than a day of drills.

Then he looks up. "You should go. Take the stones and as many people as you need to carry them for you, and go find your katsujo." He smiles then, though the expression is more than a little rueful. "I'd wanted to see it, but maybe when this is over."

"There won't be much to see." Shiara's katsujo can't be anything like the lush impossibility of Kaisuama. Varan would've found it centuries ago if there were something obvious about the place where the katsujo brushed the surface of our island.

"That's hard to believe, but you'd know better than me." He shakes his head, his expression pinching. His worry only lasts a second before he tries to hide it with a bright smile. The lines surrounding his dark eyes expose him. "Go get caravan started to carry your stones while I figure out how to get you your cannons. We'll meet you outside the city with your oversized weapons."

"I—" *don't want to leave you*, I finish silently. But that's impossible. No one but the Kaisubeh can be in two places at once. So instead of saying what almost tripped out of my mouth, I glance at Sanii. I know Sanii will want to stay with Yorri, whose strength and speed will be needed to help move the cannons, but I need em with me at the katsujo. Too few people know how to handle the desosa the way we can. "I don't know if I can let you stay here."

Let you stay here. The words echo back to me. They make me blink. *Let* em? Even before we started looking for Yorri, I never ordered Sanii to do anything. I had the right to back then, though, at least according to the Miriseh. Ey was yonin. I was a nyshin. I outranked em by plenty, but I never gave Sanii an order. It was never even an instinct. Somehow, that's changed.

Ey gathers emself as though readying emself for an argument. I shake my head once. All eir bluster collapses. Although ey glances at Yorri, Sanii sighs and nods.

"It won't be long, sukhai." Yorri takes eir hand and runs his thumb along eir knuckles. "It won't be like it was."

"I know." Sanii's hand rises, moving toward eir chest until ey notices the gesture and yanks it back down. I hate asking them to split up again so soon, but I can't take it back. It won't be for long. Sanii's skills are needed elsewhere.

When I tell Tessen we're leaving, he shakes his head. "I'm going to stay with Yorri. Chances are we'll end up moving the ship closer to the city to pull off some ingenious plan of your brother's, and they might need me." He runs his thumb over the boruikku on the inside of his right wrist.

My breath catches, unreasonable fear flooding my chest. I should be happy. He'll be safer on the ship, away from the power of the piles of weaponized stone I'm going to create, but I've become so dependent on always having him nearby. For nearly a year now, there have been so few times when he's been more than a mile from me. I can't order Sanii *and* Tessen to come, especially not when the logic for each decision is so opposed to the other.

"Be careful. And try to keep an eye to the south." It seems like the buzz in the storm has been building. Varan is closing in, and I can't keep my focus on the boruikku at all times. I don't want to be taken by surprise.

In the end, only Sanii, Zonna, Miari, and a hundred Itagamin and Denhitran volunteers—including Reeka—come north with me. Everyone else will be staying to help Yorri or to act as a translator between the Shiarans, the Ryogans, and the Khylari.

Those following me are extremely careful to follow every order I give, and to stay far away from Sanii and me with the rocks they carry.

Despite how close Shytari had been able to get to the katsujo, it takes us two hours to travel only a few miles. We must go around steep slopes instead of over them and stop to rest far more often than I expected. Our sluggish pace isn't only because of the rocks, though. A year ago, two hours carrying pounds of rock would barely have tested any Shiaran's endurance. Moons of strict rations have weakened everyone. They're quicker to tire. It's their strength of mind that keeps them putting one foot in front of the other.

"We're almost there." I shout the announcement loud enough to be heard by those closest, and they relay the words down the line. In a quieter voice, I ask Zonna, "Do you know where we are?"

"The wastelands, I think." He peers into the pounding rain through the protection of my ward and then glances at me. "It's really out here?"

"This is where it's strongest." Maybe Varan never found the Shiaran katsujos because he'd been expecting the impossibility we saw in Kaisuama. If I hadn't been led here by the boruikku, I don't know that I would've noticed the faint pulse of power rising up from the ground. Nothing grows out here. It's flat except for scattered outcroppings of rock, but when I ask Miari to find me a way underground, she soon discovers the whole plain is riddled with caves.

"The river that flows under Itagami must come this way," she says as she crawls along the ground, her dark hands sifting through the red mud to find the perfect place to break through. Even working quickly, though, it takes her several hours to create a slope down into a cavern deep enough to let us reach the underground katsujo.

Once we're inside, our bearers carefully place the stones where we direct. They step back when Sanii, Zonna, and I spread ourselves along the line—far enough away to avoid contact with the rocks—and begin to work.

It's fast. The desosa, despite being buried deeper than any I've used before, practically leaps up to meet us. It rushes through me, buzzing like the glee I felt when I held my first zeeka blade or when magic first burned through my veins. But this euphoria isn't mine. Neither is the viciously vindictive edge I sense as the power dives into the Imaku rocks.

Help me protect those willing to fight with me, and you'll have your vengeance soon, I pray to the Kaisubeh. *We'll both have what we've been waiting for.*

A scream rings through my bones. It's wordless and soundless, yet I understand. There is furious pain, bloody-minded determination, and gratitude all wrapped up together. *It's been so long*, it seems to say. *It's been too long since someone was able to hear us and since anyone was willing to help. Thank you. Thank you, thank you, thank you.*

Or maybe, I admit as the desosa's flow ebbs, those are my own thoughts echoing back at me.

The katsujo sinks back into the island like a receding flood, and I step back. The stones buzz with so much furious power they make me shiver, and I want a lot more space between them and me. They're somehow even worse than the last batch, as terrifyingly unsettling as an unexpected touch in a coal-dark room. Sanii steps away, too. Zonna, however, crouches next to the stones and picks up a fist-sized piece, running his thumb over the black rock.

Instinctively, my weight shifts forward and my arms begin to rise. I force myself to still. Zonna is fine. He's as safe as Rai or Reeka would be, but it doesn't mean I like seeing the rock in his hand. Or watching him slip a handful of smaller stones into a pouch on his belt.

Sanii and I lead the group, and the others follow at a moderate distance, though never out of range of a shout or out of reach of my wards. Despite the gap, the black rocks' power buzzes in the back of my mind like a particularly persistent bug.

Sanii's ability to create light keeps us from stumbling head-first into trenches and slamming into walls of rock, but it's not strong enough to penetrate very far into the thick storm. There are no stars to guide us. Finding landmarks through the wall of rain and the blazing flashes of lightning is unreliable at best. I must use the boruikku to keep us on course. It feels strange to need that guide when I used to believe I could navigate this island blindfolded, but I'm glad for the help. Visibility is so poor that we'd be well and truly lost without the boruikku's help.

I keep my eyes on our path, searching for pitfalls and dangers. Sanii, however, keeps looking back, tracking the position and the progress of Zonna and the others again…and again…and again…and—

"Bellows, Sanii, what are you looking for? You're making me nervous."

Eir head whips around, embarrassment flashing across eir face. It's strange to see. I don't remember ever seeing Sanii embarrassed. Curiosity piqued, I repeat the question.

Sighing, ey shakes eir head. "If life had gone a different way, I'd likely be with Reeka and the others, carrying those rocks instead of afraid of them. It's just… I don't know what it is. The thought hit me, and I couldn't shake it."

"That only would've happened if you weren't you," I insist. "You never accepted the way things were. You and Yorri are two of the only Itagamins who looked at the ocean and asked what else might be out there. It's one of the reasons you bonded, isn't it? And when you were placed yonin, and I made sure Yorri became nyshin whether he wanted it or not, you didn't accept that your time together was over. Somehow, you created a sumai bond even though everything we knew said that should've been impossible." I shake my head, watching Sanii for a moment before I admit, "People have us wrong. They think I'm the one who keeps pulling off the impossible, but most of the time it's you. I've just been there to make sure your plans work."

"Ridiculous." Sanii scoffs, but ey's smiling. "Don't pretend to be humble *now*. Without you, I'd still be running through the undercity trying to find Yorri, I'd be dead, or I'd be back there, hating you as you led us back to the city like the next commander of the Miriseh."

This time it's my turn to snort, even though there's so little about any of this that's funny. "I guess we should hope everyone else sees it that way."

Because I *have* made myself the next commander of the Miriseh, and when we reach Itagami, I'm either going to have to convince the ahdo guarding the gates to accept me in that role and give me control of the city…

Or I'm going to have to take my home back by force.

TWENTY-FOUR

Itagami is on the horizon.

I know our mesa so well I can recognize its shape even through distortions of rain and light. The bolts from the sky reflect off the massive iron gates, transforming them into a beacon. Weapons glint on the wall like the sparkle of distant stars—they're also a reminder those gates won't open for us today. This won't be a homecoming. I'm preparing to invade.

Once, seeing Sagen sy Itagami from the desert always filled me with warmth; I knew I'd be safe inside those walls the same way I knew how to breathe. It's so hard now to see the city I remember in this place. The mesa should gleam like embers under the cloudless, blue sky. I should hear the growl of teegras and the calls of mykyn. There should be squads returning from a hunt or patrol run with the Kyiwa Mountains as a formidable and familiar backdrop.

I burn with the desire to reclaim the home I once had. And I will. I *will*. Settling my shoulders, I push down the sense of loss and grip resolution. I'll return Itagami to what it once was. I'll make it better. This time, the city will be founded not only on stone but on truth.

The pouch on my belt pulses, and I remove the garakyu. Tessen's face appears inside, and he immediately says, "Your brother lived up to his reputation, Khya. We have an idea."

There will be two groups, according to Tessen and Yorri, one that breaches the city from the inside and one attacking from the desert. Yorri will be one of the many joining my force. He's supposed to be dead, and at least some people will remember that. He's exactly the kind of immediate proof we need to convince those in the city to join us. Tessen's group—including Soanashalo'a, Chirida, and several Ryogans—will move into the city through the tunnel Tyrroh once used to escape the city.

The waiting aches. Itagami is so close, and I want to reach out and touch it.

Yorri reaches us first, well before the others. While we wait for them to catch up, he gives Reeka instructions and large landmarks to follow. She commits them to memory and leaves immediately, guiding those carrying the stones to the places around the city where others are guarding the cannons. Her group is long gone by the time the other andofume, the rest of my squad, and several dozen Denhitrans run into view.

It seems like hours before my garakyu lights up and Tessen reports in. "We're in the bikyo-ko."

"Good. Can you see anyone moving on the wall?"

His face vanishes; only the swirling colors tell me the connection is active. It won't be easy for him to see through the raging storm, but anything he tells me is more than I know.

Several minutes later, he reappears. "If the spacing of what I saw is consistent, there's a couple of squads stretched out around the city. Maybe less."

"It makes sense," Zonna says. "Reeka said rations have been extremely limited for moons. None of them can be healthy, so it's probably smaller groups working shorter shifts."

"Only one question left, then." Tessen lifts his garakyu until it feels like he's staring straight into my eyes. "Overrun them or talk our way in?"

"A little of both. If we surprise them, it might shock them into listening. Once you get inside, though, I want your group to focus on isolating the leader." While his group does that, my force will climb up the sheer outer wall. That approach would never be possible if the whole clan were in the city; guards wielding fire, lightning, stone, and arrows would've battered us as soon as we were within a mile of the city. Now, with the storm's darkness to hide in and the citizens' exhaustion to exploit, I doubt they'd be able to stop us even without my wards.

I spread my wardstones out to as many people as I can. Each glows like a distant bonfire in my mind. I can use them as anchors for my shield once we begin to climb, but none of us can move from this spot until Tessen's team is in place. I eye the landscape, planning the path between the towering rocks hiding us from view and the city itself. Lightning strikes have left gouges in the ground. Rain has created rivers of slick mud where there was nothing but dust before.

"Khya, look." Yorri points up. In the distance, a cannon fires, its spark flying like a star falling up from the ground—our signal.

We surge forward, sprinting straight for Itagami's wall. The river is too wide to leap, but as soon as I step into its flow, the ground shifts under me and I nearly fall. Knee-high water slows my steps, and the drag of the current tugs me off course until I dig the southern edge of my ward into the ground, holding the river back and freeing us to run for the base of the mesa.

Miari and anyone else who can shape stone add handholds and footholds in the wall, allowing us to climb with speed. From ground to top, the Itagamin mesa is well over a thousand feet tall. Though I've thought about scaling its sides more than once—purely for the challenge—I never thought I'd do it. And I definitely never guessed I'd be able to climb it as fast as this. I smile when I watch Miari's magic reach farther than I've ever seen. I'm not the only one whose abilities have grown, and I'm not the only one to notice her incredible skill.

Rocks and arrows fall, but they go awry, sailing over our heads and down or ricocheting off the wall to tumble harmlessly away. I frown when another arrow whizzes out into the drowning desert, well away from anyone. The guards should be able to at least get close to us.

I bite my lip and climb faster. At the top, I launch myself over the wall and draw my zeeka sword in one quick motion. "Surrender now. You won't get a second chance."

The pair of guards on the wall have their weapons raised in trembling grips, but they're not afraid; they're exhausted. Their expressions are nearly vacant, as though they're exhausted to the point of mindlessness and only training has kept them on their feet. Neither ahdo attacks, but neither surrenders. For a long moment, they simply blink in the strong wind.

"Miriseh bless it." One ahdo's sword falls from limp fingers, clattering to the stone. "Tell me you have food, Khya. Please."

Words shrivel on my tongue on hearing my name. I'd become fairly recognizable during my last moons in Itagami, but I hadn't expected to be recognized now.

"Are you going to kill us?" The second ahdo's question is devoid of true fear. They don't drop their weapon, but they do lower the tip of their blade.

"We're taking control of the city. We'll only hurt you if you try to stop us." I reach into my bag and pull out strips of dried meat. Their eyes widen when I offer it. "Do you surrender?"

The second weapon falls. This is the first time in Sagen sy Itagami's history that the city has been invaded, and it was accomplished by its own people and a few strips of meat.

I pass out several pouches of dried teegra and niora meat, and every ahdo within shouting distance closes in like a flock of mykyn. Their cheeks are hollow, their eyes sunken, and the bones in their hands stretch their skin. Food was tight in Denhitra, carefully monitored and rationed, but the city wasn't on the point of starvation, not even with so many extra people to feed. Bellows, exactly how little has there been to eat since Reeka and the others left?

I bite back the question. We can give those in Itagami at least one decent meal, and a full stomach after moons of hunger can earn forgiveness and surrender faster than threats and force.

"You don't recognize me, do you?" The question comes from the one who knew my name, and who surrendered instantly. I blink in surprise and look closer. If they know me well enough to recognize me so fast, I must have known them as well. They laugh, the sound barely stronger than a huff of air. "I've changed more than I realized if one of my best students doesn't know who I am anymore."

Students? "No. You can't— *Sotra?*"

Her cheeks are narrower, her eyes glazed over, and her hair scraggly and lank instead of neatly trimmed and tightly curled, but there's no mistaking her now. This is Ahdo-mas Sotra, the woman who taught Yorri, Tessen, and me much of what's kept us alive this long.

"It's so good to see you, Nyshin-ten," she says with a lax, but genuine, smile.

"Nyshin-lu," Sanii corrects. "Tyrroh promoted her to his second after Daitsa died, and now she's leading an army. We've been calling her nyshin-lu behind her back for weeks now."

A bright smile spreads across Sotra's face. "I always knew you were going to do big things, Khya, but *bellows*. And where is—" She turns as though she's looking for something. Her balance falters. When she lists dangerously close to the inner wall, I loop my arm around her waist and place her arm over my shoulders.

"Let me help, Ahdo-mas," I say. "Where is everyone else?"

She opens her mouth, but words seem beyond her reach. It's another ahdo who directs us—to the northeastern zon's nursery, of all places.

When the city was full, the building had been used by yonin caretakers and dozens of the young children; now what's left of my clan has gathered here. I take out my garakyu and, as my gaze roams the room, I tell Tessen to meet us here when he can.

The air smells of damp, mold, and sick. Sleeping mats cover the floor, and every mat is occupied. Some people leap up when we enter, reaching for weapons, but most simply watch us, bleary-eyed and listless. I'm sure I know several people in this room, yet they're almost unrecognizable, many of them barely clinging to life. It makes it easy to decide what needs to be done first—dispensing food and healing injuries.

Setting Sotra on a mat, I issue orders. Zonna takes charge of the hishingu, Etaro passes out small rations, and I get a chance to take everything else in.

More people are stumbling down the stairs from the upper levels. Some stop in surprise when they see us. Others are so drawn by the scent of food they don't seem to care who's handing it to them. Blood-spattered bandages are wrapped around limbs, heads, and chests. It's a strange sight within Itagami—hishingu should've healed these wounds before anyone needed bandages—but the hishingu left here are as exhausted and starving as everyone else. How can they heal when they're in need of a healer themselves?

A chill colder than the wind in Nentoado fills my body. It stiffens my muscles, vibrates along my skin, and turns my heart into a rock. Varan is going to pay for this. He left these people—all too loyal to the "Miriseh" to abandon the city—without the basics they needed to survive. It infuriates me, but it's terrifying, too. If this is how he's willing to treat his devotees, what will he do to the andofume if we lose this fight?

"Why the nursery?" Rai's question is so quiet I barely hear it.

I wonder the same thing. We've always hidden from storms in the undercity before. Here, winds rattle the shutters and rain seeps through the cracks. There's no protection up here from lightning or tornados. Everyone is so weak. Why wouldn't they stay in the caves beneath us?

"It's closest to the kitchen," one ahdo answers.

Someone else nods. "And parts of the undercity flooded."

"And it gets worse with the tides," another adds. "It's...it's been bad."

The first sighs. "We should've left moons ago."

I agree, but Reeka speaks before I can say anything, anger ringing in each word. "I doubt Denhitra would've taken you all in after what you did to us."

Several frown. More look away, but not fast enough to hide the shame on their faces.

My heart lurches. "What did they do?"

Reeka had been so vague before. I'd nearly forgotten about it with so much else on my mind, but now every nuance of that conversation rises in my mind—the hesitations, the imprecise descriptions, and my certainty that Reeka was holding something important back.

"Show me," I demand, knowing there's something to see even if I don't know what it could be. For a second, I almost think she'll say no. Then Reeka sighs, the anger on her face replaced by deep grief, and she nods toward the door.

I follow her out. Sanii, Yorri, and Sotra come, too. Tessen's group is coming up the street when we leave, several dozen ahdo walking behind him with their hands bound. The ahdo and their guards head into the nursery, but Tessen turns and follows us toward the center of the city.

Memory threatens to overwhelm everything else when the bikyo-ko comes into sight. I was named a nyshin here. I said goodbye to Yorri. I discovered the lie of his death. Each image feels ancient. It's also as fresh as what happened today.

I expect to head around the front of the building, to the courtyard and the main entrance, but instead Reeka heads for the back and the saishigi door. The past gets stronger the instant I see that door. It's as though everything I've learned and gained in the past six moons is being eroded. I feel like I'm unbecoming with each step, falling back into the girl I was a year ago. Before losing Yorri. Before seeing Ryogo. Before learning from Soanashalo'a. Before discovering Kaisuama. Before imbibing immortality.

We open the door, walk down the short hall, and open the door to the saishigi core.

Heat and a rancid, inescapable smell smacks me in the face.

Tessen curses and stumbles back a step. It's hard not to do the same. I expected it to be hotter than the desert at midday, but that *smell*. I rush forward, praying to be wrong. Then the core comes into view.

The usual layer of dirt, broken plants, and leftover food is missing. There are only bodies. I put my hand over my mouth and swallow my rising bile as my pulse picks up, sending blood racing through my veins and desosa tingling across my skin. Ten. Twenty. I stop counting and look away when I realize I can't be sure where one carcass ends and the next begins. And they are carcasses, not bodies anymore. Not people. The skin is decaying, the muscle is withered and foul. Where bones are visible, they're stained by the meat rotting around them. Bits of remaining cloth and leather tell us at least six were yonin, but I don't know enough about the breakdown of a body to guess at when they died—before Varan abandoned Itagami or after.

The urge to vomit rises again. I barely suppress it. From the noise behind me, Tessen lost that fight. For the last few weeks, I've been worried about what I was leaving the Ryogans to face under Varan's control, but clearly, I should've been more worried about leaving Itagami under its own control.

Sotra clears her throat. "The people who ordered this are gone."

"Gone." I repeat the word, trying to understand. The good of the many always came first. If someone ordered rations stolen from the yonin, they were breaking one of our most important laws. If they did *this* with the dead, they'd lost all grip on every good part of being Itagamin. "Did you kill them?"

There's only the slightest hesitation before Sotra nods. "They were a danger to all of us. But we didn't put them here. We threw their bodies over the north wall."

And into the ocean below.

I close my eyes, relief, grief, and surprise all swirling in my chest. How many did she have to kill to break that pattern? Had I known any of them? I don't want to believe anyone I knew could be responsible for this, but chances are I would've recognized them. They would've been higher ranking ahdo. I would've interacted with them at least once.

I'd worried that, no matter how easily most of the city surrendered in exchange for food, I'd still have to deal with whoever had driven Reeka and the others into the merciless, storm-ridden desert, but Sotra already did.

Unable to bear it anymore—the sight or the smell of this place—I order everyone out and close the door behind us. The people who did this are gone, so I must focus on other things. Like adjusting the plan. Originally, I'd intended to have those who surrendered help fortify our position and set things in place. Despite how badly the ahdo need to redeem themselves for the atrocity behind us, most can barely stand. Forget working.

I look at Sotra. "Make sure everyone eats, and then you all should rest."

"And what are you going to do?" she asks.

"Prepare to kill the Miriseh," I say as I brush past them and out into the stormy streets.

TWENTY-FIVE

The next twelve hours test my ability to be everywhere at once. The garakyus keep me in contact with my squad and spread my orders across the city, but the work is constant. Even *my* stamina is strained. It's worse for Reeka and everyone who carried pounds of stone through the desert and the ahdo who, despite a full meal, aren't anywhere close to recovered. I don't want them collapsing when the battle actually comes, so I split the hardiest into squads and rotate each out after six hours of work. They place the cannons and, once the ishiji turn the stones into shards, pack them into balls that can be blasted from the cannons. I offer the same rest cycle to the immortals and my squad, but none take it.

While I work alongside the others, my mind circles endlessly around the concept of immortals. Is that even what I am? If anyone is truly immortal it's Zonna, Yorri, and the others born with it in their blood, but what should I call myself? Miriseh is an ugly word now. Bobasu is for those exiled from Ryogo. Andofume has become the word to describe those born to immortality. The rest of us don't fit anywhere.

We've been working for three rotations straight when I finally stop in the center of the courtyard to look at the progress we've made. It doesn't seem like enough. I'd hoped the cannons' dark metal would camouflage them, but it's just reflective enough to gleam with each flash of lightning, and those bursts of illumination mark the weapons' massive silhouettes out in glaring clarity on the roofs and in the alleys. Which means I need to hide them.

When Tessen stops next to me, I turn toward him. "What are we missing?"

"I'm not sure, but I *am* worried he'll notice the changes too soon." Lines of worry spread out from the corners of his eyes. "Varan knows the city very well."

Varan also knows we came here ahead of him, and we can't let him see we made it inside Itagami before him. It's probably one of the reasons he moved Yorri so far inland—even if I had come into the city looking for him, I would've had to leave it again almost immediately.

Wardstones are going to be necessary if we're going to fool him. Over the past few moons, we've used wardstones, lost them, made more, and lost more, and now I honestly cannot remember the number we have left. I need more, and they need to be katsujo-strength.

I use the garakyu to call Yorri and Wehli. But even if they can get me and as many crystals as we can carry to the katsujo faster than they've ever run before, do we have the time? The thrum of panic in the air is getting stronger with each hour that passes. There are too many unknowns. It's like being in a footrace and not ever seeing the opponent. Or the finish line.

Yorri arrives first, Sanii on his back, and Wehli isn't far behind. It only takes a few minutes to explain to them—and Tessen—what I need. Sanii and Yorri share a long look, but neither of them protests the plan despite knowing it will separate them for a short while again.

A brutally high-pitched scream pierces the air; it's instantly swallowed by a *crack* of thunder. I reinforce my wards. My hand falls to the hilt of my zeeka. My skin tingles with energy as I search for a source.

"Here, he's here, they're here!" Arinri bursts out of the bikyo-ko, yanking at her hair. "Have to run before he comes. It'll be too late once he's here. On the water and coming closer and closer and closer and—"

On the water. Which means he isn't on Shiara yet.

I press my hand over the boruikku anyway, flooding desosa through the magic of the symbol and locating him myself. Closer than he was before. Not at Shiara's shoreline yet.

Blocking out Arinri's screams, I try to think. If she sensed what was happening in Denhitra from the valley she'd been trapped in... I pull out the garakyu and connect to Zonna. When he answers, I ask, "How far is Denhitra from where we found Yorri?"

"At least fifty miles, but definitely not more than seventy. Why?"

"Because Varan's within her range now, and we know her powers reach at least that far."

Zonna swears—in several languages. "I guess we should be glad the wind isn't blowing straight south. It'll take him at least a full day to sail that distance."

"Bellows. I knew we were running out of time, but I wanted at least twice that to finish."

"When have things ever gone the way we want?" Tessen's tone bleeds sarcasm.

I huff half a laugh and then explain things to Zonna. "I'm going to gather as many crystals as I can from the undercity, then Yorri and Wehli are going to help me get them to the katsujo and back."

Zonna's gaze turns wary. "You'll be cutting it close, even with their help."

"I know." But it's the only way to surprise Varan inside the city he literally carved from the ground. "You, Sanii, and Tessen have to oversee things while we're gone."

"Then go. And hurry back." Zonna closes the connection.

"Do you still remember how to pick a lock?" I ask Yorri.

"Do *you*?" He seems honestly curious. "You never wanted to learn in the first place. Too afraid of getting in trouble."

"Trying too hard to keep you out of it," I correct. "For all the good that did. But yes, I remember. It's proved useful more than once."

A broad smile spreads across Yorri's lips, delight I haven't seen in too long kindling in his eyes. "Well, show me how good you've gotten, then."

Every minute matters, so Yorri offers me his back. I climb on, pressing my legs against his sides, looping my arms around his shoulders, and hiding my face against his neck. I've been carried by him before; it's disorienting. I don't want to watch the city blur past as he runs. The rush of wind in my ears is bad enough.

I spend several minutes trying not to flinch as we shift unpredictably, but it's worth it. This trip should've taken five times as long. In moments, Yorri is gently disengaging my stranglehold on him. I take a second to clear my head before I reach for my lockpicks—a set of bent metal pieces

Yorri created years ago. He smiles when he sees them, reaching out to touch their leather wrapping before he steps back to watch.

"This is never not impressive," Wehli says as I stick the tools into the heavy lock.

Yorri is silent until the lock clicks open. "Bellows, Khya, you *did* pay attention."

"You really thought I didn't?" I frown and push the door open, bothered by the comment. Wehli, after a quick look between the two of us, ducks his head and moves into the room.

"You always humored my oddities, but that's what you were doing. Humoring. If you'd had the choice, we would've been running extra drills every day instead of spending half our limited free time stealing scraps of metal for me to play with." Yorri's words sting, but his smile is full of exasperated affection. "Don't pretend I'm wrong."

I won't, but I don't know what to say now. Yorri walks into the room, opening the large pack he brought and filling it with crystals. Guilt settles on my chest like a heavy hand as I follow him in. I had always pushed him to be stronger. Better. Smarter. Faster. I wanted him to live up to my plans and expectations, and I rarely asked what he wanted. I assumed he wanted the same things.

After a while, I notice the glances he's sending me. His frown gets deeper each time. I focus on the crystals, but once we can't fit any more in our bags, I have to face Yorri again.

I heft my pack onto my back, wincing at the sharp corners that dig into my spine, and then I help Yorri strap his bag to his chest. When I take a breath, apologies and explanations planned and ready, Yorri cuts me off and says, "You've changed more than I realized."

My words fall away, suddenly useless.

"I think I might like you even better this way, but I don't know you yet." He smiles, and it looks like an apology. "A year ago, what I said before would've made you laugh, not make your eyes go dark. It'll take me a while to figure out where the new fault lines are."

Fault lines. It's an interesting choice of words, one that—unexpectedly—almost makes me laugh. That's what I was trying to figure out—fault, and how much of it is mine.

"We'll worry about all that later," I make myself say. Then, loudly enough for Wehli to hear, too, I ask "Are you ready to go?"

In answer, Yorri turns, allowing me to cling to his back again. The crystals' additional weight doesn't seem to bother him. Then again, it wouldn't—he's kynacho, even if he hasn't yet had much of a chance to test the limits of his strength or his speed. Today's task should be easy. Hopefully for Wehli, too. The loss of his arm had imbalanced him for a while, but he's recovered well since then and is almost back to his old speed. Still, the ground is uncertain, and visibility will be bad. If either of them takes a poorly placed step, it'll hurt. We'll recover, but we'll lose time. And it'll *hurt*.

When we reach Itagami's main gate, ahdo guards open it for us. Then, we're off. Although I ensure my wards are up, I don't watch our trip. Every time I travel like this, I like it less and less. I keep my face tucked into Yorri's shoulder and don't shift until I can feel the katsujo's energy buzzing in the air and Yorri's pace is slowing down.

When we stop in the cave Miari had found, it takes a few seconds for me to be certain my legs will hold. I drop my pack to the ground as soon as I'm stable and begin laying the stones along the cave floor where the katsujo's energy is strongest. I'm nearly finished emptying the third bag before I remember the warning I need to give them before I start working. "Don't let me lose track of time."

"I've rarely been able to stop you from doing anything, but I'll try." Yorri attempts a smile, but he flinches when a percussive boom of thunder makes the stone rumble around us. Inside Itagami's walls, he barely seemed to notice the storm. This must feel too much like the valley. He pulls himself together quickly, his forced smile returning.

I nod, trying not to worry. It's okay. I can do this alone. I don't need anyone else with the ability to navigate the powerful currents of energy. I won't get lost in its pull. If I do, I'll have to hope that Yorri is strong enough to pull me out.

Sitting down over the strongest point of the katsujo, I grip the desosa and begin to work. Nearly four hundred crystals of varying sizes surround me. I can't simply shove power into them. They'll burst if they're filled too fast, so I weave a thread of power through one and into the next and the next. Eventually they're all connected by one long thread. I push desosa along the path, and it bleeds off along the way as each crystal absorbs a portion of the power.

It's not enough. These wards must hold Varan inside the trap. They must protect my friends and everyone risking their lives to fight alongside me, as well as the city we're trying to reclaim. I can't watch Sagen sy Itagami collapse like Jushoyen. I need more power.

I work and keep working, sinking deeper into the katsujo until I'm floating in white light. The desert and the storm and everything else are obliterated by the burning brilliance of the katsujo's glow and the purity of my focus. This must be finished, and it must be perfect.

Perfect. Perfect. Must protect. Must save. Make it perfect or it'll be your fault if they die.

There's a whine in the air. It's harsh and getting louder. Louder. It hurts.

I pull more power from the katsujo, guiding the flow through my web.

The noise gets louder and higher until it's a dagger through my ear.

Crack. A flash of light, red in the whiteness of the desosa. Shards slice my skin. I flinch.

It doesn't end. *Crack. Crack. Crack.* Another flash of light each time. Sharp lines of pain slice across my arms, my chest, my face.

I pull more power.

Pressure on my shoulder and an inexorable weight keeping me on the ground. Words in a whisper, barely audible under the aggravating, painful tone.

"Let it go, Khya!"

I gasp. My eyes snap open. My connection to the katsujo shatters. All that beautiful light falls away. I nearly fall with it, but arms wrap around me, holding me up and helping me reconnect with my body. I slowly remember where I am and who I'm with.

It's strange coming out of it this time. Different. My mind didn't split away like it has before, but it still takes several minutes to remember how to move, how to breathe without thinking about every inhale, and how to make sounds that are actually words.

And how to understand Yorri's increasingly frantic words. "It's past time. Blood and rot, Wehli, we might have to find a way to strap her to my back if she doesn't wake up soon!"

"At least the rot-ridden stones stopped exploding." Wehli's voice trembles, snagging my attention. It's hard to unsettle him anymore. "She's not hurt other than the scratches, is she?"

"I'm here. It's fine. I'm…" I force my tired body to move, sitting up and blinking in hopes it'll make the ground stop shifting. "How long?"

"Hours. Too long." The muscles in Yorri's jaw jump as he clenches his teeth. "I was already thinking about interrupting when your crystals started trying to kill us. We heard from Tessen. Varan's almost here."

Fear sparks through my body like fire. The wardstones are finished, but my work isn't. I grab the closest wardstone. It's so full of power it's nearly vibrating. That's what the whine was—the crystals reaching their limit. I'd been so deep in the katsujo, I lost sight of the work. If Yorri hadn't pulled me out, we might've lost more than just a handful of the stones.

Carefully, I reach for a thin thread of power and wind a web through the stones again. Yorri takes my hand as soon as I offer it. Wehli is harder to convince, but as soon as he does I push a tiny particle of Yorri's and Wehli's essence into the wardstones. *Don't hurt them*, I tell the stones. *Protect these two.*

As soon as I'm sure they can touch the crystals without getting a sharp, painful shock, I release their hands and stand. Thankfully, my balance is almost back to normal. We quickly scoop up the stones, pile them back into our bags, and prepare to leave.

Whatever caution Yorri and Wehli had on the trip out is gone now. Yorri runs so fast I barely feel his feet hit the ground. We're in no danger this time. The wardstones' power makes it as easy as blinking to shield us. The wind barely touches us. The only water I feel is what Yorri kicks up as we blur across the plains.

"The watchtower fires are still lit." Yorri's words rumble through his body. I feel them more than I hear them. It's enough to make me look up.

Before we left, Tessen promised to douse the two watchtower fires over the gate if anything had gone wrong. The shifting firelight spilling from the narrow windows is still there, and an anxious knot in my chest unties. We're not too late.

"We were starting to worry you wouldn't make it back in time," one guard says once the gate is closed behind us.

"Tessen's on the north wall," the other adds before I can ask. "He wanted you to join him as soon as you got back."

"Go." Yorri nudges me north.

I cast a look at the bags. "I still have work to do."

Yorri hooks his fingers under my strap and pulls. "We'll get them in place. Trust me with this, Khya. I can do it."

My heart lurches. "I do trust you. Bellows, Yorri. For a long time you were the *only* person I trusted."

Which, if the stillness that settles over him and the instant of blank surprise on his face are any indication, he never realized before. But there's no time to deal with this now. I pull him in for a hug, one he returns so tightly I think he leaves bruises, and then I shove him toward the courtyard. "I'll come help soon. And make sure no one else touches them!"

He takes my bag and then Yorri and Wehli bolting toward the center of the city. I follow as fast as my legs can carry me, heading the same way despite the knot of worry driving me toward Tessen. The progress that's been made in the courtyard is better than I'd feared. Cannons sit on every other rooftop along the main road and every rooftop surrounding the courtyard. They're also hidden in the shadows of most alleyways. On the dais of the bikyo-ko, Rai is coordinating a group carrying small bags out to every cannon—probably either black powder or the stone shards—while Soanashalo'a and Sanii are working on something on a nearby roof. Either way, seeing it all settles at least one worry. Varan may be almost here, but we're almost ready for him, too. All I need is the time to finish the trap that will bury him in the consequences of his own choices.

The thought sends me sprinting up the north wall steps. I nearly get blown off my feet as soon as I reach the top, even with my wards in place. The wind howls in from over the ocean. I have to push my ward into the outer edges of the wall and dome it above my head before the pressure finally stops. The wind is still screaming, but it can't touch me anymore.

The stairwell I came up is directly between two watchtowers. There are several people in both, but I don't see Tessen until one of the ahdo gestures to the left. I jog that direction, spotting Tessen easily once I'm closer. He's a spot of stillness in the middle of constant motion, watching the ocean through the tower's narrow, protected windows.

"What's happened, Tessen?" I stop close by, looking at his face instead of into the storm.

"They'll land soon. Arinri is so scared she won't leave the undercity." He glances at me, a tense smile on his face. "I was worried you wouldn't be back in time, oh deadly one."

I almost wasn't. I keep those words inside my head as I lightly grip his arm. As soon as I touch him, his rigid posture eases. He closes his eyes and leans into my hand, and I find myself thinking of our last conversation about the sumai. He spent the whole time I was gone worried about me, worried—despite how little can hurt me—that I might truly be gone.

Tessen covers my fingers with his, still watching the horizon. "I hope whoever's with him is ready for what's waiting here."

"I doubt Varan would risk bringing anyone back who doesn't already know about Imaku. Anyone who knows that truth deserves whatever might happen today."

"Let's hope you're right; we're officially out of time."

I hold my breath, peering through the dark storm and searching for any sign of ships. I nearly give up the search. In this Kujuko-cursed storm, a ship could be about to crash into Shiara and I still wouldn't see it. Then a plume of fire rises into the sky, thick bursts that pulse upward and then dissipate into steam. It illuminates all the ships. Ship*s*. White sails billow over the hulking forms of three large vessels.

"What is that?"

"The signal." Tessen's body is taut and his words clipped. "After you left, we got more details from the ahdo. This is Varan checking in with the guards, asking for the all-clear."

"And he believes they're too loyal to betray him." I smile. "Are we going to answer?"

Some of his tension eases. "Yes."

At his order, kasaiji in the northern watchtowers send flares out over the ocean. Immediately, the vessels veer west. I lose sight of them, but Tessen tracks their path.

"They're on the beach," Tessen says, and I can guess exactly where—a strip not far to the west that's partially protected by a rock wall. Varan stood there once and tried to drag my squad back to land. It's where Daitsa, Thelin, and Keili died.

I shake off the memories and focus on the landscape. From there, they'll likely take the path along the cliff, and Tessen should be able to watch their progress. "I have to go, but let me know as soon as you can see Varan."

"Like you let me know you were on your way back from the katsujo?" Before I can retort, he nudges me away, his eyes never leaving the ships anchoring close to shore. "Keep your garakyu out. I'll tell you if I see anything useful."

"Okay. How much time do you think we have?"

"An hour. Maybe." His gaze flicks to meet mine, and despite how unshakably calm he's seemed, there's an unsettling amount of worry in his eyes. "Be careful, Khya."

"You too." I don't want to turn away from him, but I can't stay. The first step is hard. Momentum carries me forward until I'm sprinting down the stairs and through the empty streets.

These are paths I've traveled so many times. I've always had to dodge people or carts. Not today. Most people are already in position, and the few still moving are heading toward the western wall.

Sanii is waiting in the center of the courtyard, nervously shifting as ey watches Chirida and several tyatsu work on one of the cannons. When I stop next to em, Sanii asks, "Are you sure you can hide everything?"

"Yes." I can feel the buzz of the wardstones Yorri and Wehli spread through the city. It's like they're waiting for me to bring the power simmering inside them to life. I reach out and activate them. The cannons and everyone working on them disappear. "Can you sense the wardstones?"

Ey closes eir eyes to concentrate. Overhead, the storm rages. Flashes of lightning from different points of the sky cast conflicting shadows on eir sharp face. Then eir eyes open, expression radiating grim satisfaction. "They won't sense a thing."

The garakyu I slipped into my pocket vibrates against my waist. I draw it out and Tessen is there, quickly proclaiming, "He's here. Varan and two other bobasu are at the center of the line. I think I see two others, but it's hard to get a look at faces."

Relief sucks the tension out of my body. I let my chin drop to my chest and revel in the feeling before giving a signal that ripples through the city—final positions. Then, before I sever the connection, I give one last order. "Hurry up, Tessen. You know where to find me."

I use the garakyu and reach out to Yorri and the others next. Everything is as ready as we can make it, according to them. There's only one more problem left. I have less than half an hour to solve it.

Yorri and Wehli placed some stones in rings encircling the bikyo-ko, others are surrounding cannons, and more line roofs around the courtyard. The wardstones give me access to power, but I don't know how to separate them in my mind when they weren't attached to individual people. When I send my power out, it slides into all of them. I've taught myself how to do a lot with wardstones in the past year. However, I haven't yet learned how to simultaneously do different things with different groups. There must be a way. I figured out how to attune the crystals to specific people, so I can figure out how—*oh*.

I learned soon after I made my first wardstone that a person's energy has a tone to it that makes me think of colors. If I code each of the stones to shine like a color in my mind, I might be able to direct my power with the accuracy I need.

So long as I have enough time to get to them all.

I run for the bikyo-ko, sprinting up the stairs and then climbing up to the roof. There, in a perfect line, are twelve wardstones sunk into the stone. I place my hand on two and twist the energy running through the row until the sense of it shifts. Somehow, it feels red.

I paint the crystals on each roof red. I choose yellow for the smallest of the rings surrounding the courtyard, the same shade as the desert sun. The second one becomes the deep green of leaves on a Ryogan tree. Last and largest of the three? Pale blue, the color the sky used to be. When I'm done, Itagami glows like a mural, but only in my mind.

I race back up the bikyo-ko steps, through the double doors, up to the third floor, and over to a window overlooking the courtyard. Settling in to wait, I pull my second garakyu out. As soon as I activate it, colors swirl inside and multiple voices rise from the globe. Sanii, Soanashalo'a, Miari, Etaro, and several of the ahdo will send me information through garakyus of their own, like we did in Atokoredo. It's nearly funny; the lessons I learned in Ryogo are what will—*Kaisubeh willing*—help me defeat Varan. By taking my brother, Varan ultimately armed me with everything I need to destroy him.

"They're less than half a mile northwest, Khya." The report comes in from Otsyni, one of the ahdo stationed on the wall, an uniku known for her exceptionally sharp vision.

"We are in position, Khya," Soanashalo'a assures me.

I run my thumb along the curve of the glass. Varan will have riuku mages looking for anything out of the ordinary. Looking for *us*. Itagami, however, has never been breached. Varan thinks he's safe inside these walls. Today, I'm going to prove him wrong.

"I count ten squads," comes the report from Rai. "At least two hundred twenty."

"They don't seem suspicious yet," Otsyni says through the garakyu.

And no one in those squads seems to have figured out how to use a ward to stop the wind, so their progress is so much slower than I expected. The constant updates from Otsyni almost make it worse. A third of a mile out. A quarter. An eighth. Every time a voice rings through the garakyu, my heart clenches. I hold my breath. I'm waiting for the first sign of things going wrong, listening for the moment the plan falls to pieces around me.

Then Otsyni says, "They're at the bottom of the path, Khya."

Relief and fear clash in my chest, the collision sending sparks of energy down my arms until it feels like there's lightning in my fingertips.

"You in place, little brother?" I ask through the open connection.

"We're watching your back, don't worry." He, Sanii, and squads of Denhitrans are one floor below, guarding me. "Just don't start anything I can't get you out of. Even I have limits."

I laugh, mostly because I know that's what he wants, but my mind is anxiously churning. This is our chance to make this city ours for the first time. So much could go wrong, but oh what might be possible if we somehow get this right.

On my signal, drummers raise their mallets and begin to play. The sound echoes through the city. Each percussive thud bleeds into the next until it's like one constant peal of thunder. This is the beat played during the bigger, yearly celebrations, specifically during the ceremony recognizing the leaders and celebrating all they've done for Itagami. To Varan, this rhythm should seem like a sign of his citizens' joy at his safe return.

To us, it's a message—the next phase of the plan is about to begin.

"They're halfway up the path." Otsyni speaks so quietly I barely hear her. "Get ready."

"'Get ready,'" Tessen mutters as he joins me. "How much more ready can we be?"

"Let's hope that answer doesn't matter." I reach for his hand. He twines his fingers through mine, but his smile is strained. I don't think my smile is any more believable.

"We've made it this far." He seems to force resolution into his voice. "What's facing Varan next to everything else?"

Literally the end of everything we ever believed in our whole lives, and the start of something unknown. I keep the thought in my head.

Closing my eyes and hoping the Kaisubeh are listening, I beg for one more thing: *Please don't let me make things any worse than they are, than they were, or than they ever should be.*

There's a clang, and then the familiar grinding crank of Itagami's massive iron gates. Otsyni warns us they're closing in, but I don't need it. I can see them.

A cheer rises from the wall. I smile. I'd told the ahdo to act as if this truly was a triumphant return. Cheer, I instructed. Take their bags, gear, and weapons. They clearly took me at my word.

The iron gates close. The lock falls into place with a *thunk*. It's the next signal. I find the crystals that shine sky blue, raising the ward and locking them in with us. My ward is strong. To anyone who can sense the desosa, it should be loud and bright—like drums or a bonfire on a clear night.

Come on, I silently urge. *You know I'm here now. Find me. Hunt me down. I dare you.*

Varan bellows an order. His force races toward the bikyo-ko. Maybe he's aiming for the weapons hidden in the armory here. Maybe he's hoping to escape through the saishigi core under the building. Maybe he knows this is where I'm hiding. I hold my breath, barely able to restrain myself from reacting. Too soon. I need to wait for the signal.

The drumbeat shifts. I raise the green ward, and then I lean out the window to watch as the front line slams into the invisible wall. The impact vibrates under my skin. Behind them, the others skid, barely stopping themselves in time.

All of them are trapped. There's a barrier at their backs, reinforcing Itagami's wall, and another separating them from the bikyo-ko. Like cornered teegras, they lash out. Jets of flame, bolts of lightning, and blocks of stone all slam into my wards. Each attack makes me flinch, the impacts like tiny embers landing on my skin. I endure it gladly, especially when several nyshin try to smash through the buildings on either side of the street. As though I hadn't thought of that already. Not even the ishiji can do more than dent the stone. In the middle of the thrashing crowd is a spot of stillness. Varan looks through the ward, staring up at the bikyo-ko.

I wish I had Tessen's sight—I want to see the expression on Varan's face.

I reach for the lines of red crystals on the roofs, but I don't create a ward, I create the illusion of force—dozens of Itagamins with weapons drawn. Most of the figures are impossible to identify, their faces covered by an atakafu, but the illusion on the bikyo-ko is different. When Varan points at those figures, I smile—he believes that's me. I can physically *feel* his fury crackling and flaring like it's affecting the very desosa. I know Varan would rend me to pieces if he could, tear my body and soul into a million parts, put me back together, and then do it all again just for the pleasure of watching me suffer.

Is this what Tessen senses when he's reading emotions? I don't like it. It burns.

I focus on the green ring of wardstones, the ones keeping Varan out, and shove more desosa in just as Varan's shouted orders launch a new barrage of strikes. Faster and faster the onslaught comes until sparks and ripples fill the air.

My barrier falls. The courtyard is overrun. On the roofs, the fighters retreat. It looks like a defeat in every single way. Until I activate my last ward.

The protective dome grows from the yellow crystals, encasing the bikyo-ko and reaching deep into the mesa. This will not be another Jushoyen. Varan will *not* destroy Sagen sy Itagami.

I shift the illusions on the roofs. More fighters. The image of an army is meant to keep him from noticing the actual fighters approaching from every direction, blocking the exits and preparing to destroy him. Then, I raise my garakyu and give one last order.

Varan bellows again.

Tessen screams a warning.

Too late. All my wards shatter. It's like someone reached into my chest and tore my magic out of my soul. I feel shattered, and the pieces I have left slice when I try to hold them.

An arrow pierces my arm. A blast of fire smashes into the bikyo-ko, so close the heat singes my skin through the window. I barely feel either. The loss of my magic overwhelms everything else. Tears stream down my face. I gasp for breath around the cry of agony I can't stop. I'm screaming. Tessen bellows so loud his voice cracks. Dozens, maybe hundreds of voices fill the city, ringing with fear and pain. That is what death sounds like.

Run, I want to order everyone, but I dropped the garakyu. The tips of my fingers brush the glass, and it rolls away. I'm sobbing. Tears course down my face.

Get up! I order my failing, pain-wracked body. *You have to make this work. Get up, get up, get up!*

Desosa rushes into my body, but whatever Varan did has left a hole at the center of me no amount of power seems able to fill or heal. Every motion sends icy agony shooting through me. I manage to rise a few inches before my elbows buckle and I crash. I try and fail again. And again. Tessen is a few feet away, curled into a tight, trembling ball. The sight of him in such agony sends a fresh flood of tears down my cheeks, and anger adds a small measure of strength into my arms.

"People are coming, Tessen. We've got to go." My voice is harsh and hoarse. Tessen doesn't move. The voices are louder, and outside people are screaming. People *I* was supposed to protect are dying. I made them believe in me, and I doomed the mortals to death and the andofume to endless pain because I thought immortality was all I needed to win against Varan. I'm not any better or smarter than I was a year ago. All I am is harder to kill.

A hand grabs my throat, gripping with enough force and strength to lift me off the ground. My lungs burn. My vision goes white on the edges except for the black sparks that ring the only thing in focus—Varan, his dark eyes gleaming with rage.

"You are a speck. You should be nothing, and yet you've caused me so many problems." His grip tightens. I want to kick and scratch at his wrists until he lets me go, but even blinking is hard. My eyes are stuck open, my attention locked on Varan's face. "Die knowing I'm going to make your brother suffer for everything you've done."

I can't breathe. I can't move. I can barely see. But I start laughing. Wheezing and shaking, I sound like I'm dying and feel like knives are slicing the inside of my lungs. Still, I laugh, and I can't stop.

I hadn't been sure until now, but there it is. He doesn't know. He doesn't realize that we didn't just find Kaisuama, we recreated the susuji and *used* it. He doesn't know, and I can't tell him, and none of this is funny. I can picture too clearly what will happen once he realizes he doesn't just have Yorri to take his rage out on; for as long as he chooses not to use the weaponized Imaku stone to slit my throat he has me and everyone I love. Even as I wonder how long I'll last under Varan's control, I *cannot stop laughing.*

Varan's grip tightens. Darkness engulfs my vision. I can't breathe, can't think, can't feel my hands to fight him off. A loud, terrified voice in my mind screams, *You're dying!* But I'm not. I hang on the cusp of death, surrounded by shadows spotted with dancing colors.

Until something slams into me. I fall, but my airways open. Sparks burst in my peripheral vision as I finally suck in air. Varan screams curses, his normally resonant voice cracking.

"Run!" Tessen orders.

I cough, breathing too fast and shallow as arms close around me, lifting me up. Yorri. Air rushes past as he runs. I force another breath through my bruised and battered throat, and my vision clears a little. Just as Yorri bursts out the front of the bikyo-ko and straight into a battle.

My allies are blocking the exits my shattered ward left open, keeping the enemies in place. We're moving so fast it's hard to see more than flashes. The gleam of an iron blade lit by a jet of powerful fire. The spray of dark blood mixing with the crystalline drops of rain. Shouts in three languages overlap, all carrying the same taint of fear. Denhitrans, Itagamins, and Ryogans work alongside one another, facing off against Varan's warrior mages. My army is larger, yet the nyshin outmatch and overpower so many of my soldiers. My people are dying. Fast.

This wasn't supposed to happen. Battle was a last recourse only if everything else went wrong. That's not why we're in this position. This is happening because our plan relied on *me*, and Varan found a way to take me out of the fight.

But if he thinks I'm the only threat here, he *still* hasn't learned what he's up against.

"Gara—" I cough. My voice is barely more than rasp and breath. "Garakyu."

"Bellows. You can barely talk and you still give orders." But even as he says it, Yorri turns for a narrow alley, punching a nyshin so hard they fly back and land several feet away.

My first try to activate the globe is so garbled it fails. I try again. Again. The fourth time, colors swirl inside the glass.

Rai's face appears, lax with relief. "*Oh,* you're not dead!"

"Fire, Rai!" My voice is harsh—it's been several minutes, but I still can't take a breath that doesn't feel like trying to swallow the spines of a kicta plant.

"Blood and rot, I'm *working* on it, Khya." Somehow, she looks concerned despite the frustration clearly laced through her words. "Something happened, and almost everyone just *dropped*. Most of the other kasaiji are busy, and—"

"Give me that!" The image jerks. Soanashalo'a appears, Sanii's face barely visible over her shoulder. "We need two minutes. Sanii and I are working on a spell. And some of our friends are in the courtyard."

Our friends, she says. Everyone who was with me when I first met her. All of them, except Rai, are as vulnerable as Varan to the shards of Imaku stone about to blast down on them. Can I really bring myself to order the final blow knowing it will kill my own, too?

The ground trembles. My stomach drops. "I don't think we have two minutes."

"Do your wardstones still have power?" Yorri asks.

"I—" Blood and rot, I haven't checked. I do now, and there they are—the pure white of the uncolored crystals, and the red, green, blue, and yellow rings mix like the strangest of sunrises. The wardstones' power feels nearly as far away as a sunrise, but it's there. Waiting.

The shaking under my feet gets worse. Cracks form in the walls. One climbs up the building I'm bracing against. Time is running out.

Reaching for the rings of color, I touch the katsujo-fueled power at their cores and send it deep into Itagami, binding the layers of power into the city. Though the desosa jumps to obey, the effort of giving the order sends burning sparks of agony through my chest. Varan's attack scraped me raw from the inside out. This feels like falling into the salty ocean with thousands of open wounds, but the tremors shaking Itagami weaken.

My teeth are clenched so tight they creak. Pain sparks and flares through my muscles, but I clutch the desosa harder. I shove the garakyu into Yorri's hand. Forcing words out, I pray he understands. "Warn them. Find a way. They have one minute to get out. Then, fire."

He searches my face, seeming confused, then resigned determination wipes everything else away. I sag. He understands and immediately uses the active garakyu to relay the warning. When he's finished, I have one more request. "I need to see."

Though he mutters under his breath, Yorri picks me up and runs, shifting me to his back as we move. I force my muscles to grip him tight so his arms are free.

"Brace." His warning barely gives me enough time to tighten my hold before he puts on a burst of speed and leaps. His feet land on one wall. Pressing off hard, he lands on the opposite surface. He grabs a window ledge on the third floor; the impact of the sudden stop almost breaks my hold before he hauls himself up to the roof Rai, Sanii, and Soanashalo'a have been working from. Yorri carries me to the front corner and helps me sit down behind the low wall.

"Just stay behind your wardstones." His voice is harsh, but his hands are gentle.

"You had to carry me up." At least it's getting easier to talk. "Where can I go?"

Below, the city is consumed by chaos. Iron weapons slice through the air, their arcs cutting paths through the thick rain. Bursts of fire create billows of steam that obscure the view for precious seconds. Bodies lie where they fell, left to be trampled by those still fighting.

The battle is spreading, pushing past the borders of the courtyard and into the streets. Nyshin ishiji keep trying to crack the city open, but my wardstone web holds, the katsujo-fueled power strong enough to keep their magic from sinking in. We're running out of time. My allies—my friends—are falling because my wardstones may be holding Itagami together, but they can't do a thing to save them. Enemies are climbing the buildings to reach those firing arrows from above, and if they take control of the roofs, we'll lose the cannons. We have to fire, but so many of my friends are still down there.

"Can't you ward them?" Yorri asks.

"Against *that* rock? I don't know." Maybe on a good day. It feels like too much of a risk when even guiding the wardstones' desosa *hurts*.

"You could block the arrows. This might work, too." Soanashalo'a's voice shakes.

"*Might?* Blood and rot, no!" Rai swings around, furious. "Etaro is down there! You're not risking em on something you don't think will work." I try to protest, but she cuts me off. "Don't. I know that look! You're pretending you know what you're doing, and it'll kill them."

"I never promised we'd all live through this!" I shout at her. I regret the words instantly, heartache blooming when I see the shock in Rai's round eyes. I can't hold her gaze. Swallowing, I look down at the fighting as it spreads farther into the city. There has to be something I can do.

"Lo'a." I hold out my hand. She kneels at my side and slides her palm against mine, intertwining our fingers. As I tell her what I need, I miss Natani. He was a bolster, stable and strong, and a zoikyo's strength might be exactly what I need now. If I can't, at least I have Soanashalo'a.

"Rot take you all. I'm not waiting here for this to fail." Rai runs for the front of the building, grabs the ledge of the low wall, and launches herself over the side. I silently curse as she quickly climbs down the opposite building and safely drops to the ground.

"Yorri, go with her," I order. "Warn our people to run. Sanii, can you fire the cannon?"

Sanii flinches when Yorri drops into the fighting below, but nods. "Just tell me when."

"You are in the lead this time, Khya." Long strands of dark hair stick to Soanashalo'a's round face, their paths blending with the designs tattooed around her eyes. Those golden-brown eyes are absolutely sincere when she says, "Take what you need."

And I do. Drawing from her, I use the boruikku to find my squad. That connection lets me draw power from the wardstones—the magic inside myself is still broken, nothing but shards—and build a shield around everyone who followed me into immortality.

Stay safe, I beg as Yorri bodily lifts someone up and tosses them into an alley. Rai screams, blasting her path to Etaro clear with a column of fire so hot I feel it from across the courtyard. *Please stay safe, because there's no more time to run.*

"Now, Sanii!" I order as soon as my thin protections are in place.

Boom after shattering *boom* fills the city. The scent of sulphur and blood stings my nose. Stone shards pelt down like black raindrops, striking everyone. The mortals simply bleed. The bobasu are screaming. Rai throws herself on top of Etaro, slamming em to the ground and shielding em with flesh and fire. Those nyshin able to move do, backing away with fear-filled eyes. Their so-called immortals are dying before their eyes. Then shock turns into panic. They try to run. Closing my eyes and praying for my friends, I activate the second ring of wardstones—the one I'd let Varan think he broke—and trap everyone in the courtyard.

Cannons fire blast after blast. *Boom. Boom. Boom.* From the roofs, from the alleys, the blasts of stone and black powder shred skin and leave destruction behind.

"Khya!" Sanii's pointing west of the bikyo-ko.

What was once a cannon is a lump of twisted metal. Three people are fighting in the middle of the destruction, two against one. Their swords clash in a blur of silver. My heart stops when I realize who they are. Tessen and Nairo are battling Varan. And they're losing.

"Yorri!" I point as soon as his gaze snaps up to me. "Go!"

He sprints across the courtyard in a blur, shoving people aside when they don't move out of his way fast enough. Near the building, he leaps, grabbing on to the ledge of the second-floor window and quickly climbing the rest of the way. On the roof, Varan's sword slashes Nairo across the abdomen and shoves him off the roof, straight into the blasts of black rock still firing from every cannon. Tessen tries to stop our friend's fall. He's too late. The moment gives Varan the advantage. Screaming, he slices deep into Tessen's upraised arm and comes back an instant later, slashing across Tessen's throat.

"No!" I force myself to stand, desperate for a better view. Only Soanashalo'a's grip on my hand and my wards keeps me from faltering. Nairo is already lost, devoured by the pain of the stone shards' draining power, but Tessen must be okay. Please, Tessen, be okay.

Then Yorri is there. He moves with speed Varan can't match and strikes with strength Varan can't withstand. In seconds, Varan is weaponless. Exposed. Defeated. Yorri punches him in the stomach, catches him when he folds, and tosses him into the bloodstained courtyard.

I watch Varan twist and reach for something to slow his fall as he crashes to the ground. Sanii laughs and fires eir cannon again. Every working cannon fires again, too.

Varan is hit with hundreds of black stone shards. He bellows, the scream almost as loud as the cannon's blast. The rest of the bobasu have already collapsed into writhing heaps. Some have stopped moving entirely. Although he's bleeding badly and unsteady, somehow Varan forces himself to his feet and searches the roofs, glaring defiantly at us. Until his eyes meet mine. He falters. I'm alive, and he knows I shouldn't be. He'd all but crushed my throat.

Face flushed from either pain or fury, he runs toward my building. Yorri screams a warning, but he can't leave Tessen yet. I wave my hand, trying to tell them it's okay. Varan is coming, but he's already dying. Nothing and no one can save him now. All I have to do is keep myself, Soanashalo'a, and Sanii alive until Varan is too weak to move.

He lands only a few feet away, jaw clenched tight. Somehow, he's holding back the pain, but black lines are climbing up his throat. He rasps, "You..." but nothing else comes.

"Do you feel it? The Kaisubeh are taking back what you stole, Varan Heinansuto. You had your time. Now, it's our turn." I take a step closer, drawing power from the closest wardstones around me like a cloak. I risk letting go of Soanashalo'a's hand, leaning against the wall to keep my balance. I can't touch Varan—shards of stone are caught in his clothes and stuck in his skin—but I want to watch the spark of life in his eyes go out. "You built something beautiful here, but it was never enough for you because it wasn't what you thought you deserved. You could've had Shiara forever. You kept chasing Ryogo, though. Now, you have nothing."

He opens his mouth, but all that escapes is a long, pain-racked groan. His knees hit the ground, and then his hands. Tremors shake him. The black lines crossing Varan's face blister and burst as the desosa that's kept him alive for so long drains away.

Miriseh Varan, the immortal gatekeeper to the paradise of Ryogo, finally dies.

I brace myself on the low wall and let my head hang. The city has fallen quiet. Even the storm seems to have lost some of its fury. I can hear my heart pounding, and each breath scrapes like the air is full of sand, but Varan lies unmoving below me. I think he's dead.

Think, but don't believe. For most of my life, I believed in Varan's invincibility with the same implicit faith I had in sunrises and desosa. I've worked so hard to make this possible, yet even as I stare at his desiccated, motionless, unhealing body, I can't quite trust that we won. I'm responsible for the carnage covering the courtyard and the fear in the eyes of the nyshin crowding the edges of the square but I find myself watching for motion, for the smallest twitch of a muscle to prove Varan had been right all along and he truly is immortal.

Motion nearby makes me look up. Soanashalo'a is easing closer, her tan skin paler than usual and her eyes a little red rimmed, but otherwise fine. "Are you all right?"

"If it's really over, I will be." I turn back to the courtyard, irrationally afraid Varan won't be there. A small part of me is sure he'll somehow get to his feet and attack again. "Tell me it worked. Tell me it's over."

"He is not breathing. It is over." She rests her hand on my shoulder. "But whatever Varan did…I felt it, but it did not gut Sanii or me the way it seemed to drop Etaro and the other mages. Are you really okay?"

"I will be." If Varan is truly gone, everything is wonderful.

I put my hand over hers for a second before I force myself to straighten. The muscles along my spine feel tight enough to creak like old leather, but so much of the pain that hit me when Varan shattered my magic and tried to break my neck has already been soothed by the desosa pooling in my body. Soon, the only proof any of today happened will be the ash of the bodies we'll burn to feed to the land and the memories seared into our minds.

What worries me now is my magic. I managed to protect the others because of my wardstones and Soanashalo'a, but the energy I've felt at my core for years is still splintered and painful to pull power from. The blowback from every other time my wards shattered has only lasted minutes. Now, despite the desosa in the air, my power well is so cracked it can't seem to refill; desosa drains out of me as soon as I draw it in. It raises a quiet terror that this will be something even immortality can't heal.

But not even that fear can outweigh my relief. We don't have to run anymore.

The courtyard is too dangerous for my squad, so the andofume and the Itagamins who can skip a visit to the hishingu are working on identifying the dead. They separate the Denhitrans and Itagamins from the Ryogans, taking equal care with each. Names are only called out when they find a bobasu. I close my eyes, not even opening them when Tessen joins me, and listen to name after name. Four of the bobasu found. Five. Six.

Six, including Varan. Not seven. Elyini is missing.

"We knew it was a possibility," Tessen says. "He probably left her in charge on Ryogo."

And no matter how powerful an akuringu Arinri is, and no matter how much I boost the range of the garakyus, we can't reach across the ocean to find out what's happening there.

"She's only one. We'll find her." I look into his eyes and smile. It feels tired and uncertain, but it's genuine. "It's not like we don't have time."

For the first time in a year, I let myself take this moment and simply be. The wind doesn't seem to be gusting as hard as earlier, the flashes of lightning are far enough apart for darkness to settle between them, and the rain pouring down on me now feels cleansing rather than bruising, like it's washing away so many of the mistakes I've made and giving me a chance to start anew.

We won, and beginning today, I can create for Sagen sy Itagami the future I always believed we would have. All I can hope is that this victory didn't cost us too much.

TWENTY-SIX

Over one hundred eighty people are dead.

Nairo. Vysian. Reeka. Sotra. Nearly Etaro and Miari, too. They'd escaped the same fate by luck and by Rai's recklessness.

Miari dropped when the first cannon sounded, desperately trying to reshape stone to cocoon herself until the worst was over. My web of wards had still been in place, though, and she couldn't do it. She would've died if one of the kaigo hadn't tripped over her, falling across her and accidentally saving her from the shards. Even after Miari killed them, she stayed under the corpse until someone cleared a safe path for her to use.

Strangely, the same thing saved Etaro, only Rai shielded Etaro on purpose, and both were alive at the end. Wounded and angry at me for the order that killed three of our friends, but alive.

Collecting and containing every miniscule shard of Imaku stone will take time, probably days, but we can't leave the courtyard full of the dead for long, so while the mortal ishiji work on that, everyone else tends to bodies the battle left behind.

I wish I could help clean and prepare my clan for final rites, but all I can do is watch from a rooftop. The Denhitrans claim their dead when they arrive, and Chirida takes charge of the few Ryogan losses. Everyone who belonged to Itagami is wrapped in clean cloth and laid out in the courtyard. The bobasu are laid out on the dais of the bikyo-ko and left there for now.

I use the inner ring of wardstones to create a shield high above the courtyard to keep the rain away, and Rai and the other kasaiji light the pyres, sending plumes of smoke and coils of steam rising into the air. The smoke slides along the ward and out the open sides, dissipating into nothing. The questions filling the space between my ears aren't as easy to quell.

Who will sail back to Ryogo with us? Where should we land? What will draw Elyini in? How can we get the army to follow us to Shiara? How will we feed everyone on the trip back?

At first, planning the next step is simply a way to ignore the reality "winning" has left me facing—the devastation etched into Miari's and Wehli's faces, the sheer amount of blood that coated Itagami's stones, the times I turned to ask Reeka a question and remembered she'd fallen giving others the time to get away—but soon the work is being done in earnest. Waiting only gives events in Ryogo time to get worse.

The trip won't be easy, though. Before I can lead anyone across the ocean, I have to figure out how to feed those coming and everyone staying behind, who to leave in charge of Itagami while we're gone, and what to do once we get where we're going. Practicalities. Logistics. Constant questions. Even with the help of Soanashalo'a, Chirida, Shytari, and the Denhitran elders, it all seems endless.

"I'd be bored with all of this if it didn't keep me so busy," I mutter to Tessen on the second day spent mired in nothing but delegation and organization.

He laughs. "No, you wouldn't. You wanted to lead. You wanted people's respect. This is what happens when you get both, and there's no way you don't enjoy everyone coming to you because they think you'll have the answers. Because they want your opinion."

I scoff at him, but I soon have to admit he's right. People who once would've given me orders come to me to propose solutions, and they seem proud when I approve their plans. I do find myself liking it, especially since it's the only way I'm allowed to help.

My magic still hasn't healed, not completely.

It's strange to relax my vigilance after so many moons doing everything I could to keep my wards up even when I was sleeping, but now I can't create a shield without using wardstones. After the first few days, I don't even try. I don't reach for the desosa at all. Instead, I let it soak into my skin and slowly heal the cracks Varan's attack left on my core.

The few nyshin who survived the battle told me Varan had been working on a way to break my wards ever since Jushoyen. It was one of the reasons he'd gone to Kaisuama. Apparently, he succeeded even without a katsujo's power. None of them understood how it worked, but what they told me gave me enough information to guess Varan had combined an old Ryogan spell and the power he'd developed in exile on Shiara. If I were mortal, the shock of my magic shattering probably would've killed me. Even with the susuji's healing power running through my blood, the damage lasts for days longer than my scratches, bruises, and aches.

As unexpectedly calming as the days are, the nights help even more.

For the first time, Tessen and I have a room to ourselves. When our work is done and most of the city retreats to rest, so can we. In the room Varan once claimed, we spend hours alone. Some nights we talk, going over the day and listening to the rain fall. Other nights we don't say anything—I'm too busy testing exactly how sensitive Tessen's skin really is.

Heat courses through my body, pooling in my chest as I hold his face between my hands and pull him into a devouring kiss, all fire and crackling energy. I rake fingernails over his scalp and down his back, and I hold on when he shivers so hard it almost seems like he'll shake apart. I swallow the sounds he makes and do everything I can to make him make more. He writhes and clings, and I push him further and higher until it feels like we're standing at the tipping point.

We have to fall eventually, and when we do, the impact is beautifully shattering.

For a long while after, we lie side by side, and I trace patterns on his damp skin. The temperature is cooler than I remember Shiara being, but it's still far warmer than any part of Ryogo. I'm glad, because getting up to rush back into our clothes isn't exactly appealing.

"I knew I wanted to see how far I could push you," I murmur against his throat one night when we're both sweat-soaked, wrung-out messes. All Tessen does is groan and laugh as he presses closer.

Eventually, I turn in his arms. He rumbles contentedly, sliding one arm in to pillow my head and draping the other over my waist. His hand presses flat on my stomach with enough pressure that it seems like he's trying to hold me in place. I almost laugh. I'm certainly not going anywhere tonight. Possibly ever, if I can help it.

Comfortable and secure in his hold, I let my mind wander. When his fingers begin tracing the lines of my muscles, a question rises through my thoughts.

"Will you regret it, do you think?" I place my hand over his on my abdomen.

Years ago, Varan's healers had changed all of us to make it difficult, though not impossible, for any of us to have children. The susuji changed us back. When Zonna told me that, I spoke to the others. We decided to ask Zonna to replace the changes that had been made. The clan can make their own choice. With us, the chances are too high more immortals would be born. There are already more than forty living in one city, and I have no idea how that will impact the clan. We can't stop more being born from whatever magic is in our bloodlines already, but there's no reason for us to make the chances of it happening any higher.

Tessen shakes his head and presses a kiss to the base of my neck. "I remember what Tsua said. Watching someone I love die is too painful, and there's no guarantee our children would be andofume. It's not worth the risk. Especially not when we'll be raising the clan for generations."

"I hadn't thought of it like that." I smile; it doesn't last. What else haven't I thought of?

"Whatever you're thinking about, don't," Tessen murmurs against my skin.

"Can't help it," I whisper back.

He sighs and pushes himself up on his elbow. The lamps on the walls cast a warm glow on his brown skin and make his eyes look like embers. "You have done everything in your power for everyone who's placed themselves in your care, and that's all anyone can ask."

"Stop reading my mind," I grumble, tapping the end of his nose.

"No." He captures my hand and kisses the tips of my fingers. "You have to figure out how to accept it all, Khya. You're powerful, arguably one of the most powerful mages this clan has ever seen, and you're immortal, but you can't see the future. You're barely past your eighteenth year, and you—all of us—have a lot to learn. Are there still problems we're going to have to deal with from the past year? Of course. We don't know what they are yet, though, so stop." He kisses my lips. "Worrying." He kisses me again.

"It doesn't seem like it should be that easy."

"Nothing you've done is easy, and I don't think much of what we'll have to do in the next few decades will be easy, either, but that doesn't mean you can't do it."

"We." I grip his hand and use my hold to pull his arm around me tighter.

The smile he gives me is as bright as a sunrise, and more beautiful. "Always, Khya."

He kisses me again, a long and lingering caress, and then he settles back down behind me, pulling me closer until my head is resting on his shoulder and my leg is slung over his. Then he leans his head against mine and murmurs, "Now, sleep, okhaio. You've done everything you can do tonight."

It takes a while longer, feeling his heartbeat against my back and listening to his even breaths, but eventually, I do.

The tornadoes stopped appearing the day Varan died. Two days later, the wind calmed. After a week, although the rain hadn't broken yet, the lightning was less frequent. By the time the ships are finally ready to sail, the rain is lighter. It's still constant, but the fall isn't so thick it distorts our vision. Good. I'd been worried about being able to protect the ship as we sail. I can build a ward without a wardstone again, but I don't trust my own strength. Wardstones on the ships—Shytari's and the three Varan arrived on—should be enough to protect us against the stormy seas.

Yorri is grinning when we board the ship. "I can't believe I get to see proof."

"Of what?" I ask.

"Of somewhere other than Shiara. And that I was right."

"You're never going to let that go, are you? Besides, I showed you the map," I remind him.

He scoffs. "Anyone can draw lines on paper. I want to see those statues on the coast, and the cities, and *trees*."

If those statues are still standing, and the cities haven't all been destroyed, and the trees haven't all been blown over or burned to charcoal. He heard our stories, but he hasn't felt that bone-biting cold or watched a city engulfed in flames and terror. He doesn't seem to understand that, unless we hit a stroke of Kaisubeh-blessed luck, our next trial will be as hard as the one we just finished.

One more time—maybe one last time—I leave Shiara. At least I have Yorri. He leans into the wind, giddier than I've ever seen him. This time, I know where we're headed and what my mission will be—even if I'm not entirely sure how I'm going to accomplish it.

This time, I also know I have a way home, and that, apparently, changes everything.

We're only a few hours into the journey when Tessen's focus shifts from a roving scan to a sharp focus on the northwest. I'm about to ask what he sees when the garakyu in my pocket vibrates. It nearly startles me into jumping. Oh, no. Something must have gone wrong on one of the other ships. Either that, or someone on Shiara is calling us back.

I wave to catch Tessen's attention and point toward the lower decks when he glances my way. He nods, his focus instantly shifting northwest again. The storm is less, but the ship still tilts dangerously at times, so I grip ropes and rails until I'm safely behind closed doors. I pull the garakyu out and answer the call.

"She's here!" The face is unfamiliar. The words are Ryogan. Their shock at seeing me is the strangest of all.

Then, the image shakes and shifts, like the globe is being passed to another, and a new face appears. "Hello, Khya."

"Ryzo?" My eyes go wide. This doesn't make sense. "Where—"

"Where are you?" he asks before I can.

"Less than a day out from Shiara. We're heading back to Ryogo. To find *you*."

"Turn around." A smile spreads across his strong face. "We'll meet you at home."

"Home? *We?*" My own smile answers. "You're heading to Shiara?"

"Better. If this ball is able to reach you, we must be almost there."

The door behind me slams open. Wind and rain blasts through, pushing Tessen in with it. His eyes are filled with a near panic as he shoves the door closed. "There are ships, Khya. Ryogan ships."

"Is that Tessen?"

Tessen's head tilts. His expression drops into blank shock. "Ryzo?"

I have so many questions buzzing in the back of my mind like insects, but I hold them back. It can wait until we're home.

WAR OF STORMS

Forty-seven ships, including my four, anchor along the coast in coves and bays. From there, everyone makes their own way across the land, slowly converging on our home.

We're approaching the city gates when Tessen laughs. "This can't be happening."

"It had better be happening," I grumble. Timing and coincidence have worked against me for too long. It would be nice if this is coincidence twisting in our favor. Or maybe this luck truly is Kaisubeh blessed.

It takes hours for shipload after shipload of nyshin to return to the city. None of them seem wounded—no bandages and no blood—but each walks like their next step might be the last they're able to take. They look around as they enter the city, tired eyes tracing the lines of the streets and the buildings. Most of them look at Sagen sy Itagami as though they never expected to see it again, and as though they've forgotten the feel of the city they once knew so well.

I recognize the look. I was in their place not long ago.

Ryzo is among the last to arrive, and he comes with two people I never expected to see again—Kaibo'Ma-po Yonishi Tsukadesu and Jintisu Gotintenno. Tyatsu surround them, eyeing their surroundings with wary, weary awe.

"We were coming to help, but it seems we're too late," Jintisu says with a smile. "The construction of this place is…"

"Impressive doesn't seem enough to describe it, does it?" Yonishi is studying the buildings around us. "It's practically seamless."

"It is. According to the stories, Varan carved Itagami out of the mesa." I used to be proud of that, and I suppose I still am, but the feeling has been irreparably tainted.

But I don't want to think about the past. There's way too much happening now that I need to figure out first.

"What happened after I left?" I ask as soon as everyone is gathered around the large table in my room. "And do you know where Elyini is?"

"I killed her," Ryzo flatly states. "You were right about the army—watching her death made it incredibly easy to convince the army to surrender."

All the air rushes from my lungs, and I let my head drop forward, pressing my clasped hands to the center of my forehead. She's dead, and the army's out of Ryogo. It really is over.

I take a breath, place my hands on the table, and ask them to start at the beginning.

The conversation moves slowly, especially since it's broken by constant pauses for translations. There are four languages spoken by the people in this room, and few here are fluent in more than two, but *everyone* needs to understand what's being said.

Ryzo, Yarzi, Donya, and Remashi seeded doubt through the army with whispers and stories and—in a stroke of brilliance—by leading a squad into Uraita, Varan's home village, so they saw Varan's legacy for themselves.

"We saw that the army was beginning to break." A tyatsu picks up the story. "Squads left the main army, and we thought it was for missions, but they never rejoined the force."

Ryzo nods, but adds, "The worst damage was already done, though."

Their descriptions turn my stomach, reminding me too much of walking into the saishigi core and seeing nothing but waste and loss. So much of Ryogo has become a hollow shell, streets empty and buildings crumbling. People have nowhere to go. Fire cut swaths across the land.

Jintisu looks immeasurably sad, but smiles when she says, "Thankfully, the rain made the trees exceptionally hard to burn. None of the fires spread as far as they could've."

I tell myself I did the best I could with the skills and information I had; I couldn't have prevented any of this. It's hard to believe. Ryogo and Shiara haven't survived this war whole. Both lands are broken and reeling. Going back to what we were isn't possible, and I don't know how we'll figure out where to go from here.

Tessen places his hand over mine, his fingers tracing gentle patterns on my skin. I let his touch settle me.

"The splintering of the army made sneaking back in easier," Ryzo says. "Once I was sure Varan and the others were gone, we grabbed Elyini and dragged her to the middle of the camp."

"No one knew what to do," Yarzi says when Ryzo doesn't continue. "Training said to protect the Miriseh. Logic told them to wait and see."

"We didn't give them time to think about it," Ryzo admits. "I said something—I don't remember what, honestly—then I sliced Elyini's throat with one of the stones you left with me."

Yarzi looks at Ryzo, frowning and placing eir hand on the table between them. Ey relaxes a bit when he sighs and links his fingers with eirs. Then ey shrugs. "They gave up the fight. After, we found Gentoni again and worked on getting back here."

"He wanted to come himself, but he was needed at home," Jintisu says. "He sends his greetings, though."

"And he looks forward to hearing your story when we get back," Yonishi hints.

Even though I haven't told *this* story before, the scenario feels intensely familiar. I fall into the pattern I've learned so well in my moon cycles on Ryogo.

When I finish, the conversation slows down and becomes a lot harder to navigate. Shiara is already on the brink of starvation, Ryogo has years of rebuilding ahead, and the hanaeuu we'la maninaio are being given a voice for the first time. We talk about peace, trade, and the future for hours, and it feels like we get nowhere. There's so much anger in Ryogo and a deep desire for everything to be the way it was before. I doubt it'll be an easy time as they come to terms with the reality that no one but the Kaisubeh has such power.

Eventually, once everyone has sworn there will be no reprisals against any other for the damage Varan caused, plans begin to unfold. Trades are tentatively offered. Soanashalo'a agrees hanaeuu we'la maninaio ships will take on the risk of journeying between Shiara and Ryogo in exchange for a part in all future trade negotiations.

When the others break for a meal—the immortals limit ourselves to one small meal a day—I get up and walk to the window, watching the city below. I left my wardstones on the outer wall, and they're keeping the light but persistent rain and wind at bay to give the city a chance to dry. What's better is the life inside these walls again. Dozens of people are in the courtyard, some talking and others simply passing through, and the sight helps erase memories of an empty, abandoned Itagami.

"Do you think we can stay here and make it work?" I ask when Tessen joins me.

"It won't be easy," Tessen hedges. "But it's far less impossible than our last mission."

"You say that now." We haven't even begun, though, and we're going into this inexperienced and overloaded. We'll be interacting with a world Varan taught to fear and revile us, yet we'll have to rely on them for essentials. Like food. The rains destroyed Shiara's crops, and until the sun returns, all we can gather is mushrooms and fish.

"I say it, and I believe it." Tessen wraps his arm around my shoulders and tugs me to lean against him. "And you may be leading, but you're not alone. You never have been. We'll fight to save Shiara, and if we one day realize we can't win, you'll make a new decision and the rest of us will help you figure out how to make it work."

Maybe it is that simple. We've gotten this far because I've made decisions, and my friends have figured out how to make those choices work. A few moons ago, I would've balked at the implication of such deep reliance, that I couldn't succeed without help, but I've never been alone in this.

Together is what saved us in the end. Together is going to be what keeps us going, too.

EPILOGUE

I wake to the sound of drums.

The beats are quick and rhythmic, like the pulses of a dancing heart, one nearly running into the next. It's so loud it seeps into the stone of the city and vibrates through my body. A year ago, I might've mistaken it for thunder, but that was before I spent moon after moon with thunder constantly underlying everything else.

I dress quickly and run toward the stairs, frustrated that Tessen's already gone. Without his help, I have to decipher the rhythm itself. The pattern isn't right for trouble. It reminds me of a homecoming beat, the one we used to welcome back a squad after a long, successful hunt.

Oh. My breath catches. I can't believe I didn't notice it as soon as my eyes opened.

The sun is rising. The *sun*.

It stopped raining about two weeks after Ryzo returned, but the clouds remained. Weeks passed, and then moon cycles, and still the clouds were thick enough to block all but the faintest hints of light. Now, there isn't even a wisp in the sky, and I see true daylight on the horizon for the first time in far too long.

I sprint toward the eastern wall, effervescent warmth rising in my chest. Hope, I realize. This is hope mixed with happiness, and it's been ages since I felt it so pure and strong.

Throngs of people crowd the stairs and the wide wall, so many it slows me down trying to get through. Until they notice who's nudging them aside. Everyone parts, all of them giving me the same salute they once gave Varan and Suzu, arms crossed to press their clenched fists against opposite shoulders. I'm not used to these displays—each time I fight off the instinct to peer around and see who they're looking at— but I've taught myself to simply nod and move on. Especially since I'm never entirely sure how genuine the gesture is.

There's been a rift in our society, albeit a small one, because not all of the clan is grateful. The truths my squad discovered and the actions we took changed everything the clan understood about where we came from and who we are. Although they've stayed in the city and haven't disobeyed any of my orders, they talk. Tessen has taken up eavesdropping again like it's his official responsibility, and the conversations he reports to me make it clear a portion of the clan would leave if there was anywhere else to go. Yorri and Etaro both believe things will settle in time, once we get the city back to some semblance of normal. I'm not so sure.

Most days, this problem is one of several dozen swirling through my head demanding attention. Today, I'm only peripherally aware of anything but the sky.

I aim for a less crowded section of wall and watch colors spread across the horizon. Warmth sinks into my skin like a blessing, and my eyes burn with tears. I missed that fiery orb.

"It's beautiful." Yorri joins me, his eyes on the sunrise. "I'd forgotten, somehow."

I have as well, but no matter how long it's been, *this* is exceptional. Deep red pools along the mountains, and the color fades through shades of orange and gold before bleeding into a bright, brilliant blue. I tear my eyes away and turn around to see how the light fills Sagen sy Itagami.

The sunrise spreads a fire-red glow over the mesa, enhancing the color of the sandstone, and the members of the clan not crowded on the wall stand on rooftops where gardens once grew to stare at the sky with delight. Even so, work continues. Forge fires have been lit, the miners are heading down to work, fishers are spread along the coast, and the first squads of hunters are leaving the city. Pride swells my chest. I wouldn't have faulted anyone for being late today of all days, but those with duties are carrying them out. Because Itagami needs them to.

"Maybe they think you'd restrict their rations if they didn't get to work on time," Yorri says when he notices where my attention is focused.

"I hope I haven't become *that* scary yet."

"You're terrifying," he insists. "The last person anyone wants to face if they've done something wrong, especially after you restricted that nyshin to half rations for a whole moon."

"He was hoarding food!" I refuse to believe that punishment was unfair.

"And you were right." Yorri nods, his expression serious despite how his eyes are laughing. "That doesn't mean people aren't afraid of you. If they need something, they come to pretty much anyone else first."

That doesn't feel true, because dozens of people come to see me every day about one thing or another. Still, if he's right, it makes me glad I'm not the only one the clan has accepted as a leader. Rai, for one, has gained quite a devoted following.

Maybe that's what Yorri means. Immortality raised most of my squad to positions of power, but it also created distance. Rai is mortal still, and so more approachable. The people need someone like that right now, because nearly everyone who once held power in Itagami is either dead or still reeling from the war and far too lost to lead anyone. The nyshin elders who returned from Ryogo offer advice when we ask for it, but necessity has changed a lot. Most of those old ways simply don't work anymore. Thankfully, there's been surprisingly little resistance to the changes, especially after we revealed all Varan's lies and secrets.

"Don't worry, Khya." Yorri chuckles and turns back to the sun. "They respect you more than they fear you, and I think what they fear most is letting you down."

Something warms in me, deeper than sunlight can touch, and I'm glad Yorri's not watching me anymore. The smile on my face feels ridiculous.

"A sunrise today of all days." I face the sun, too, reveling in its beauty. "What do you think: coincidence or a sign the Kaisubeh are watching us?"

His head tilts as he considers the question. "I'm not sure. Tessen's been noticing the clouds thinning for a while, and even the rest of us could see it the last few days. It's part of why you planned the celebration, isn't it?"

"Partly." It was also partly because we sent off the tenth hanaeuu we'la maninaio trade ship yesterday. I decided the milestone deserved a celebration.

Soanashalo'a has been a friend in more ways than I could have anticipated, and her people are the only reason my clan has survived. Shiaran metals, stone, and crystals are being traded to the rest of the world, and the hanaeuu we'la maninaio bring us food, cloth, and other staples we won't be able to produce ourselves for a while yet.

It's been hard for the clan to adapt to the new demands. Before, we only needed to excavate enough ore and crystal for our own use, and we never needed to quarry sandstone. Before, we didn't have to constantly watch the northern horizon for ships—those carrying food *and* those carrying revenge. No matter what the Ryogan elders decided, some citizens vehemently disagreed. Twice now, we've had to turn ships away from our shores, and it'll likely happen again. Yorri has been a steadfast support through it all.

"Have I said thank you yet, Yorri?" I quietly ask.

His thick, straight eyebrows furrow. "For what?"

"Forgiving me, for one. But everything, really. I don't think we would've been able to accomplish half as much as we have these last few moons without you."

"You're underestimating yourself," he says, shaking his head. "Your friendship with the hanaeuu we'la maninaio saved our lives, and you're the one who worked out the deal with the Ryogan leaders. I'm just glad I can help you with it all."

I shift my weight, letting my shoulder brush his. "I missed you, Yorri. This wouldn't be the same if you weren't here."

"I know what you mean." He's smiling, but the expression is sad. "Some people change the shape of the world just by being in it, and their absence is fundamentally wrong. The world becomes warped without them."

"So much so that you wonder how it doesn't change the pattern of day and night."

His expression fills with amusement, then. "I wouldn't go that far. Not even you have the power to impact the sun, Khya."

"Are you sure?" I ask, arching my eyebrow.

He laughs and shakes his head.

For the first time in moons, I feel like the good finally outweighs the bad. I grin. We finally have more than one reason to celebrate.

Under the glowing light of a Shiaran sunset, the clan lines up in neat columns and rows. I stand on the bikyo-ko's dais with my squad, Zonna, and several nyshin elders. I'm in the center, looking out over my family, and for a second, I have to swallow laughter. A year ago, I believed I was about to either be exiled or killed, and yet I'm now in charge.

I lived through it all, and I'm still not sure how the bellows I ended up here, with several thousand people waiting for me to speak.

Ever since we decided we had the reasons and resources to rejoice, I've been thinking about what to say. I've changed my mind dozens of times. Stories about our journey have circulated already, so everyone knows a version of the truth. I finally decided to focus on the one thing that isn't clear to any of us—what our future looks like.

"For centuries, our leaders seemed eternal, and they kept us on their path. We only knew what they taught us. We only saw what they allowed us to. They fundamentally changed us, and there's no way for us to truly know what their interference has taken away."

More than one person shifts, some uneasily, looking at their feet or up at the color-streaked sky, and some eagerly, leaning toward the dais.

"We have always been strong, though, and we need that strength more than ever." I pause, watching chins rise and postures straighten. It's like watching a wave of determination ripple across the clan. "If I believe in anything, it's in us."

"Urah!" The clan raises their left arms, where we used to wear the tokens designating our class. Our wrists are bare now. One of my first orders disintegrated the classes Varan used to separate us. I refuse to continue on Varan's path.

"Over two thousand lives were lost in the battles on Ryogo and Shiara. That's a hole we can't ever fill." I step closer to the edge of the dais and take a deep breath. "Tonight, though, we celebrate the steps we've taken toward transforming Itagami into what *we* decide it should be."

I emphasize each word and put even more power behind my voice. "We know how to persevere against seemingly insurmountable odds.

We've been doing so for centuries. Even the fact that we've survived the aftermath of the Bobasu Invasion is a testament to what we're capable of. So celebrate tonight! Celebrate everything we've achieved. The sun has risen over Shiara again today, and I know we will see a thousand more."

"Urah!" they cry again before the unified call devolves into a chorus of cheers.

I raise my arm, signaling those stationed at the corners of the courtyard. Quickly, they dash off, returning with the surprises we prepared. Wagons of food are rolled in, a veritable feast compared to what we've been subsisting on. What really makes the citizens cheer, though, is the casks of ahuri wine Tessen found in a hidden storeroom. It's the last any of us will have for a long time. Tonight, therefore, we'll drink to everything we've been forced to leave behind, with the alcohol we might never drink again. It seems appropriate.

"I always knew I'd see you up here for one reason or another." Rai brings me a plate of food. It's a meal more Ryogan than Shiaran—tiny white grains instead of the fluffy nyska, fish instead of teegra meat, and milder spices—but it's hot, it's well cooked, and there's plenty. I haven't had a meal this big in weeks. She hands me the plate and then, smirking, flicks one of the short, black curls hanging over my forehead. "Honestly, though, I thought you'd at least have one gray hair before you made it onto this dais."

"Now I won't ever have gray hairs." I shake my head. "You must be so disappointed."

I expect another Rai remark, something full of wit and sarcasm, but instead her smile softens and pride glimmers in her eyes. "Rarely by you, Khya."

The words stun me. I blink, my mouth opening as I try to figure out what I can say.

"Rai!" We turn. Etaro is standing a few feet away, a plate in one hand and eir other pointing toward the crowd. "I say you should try for her."

"My love may be ushimo, but there is no one better at picking out potential partners," Rai says with a lascivious grin. Winking, Rai jogs to Etaro's side. They stand there, heads tilted toward each other but eyes on the crowd, and one of my worries settles. It's a little thing, but Rai's been too serious and distant, snarking back at me more sharply than usual, gossiping rarely, and never looking for anyone to keep her up at night. Seeing her relax enough to go back to something I know she's missed is one more element of life as it should be. I grin as I watch the girl Rai approaches blink, stammer, and then grin as my friend turns on the charm. My smile widens when I catch sight of Ahta sprinting past with a pack of the other children; the little ebet has been settling in even better than I'd hoped ey would.

The sun has set farther, deepening the colors overhead, and the kasaiji have lit the lamps hanging on the walls. A word from me activates the crystal lamps we've added overhead, large clusters attached to chains crisscrossing the courtyard that cast a soft, steady glow.

After a few minutes, the drumbeat shifts. The base mimics a pulse, the steady rhythm of life. Higher-pitched drums overlay it with flourishes that grow more and more complex. The new rhythm jolts the clan into motion. Pairs claim the circles marked in the stone, and spectators gather close to watch them. Excitement ripples through the crowd, and the volume of their talk rises with each passing second. There's an incredible thrill to watching tokiansu pairs challenge each other, and although I rarely participated, I dreamed of performing this dance with someone who was both a challenge and an equal. Plus, I made a promise. Tonight, I'm going to keep it.

Nearby, Tessen is watching the tokiansu with wistful longing. His lips roll between his teeth, he takes a breath, and I think for a second that he's going to speak, but then he exhales and minutely shakes his head. I smile to myself. He's resigned himself to keeping his thoughts in his head out of some strange sense of... I don't even know. Honor? Defeat? Self-deprecation?

Adorable fool. He still hasn't quite learned how to ask for what he wants from me. Thankfully, I have all the time I need to teach him.

"Tessen, I need to ask you something."

"What?" He smiles back, but he seems wary.

"How are you feeling? Are you warmed up? Not too tense or out of shape?"

"I'm getting tense now," he says drily, his gray eyes glinting with humor. "What are you up to, Khya? I'm starting to think I'm going to have to talk you out of something dangerous."

"Well..." I step closer. His breathing hitches when I brush my nose against his cheek. I love that moons of spending nights together hasn't inured him to me at all. If anything, he seems *more* aware and *more* sensitive to my touch than ever. "It might be dangerous, but I don't think you'll want to talk me out of it."

"Tell me and I guess we'll see," he says shakily.

I stay quiet for long enough that Tessen begins to fidget, shifting his weight.

"I made you a promise." I pull back and look into his eyes. "And, for a long time, I couldn't keep it."

When he catches on, his gray eyes light up and a wickedly delighted smile spreads across his face. "You did. I was starting to think you'd forgotten."

"When have I ever broken my word?" I step back, raising my eyebrows. "If you go find us some surakis, then maybe tonight we'll—"

Tessen pulls me in, kissing me quick and hard before spinning around and running for the weapons rack.

Behind me, Yorri laughs. "Finally! Bellows, Khya, I've been waiting for you to dance with him for *years*."

"It's a good thing she didn't," Sanii says. "She probably would have 'accidentally' tried to slice his hand off the first few moons he started chasing her."

"Who says I won't do that now?" I ask, smirking.

"No. Not happening," Etaro says as ey walks closer, part of eir attention still on Rai, who's jogging back up to the dais.

"Why not?" I raise my eyebrows.

"Because I know you've already made use of his hands—"

"Which I can't believe took you as long as it did," Rai breaks in, grinning as she rejoins us. "He has very talented hands, from everything I've heard."

Etaro picks up again, "—and you will again, probably often. Which means they should probably stay attached."

"You are all too obsessed with my sex life," I mutter, fighting the urge to roll my eyes.

Tessen is running back with a suraki in each hand. They're vicious weapons, five feet of thick chain connecting a curved, double-edged, clawlike dagger on one end and a palm-sized iron ball with four-inch-long spikes ringing the globe on the other. Most Itagamins never pick one up, choosing weapons that are less likely to leave them with scars. It's the weapon I always tested myself with. The design intrigued me, the difficulty fascinated me, and the challenge kept me working until I had mastered it.

Grinning widely, Tessen hands me a suraki and leads me to the empty tokiansu circle directly in front of the bikyo-ko. Traditionally, only the highest-ranking members of the clan used this ring, and they rarely showcased their talents in public, so it remained empty during most celebrations. Habit has held—it's still empty. As soon as Tessen and I step into the space with intent, though, people notice. Word spreads in whispers, then shouts, then a rush of motion. Within seconds, our exhibition space is surrounded, and more people press in from all sides.

I ignore the attention and refamiliarize myself with my weapon. I feel the weight of it, the way it fits in my hand. I've used one in the training yard recently, mostly when nightmares made sleep impossible, but this will be the first time in a year I've used it against an opponent.

Tessen throws the dagger out like a dart, jerking the chain to spin the blade in a circle above his heads before tucking his elbow into the chain, changing the direction of the arc, and catching the hilt in his hand. It's impressive. And it's almost enough to make me wish we didn't have quite so large an audience. Tessen is never more appealing than when he reminds me how annoyingly good he is at *everything*.

"You're both set on this?" Sanii asks. "The last thing we need is for you to bleed all over the place just because you can't tease each other like normal people."

"If you talk her out of this, I might hurt you," Tessen mutters.

Sanii smirks. "You're welcome to try."

I grin across the circle at Tessen. Attraction, adrenaline, and more apprehension than I want to admit stir in my chest. I catch his attention, silently asking, *Ready?*

Eyes alight, he nods and settles, mirroring my posture. I let the percussive beat of the drums vibrate through my bones for several seconds. Then, I extend three fingers and close them around the leather-wrapped hilt one by one to count down.

Three. Two. One.

Tessen and I circle each other. With the hilt in my right hand, I draw the chain through my left, gripping tight near the metal sphere that caps the opposite end. The spiked iron ball is a weapon in its own right, but not in the tokiansu. Dancing with the surakis is all about speed, grace, and the flowing arcs of the blades' flight.

He takes a step. I toss the dagger up then jerk it back, arcing the trajectory over his head. It misses his hair by an inch. Tessen's grin widens. I barely twirl aside in time to escape the arrow-like flight of his blade. As I come around again, I swing my chain in a waist-high circle. Tessen springs off the ground, flips over my weapon, lands on his feet, and jerks his chain to bring the dagger down on my head.

Each arc of our surakis is a near-hit. We dance between close combat—gripping the hilts of the daggers in our fists and throwing killing blows that barely miss their mark—and the wide-reaching swings of the chains. He isn't just good, he's nearly unstoppable. In close quarters, his strikes jar my shoulders. Apart, his aim is so accurate I know at least one would've found its mark if he wanted it to.

Tessen is a challenge, and the longer this bout lasts, the wider my grin gets. He's not holding back. But I still think I can beat him.

His smile shifts, becoming the crooked grin I've seen since on his face every time some fool issued a challenge Tessen knew he could match.

Gripping the chain just below the dagger's hilt, he tosses the metal sphere instead. I try to pull back. The chain catches my wrist, wrapping around twice and weighing down my arm. Tessen lunges, bringing the chain around my back and locking my arm behind me. I slash at his chest, my heart pounding harder than ever, but he brings his chain up, over my arm, and down.

The chain pins my hand to my side. Tessen yanks me forward, and I stumble, crashing into his chest. Our bodies are pressed tight together, and his dagger is at my throat.

"Does this mean I win?" Tessen asks, breathing deep and fast.

Though it strains my wrist, I trace a line across Tessen's stomach with my blade. "I think it's a draw."

His eyes flick down, and his smile widens. "I could break your wrist."

"I could show you what you had for breakfast."

When his eyes flick down again, Tessen's breathing hitches. It's slight, barely audible, but it's there. The gleam in his eyes brightens, and my pulse jumps as heat rushes under my skin. I've never handled defeat well. Or ties. Around Tessen, a tie seems to be the best I can hope for, and I'm okay with that.

But I still raise one eyebrow and tap his stomach with my blade. "Are you waiting for me to concede? It won't happen."

"No, I—" He cuts himself off, glancing at the watching crowd. Exhaling, he shakes his head. "Like you said. A draw."

I pull him closer and whisper, "Wishing we were alone?"

"More than a little. But this was worth it." He softly kisses my cheek. I feel him take a deep breath. "I've been wanting to...to dance with you for years, oh deadly one."

I don't miss his hesitation, and curiosity grabs me. What had he been about to say?

We carefully disentangle ourselves from the weapons and each other, and I pass both the surakis to a watcher to be put away. Then, I offer Tessen my hand. He watches me with amused speculation as he clasps his fingers around mine and follows me without question.

Bravery is a strange thing. I faced down armies and oceans and storms, but the fear of losing someone I love is enough to lock my body in stone. Thinking about what *my* loss would do to the person who'd claimed me as their other half terrifies me even more.

Tessen sees the sumai so differently. He looks at Sanii and Yorri with such deep longing sometimes—and other times with rueful resignation—and I know he desperately wants a bond that deep. Instead of a vulnerability, he sees it as reassurance and an anchor in the constant tumult of his senses. His fear, as far as I can tell, is me telling him no and meaning goodbye.

So I gather up my courage once we're in our room, refusing to let fear stop me. "You know, we have time. Years and years. If there's something else you want, something more than a dance, you can always try to convince me."

"What if I didn't want you to need convincing?" His words are quiet, and the fingers he brushes over my hair gentle.

I close my eyes and lean my forehead against his, brushing the tips of our noses together. "Then you might have to wait a while for me to get there on my own, okhaio."

"I've been waiting for you all my life, oh deadly one," he says with a soft laugh. "It'd make no sense to change that now."

Brilliant, beautiful boy. I close my eyes and try to relax, focusing on the rhythm pouring in from the courtyard below. It's the sound of celebration, a revelry we had a hand in bringing back to the city we love so much, and for tonight, everything is beautiful.

Trouble will definitely find us again. We made some friends in Ryogo and found an ally in the hanaeuu we'la maninaio, but we have enemies, too. Ryogans who disagreed with the Jindaini's ruling. Other lands whose people fear what we might one day do to them and plan to strike us while we're weak. There's also drought, rot, plague, and a hundred other natural disasters that could befall us.

Maybe we'll face all of it, maybe none, but it doesn't matter. The only thing I have power over is my clan, helping them heal and then preparing them to face whatever challenges the world throws at us next. So long as the Kaisubeh will it, that is exactly what I am going to do.

And this time, with Tessen, Yorri, Sanii, and the rest of the clan standing behind me…maybe I actually can.

INDEX

Cast of Characters

AHNATIOLIO – one of the Denhitran elders and leaders and married to Ralavanonav; he/him

AHTA – a Ryogan child living in the Mysora Mountains with eir mother Dai-Usho; ey/em

AKIA – one of the elders of Soanashalo'a's family, a responsibility shared with her husband Hoku, and a citizen of the hanaeuu we'la maninaio tribe; she/her

AMIS – an original member of Tyrroh's squad; oraku mage; he/him

ANDA – Khya and Yorri's blood-mother and a kaigo councilmember; rikinhisu mage; she/her

ARINRI – one of the born immortals trapped on Imaku with Yorri; akuringu mage; she/her

ATSUDO – a tyatsu guard serving in Jushoyen; she/her

CHIO HEINANSUTO – Tsua's husband, Varan's brother, and one of the original twelve immortals; dyuniji mage; deceased; he/him

CHIRIDA JOSENSHI – the general of the Ryogan army and the Jindaini's military advisor; she/her

DAITSA – former second-in-command of Tyrroh's squad; dyuniji mage; deceased; she/her

DAI-USHO – Ryogan woman who lives in the Mysora Mountains with her child Ahta; deceased; she/her

DONYA – an original member of Tyrroh's squad; kasaiji; ey/em

ELYINI – one of the original twelve immortals; he/him

ETARO – an original member of Tyrroh's squad and currently platonically partnered with Rai; rikinhisu mage; ey/em

GENTONI GOTINTENNO – the elected leader of Ryogo who holds the title of Jindaini, he is married to Jintisu; he/him

HOKU – one of the elders of Soanashalo'a's family, a responsibility shared with his wife Akia, and a citizen of the hanaeuu we'la maninaio tribe; he/him

HYKIN – Tyrroh's childhood best friend who was imprisoned on Imaku by Varan; kasaiji mage; he/him

JINTISU GOTINTENNO – a leading figure in Ryogo and wife of Gentoni; she/her

KAZU – commander of the Ryogan ship that carries Tyrroh's squad to Ryogo; he/him

KEILI – an originl member of Tyrroh's squad; deceased; he/him

KHYA – an original member of Tyrroh's squad, Yorri's older sister, and Tessen's current partner; fykina mage; she/her

MIARI – an original member of Tyrroh's squad and currently partnered with Nairo and Wehli; ishiji mage; she/her

MYTUA – one of the original twelve immortals; ratoiji mage; she/her

NAIRO – an original member of Tyrroh's squad and currently partnered with Miari and Wehli; kasaiji mage; he/him

NATANI – an original member of Tyrroh's squad; zoikyo mage; he/him

NEEVA – Tessen's blood-mother and a kaigo councilmember; rusosa mage; she/her

ONO – Khya and Yorri's blood-father and a kaigo councilmember; oraku mage; he/him

OSOTA TARUSUTA – Ryogan smuggler and descendent of Suzu's family; married to Shiodeso; she/her

OSSHI SHAGAKUSA – Ryogan historian who sailed to Shiara looking for proof of the bobsu's existence; he/him

RAI – an original member of Tyrroh's squad and currently platonically partnered with Etaro; kasaiji mage; she/her

RALAVANONAV – one of the Denhitran elders and leaders and married to Ahnatiolio; ey/em

REEKA – a yonin attendant whose partner Taya was killed by Varan and who helped Sanii and Khya look for Yorri; she/her

REMASHI – an original member of Tyrroh's squad; rikinhisu mage; she/her

RYZO – former second-in-command of Tyrroh's original squad, but one who initially remained on Shiara; hishingu mage; he/him

SANII – Yorri's sumai partner and the one who discovered the truth about Yorri; hyari mage and tusenkei; ey/em

SHIDESO TARUSUTA – Ryogan smuggler; married to Osota; he/him

SHIU - one of the elders of Soanashalo'a's family and a citizen of the hanaeuu we'la maninaio tribe; he/him

SHYTARI LEOWESA – captain of a Khylari cargo vessel; she/her

SOAHOLIA – one of the Denhitran elders and leaders; she/her

SOANASHALO'A SHUIKANAHE'LE – Osshi's friend and the voice of a hanaeuu we'la maninaio caravan; she/her

SOTRA – the ahdo training master who taught Khya, Yorri, and Tessen in Itagami; kyneeda; she/her

SUZU – a leader of Sagen sy Itagami and one of the original twelve immortals; sykina mage; she/her

SYONI – an original member of Tyrroh's squad; ishiji mage; she/her

TESSEN – a one-time member of Tyrroh's squad and Khya's current partner; basaku mage; he/him

THELIN – an original member of Tyrroh's squad; deceased; she/her

TSUA – Chio's wife and one of the original twelve immortals; rikinhisu mage; deceased; she/her

TYRROH – an original member of Tyrroh's squad; oraku mage; deceased; he/him

VARAN HEINANSUTO – leader of Sagen sy Itagami and one of the original twelve immortals; ishiji mage; he/him

VYSIAN – an original member of Tyrroh's squad, but one who initially remained on Shiara; rikinhisu mage; he/him

WEHLI – member of Tyrroh's squad and currently partnered with Miari and Nairo; ryacho mage; he/him

WYRIN – one of the original twelve immortals; hishingu mage; he/him

YARZI – an original member of Tyrroh's squad, but one who initially remained on Shiara; ratoiji mage; ey/em

YONISHI TSUKADESU – the leader of the group of kaiboshi (priests) who serve the goddess Masya-Mono and also acts as a confidante and counselor to Jindaini Gentoni; he/him

YORRI – Khya's brother, Sanii's sumai partner, and a born immortal; kynacho mage; he/him

ZONNA – Chio and Tsua's son and a born immortal; hishingu mage; he/him

Cities and Places

Ryogo

Arayokai Sea – the stretch of water between Shiara and Ryogo

Atokoredo – a city in northwestern Ryogo within the Soramyku Province

Hopo'ka River – a river running north from Jushoyen toward Atokoredo

Jushoyen – the capitol city of Ryogo, located in the center of the country

Kaisuama – the Seat of the Gods; a valley hidden deep within the Nentoado mountain range where one of the strongest katsujos in the world surfaces

Khylar – the country directly to the north of Ryogo, separated by the Mysora Mountains

Masu'iro Channel – the strip of water dividing Ryogo and Menlai, their neighbor to the west

Mushokeiji – a prison for mages located within the Soramyku Province in northwestern Ryogo, specifically the Suakizu region

Mysora Mountains – the northernmost range of mountains that separates Ryogo from Khylar

Mysora'ka River – the river that runs from the eastern half of the Mysora Mountains to the eastern coast of Ryogo

Nentoado – the section of the Mysora Mountains known for being harsh and impassable

Po'umi – a port city on the southeastern coast of Ryogo within the Namimi Province

Rido'iti – a port city on the southern coast of Ryogo within the Namimi Province

Ryogo – the country north of Shiara where Varan, Chio, and the other immortals are from

Ryogan Provinces – (clockwise from the southwest)
    Minowa – southwestern-most coastal region
    Azukyo – central western coastal region

Soramyku – northwestern-most mountains
Kyo'ne – northeastern-most peninsula
Okasuto – northwestern coastal region
Hynochi – central plains
Tomi'ishi – central eastern coastal region
Namimi – southeastern-most coastal region

SUAKIZU – the region within the Soramyku Province where the Mushokeiji prison is located

URAITA – a village in northeastern Ryogo within the Kyo'ne Province and the hometown of Varan and Chio

ZUNOATO – a city in the Okasuto Province that sits just north of the Mysora'ka River

Shiara

DENHITRA – the city in the southern mountains of Shiara

IMAKU – the black-rock island off the northeastern coast of Shiara

KYIWA MOUNTAINS – the range along the eastern coast of Shiara, just beyond Sagen sy Itagami

SAGEN SY ITAGAMI – the city in northeastern Shiara; often simply called Itagami

SHIARA – the island nation south of Ryogo

SUESUTU PASS – a narrow passage between two mountains within the Kyiwa range

TEEDIN MOUNTAINS – the range along the southern coast of Shiara where Denhitra is hidden

TSIMO – a city on the western peninsula of Shiara

MAGIC OF SAGEN SY ITAGAMI

Soyiji Mages – Elemental Manipulation

ISHIJI – Stone Mage – Ability to reform, lighten, move, and meld stone

RYIJI – Earth Mage – Affinity for plants and soil that helps these plants grow in the desert

KYSHIJI – Water Mage – Ability to find, clean, and sometimes manipulate water

MYIJI – Weather Mage – Extremely rare ability that can manipulate wind and detect or, sometimes, call up storms

Desosa Mages – Energy Manipulation

ASSISTIVE:

DYUNIJI – *Kinetic Mage* – Ability to use their own kinetic energy, or sometimes someone else's (for example, blows landed during battle) to augment their own strength

ZOIKYO – *Augmenter* – Ability to boost other people's powers by funneling desosa to them

HISHINGU – *Healer* – Ability to use the desosa to heal themselves and others

WARDING:

SYKINA – Ability to use their own energy and the universal desosa to shield themselves from other magic

FYKINA – Ability to shield themselves and others from both magic and the physical world

OFFENSIVE:

KASAIJI – *Fire Mage* – Ability to use the desosa to create sparks and/or fire

RATOIJI – *Lightning Mage* – Ability to use the desosa to create lightning

Okajin Mages – Enhanced Humanity

PHYSICAL ABILITIES:

KYNEEDA – Enhanced strength, stamina, and endurance

RYACHO – Enhanced speed and ability

KYNACHO – Enhanced speed, ability, strength, stamina, and endurance

SENSOR MAGES:

UNIKU – Enhancement of a single sense, usually either vision or hearing

ORAKU – Enhancement of three senses: sight, smell, and hearing

BASAKU – Enhancement of all senses, plus the ability to sense magic, and, rarely, the impact emotions have on the desosa

Shinte-kina Mages – Psychic Abilities

RIKINHISU – *Telekinesis* – Ability to move objects or people without touching them

RUSOSA – *Mental Manipulation* – An uncommon ability to create, among other things, illusions in other people's minds

AKURINGU – *Scrying* – Ability to use a reflective surface to see across great distances or, rarely, a short period of time into the past or future

RANKS AND HONORIFICS

Ranks of Sagen sy Itagami

Highest rank listed first

Miriseh

Kaigo

Nyshin-lu	Ahdo-na	Yonin-na
Nyshin-ri	Ahdo-mas	Yonin-mas
Nyshin-co	Ahdo-sa	Yonin-sa
Nyshin-ma	Ahdo-po	Yonin-po
Nyshin-pa	Ahdo-li	Yonin-li
Nyshin-ten	Ahdo-va	Yonin-va

Military Ranks of Ryogo

Highest rank listed first

Navy – Taikan
- Admiral: -da
- Commander: -co
- Captain: -yi
- First Officer: -fu
- Petty Officer: -pa

Army/Police – Tyatsu
- General: -ge
- Colonel: -ne
- Lieutenant: -lu
- Sergeant: -sa
- Private: -va

Government Ranks of Ryogo

Rank is added to the branch name

Prime Minister: Jindaini
Branch name: Jinlo
Council of Territories: -ya
People's Council: -vi

Ministry Officials:
Fusai
Ministers of departments: -ry
Directors of Territory offices: -si
Directors of local offices: -lo

Judicial Branch:
Supreme Court Judges: -su
Territory Judges: -te
Local Judges: -ju

Civil servants: -sa
Anyone who is not of a high-rank but works for a branch of government would use this honorific

Religious Ranks of Ryogo

Rank is added to the priest-servant name, for example Kaibo'Ma-po or Kaibo'Ni-chi

Kaiboshi Council:
Pope: -po
Cardinals: -na

Adherents to a specific god/goddess:
Archbishops: -sho
Bishops: -bi
Priests: -ri
Deacons: -de
Students: -tu

Religious police/guards:
Chief: -chi
Inspector: -to
Deputy: -ty
Officer: -fo

Social Honorifics in Ryogo
Added to a given name, for example, Osshi-tan

Family honorifics:
Elder male within a family: -liu
Younger adult males: -lo

All female family members: -la

Your father: oto
Your mother: onyo
(neither is attached to a given name)

*Lower strata men and women do not get honorifics. Neither do children of any rank (not even those within your family).

Social:
Unrelated higher rank/elder male: -ti
Unrelated females from ranking families: -ja

Teacher: -sei

Close friend: -mi *(usually only used from male to male or female to female)*

Lover: -itzo *(usually only used male to female; there's a close bond implied here, but there's also a vague sense of derogatory ownership with this honorific)*

Equal acquaintance: -tan

Kaisubeh of Ryogo

Anshi – *God of Death/Judgement/Pain*
- Title for their adherents: Kaibo'An
- Robe colors:
  - Base - White
  - Border - Rose pink
  - Pattern designs - lavender and deep eggplant

Byfuto – *Goddess of Art/Weavers/Crafts*
- Title for their adherents: Kaibo'By
- Robe colors:
  - Base - Tea rose orange
  - Border - Salmon
  - Pattern designs - sky blue

Chaiwo – *God of Love/Harmony/Beauty*
- Title for their adherents: Kaibo'Cha
- Robe colors:
  - Base - Eggplant
  - Border - Mauve
  - Pattern designs - pear green

Chihiru – *Goddess of Healing/Medicine*
- Title for their adherents: Kaibo'Chi
- Robe colors:
  - Base - Navy blue
  - Border - Beige/Cream
  - Pattern designs - Slate blue

Dosuori – *God of Animals/hunting/husbandry*
- Title for their adherents: Kaibo'Do
- Robe colors:
  - Base - Doe skin brown
  - Border - Tree bark brown
  - Pattern designs - blood red

GIJUSUMEI – *Goddess of Intelligence/ Inventions*
- Title for their adherents: Kaibo'Gi
- Robe colors:
    - Base - Buttercream yellow
    - Border - Royal purple
    - Pattern designs - pale violet

KYGAONA – *Goddess of Music/Dance/Grace*
- Title for their adherents: Kaibo'Ky
- Robe colors:
    - Base - Soft pink
    - Border - Royal purple
    - Pattern designs - Cream

MASYA-MONO – *Goddess of Justice/Law/Magic*
- Title for their adherents: Kaibo'Ma
- Robe colors:
    - Base - Black
    - Border - White
    - Pattern designs - cobalt blue

NENSO – *God of War/Warriors*
- Title for their adherents: Kaibo'Nen
- Robe colors:
    - Base - Iron gray
    - Border - Ash gray
    - Pattern designs - Black and pink

NIZOKEN – *God of Fire/Metal/Guardian of Hell*
- Title for their adherents: Kaibo'Ni
- Robe colors:
    - Base - Rust Red
    - Border - Brown-black
    - Pattern designs - Ash gray

REIRO-JIN – *Goddess of Time/Old Age/History/Fate*
- Title for their adherents: Kaibo'Rei
- Robe colors:
    - Base - Ice blue
    - Border - Charcoal gray
    - Pattern designs - Slate blue

SEISHO-FU – *God of Fertility/Earth*
- Title for their adherents: Kaibo'Sei
- Robe colors:
    - Base - Forest green
    - Border - White
    - Pattern designs - Spring Green

TENSOKI – *God of Sky/Weather*
- Title for their adherents: Kaibo'Ten
- Robe colors:
    - Base - Royal blue
    - Border - Slate blue
    - Pattern designs - sky blue

ZUMI-UTSU – *Goddess of Water/water animals*
- Title for their adherents: Kaibo'Zu
- Robe colors:
    - Base - Sea green
    - Border - Navy blue
    - Pattern designs - Pale mint

GLOSSARY

Terms and Phrases (all languages):

AHDO – *Itagamin* – Sagen sy Itagami's second citizen class; includes the following ranks (sorted highest to lowest):
Ahdo-na | Ahdo-mas | Ahdo-sa | Ahdo-po | Ahdo-li | Ahdo-va

AHOALI'LONA – *hanaeuu we'la maninaio* – the small, furry animals kept as companions

AKILOSHULO'E KUA'ANA MANANO – *hanaeuu we'la maninaio* – the universal energy of the world and the source of magic

AKUKEIJI – *Ryogan* – a derogatory term that literally translates to "evil mage"

ALUA'SA LIONA'ANO SHILUA'A – *hanaeuu we'la maninaio* – the gods or power responsible for the creation of the world

ANDOFUME – *Ryogan* – those denied death; a word Tsua and Chio invented to describe their lifespans

ANTO – *Itagamin* – a short, slightly curved dagger used in Sagen sy Itagami

ASAIRU – *Ryogan* – a fire spell to burn everything within a designated space

ATAKAFUS – *Itagamin* – a headscarf worn on Shiara as protection from the desert winds

BASAKU – *Itagamin* – a mage whose five senses are enhanced and who also has the ability to feel shifts in the desosa; in rare cases this includes the impact emotions have on that energy

BIKYO-KO – *Itagamin* – the armory and the barracks for the two councils within Sagen sy Itagami

BOBASU – *Ryogan* – the exiles; a word used for the twelve immortals and numerous mortal followers who were exiled from Ryogo

BORUIKKU – *Itagamin* – a word created by Rai and Etaro to describe magic that uses symbols to guide and control the flow of the desosa

DESOSA – *Itagamin* – the universal energy of the world and the source of magic

EBET – *Itagamin* – the designation for one of Sagen sy Itagami's three recognized sexes

GARAKYU – *Ryogan* – a clear, spelled globe that allows anyone to communicate across miles

GENSU – *Itagamin* – a woman's monthly menstruation

GOA'WA UITA – *Ryogan* – the spell to unseal a protection against the elements

HANAEUU WE'LA MANINAIO – *hanaeuu we'la maninaio* – a group of nomadic traders who travel either by wagon caravan or by boat; the name translates to "souls carried by the wind"

HERYNSHI – *Itagamin* – the trial undergone by all Itagamin citizens the moon of their sixteenth birthday

HINOSHOWA – *Ryogan* – an incredibly derogatory word for a wretch, someone lower than the peasant class; often used synonymously to mean someone who is neither male nor female

HYARI – *Ryogan* – a mage who specializes in producing and manipulating light

JINDAINI – *Ryogan* – the title held by the elected leader of Ryogo

KAIBOSHI – *Ryogan* – the priests who serve the Kaisubeh, the gods Ryogans worship

KAIGO – *Itagamin* – the council of elders who serve the Miriseh in Sagen sy Itagami

KAIJUKO – *Ryogan* – the place Ryogans believe souls are trapped for punishment in the afterlife; also, what Ryogans call the black rock that helped them trap and defeat the bobasu

KAISUAMA – *Ryogan* – a mountain in the Mysora range where the Kaisubeh convened to observe their followers, according to an old legend

KAISUBEH – *Ryogan* – as a whole, the gods and goddesses that the Ryogans believe created and control the world

KAMIDI – *Itagamin* – a large lizard with venomous spit

KATSUJO – *Ryogan* – a vein of concentrated power and energy

KUJUKO – *Itagamin* – where Itagamins believe souls are trapped for punishment in the afterlife; Varan introduced this to his city, a twisted version of Ryogo's belief in Kaijuko

MIRISEH – *Itagamin* – the title Varan gave himself and the other immortals after he built Sagen sy Itagami

MURA'INA – *Ryogan* – a purple flower with healing properties that only grows in specific climates within Ryogo

MYKYN – *Itagamin* – a large, predatory bird that lives on Shiara

Niadagu – Ryogan – a powerful binding spell using specially made red cords

NYSHIN – *Itagamin* – the first and highest of the citizen classes within Sagen sy Itagami; includes the following ranks (sorted highest to lowest):
Nyshin-lu | Nyshin-ri | Nyshin-co | Nyshin-ma | Nyshin-pa | Nyshin-ten

NYSKA – *Itagamin* – one of the tallest shrubs on the island, which bears pods that can be dried and used to make grain; the plant itself is also used to make cloth, bowstrings, paper, and other useful items

OJOKEN – *Ryogan* – a plant whose stem and roots are used for powerful healing potions

OKHAIO – *Itagamin* – a strong, sparingly used term of endearment meaning dearest one or treasured love

RIANJUKO – *Ryogan* – a rare flowering plant used in a variety of ways depending on which part of the plant is used; powerful when added to magic work

Riuku – *Itagamin* – a group name for all classes of sense mages (uniku, oraku, and basaku) who have one or more of their physical senses enhanced

Saishigi – *Itagamin* – the last rites for citizens of Sagen sy Itagami

Shuikanahe'le – *hanaeuu we'la maninaio* – a family name of the hanaeuu we'la maninaio

Sukhai – *Itagamin* – a bondmate or one partner in a sumai soulbond; often used as a term of endearment between bonded pairs

Sumai – *Itagamin* – a magical bond that ties two souls together beyond death

Suraki – *Itagamin* – a weapon with a blade on one end, a weighted, sometimes spiked ball on the other, and a five-foot chain connecting the two

Susuji – *Ryogan* – a potion used to heal

Teegra – *Itagamin* – a large, scaled cat that lives on Shiara

Tokiansu – *Itagamin* – the warriors' dance, performed once a moon cycle in Sagen sy Itagami during their celebrations

Tsimo – *Itagamin* – the westernmost clan on Shiara

Tudo – *Itagamin* – a long, slightly curved sword used in Sagen sy Itagami

Tusenkei – *Ryogan* – a term of respect used for those who weild magic in Ryogo

Tyatsu – *Ryogan* – the soldiers of the Ryogan army as well as the army itself; includes the following ranks (sorted highest to lowest): Tyatsu-ge | Tyatsu-ne | Tyatsu-lu | Tyatsu-sa | Tyatsu-va

Ukaiahana'lona – *hanaeuu we'la maninaio* – horned herbivorous beasts with tough, mottled gray hides that the hanaeuu we'la maninaio use to pull their wagons or cargo loads

Ureeku-sy Rii'ifu – *Ryogan* – the spell Tsua and Chio think might break the magic binding Yorri and the other prisoners to the stone platforms

USHIMO – *Itagamin* – describes those on the asexual spectrum; someone who feels little to no sexual desire for anyone, regardless of gender, appearance, or personality

YONIN – *Itagamin* – the third and lowest of Sagen sy Itagami's social classes; includes the following ranks (sorted highest to lowest): Yonin-na | Yonin-mas | Yonin-sa | Yonin-po | Yonin-li | Yonin-va

YUGADAI – *Ryogan* – describes the system Varan enforced in Itagami requiring approval for all births and lifetime partnerships

ZOHOGASHA – *Ryogan* – the massive statues guarding the Ryogan coastline; each set contains fourteen statues

ZON – *Itagamin* – a district or zone within Sagen sy Itagami

ABOUT THE AUTHOR

After a lifelong obsession with books, Erica Cameron spent her college years studying psychology and creative writing, basically getting credit for reading and learning how to make stories of her own. Now, she's the author of several series for young adults including The Ryogan Chronicles, the Assassins duology, and is co-author of the Laguna Tides novels.

She's also a reader, asexuality advocate, dance fan, choreographer, singer, lover of musical theater, movie obsessed, sucker for romance, Florida resident, and quasi-recluse who loves the beach but hates the heat, has equal passion for the art of Salvador Dali and Venetian Carnival masks, has a penchant for unique jewelry and sun/moon décor pieces, and a desire to travel the entire world on a cruise ship. Or a private yacht. You know, whatever works.

You can find her online in all the following places:

Website: http://byericacameron.com
Twitter: http://www.twitter.com/byericacameron
Tumblr: http://byericacameron.tumblr.com/
Instagram: http://instagram.com/byericacameron
Goodreads: http://www.goodreads.com/ericacameron

Manufactured by Amazon.ca
Acheson, AB